Alison Roberts is a New Zealander, currently lucky enough to be living in the South of France. She is also lucky enough to write for the Mills & Boon Medical Romance line. A primary school teacher in a former life, she is now a qualified paramedic. She loves to travel and dance, drink champagne, and spend time with her daughter and her friends.

Traci Douglass is a *USA TODAY* bestselling author of contemporary and paranormal romance. Her stories feature sizzling heroes full of dark humour, quick wit and major attitude, and heroines who are smart, tenacious and always give as good as they get. She holds an MFA in Writing Popular Fiction from Seton Hill University, and she loves animals, chocolate, coffee, hot British actors and sarcasm—not necessarily in that order.

FALLING FOR THE SECRET PRINCE

ALISON ROBERTS

NEUROSURGEON'S CHRISTMAS TO REMEMBER

TRACI DOUGLASS

MILLS & BOON

First Published in Great Britain 2020
by Mills & Boon, an imprint of HarperCollins*Publishers*
1 London Bridge Street, London, SE1 9GF

Falling for the Secret Prince © 2020 by Harlequin Books S.A.

Neurosurgeon's Christmas to Remember © 2020 by Harlequin Books S.A.

Special thanks and acknowledgement are given
to Alison Roberts and Traci Douglass for their contribution
to the Royal Christmas at Seattle General collection.

ISBN: 978-0-263-27986-3

Printed and bound in Spain
by CPI, Barcelona

FALLING FOR THE SECRET PRINCE

ALISON ROBERTS

MILLS & BOON

CHAPTER ONE

Trauma Team to ER. Stat.

Yes... DR EMILIA FEATHERSTONE keyed in the response on her pager that she was available and that she was on her way to the ER and then found an apologetic smile for all the other members of Seattle General Hospital's orthopaedic department, who had gathered in this small lecture theatre to present and discuss current challenging cases.

'Sorry... Gotta go. Trauma team code.'

She wasn't really sorry, of course. Emilia was already pushing open the wide door of the lecture theatre and she would be running by the time she hit the stairs. She loved a trauma team code. She loved the buzz of an ER dealing with an incoming major trauma case and she loved being the surgeon who was the 'go-to' expert for orthopaedic injuries. This was exactly what she'd worked so hard for, ever since those first days at medical school. And here, at Seattle General, was exactly where she wanted to use her expertise—a bustling, state-of-the-art, big-city hospital that attracted the best of the best.

Like she was now.

Like Domenico di Rossi was. As the head of the ER
and the trauma team leader, she knew he'd be waiting
outside the main resuscitation area to perform a pre-
arrival team briefing. He'd have a trauma checklist in
his hand, that had items like allocating roles to key per-
sonnel, including the airway doctor, circulation nurse
and a scribe. He would be ticking off things like appro-
priate personal protection equipment for each person
such as gowns, gloves and goggles and making sure that
drugs were drawn up and monitors prepped along with
the kind of special equipment that might be needed like
a rapid infuser or chest drain. Not that Dom actually
needed a clipboard with an attached checklist at all because this was *his* area of expertise and he had always
been determined to be the absolute best.

They'd had that ambition in common from the first
time they'd recognised the other as their main competition for the top position in their class at medical school.
It had been a bonus to discover that her old rival was
working here when Emilia had joined the staff at Seattle
General recently. And it had been even more of a bonus
to find not only that their respect for each other's abilities was still intact but also that oh, so enjoyable banter
that had softened the edges of their competitive relationship seemed to be still very much alive and kicking.

Judging by the gleam in those dark eyes of his, Dom
was also sharing Emilia's love of the challenge of a
trauma team code. She knew the satisfaction he would
have in orchestrating what could turn out to be a complicated response to someone who was critically injured. She suspected there might be another element,

whether conscious or not, adding to that satisfaction because, for the moment, he had the advantage over Emilia. This was his space and, as always, he was owning it.

'Out of breath, Emmy?' He kept his voice down so that other members of the team, who were already busy donning their PPE couldn't hear him. 'Have you thought of taking up a fitness programme?'

He was the only person who called her Emmy. It was like a signal that he was tapping into that old banter and he only did it because he'd found it had bothered her so much all those years ago. It had a familiarity that was almost welcome now, however. Maybe because it had been nice to find a familiar face when she'd started working in a new hospital. Or perhaps it was because her past was so far behind her now, it was another lifetime.

'Come to the park with me any day, Dom, and I'll show you who's fitter.'

Lucas Beaufort, another ER doctor, was tying the strings of his gown as he appeared beside Dom.

'Another challenge?' He was grinning. 'Are you two ever going to stop competing with each other?'

Dom just shook his head. 'Lucas—you're on airway, as usual.'

Lucas nodded. 'All set. Equipment list ticked off and drugs drawn up. We're good to go.'

Dom mirrored the single nod. 'Don't forget your lead apron, mate. You too, Emilia.' Dom turned away. 'Where's our radiographer?' he called. 'And has someone put CT on standby in case we need them? What's the ambulance ETA? Okay...let's get everyone into Resus, please...'

Lucas and Emilia shared a glance as they reached for the lead aprons that would protect them when X-rays were taken in Resus. They might not know each other particularly well yet but they were the two people in this hospital who probably knew Domenico di Rossi better than anyone else. Emilia because of their shared years at medical school and Lucas because he was Dom's closest friend. They also had two of the critical roles in this trauma team. The airway was the first step in assessing and stabilising any patient and Lucas would have to deal with any obstruction and perform an intubation if necessary. Emilia would be assessing any injuries that might need surgery and deciding how urgent it was to get someone to Theatre. She was also the team leader support so she could share management with Dom if victim numbers meant that the team would be divided.

'It's an MVA,' Dom informed the medical staff gathered around him moments later. 'Relatively high-speed skid on black ice, apparently, and the vehicle hit a concrete barrier. There are three, maybe four incoming patients and at least one of them is Status One with a compound femoral fracture and haemorrhage. He's unconscious which could be due to blood loss but could also be due to a head injury.'

Dom didn't need to catch Emilia's gaze to warn her that her input into the assessment and treatment of this patient would be a priority. An open fracture of the femur was a serious enough injury for anyone. If it had severed the femoral artery to cause a haemorrhage the blood loss could well be significant enough to not only explain his level of consciousness but also to give the patient an immediately life-threatening designation.

Someone from Neurology was the last person to join the group, just as the double doors that led to the ambulance bay slid open on both sides of the emergency entrance way. With the doors to Resus One folded back it was possible to see the flashing lights of ambulances against the deep grey of a late November morning sky. They could also see the gurneys starting to roll in and the first one clearly held the case that needed the most urgent attention. The patient was still unconscious. Covered in blood. A man hanging on one side of the gurney, who wasn't an ambulance officer was also covered in blood and seemed to be holding a pressure bandage in place on the patient's leg. An older patient, Emilia noted, as the gurney reached the doors of the resus area where the trauma team were waiting to receive the handover.

'This is Roberto Baresi.' The lead paramedic started speaking the moment he was within earshot of the team. 'A seventy-five-year-old male who's just arrived from Europe. His daughter tells us he speaks both Italian and English. He was a back seat passenger in the MVA and he took the brunt of the impact with a concrete barrier wall.'

The gurney was being positioned beside the resus trolley so that the patient could be transferred. As Airway Doctor, it was Lucas's job to oversee the transfer, using a log roll so that the plastic slide could be positioned beneath the elderly man. There was a tourniquet in place, Emilia noted, but it didn't seem to be a hundred percent effective and the face of the man who was trying to keep pressure on the wound was grim enough to suggest that it had already been a battle to control blood loss. Who was he, she wondered, and why had he been given such a critical role in caring for this badly injured man?

'Open femoral fracture and heavy blood loss estimated at two litres, possibly more,' the paramedic continued. 'Patient unconscious with a GCS of seven on arrival. Airway clear and breath sounds equal. Blood pressure was unreadable. He's had two units of saline and currently has a systolic pressure of eighty.'

Still too low. Emilia glanced at the bags of intravenous fluid now being transferred to hooks over the trolley. Lucas had the patient's head tilted back to ensure his airway was open, had transferred his oxygen supply to the overhead outlets and was now listening to his chest with a stethoscope. Other staff were working fast to put monitoring in place for heart rate and rhythm, blood pressure and oxygen levels.

The man who'd been doing the haemorrhage control was being moved aside as a new tourniquet was placed and it was possible to see the extent of the wound on the man's leg which looked serious. The femur—the longest bone in the body—had been broken with enough force to send the ends through tissue and skin, obviously causing damage to important blood vessels on the way.

Emilia's brain was working as rapidly as it always had. She had the ability to pose questions and then instantly provide a list of what needed to be done to get the necessary information. In a matter of only seconds, she was assessing what she could see of the soft tissue and bone damage, wondering what type of fracture she would be dealing with and getting ready to request X-rays of the entire femur, hip and knee. She would prefer a CT scan of the femoral neck as well.

It might be necessary to scan the man's brain before she took him to Theatre, too. The gold standard repair using a rod inside the bone to repair a femoral fracture was contraindicated if the patient had a closed head injury because it was critical to avoid low blood pressure or oxygen levels. If that was the case—and both Lucas and the neurosurgical resident were assessing the man's pupils now—Emilia would have to consider a provisional external fixation for this serious fracture.

More gurneys were in the ER now. A glance over her shoulder showed that one of them had a woman about Emilia's age on it, who had long, curly black hair. She was sitting up and conscious and another man coming in was walking so neither of them were injured seriously enough to mean it would be necessary to disperse members of the trauma team. They probably wouldn't even attract the attention of more than the triage nurse.

Or...perhaps they would.

For the first time since this critically injured patient had been rolled into the resus area, Emilia looked towards Dom. He should be at the foot of the bed, watching and processing everything that was happening, ready to direct the team, locate whatever extra resources were needed and to step in at any time if necessary.

He was at the foot of the bed, all right, but his head was turning from one side to the other, looking, in turn, at both the man on the trolley and the girl on the gurney as if he was observing a slow motion game of tennis. And…something was wrong. So wrong that Emilia could feel the hairs on the back of her neck prickle.

This wasn't the highly skilled and totally focussed team leader that she knew and respected so much. This was a man who was clearly so rattled, for whatever reason, that he was facing a challenge that appeared to be momentarily overwhelming. She knew he was more than capable of pulling himself together well enough to stay on top of the situation but Emilia's heart went out to him because she knew how much he would hate to feel like this, let alone to have any of his colleagues seeing it. Plus, he was pale enough for her to wonder if he was unwell in some way himself.

Emilia didn't hesitate. She could only hope that she had noticed Dom's predicament before anyone else. She stepped close enough to touch his arm and make sure she had his attention.

'I'll take this one, Dom,' she said. 'Go… Take as much time as you need…'

Oddio…

It was every doctor's worst nightmare to have members of their own family brought into an emergency room with potentially life-threatening injuries but, for Dom, it was on a whole next level of complicated.

Nobody could know that this was his family. That this was his father on the resus trolley and it was his sister, Giada, who was on the second gurney. Lucas was the only person at Seattle General who knew why he had such a strained relationship with Roberto but his best friend was the brother Dom had never had and he knew that Lucas wouldn't dream of breaking that confidence. Besides, as the airway doctor, he was totally focussed on stabilising his patient's condition right now. He hadn't looked up so wouldn't have seen, and recognised, Giada and he probably hadn't realised the connection between Dom and Roberto thanks to the difference in surnames.

But Emilia had noticed something odd was going on with the same kind of lightning fast mental reflexes he'd learned to expect from her long ago. Not that she could have the slightest idea of what it was about but her concern for his wellbeing was obvious and Dom could feel a wash of gratitude softening the edges of the shock he was still grappling with.

It could have been enough to allow him to push past the personal connection with these patients. To let him stay where he was and not let it affect his clinical judgement but, beyond where Giada was talking to the triage nurse, Dom could see someone else moving calmly, but swiftly enough to suggest urgency, into the ER. Ayanna Franklin, head of PR for Seattle General. Somehow, she must have already found out who was involved in this accident and she knew she had to safeguard their identities.

No wonder she was looking stressed. It would be a PR disaster if it became known that Seattle General was incapable of protecting the privacy of patients who were depending on it because negative publicity could have wide-ranging and very damaging effects. While a small, Mediterranean kingdom might not be globally well known, the fact that Seattle General currently had both a king and a princess as patients would be deemed more than worthy of intense media attention. Dom had

been satisfyingly successful in flying under the radar
and avoiding that kind of attention for a long time but
he hadn't forgotten how intrusive it could be. Or how
far-ranging the effects could be.

Ayanna was speaking quietly to senior nursing staff
and Dom needed to know what was being decided. He
also needed Ayanna's help to ensure that his father's
medical history was available to those that needed to
know without revealing his own connection. There were
three other patients who'd been brought into his ER at
the same time as his father so it was perfectly reasonable for Dom to be seen leaving Resus to check up on
them, especially when he had someone as competent as
Emilia Featherstone to be the team leader for manag-
ing this particular patient. Staff members were stepping
back anyway, to allow for the radiographer to get the
images needed, so it was easy to keep moving.

Emilia had known what he needed more than he did,
apparently, and that was enough time to get his head
around what was happening. And to find out why his
father was even in the country way before his planned
visit in a few weeks' time. Dom needed the sanctuary
of his own office so he could make some private phone
calls to the palace but he couldn't go there yet. Not until
he could be sure that the other people involved were
being taken care of, and his younger sister was obviously going to be at the top of that list.

Except that she didn't seem to want his attention. He
couldn't even catch her gaze as he walked towards her.
The gurney she was on was already being wheeled towards one of the private examination rooms rather than
the curtained cubicles that were the usual destination

for minor to moderate cases. If that had been something Ayanna had suggested to the staff to protect privacy then Dom approved of the plan. It also meant that he could have a private conversation with her but, as he got close enough to speak to her, she shook her head.

'I'm fine,' she murmured, the assurance definite but so quiet that no one else could hear. 'Just look after Papa and the others. *Go...*'

She was the second woman to tell him to 'go' within the space of only minutes. Emilia had only been worried about his own wellbeing but Dom knew that Giada would be concerned about so many others. She had devoted her life to being the perfect Princess and their father's closest aide and she would know how devastating it would be to their people to hear what was happening when the family members weren't in a position to offer any personal reassurance.

The other people involved in this accident, his father's driver Giorgio and his bodyguard, Logan were still waiting for triage and perhaps, they would also be given the shelter of more private rooms. Dom wanted to thank Logan for the potentially life-saving treatment he'd provided for Roberto in controlling that haemorrhage but, again, it would have to wait because he couldn't allow other staff members to realise they had a personal connection. Besides, Ayanna was clearly keen to talk to him as soon as possible. He followed her into another private room and closed the door behind them.

'It's okay,' was the first thing Ayanna told him. 'For now, we've got this covered. Nobody knows that the royal family is here. It's still a secret, as originally planned, and all hospital staff are under strict instructions not to talk about their identities, as per the King's demand.'

'Why are they here so early? It's three weeks until his scheduled surgery.'

'I don't know. Perhaps he wanted to settle in and feel comfortable in the place he's going to be recuperating?' Ayanna shook her head. 'At least we already had all the plans in place. I've contacted his neurosurgeon as well. Max Granger?'

Dom's nod was curt. Without revealing his own relationship with the foreign dignitary who'd chosen Seattle General for his medical treatment, Dom had used his connections to secure the interest of one of the best neurosurgeons the world had to offer. It was at least something he could do to help his family, after his father had received that shocking diagnosis of a brain tumour. Suggesting his own hospital for the surgery had been a way to keep the news private for longer. It also meant that Dom could be sure that Roberto would get the best of care.

'He was attending a conference in Vancouver but he's already on his way back. He was very concerned to hear that the King may have a head injury.' Ayanna glanced at her watch. 'I've got to run. I'm going to collect him at the airport and bring him here.'

Stepping out of the private room, Dom's progress towards his office was interrupted by another young woman—one of his ER nurses, this time.

'What's up, Kat?'

'It's one of our patients from the MVA. Giada Baresi.'

'Is there a problem?' Dom was careful to keep his tone as neutral as possible.

'Could be. She's got a bit of bruising from a seat-belt but she's also injured her wrist. It's not an obvious fracture but we'll need an X-ray to be sure and she's refusing to have one.' Kat was frowning. 'And that's not the only thing...'

'Oh?'

'Well...it's strange but she's insisting she'll only see one doctor from the department. Lucas Beaufort?'

This time, Dom simply raised an eyebrow as a response because he needed a moment to process yet another level of complication. He looked across the department to where the doors of Resus One were folded back again. Roberto was obviously stable enough to be moved—probably to have a CT scan, unless he was going straight to Theatre, but in either case, Lucas would be available very soon. Giada knew Lucas because he'd helped to entertain her a few months ago, when she'd arrived for a visit on a weekend when Dom had an obligation to be out of town to deliver a keynote address at a conference. Was this another attempt to protect Dom's own identity because Giada was afraid she might accidentally say something revealing?

He nodded to Kat. 'That's fine,' he told her. 'And, yes, I know it's unusual but this is a special case.'

A special, rather chaotic case right now but his department was working like clockwork and he knew that everyone involved was getting the best of care. Dom wasn't needed and, in all honesty, he would not be at the top of his game with so many things hammering at his brain from so many directions. Even if it was only for a few minutes, he simply had to escape.

He had phone calls to make. Both he and Giada

needed to be kept informed, about their father's condition but it had to be done discreetly for everyone's sake. She had Lucas with her now which was a good thing because Dom had a lot to do. Palace officials needed to be informed about the accident and there were undoubtedly plans already in place in case the upcoming surgery didn't turn out to be the success they were all hoping for. Succession plans that were inevitably going to turn Dom's life upside down. He suspected that the reason his father had arrived in Seattle so early had been to ensure that he was going to be ready to do his duty—to his family and to his country. That, even if the surgery was successful enough to give Roberto many more years, it was still time for Dom to return home and become the new King. That the time had finally arrived when he had to give up the career he was so passionate about.

The calm space of his office was a complete contrast to the controlled chaos of a busy ER but it wasn't enough to relieve the tension Dom was under. If anything, as he lifted the phone to make his first international call, it was steadily increasing. Call after call needed to be made. Shocked people had to be spoken to at length and arrangements had to be planned, confirmed and double-checked. It was astonishing how much time it took and how little it was doing to ease the tension. How was his father?

Was he even still alive…?

Fear that he might never be able to speak to his father again ramped up that tension even further. The need to tell Roberto that, despite the distance Dom had kept for so many years, he still loved his father very much.

Guilt was snapping at the heels of that fear as well. If he'd done his royal duty all along instead of insisting on following his dream of becoming a doctor, this accident might never have happened in the first place. He could have lost his sister along with his father if that accident had been any worse and his country would have never forgiven him. He would have never forgiven himself.

With a groan, Dom buried his face in his hands, his elbows on his desk.

Oh…dear Lord…

She should have knocked before opening the door of this office. For a horrified moment, Emilia stared at what seemed to be a more broken version of Domenico Di Rossi than she could have ever imagined.

She ducked backwards just as quietly, pulling the door with her and then knocked on it loudly enough to be a warning. As she opened it again, in response to his call to enter, she knew her instincts had been correct. Dom would have been as horrified as she was to know that she'd seen him like that. He'd dropped his hands from his face now and he was watching the door to see who was coming into his office with an expression that suggested he was ready to deal with anything.

'I was told you wanted an update on Roberto Baresi.' Emilia kept her tone completely professional. 'I didn't realise that he was such a VIP until I came out of Theatre. It's all very hush-hush, though, isn't it?'

'How is he?'

Dom seemed to freeze after his curt query, waiting for her response, and the tension in this office was palpable enough to make Emilia blink. What on earth was going on, here?

'I'm not sure. He's still in Theatre.'

'What?' The frown on Dom's face turned his focus on her into a glare. 'What are you doing down here, then?'

'Because my part in his surgery is completed. We had to rush him to Theatre because he was still losing blood. We got some X-rays but there was no time for a CT scan—of either his leg or his head. We controlled the haemorrhage, repaired the artery and stabilised the fracture but his condition was deteriorating. He's now with a neurosurgeon who was apparently flown in specially to treat him.' Emilia was still astonished by this superstar treatment. 'Right now he's being operated on to deal with a subdural haemorrhage due to his head injury.'

'Oh, no...'

Dom closed his eyes and Emilia could see him dragging in a deep breath as if this news was a body blow of some kind.

'What's going on, Dom?' she asked quietly.

His eyes snapped open. 'Nothing. Why do you ask?'

It was her turn to glare at him. 'Something's being covered up,' she said. 'And, if there's one thing I can't stand, it's dishonesty. I've known you long enough to know that you're lying, Dom, and...and I don't think I deserve that. Do you?'

They'd always been rivals rather than friends but that didn't mean there wasn't a connection between them. A connection that was strong enough to make Emilia want to help Dom. Perhaps she cared about him more than she'd ever realised, in fact?

And maybe he could feel that connection, too. Because he was shaking his head in response to her query. The shake morphed into a slow nod.

'You deserve to know. Maybe I should have told you a very long time ago.'

'Told me what?'

This was something serious, wasn't it? Something that she was somehow involved in already, if it went back into their shared past? There was a beat of something darker than curiosity for Emilia now. She didn't like secrets. They could be considered a form of lying by omission as far as she was concerned. Dishonesty was more than simply something she disapproved of. It was right up there with not being able to trust someone and she knew, all too well, how that could destroy someone's life.

'I can't talk now.' Dom shook his head. 'There are others who need to know what's happening with Roberto and I need to talk to his surgeon when he comes out of Theatre.'

'That might not be for ages—he's only just gone in. You'll know a lot more about what's happening if you wait a while.' She held his gaze. 'And maybe whatever you think I "deserve" to know is something I should know before I see him again myself.' Surely Dom couldn't miss the hint of anger in her tone—a warning, even—but it was justified as far as Emilia was concerned. If the information that she hadn't been told meant that her patient hadn't received the best care she could possibly provide then Dr di Rossi was going to find out just how angry she was capable of getting. 'And that will be as soon as Roberto's been admitted to post-operative intensive care so the clock's ticking.'

Quick analysis of a situation and then decision making was more like the man Emilia knew. He barely hesitated.

'Fair enough.' This time, the nod was as curt as the tone. 'But we can't talk here. It's not private enough.' Dom moved swiftly to open the door of his office. 'Come with me.'

CHAPTER TWO

EVEN CLIMBING STAIRS automatically became some kind of competition between Emilia and Dom. They just couldn't help themselves. Emilia had to run to keep up with the way Dom's long legs could easily take two steps at a time and, despite still wearing her theatre scrubs, she was a little out of breath and overheated by the time they reached the top floor of Seattle General. Even so, the idea of going outside onto the roof space seemed ill-advised but Dom was definitely heading for the doors that led to the helipad.

'Are you crazy? It's single figure temperatures out there. The ice from this morning hasn't even melted yet.'

'It's okay.' Dom had already opened the door to let in a blast of freezing air. He was also wearing scrubs but didn't seem at all perturbed. 'Trust me.'

The wind chill factor felt like it was taking the temperature unpleasantly close to zero but, if Dom could handle it, Emilia wasn't about to start whining. She was familiar with this part of the roof space, having been with the trauma team on occasion, meeting critically ill patients coming in by helicopter but Dom was striding past the helipad and around the structures that housed the elevator mechanisms even though they could have provided some shelter from the biting wind.

Emilia wrapped her arms around her body, wondering how far they were going on this vast roof space but then she was totally distracted by the spectacular views she hadn't known were available up here on this side of the roof. In one direction, the dramatic mound of Mount Rainier could be seen, and in another, the distinctive tip of the Space Needle stood out amongst the high-rise buildings of the city centre. The waters of Elliot Bay had tendrils of mist that made the islands look dark and mysterious and beyond them, the impressive range of the Olympic mountains had snow and glacier-capped peaks that were touching the heavy, grey clouds.

The gorgeous landscapes of Seattle had attracted Emilia to work here just as much as the prestigious position she'd won as head of the orthopaedic department in this hospital and, already, the Olympic National Park at the foot of that mountain range had become her favourite place in the world.

A sunrise or sunset from this vantage point would be something to see. Romantic, even, if it wasn't so incredibly cold. Except...to her astonishment, Emilia could now feel the caress of warm air. A few steps more and she was surrounded in the warmth that was coming from the cluster of huge bent funnels that had to be vents for the hospital's central heating system. The noise from the system was enough for the need to raise your voice to be heard by someone standing right next to you which probably guaranteed that nobody else would hear what was said. She found herself giving Dom a surprised glance. Had he come here before to know of such a private place to have a conversation? If so, why? How much did she really know about Domenico di Rossi?

With its usual efficiency, her brain rapidly scrambled to supply the information she had available, the collection of which had begun well over ten years ago, at medical school. With his tall, dark, Mediterranean looks, Dom had been, without doubt, not only the best looking male in her class but with the faint but cute Italian accent to his perfect English she could see that most of the women around her were instantly distracted.

Emilia hadn't been about to let herself be distracted, however. It was nothing short of a miracle that she had this opportunity to follow her dream of becoming a doctor and she owed it to the person who had believed in her and made this possible to make sure she gave it her very best shot. So she'd ignored the handsome Dom, right until the day that his name had appeared above hers at the top of the list of class marks in an anatomy test. Emilia had adjusted her view of Dom at that point. She wasn't going to ignore him now. She was going to rise to the challenge he presented and do whatever it took to stop him beating her again. He couldn't have known the gift of motivation he'd provided but it got her through the tough patches when she was feeling unbearably lonely and out of place so, even though she steadfastly refused to allow any kind of personal relationship with Dom, and they went their separate ways after medical school, she hadn't been about to forget him, either. She could, in fact, probably remember every test or exam in which he'd scored a higher mark than herself but apart from that, she didn't know very much, did she?

His first words were also about something she knew nothing about.

'Have you ever heard of a country called Isola Verde?' he asked.

She shook her head.

'It means "green island" in Italian. It's an island nation in the Mediterranean. Independent. Has its own government and royal family who can be traced back to sometime in the twelfth century.'

Emilia couldn't think why Dom was telling her this but his expression was deadly serious. This was important. She remembered that the paramedic had said that her patient spoke both Italian and English. So did Dom, for that matter. She refocussed on what he was saying.

'So it's like Monaco? In France?'

'Monaco's a principality, which has a ruler or a prince, rather than a kingdom that has a king or queen, but, yes, there's a similar structure.'

Emilia was getting used to hearing Dom's words through the background noise of the vents. 'And this kingdom of Isola Verde has something to do with Roberto Baresi?'

Dom gave a single nod. 'He's the King. The girl that came in with him is his daughter, Princess Giada.'

Emilia's jaw dropped. 'I was operating on a *king*? And nobody told me?'

Dom's gaze was steady. 'Would it have made any difference to the care you gave him?'

'No, of course not.

'But why is he here? If they're here on a state visit

or something, why don't they have some sort of protection team? And media coverage?'

'It's a private visit. Arrangements had been made for him to have surgery away from his own country. There's a new hospital that's just opened in Isola Verde but I think he thought it would be too much pressure for the staff to handle treating their own monarch. Plus, his diagnosis may not be as serious as it seems and he would prefer to reveal it after the surgery has been successful.'

'Surgery for what, exactly?'

'A brain tumour. The expert opinion is that it's not malignant and that surgery should provide a complete cure but we won't know for sure until it's removed and it's in a difficult spot which is why someone as highly respected in the field as Max Granger has been engaged as the surgeon.'

Emilia was starting to put the pieces of the puzzle together. 'So that's why he got flown in so fast. I thought it was a bit over the top for a possible head injury from an accident. The injury could be significant, then, yes?'

'Yes.' Dom's tone was grim. 'It's a bit of a catastrophe really. We'll have to wait and see if it's even possible to go ahead with the original surgery that was scheduled for December.'

'How far away?'

'The fifteenth.'

'I'll have to keep that in mind while we're watching progress on the leg injury.' Focussed again on her patient, Emilia brushed aside the question of how and why Dom knew so much about this.

'Thanks for telling me,' she said. 'I can imagine why it needs to be kept under wraps and I can understand why you couldn't say anything earlier with so many people around in the ER. It's not as if we had time to do a CT of his head when it was paramount to repair that artery in his leg.'

Maybe they were both thinking of that leg wound and how hard it had been to get control of the bleeding.

'Something else you should probably know,' Dom told her, 'is that the man who was doing the haemorrhage control is the King's bodyguard, Logan Connors, who used to be an army doctor. Or *was* the King's bodyguard. He's about to leave that position because he has, coincidentally, landed a job here in the ER. He'll be starting on the first of December.'

'Oh…so that's how you knew who they all were?'

Dom looked uncomfortable now. 'Not exactly.'

That question of how Dom knew so much about this reappeared in Emilia's head because it was obvious that Dom hadn't told her everything. Okay, maybe he'd recognised the bodyguard so he knew who the patient was, but that didn't explain why he'd been rattled enough to seem incapable of taking control.

'How do you know so much about this King?' she asked slowly. 'How did you recognise his daughter the moment they came in?'

She could see Dom's hesitation. The way he took time to swallow as if it was difficult. Significant.

'Because she's my sister.'

'What?' It made no sense.

'Roberto Baresi is our father.'

Emilia actually shook her head. 'But your surname's Di Rossi, not Baresi.'

'I go by my mother's maiden name. I didn't want my

background known when I came to study and work in America. I didn't want special treatment or media attention. I wanted to be like everyone else. Like *you*, Emmy... Being able to work hard and achieve my dream of becoming a doctor.'

Emilia's head was spinning. 'Wait... You're telling me that you're the son of a *king*? That would make you a...a *prince*?'

He was holding her gaze again and she could see the absolute honesty in his eyes. 'Yes.'

A single word but one that suddenly opened a gulf between them that was wider than any ocean. He was nothing like her. They were suddenly so far apart that they could have come from different planets. He was a *prince*. Part of a royal family that could be traced back for centuries and she was a girl who hadn't even known who her father was and had had to be taken away from her mother's damaging lifestyle. He was a man who'd always had a privileged lifestyle and a future to look forward to, whereas she'd been a girl who'd been labelled wild enough to get shunted from foster home to foster home, becoming more and more lost until someone— that amazing teacher she'd had in the eleventh grade— had finally believed in her enough to let her dream of a different future.

So she'd been bang on the mark in thinking she didn't know very much about Dom, hadn't she? It was, in fact, so much of an understatement that it should have laughable. But it wasn't. This wasn't remotely funny. Emilia couldn't quite identify the swirl of emotion that she could feel building inside her head—and her heart—but it wasn't pleasant. And it was powerful enough to be preventing any speech right now. Having opened her mouth and then closed it again, she had to give in and wait for the initial shock, or whatever it was that was paralysing her, to wear off.

Emilia looked stunned, as Dom had known she would be but there was more to see in those wide, blue eyes. She looked...*hurt*, dammit—as if he'd delivered a personal blow. Because he had never trusted her enough to share his secret?

But why would he? They'd never been that close. It wasn't that he'd never found her attractive, mind you. Quite the opposite. He'd recognised the potential for not only distraction but destruction as well. He couldn't afford to fall in love with anyone because that might have led to complications that involved publicity and an early end to his career and Dom had no intention of letting that happen.

It had been so much easier to keep any liaisons with women, sexual or otherwise, on a strictly casual basis. And to keep them infrequent and as discreet as possible, of course. It didn't matter that he became labelled as something of a playboy and perennial bachelor because, if it came out later—and it most likely would—it wouldn't be a damaging scandal for the royal house of Isola Verde. He was never unkind, either, and perhaps that intent not to hurt anybody had also been a reason to steer well clear of Emilia Featherstone as anything more than his biggest academic rival.

But had he ended up hurting her anyway? It would appear so, given that she seemed to be struggling to find something to say and the silence was startlingly obvious, even with the background noise of those air vents. Dom was already feeling the weight of guilt today so he might as well add a bit more to the burden but he didn't like this. Not at all. He'd said that she deserved to know the truth. Maybe she deserved something a bit more personal as an explanation?

'I didn't tell you back then,' he said. 'I didn't tell anyone.'

She was just staring at him. Not saying anything. The wind teased a tress of her bright auburn hair out of its clasp but she didn't bother pushing it off her face. Oddly, Dom had to stifle an urge to do that himself. Instead, he chose to release words that came straight from his heart.

'I wanted a chance to be *me*,' he told Emilia. 'The person I am in here.' His fingers clenched into a fist as he thumped the left side of his chest twice. 'As a man. As the doctor I'd always dreamed of being.'

He took a deep breath, surprising himself by how shaky it felt. 'Not as Crown Prince,' he added, his words gathering more emotion. 'On borrowed time and knowing that one day I was going to have to give up a career that means everything to me and take over ruling a country just because of where I happened to be born. Even if...' He had to suck in another breath. 'Even if it's the last thing I really *want* to do.'

The expression on Emilia's face was changing. A frown line was appearing between her eyes. He might have hoped for her understanding, at least, after that very personal revelation. Sympathy, even. But no. Surprisingly, the way she was looking at him now suggested that she was...angry?

'You lied to me,' she said.

'How?'

'By not telling me the truth.'

'Nobody knew the truth. How long do you think I would have lasted if it had come out? I would have been hounded by the media until I was driven home again. I needed to be safe to achieve what I wanted so much and keeping it a secret was the only way.'

'So you're saying you've never told anyone, in all these years? That no one here knows who you are and that no one from your country knows where you are?'

'Not exactly,' Dom admitted. 'I haven't been home for many years but my sister's been to visit me more than once. And Lucas Beaufort knows... We found we had something in common with...um...some family issues.'

Emilia's breath came out in a dismissive huff. 'Family issues? You have *no* idea what family issues really are. People kept secrets from me all my life and, as far I'm concerned, they're just as bad as outright lies. They damage people. They damage lives.'

Oh, man...she wasn't just angry about this, was she? Emilia was furious.

'You know what?' She didn't wait for a response. 'I don't care that you're a damn prince. I respected you for what I thought you were—as that man and that doctor you wanted so much to be—but not now...' Emilia paused to gulp in a breath. 'I don't respect anybody who lies to me. I *hate* dishonesty...'

She turned away, her arms tightly wrapped around her body. 'Don't worry,' she added, with a bitter note in her voice. 'Your secret is safe. I'm not going to tell anyone about you. I don't even want to talk *to* you, let alone *about* you.'

And, with that, she was gone. A petite, furious figure striding across this vast roof space. Turning the corner to head for the helipad and then back into the warmth and shelter of the hospital buildings. Which was exactly where Dom needed to go. There might be news of his father by now that he could pass on to Giada. He might have just ruined one of his closer professional relationships but he had his family to care for and that had to take priority. And yet, his feet refused to start moving just yet. He looked up at the sullen sky above him as he took several, slow, deep breaths to try and clear his head enough to centre himself.

Part of his brain was reluctant to let go of that last image of Emilia, vanishing behind the tops of the nearest elevators. There was something nagging at him that he couldn't quite pin down. Curiosity, perhaps, about why she was so angry with him. They hadn't known each other well enough for her to be that offended that he'd kept a secret from her, surely? It wasn't as if she'd ever told him anything personal about her own life. And maybe that was what he wanted to think about—that reference to people keeping secrets from her? Damaging her life? He wanted to know more about that. No… it felt like he *needed* to know more about that.

Except that there were other things he had to think about right now that were a lot more pressing. Dom knew it was way past time that he stepped up to do his duty. He'd had a lot longer than he'd hoped for when his father gave him permission to go to an American medical school. He'd hoped to graduate and at least have a few years to practise medicine but he'd had a good ten years to do the job he loved and he'd achieved an expertise and position that had been above any expectations.

And he'd always known that this day would come. That the shackles of his birth right would pull him back to the gilded cage that his childhood had been. He could feel them tightening already as the chains that bound him to his country were being hauled in. Dom was used to pressure. In the early years of his studies it had been to succeed. A wry smile touched his lips as he remembered how, at medical school, that pressure had included trying to beat Emilia Featherstone. The pressure of running a busy ER was something else again but it was something that Dom thrived on. This pressure, however, of facing up to becoming King, felt like a weight that threatened to bury him.

But that couldn't happen.

It wasn't going to happen because Dom knew what was expected of him by people that he loved and he wasn't about to let them down. One of those people was in danger right now and that was where Dom needed to be. He had to protect his father as much as he could. He had to support his little sister who must be extremely anxious at the moment. The driver, Giorgio, no doubt also needed some reassurance from him, even if he had been uninjured, and Logan was about to become a colleague instead of one of his father's employees. Dom had to check to see if there was anything he could be doing to make sure everyone was okay.

He certainly couldn't stay out here on the roof any longer, that was for sure. He felt cold now. And very, very alone…

* * *

Emilia did an online search on Isola Verde as soon as she got home. Of course she did. The events of the day had taken on an almost dreamlike quality, despite the reality of her post-operative visit to Roberto Baresi and seeing the discreet security that was now positioned as close as possible to where he was being cared for in the most private space available in the intensive care unit. At least Dom hadn't been there at the same time because she was still furious with him. It might be impossible to avoid seeing him again but she really, really didn't want to talk to him.

And maybe she was searching for details on the island kingdom she'd never heard of because she wanted to justify that anger. To confirm that they came from such totally different worlds it was a relief that she'd avoided any kind of personal relationship. The fact that they were colleagues was extraordinary enough on its own. That they had that competitive bond and were familiar enough with each other for the teasing and, okay, sometimes bordering on insulting banter, to feel completely normal was enough to make Emilia cringe, now. How could he do that? To pretend he was a normal person? To pretend that he was trustworthy when he'd been living a lie the whole time?

He'd said he hadn't been home for many years. Why not? The images and text that Emilia had in front of her told her that he'd been brought up in paradise. The 'green island', surrounded by the astonishing blue water of the Mediterranean Sea, was well named for its fertile land that produced olive oil, tomatoes, lemons and the grapes that were used for award winning wines. The old town, that dated back to the eleventh or twelfth century had narrow, cobbled streets and colourful market places but there was a modern city as well where a new hospital, that the country was obviously very proud of, had been built.

There were gorgeous gardens on the top of a hill in the old city that surrounded a palace built of white stone and marble and the photos that Emilia was staring at suggested that it was always reflecting endless sunshine. The images and impressions were piling up, one on the other. She could almost taste those fat, red tomatoes, and the bright lemons were actually making her mouth water. She could feel the warmth of the sunshine and smell the flowers in those gardens and imagine what it would be like to swim in that blue, silky sea and it felt like Isola Verde was the most perfect place on earth.

The place where Domenico di Rossi had grown up.

No. The place where Domenico *Baresi* was the Crown Prince. Unimaginably wealthy. Unbelievably privileged. And he'd wanted her to feel *sorry* for him? An incredulous huff escaped Emilia's throat and she slammed down the lid of her laptop but, moments later, she was bewildered by the sting behind her eyes that she remembered from long, long ago. Tears were gathering, although they would never be shed because she didn't cry any more.

From fury to feeling so sad? What on earth was this about? Emilia hadn't felt such a rollercoaster of emotion for as long as she could remember. Anger had always been her 'go-to' release for dealing with anything difficult, though, hadn't it? Even when that had got her into so much trouble in the past. Her running away, shouting and breaking things had more than likely been responsible for those endless punishments. For waiting outside those Social Services offices while discussions were taking place about what on earth they were going to do with such a difficult, unruly child.

But it hadn't stopped her hitting back at a world that had promised so much but never delivered. Not until that amazing teacher had somehow recognised her intelligence and had shifted her focus onto studying, along with teaching her that there were ways other than anger to escape something unbearable.

If she'd known there were places on earth like Isola Verde in those days, Emilia might have dreamed of being there. Maybe that was what was making her feel so inexplicably sad now. That longing to be living, or even just visiting, somewhere so perfect felt a lot like that longing to be loved that she'd lived with throughout all those difficult years. And that was something else that made Dom so different from her. He had a family. People who loved him. He had everything, didn't he?

So why was Emilia feeling haunted by that look in his eyes when he'd told her that going back to his own country to be a prince was the last thing he really wanted to do? And why was it, when her anger had faded enough for her to remember that look, she felt that there *was* still a connection between them?

That, maybe, it was even stronger than before?

CHAPTER THREE

STEPPING THROUGH THE automatic doors that linked Seattle General's ER to the rest of the hospital, Emilia found herself catching her breath.

How could everything look the same when nothing *felt* the same?

She could see the doors to the ambulance bay opening and a patient being brought in on a stretcher to where the triage nurse was waiting for them. The central desk had doctors and interns checking results like X-rays and blood tests that were coming through on one of the many computer screens available or standing beside the glass wall where patient locations and conditions were kept up to date, along with which doctor was assigned to the case. Curtains were being opened or whisked shut as medical staff, technicians or even cleaners or security came and went from the cubicles and the folding doors to Resus One were open, just as they had been when Emilia answered the trauma team code only yesterday.

But it felt very different. The head of this ER was not the person she'd thought he was. Instead, he was something so extraordinary it was still almost impossible to wrap her head around it. A crown prince. Royalty. With a background of such privilege that the gulf between them couldn't be any bigger. And that was why it felt so different. Emilia didn't know what to say to Dom any more. She felt awkward. Out of place. *Different*. The feeling was uncomfortably reminiscent of how she'd felt at every new school she'd had to go to or worse, with every new family who'd decided to take on the challenge of fostering her.

Dom was even in almost the same place she'd seen him yesterday morning but it looked as though he was merely scanning the area to make sure it was ready for use when needed. The incoming patient, a teenaged boy in a school uniform who was grinning at something the paramedic was telling him, certainly didn't look as if he was in need of critical care. Emilia didn't need to go near the resus area, either. She wasn't actually required in the ER at all at the moment but she was here and seeing Dom standing alone and not currently caught up in some emergency was exactly what she'd hoped to find.

Because she needed to apologise.

She needed, somehow, to try and make things more like they'd been the day before yesterday. So that she could feel just as excited by the challenge of answering a trauma team call and come into this ER without feeling like her stomach was tied up in knots. She'd been unprofessional yesterday, storming off like the petulant teenager she'd once been and she didn't want that to affect her ability to work with Dom. Was it possible that they could somehow get past this and go back to that easy camaraderie that allowed for a bit of banter?

Swallowing hard as she got close to Resus One,

Emilia decided to see if she could take a short cut straight back.

'Hey...' She lowered her voice to a whisper as she half smiled to let Dom know she was teasing him. 'Sorry, but my curtsey's a bit rusty.'

Oh...help... That had gone down like a lead balloon, hadn't it? Dom's smile was more like a grimace. Then he raised an eyebrow, glancing over Emilia's shoulder to where a technician was coming past, pushing an ECG trolley.

'My office?' His tone was neutral. 'If you've got a moment to spare, that is.' He didn't wait for her response, but turned on his heel and walked off. Emilia followed. This wasn't reminding her so much of a first day at school, any more. It was more like being sent to the headmaster's office to explain yet another instance of her bad behaviour.

But Dom didn't look angry as he shut the office door behind her. He looked as if he hadn't slept all night. Or maybe he hadn't even gone to bed. There were deep creases around his eyes and he might have combed his hair with his fingers judging by its tousled look. And then he sighed and the sound cut through Emilia more than a raised voice might have.

'This is exactly why I didn't tell you,' he said quietly. 'Why I didn't tell anyone. It changes things. It makes it impossible to know whether a relationship is even genuine.'

Yep...he was rubbing his forehead as he spoke and then he ran his fingers through his hair making it even more rumpled. But Emilia only noticed that in her peripheral vision because she was caught by his eyes as he spoke again.

'And what we had—what we *have*, I should say—that's genuine, isn't it?'

Emilia felt the need to catch her breath again, the way she had when she'd been coming into the ER, but this time, it didn't work. Her breath had already been caught in her chest.

Dom gave his head a tiny shake. 'It's strange because we don't really know that much about each other but I've always thought that you know me better than anyone. Because we're the same, you and me.'

Her breath wasn't caught any more. It escaped through pursed lips in a dismissive huff. 'Yeah... right...' she muttered.

But Dom ignored her. 'In here, we are,' he said softly. He touched the left side of his chest, over his heart, with the same gesture he'd used yesterday when he'd been telling her so passionately that he'd wanted a chance to be the person he truly was.

'We both had the same dream and we were both driven to be the best. We both give everything we've got—and more—to our careers. To the people who put their trust and their lives into our hands.'

Emilia had to swallow the lump in her throat. It was true. That was the connection. But something else had grown from them becoming such rivals to be the best. Genuine respect. And, while they'd kept their distance personally, there was a familiarity, if not a kind of fondness, even, in the banter they'd always enjoyed. Was that why she'd found herself almost crying, yesterday? Because she'd thought she'd lost that for ever?

'Maybe I didn't explain things very well yesterday,' Dom continued. 'I didn't mean to upset you. I'd like a chance to explain better.'

Emilia shook her head. 'There's no need. I shouldn't have reacted the way I did. That's what I came here for…to apologise.'

'There's no need for that, either, but I'd still like to talk. I want to try and put things right between us and…'

Emilia watched him take a slow breath as he hesitated. This was what she wanted, too, wasn't it? To put things right? Maybe it was going to be possible to push the rewind button, at least enough to let them work together without distraction. Except that Dom seemed to have something he was reluctant to say.

'And…?' she prompted.

'I'd like to know you better,' he said. 'I didn't sleep much last night. I was worried about my father. And my sister.'

'Of course you were. I was happy with Roberto's condition as far as his orthopaedic status is when I saw him earlier today but the brain surgery has to be a concern. Are they going to try waking him up soon?'

'They've already lightened the sedation but he's not showing any signs of waking up. It may take some time.'

'At least he's in the best possible place. And your sister?'

'She tells me she's fine. She's not in the hospital any longer and she's apparently trying to keep a low profile. She wouldn't even tell me where she is. Anyway…' Dom rubbed his forehead again. 'It wasn't just family worries that kept me awake all night. I was thinking about you, as well.'

That startled her. Not that she was about to confess she'd spent quite some time thinking about him,
mind you.

'About what you meant when you said I had no idea
what "family issues" really are.' Dom caught and held
her gaze. 'I want to know what happened to you and
why you hate secrets so much. I just...' His breath came
out in another sigh. 'I guess I just don't want to lose
what we have, Emmy. Something that's real. Something I can trust.'

'But...how can I trust *you*...?'

'You know my secret now.' Dom gaze shifted to the
closed door of his office and then back to Emilia. 'You
and Lucas are the only people here that know. Even
everybody involved in Roberto's scheduled visit and
surgery have no idea of my connection to the family.
I'm trusting *you*...'

He was. And, oddly, it made Emilia want to cry again
and she never cried. She'd decided long ago that she had
used up a lifetime supply of tears as a child.

An alarm was sounding beyond the office door and
Dom's head swerved, his conversation with Emilia shut
down as swiftly as if a switch had been flicked.

'That's the cardiac arrest code...' He was already
opening the door and, a moment later, Emilia could
hear him issuing terse instructions to get the patient
into Resus One. As she walked past the closed doors
seconds later, he was calmly asking for someone to
charge the defibrillator to two hundred joules. *Stat...*

The cardiac arrest victim who'd been rushed into resus
looked barely more than a child.

'How old is he?' Dom was watching the screen of the monitor as he held a bag mask over the boy's face to deliver a breath of oxygen. It was still showing a heart rhythm that would have been rapidly fatal if this arrest hadn't happened somewhere with people trained to support circulation by doing CPR while they used shocks and drugs to try and get a normal rhythm established again.

'Fourteen.' An intern was doing the first two minutes of chest compressions.

'History?'

'He got brought in by ambulance after fainting at school.' It was another ER doctor who answered Dom's query, as she was working to establish an IV line in the patient's arm. 'The paramedic said that the school wasn't aware of any health problems. His mother's been contacted and she's on her way.'

A fainting episode could well have been a warning sign of the sudden cardiac arrest that had occurred later but Dom didn't have the head space to be considering what might have caused this life-threatening situation. That would come later, when they'd got this boy back.

'I'll have the airway trolley, please. I'm going to intubate.' A flash of thought came and went as Dom realised that Lucas wasn't here to manage the airway component of this resuscitation but that was something else that couldn't be allowed head space yet. 'Draw up some adrenaline, thanks. And amiodarone. Charge the defib again. I'll intubate in the next cycle of compressions.' He gave another two breaths with the bag mask as the defibrillator was charging.

'Okay...stand clear... Shocking now...'

The battle was on and it was one that Dom was absolutely determined to win. He had all the weapons that could be to his advantage—the ability to deliver electrical shocks, access to blood vessels and drugs that could stimulate the heart or deal with arrhythmias, the means to control an airway and breathing, oxygen, trained staff to perform quality chest compressions to keep blood circulating and the knowledge and skills to use all these weapons to whatever degree was needed.

It was the kind of battle that Dom thrived on. It was absolutely gutting if he lost, of course, but on the other side of the coin was where there was no question that someone's life had been saved and that had always been at the heart of why he'd dreamed of becoming a doctor. A success was something the whole team would celebrate—and remember—and, this morning, fifteen minutes after Dom had answered the cardiac arrest code, it looked like that was happening.

'Look...there...we've got sinus rhythm.'

The excitement in the intern's voice made Dom wonder if this might be the first successful resuscitation this young doctor had been a part of. Dom had long ago lost count of how many he'd experienced but, even now, he could share that thrill of seeing the normal spikes tracking across the monitor screen.

'Airway and ventilation are secure,' he told the team. 'I'm going to keep him sedated for now. Let's get a twelve lead ECG. Has Cardiology been paged for a consult?'

'They're on their way. Should arrive soon.'

Someone else arrived first, however. A distraught

looking woman who was shown into the resus room, where she rushed towards the trolley.

'Oh, my God… *Jason*…' She reached out to touch his hair but then froze, her gaze fixed on Dom. 'Is he… is he…?'

'He's been very sick,' Dom told her, 'but we've got him back to a normal heart rhythm.'

'The school told me he'd just fainted. That there was nothing to worry about but they'd called an ambulance to be on the safe side.'

'It's good that they did. He was in the best place possible when his heart stopped.'

Jason's mother was pale enough to look as though she might be about to faint herself. 'It *stopped*? How? *Why?* Is he going to be okay?'

'That's what we need to find out. Has he ever fainted before? Or had seizures?'

'No…never.'

'Has he been unwell recently? With a virus, perhaps?'

Again, the woman shook her head. She had her gaze fixed on her son's still face now, her fingers pressed against her lips as if she was trying to stifle a sob.

'Is there any chance he's been exposed to drugs?'

'*No…*' She was shocked but then looked fearful. 'They can cause heart attacks, can't they? Some of those pills the kids experiment with these days.'

'Jason hasn't had a heart attack,' Dom explained. 'He's had what we call a sudden cardiac arrest. A heart attack is caused by a blockage in a coronary artery and damage to heart muscle. A heart attack can cause SCA but it's very, very unlikely in Jason's case. It's far more likely that it's been caused by a congenital defect that hasn't shown up before, or a problem with the electrical signal. The cardiologists will be able to tell you a lot more and they'll do whatever tests are necessary to find out the cause.'

'But…but what if it happens again? He…he could die in his sleep or something…'

Tears were escaping now and Jason's mother was getting more and more upset. This wasn't the time to start telling her about implantable defibrillators that could prevent it happening again. She needed reassurance right now. And support.

'Jason's safe here,' Dom told her. 'We're going to take very good care of him but he won't wake up for a little while yet. Would you like to come into one of our relatives' rooms? Can we call family to come and be with you? What about Jason's dad?'

'No…' A handful of tissues was muffling the woman's words. 'It's just me and Jase…' A nurse had come close and put her arm around the distraught mother's shoulders. 'His father hasn't even seen him since he was a baby and my family…well…there's kind of issues there, you know?'

Dom was nodding but he was hearing something else. An echo of Emilia's words.

You have no idea what family issues really are…

The cardiologist team were arriving, Jason was stable and he could see that the boy's mother was going to get plenty of emotional support from his staff so, after a detailed handover to Cardiology, Dom left the resus area. He had other things he needed to do.

He passed the triage desk first.

'Kat? Do you know where Lucas Beaufort is?'

'I heard he's had to take leave to deal with something personal. A family thing, maybe?'

Dom simply nodded and moved on but he was frowning. Why hadn't Lucas come to him to arrange the leave? Did it have something to do with his father, perhaps, and he hadn't wanted to share that with Dom when he was facing a crisis with his own father so critically ill?

Family issues were obviously the theme of the day and the tension that had dissipated to some extent this morning when he'd been told that Roberto's condition was stable was now ramping up again. He had another family member to worry about as well, didn't he? Where was Giada and was she really okay?

In the privacy of his office, Dom hit a speed dial number.

'What's happening?' were her first words. 'Is it Papa?'

'No. The last information I have is that he's stable. Still unconscious but his leg's looking good, his intracranial pressure is under control and everything else is within normal limits. We'll have to be patient. It's a "wait and see" situation.'

'That's what I was told as well. That's why I'm going home.'

'What?' Dom was shocked. 'Home? To Isola Verde? When?'

'I'm on my way now.'

Someone else who was making big decisions and taking leave without even consulting him was disturbing. Surely Giada felt the need to be close to their father at a time like this? She was certainly much closer to him than he was. Or she wanted to be, anyway. And, okay, maybe his little sister had been rebellious enough to cause Roberto some embarrassment years ago but the people of Isola Verde adored her and she'd been the King's right-hand woman for a long time now. It was entirely to Giada's credit that the fabulous new hospital was up and running.

'Someone has to be there,' Giada said into the silence. 'What if this news gets out somehow? Can you imagine the instability it could cause? What if…?' Dom could hear his sister trying to steady her voice. 'What if he dies, Dom?'

'He's stable… He's not in any immediate danger.'

Giada didn't seem to hear him. 'It's *you* who should be going home. You're the person that people need to see. They need to know that you care about the country you're going to rule.'

'I can't just leave.' The feeling of being torn between two places had been there for so long now, it was very familiar but it was stronger than ever today. Strong enough to be painful. 'And someone needs to be here for Father. He came here for care in my hospital. I'm the one who can ensure that care is the best available.'

'No, Dom…what he really came here for was to talk to you about the succession. To have enough time before his operation to persuade you to come home. In case… in case he didn't survive the surgery.'

'Why didn't you tell me? *Warn* me?' Perhaps Emilia wasn't wrong to find secrets disturbing.

'Papa forbade it. He's afraid, Dom. Of what might

happen if people find out before you're back home to take the throne.'

His father…*afraid*…? The concept was alien. He'd always been a somewhat distant figure when the royal children were young and became even more so after their mother had died. Dom hadn't even visited his homeland for years and had barely spoken to his father during that period. Did being afraid meant that Roberto cared about more than his country? That he might have difficulty showing it but he cared about his children? Yesterday's guilt came back with a vengeance.

'I've got to go,' Giada said. 'They're calling our flight.'

'Our?'

'It's not a private plane, Dom. Keep in touch, won't you? Let me know if anything changes with Papa. I'll come back as soon as I'm sure everything's fine at home but I can get straight on a flight if I'm needed and be back in twelve hours.'

He had no right to try and persuade her to stay. He had taken himself out of her life as much as their father's when he'd come to America to study and then work.

'Of course I will,' was all he said. 'Safe travels, Gigi.' Using her pet name gave him a lump in his throat. 'I'll miss you.'

He was missing her the moment he ended the call, in fact. He had his father upstairs in the ICU in a coma and the only other family he had was on her way back to Europe. His best friend wasn't available to talk to either. Or was he?

Dom hit another speed dial number but he got a voice

mail message that Lucas's phone was either turned off or reception was unavailable. He left a message.

'Don't know what's up, bro, but I'm here if you need a friend. Take care.'

Dom dropped his phone on his desk and rubbed his forehead with his middle finger. No family to talk to. No best friend. He hadn't felt this alone for a long, long time. Closing his eyes, he heard that whisper at the back of his mind again.

You have no idea…

His eyes snapped open. He had Emilia's number but he wasn't going to ring, in case she was busy with a patient. He texted instead.

We got interrupted before. I'd still like to talk.

Discovery Park.

The largest green space in the city and one of the many great assets that Seattle was blessed with. There were hundreds of acres of land with views of the Olympic and Cascade mountains that were almost as spectacular as the ones Emilia had seen from the roof of Seattle General a couple of days ago. There were miles of beach, dramatic sea cliffs and sand dunes, forests and streams and, when Emilia didn't have a whole day free that meant she could go as far as the Olympic National Park, or she simply wanted to be available within a reasonable amount of time for any seriously unwell patients, this was the place she always came. She could run, walk or simply sit somewhere to soak in the landscapes she loved and recharge her batteries.

It was normally a solitary activity but Dom's text

message yesterday struck her as being almost a plea. Maybe it had been the sincerity of what he'd said about them being so alike, even if that notion was ludicrous given what she'd just learned of his background. Or— and this had been something that had really touched Emilia—it was because he'd said he didn't want to lose what they had. Because it was *real*...

So, she'd texted back and said she had a late start today and, if he had some free time, he was welcome to join her at the park for a jog. And here they were, jogging along a forest track, their breath creating white clouds in the frosty morning air. Emilia was leading the way. Because she knew the tracks of this park so well and where she wanted to go? Or was Dom allowing her to stay in front despite how easy it would be for him to use those long legs of his and turn this into a race? Oddly, that kind of rivalry that could turn anything into a competition was absent this morning. By the time they left the forest track and headed into open space towards the beach and the West Point lighthouse, they were jogging side by side. And then, by tacit consent, they slowed to a walk. In silence to start with, as they both needed to catch their breath.

It was Dom who broke the companionable silence as he turned to smile at Emilia.

'Thanks.'

'What for?'

'Suggesting I come here. I never take advantage of spaces like this when I've only got an hour or two free but this...' He made a sweeping gesture with his arm. 'This is exactly what I needed.'

'It's gorgeous, isn't it? That over there...' Emilia

pointed to the snow-capped mountain range in the distance. 'That's the Olympic National Park. If you want to clear your head and put your world to rights properly, then that's the place to go. It takes nearly three hours to get there, though, so I don't go that often but I love it. It's my absolute favourite place in the world, now.'

'I remember you used to love running. You were a real gym bunny back at med school.'

'Only because I couldn't take the time to find places like this.'

'You looked like you were in love with treadmills whenever I got to the gym. I never used the one next to you because you looked like you could keep going for ever and do it faster and steeper than I could,'

Emilia laughed. 'That's what I wanted you to think. The truth was that I was dying inside and was scared that I'd fall flat on my face. Or have a heart attack or something.'

Dom's grin lit up his face. 'Really? It was for my benefit?'

'I was using the old "fake it till you make it" strategy. It was obvious from the get-go that if I wanted to get noticed, you were the one I had to beat.'

'We both pushed each other, that's for sure. I wouldn't have done nearly as well at school if you hadn't been—how do you say it? Setting the post? No…it's setting the bar, I think.'

The tiny slip in his command of American English was unusual enough to remind Emilia that he came from somewhere a long way away. And that that was only one of the differences between them.

'And I might not have even got through school,' she

admitted, 'if I hadn't been trying to make sure I got higher marks than you every time.'

'No...' Dom shook his head. 'Everybody knew you were a genius. You were years younger than any of us. You must have done your bachelor's degree while you were still a teenager.'

Emilia shrugged. 'I got fast-tracked. I had a teacher who coached me. Mrs Delaney. She probably saved my life, actually. If it hadn't been for her, I was probably on my way to being in jail. Or dead.' She swallowed hard. 'Like my mom.'

She could hear their feet crunching on stones as they left the path to walk along the beach. Way ahead of them were the cluster of little buildings with the peak of the lighthouse on one of them. Pretty white structures with pink roofs that had the glorious background of the Olympic mountain range behind them.

'Did you have any other family?' Dom asked quietly.

Emilia shrugged. 'Guess I have a father somewhere but I never knew who he was.'

'And your mom really went to jail?'

'Yeah...not until after they took me away when I was five. One of my foster families told me about it later. After they heard she'd died of an overdose as soon as she got out. And then they said that I was going to end up just like her and I'd better behave myself with my next family.'

'Buon delore,' Dom muttered. 'You were just a little girl.' He looked appalled but then, as he held Emilia's gaze, his expression changed to something more like admiration. 'But you won,' he said softly. 'You had such a tough start and yet, here you are—a beautiful woman.

An amazing doctor. With the kind of position that you always dreamed of?'

Emilia nodded. 'I have the perfect job. The perfect apartment. And places like this to come to when I'm not at work. I'm very lucky.'

It was true. She *was* very lucky, in every aspect of her life except the most personal but she wasn't about to confess that failure to Dom. He'd never been short of women who'd been desperate to be his partner, even if it was only a short-lived fling.

'I, too, have been very lucky,' Dom said. 'It always felt too good to be true that I was allowed to come here and study and then to work as a doctor. To be able to do it without anyone knowing who I was made it perfect and it went on for so much longer than I had dreamed it could. I've felt safe. Safe enough to suggest that this was where my father should come for his surgery but now...' He shook his head. 'Now it's falling apart. I may have to leave Seattle General by Christmas. It's past time I stepped up and became King.'

Emilia almost laughed. If someone had told her when she was young that, one day, she would be walking on a beach with a man about to become a king, she would probably have kicked them for teasing her. Here she was, doing it, and it still felt like a fantasy. Too good to be true...?

'I should have done it a long time ago,' Dom added. 'My father is seventy-five. He should have been able to abdicate long ago. He should have had the support of his family to do that. I've been selfish.'

They were almost at the lighthouse now and they both slowed their steps further and then stopped.

Emilia could see the guilt that Dom was grappling with. Shame, even, that he'd followed his dream instead of doing his duty?

'You're the one who's an amazing doctor,' she told him. 'Have you ever stopped to count how many people are still alive because of what you gave up and how hard you've worked to become who you really wanted to be? That's not selfish, Dom. It's pretty heroic, if you ask me.'

His expression was changing again and Emilia found herself watching with fascination as she saw frown lines melting and eyes becoming dark with emotion. His smile was barely there, as if he didn't want to take the compliment, but it was so warm it was thanking her for offering comfort.

It still felt too good to be true to be here with this man who was a prince and it also felt incredibly personal. This had to be the first time ever that they'd had a conversation that wasn't about anything professional at all. This wasn't even about the rivalry they'd always fostered.

This was about the connection between them that perhaps neither of them had ever tried to define. The connection that Dom had described as 'real'. It *was* real. And it went deep. It had been brought sharply into focus by the extraordinary revelations of the last couple of days but even more so by Dom saying that he might have to leave Seattle by Christmas. A matter of only weeks away and he was going to vanish from her life for ever and that thought was enough to squeeze Emilia's chest so hard it was impossible to drag in a new breath. As impossible as it was to break that eye contact with Dom.

What this was *really* about was admitting how much she cared for this man, wasn't it? She'd had her suspicions the other day when she'd seen how rattled he was in the ER and again, in his office when she'd appealed for him to tell her the truth about what was going on but this was even bigger.

So big that she knew it was about to shake the foundations of her life.

How ironic was this? To find out that she felt so strongly about Domenico di Rossi when she'd just learned how impossible it was that they could ever be together in any way?

Except…maybe that was precisely why these feelings were bubbling to the surface. Because it was safe.

Because nothing was ever going to happen between them. Or nothing more than what had already happened, anyway. Finally, Emilia was able to drag her gaze away from Dom's. She shifted it to her watch.

'I'm running out of time,' she told him. 'I'll have to run back to the car park. Feel free to take your time, Dom.'

'Ha… I don't think so.'

The way Dom seemed to become even taller reminded her of days long gone when the marks to a quiz or test had been released and her name had been first on the list. He was stepping up to a new challenge. He caught her gaze as they both turned, poised to break into a run and she could see a glimpse of sheer pleasure in his eyes. More than that, even. A new connection because there was more truth between them now?

Whatever. Emilia had a very good reason to stay in front of Dom right now. She didn't want him to guess what had been going through her mind seconds ago. She didn't want to remember it herself and running as fast as possible was a great way to put it behind her. She took off, throwing no more than a smile and a few words over her shoulder.

'Eat my dust…'

CHAPTER FOUR

AN INTENSIVE CARE unit was not the most peaceful place to be for either the patients or the close family members who were beside their beds. The level of staffing was high enough for it to feel crowded and seriously unwell people were there for the constant monitoring they needed which meant they were rarely left alone. The banks of sophisticated monitoring equipment created a background of beeping sounds, occasionally interrupted by alarms as parameters for whatever was being watched reached levels that were too high or low.

Nobody questioned the interest that the head of Seattle General's ER had in this particular patient because he often followed the progress of cases he'd been involved with. Apart from the select few that knew his father's identity, nobody thought there was anything different about the man in the far corner bed who was still in a coma following his emergency surgery for both leg and head injuries. It was a sad thought for Dom that nobody would recognise Roberto Baresi right now, with his head bandaged, eyes puffy and closed and his face half covered with the device securing his breathing tube in place and supporting the bulky connections to the bedside ventilator.

After three days, it was becoming a familiar part of Dom's routine to regularly drop into the ICU. He was also in frequent contact with his father's neurosurgeon, Max Granger, so he could pass on the progress reports to his sister, Giada. During the day, Dom's brief visits were purely clinical, but during the night in Seattle General's post-surgical ICU the staffing level was lower so that was when Dom could spend a little more time by his father's bedside—as a loving son who was grappling with both sadness and guilt at what Roberto was having to endure.

If anybody asked, Dom was going to tell them that he was a friend of the family and the only person close enough to visit, but nobody had asked yet. This was a place where people were ultimately vulnerable so privacy was respected whenever possible to afford patients just a little more dignity.

Dom was sitting quietly now, close to Roberto's bed, in the dimmed lighting of the unit, watching the screens and readouts on the monitors around his father. He was able to speak quietly to him without being overheard thanks to the background hum of the ventilator and the other sounds of the ICU. He told him that Giada was fine and that she was back in Isola Verde and there were no problems at home. He reassured him about the others involved in the accident, telling him that Logan was unhurt and ready to start work next week at Seattle General and that Giorgio was uninjured. He also told him frequently that he was doing well himself.

That they were all taking the best care of him and that he was going to come through this with flying colours.

There was still a level of tension, of course. His father had not only survived a serious car accident but had also been through not just one but two life-saving surgeries in the space of only a few hours after that. He was still in a coma and requiring support for his breathing days later with no indications yet of when he might wake up, but there was relief to be found as well. The critical period of the initial six to twelve hours, when a deterioration in clinical status was usually the first sign of a potentially fatal complication, was thankfully well past now and Roberto was stable, with good control of the key aspects of blood pressure and oxygen levels that werc so important in the care of a patient with a head injury.

Relief was one of the best feelings in the world, Dom decided, as he let a long, slow breath out, having scanned all the monitors before allowing his gaze to rest on his father's face again. He could actually feel some tension being swept away, to be replaced with a sense of peace that might not last but it was something to be savoured for as long as possible. Dom found himself smiling at his father and leaning closer so he could talk quietly. Not about anything in particular, it was in the hope that his father would be able to hear his voice and to know that someone who loved him was nearby.

'I had a big day in the ER today,' he told Roberto. 'There was just so much going on and a lot of very sick people so I had to try and be in too many places at the same time. There was a shooting victim and someone who'd fallen from a roof. Other people with drug overdoses and heart attacks and someone who was badly burned.' He leaned back to stretch. 'Do you ever get an ache between your shoulder blades from too much stress? Yes...' Dom paused for a long moment, watching his father's face. 'Of course you do. Ruling a country carries a lot more responsibility than running an ER, doesn't it? I have to admit I'm really not looking forward to that at all. The ER is the only kingdom I've ever wanted to rule.'

He let his breath out in a sigh. It was time to change the subject. This might be a one-sided conversation that nobody else could hear but he was still treading on thin ice. If this story broke, the level of tension around Roberto would escalate as private security as well as other measures would have to be installed and that would not help his recovery at all.

'Were the horses your way of defusing the stress? A fast gallop along a beach? The best thing I find is to stand in a really hot shower for a long time. Not that I'd change my job because of the stress, mind you.' He was talking aloud to himself now. He would never have dreamed of saying anything like this to his father if it was a normal conversation. 'I love it because it pushes me to perform the best I can and...when you know you've made a difference—saved a life, possibly— then that's the best feeling in the world. Like relief but bigger...because there's satisfaction in making it happen. Pride, even...'

There was no flicker on his father's face to suggest that he could hear what Dom was saying but it felt good to be telling him how important his job was to him. To say things he should probably have said long ago.

'I've never thanked you for letting me have the opportunity to do this. You could have stopped me from coming here to study in the first place and…and I know you've let me continue working for longer than you wanted to. I'm sorry I haven't been home in so long but it was because I didn't want to have that discussion. I didn't want to feel any more guilty than I already did, that I was putting off doing my duty. Hoping for just another year of being here and being able to be true to myself—as a man. And a doctor. Not as a crown prince who should have stood up to do his duty a long time ago. I've felt so guilty about that…'

Dom let his breath out in another sigh. He shouldn't be talking about this again but it had been bottled up for too long. 'I've felt guilty about keeping the secret of who I am, too. At first it was so good to be able to live like a normal person here and never have to worry about someone taking a picture that might reflect badly on the family but, you know what? Keeping a secret like that meant that nobody really knew me. I think it's actually been a much bigger barrier than I realised. To all sorts of things…'

Because there was the most astonishing relief to be found in the fact that Emilia Featherstone now knew that secret. He'd always been himself with her—or what he thought of as his real self—but that secret was also part of himself and it had created a solid wall between them. A gap that could never be bridged. Now it was gone and, while the smashing of that barrier had created a bit of damage and he couldn't blame Emilia for having been so angry he was hopeful that, given time, she would trust him again and they would be on new ground.

Astonishing new ground, for both of them, but most significantly, for Dom.

He'd never had a relationship with anyone that felt as honest as the one he had with Emilia. She'd never held back, either in competing with him all through medical school or giving as good as she got in their personal banter that was often a little too close to being insulting to be acceptable with any other people and totally unthinkable with anyone he might interact with as a prince.

A nurse came into the space Dom was occupying by his father's bedside. 'Excuse me, Dr Di Rossi, but I need to take an arterial blood sample to check Mr Baresi's oxygen levels. We're due to reposition him soon, as well.'

'Of course. I'll get out of your way.'

'There's no need—it won't take too long and it's nice to see Mr Baresi with some company. It's sad that his family can't be with him.'

'Mmm…' Dom stood up as he made the noncommittal sound. 'It is. But I can't stay any longer. It's good to see that he's stable. He's doing well, given all that he's dealing with.'

The nurse smiled, nodding, as she moved in with the small syringe to take a sample of blood from the arterial line—one of the many ways his father's condition was being monitored closely. Dom left the unit. It was late but he was going to go back to his office in the ER and catch up on some paperwork, his head a lot clearer now that some of the day's tension had evaporated.

Taking the stairs instead of an elevator, Dom found

his thoughts tracking back to Emilia again. To the unique relationship they had that wasn't exactly friendship but it was, nevertheless, remarkably close. His friendship with Lucas was the closest relationship he'd ever had with anyone outside his family and that had been forged from the things they had in common. They were both men who had issues with what was expected of them by their families. They worked together. They relaxed together whenever they could, over a beer and a pizza. They were like brothers—they had each other's backs and, while they might have disagreements, ultimately they were on the same side.

His and Emilia's history was pretty much the opposite. Years of battling with each other to be seen as the best. An unspoken understanding that it was of the utmost importance to succeed and it hadn't mattered that neither of them had known exactly why it was so important to the other.

For Dom, it had been about being true to himself.

And for Emilia? Had it been about escaping her background?

He pushed open the internal doors to the ER and walked through a department that was quiet enough for the moment to seem a totally different world from the space he'd been working in all day. There were no distractions on the way to his office that disrupted his train of thought.

He and Emilia were actually far more alike than he'd realised. They'd both been escaping their backgrounds. Okay, from the outside, it would look like they were total opposites because she was escaping poverty and the lack of anyone who cared about who she was or what her future might hold and he'd been surrounded by unlimited wealth and people who cared too much about who he was and a future that was inescapable.

But…at a level that was soul-deep, they were kind of the same thing, weren't they?

And if Emilia could see that, maybe she would forgive him for having kept that secret. Not that it should matter so much but…it did…

Because he'd never had a relationship with anyone that was like what he had with Emilia and he certainly would never get the chance to have another one when he stepped up to take on his responsibilities as King. Knowing that he was soon going to lose what he was only just discovering was disturbing because it felt… important. Special.

The paperwork on his desk was ignored. Dom pulled out his phone instead. It was after midnight and it would be rude to wake someone up by sending a text message… But that feeling of something important about his relationship with Emilia was morphing into a sense of almost urgency.

Have just realised it's almost Thanksgiving. Do you have plans for dinner?

Her response came swiftly enough to let him know she hadn't been asleep.

Ha-ha. I've always thought I should cook a turkey and a pumpkin pie, etc., etc., but I've never been inspired.

Can you actually cook?

A lot better than you, I expect.

Want to put that to the test?

There was a minute's silence but then Dom's lips curved into a smile as her response pinged in because it felt like normal service was being resumed, here, between himself and Emilia. A bit of banter. A whole lot of friendly competition.

I'll do the turkey. You do the pumpkin pie. Your place or mine?

Mine. And bring the ingredients so we know there's no cheating and buying ready-made.

Don't need to cheat, mate. I'll be surprised if you can even boil water.

An emoji of a winking face had been added to the end of her message.

Wanting something that you knew you were never likely to have was like pressing your nose against a glass window as you gazed longingly at what you could see on the other side.

For Emilia Featherstone, the sense of desperately wanting what other people all seemed to have but was always out of reach for herself was almost a comforting feeling because it was so familiar. Because she knew that she'd experienced it often enough in her lifetime to know that, no matter how overwhelming it might seem, she could deal with it. She would probably end up being stronger because of it, in fact.

The most overwhelming longings were the emotional things, of course.

The need to belong somewhere. The need to be loved. The kind of windows that were always lit up extra brightly around celebrations for Thanksgiving or Christmas—those family celebrations when everybody else seemed to be enfolded in loving gatherings.

Maybe there was a new longing Emilia could add this year—the need to be with the person that *she* loved?

No…she needed to qualify that. It wasn't just a random need to be with someone she cared deeply about, it was a specific need to be with Domenico di Rossi. It wasn't just an aftershock of realising how much she cared about him because this was very different from having a crush on someone, or even falling in love. She'd been in love before and, although her last relationship had carried on for far longer than it should have and any memories were now tainted, Emilia knew that even at the beginning it had been nothing like this.

She'd never felt connected to anyone in quite the way she did now to Dom. But the glass in this new window was impossibly thick. It wasn't simply the idea of a relationship that was equal enough to have respect on both sides, or to be able to trust the other with a raw honesty that made the connection tight enough to be unbreakable, it was the whole royalty thing. As crazy as it seemed, Dom was a *prince*. Soon to become a *king*. And that was enough to make that window so thick it actually felt like a safety barrier. Or one of those glass bridges they had in places like China where you could walk over a chasm and experience the thrill but know that you were perfectly safe and that you could trust that the glass was never going to break.

So maybe that was why Emilia was here now. In Dom's apartment. Taking over the bench space while he'd marked out his own territory on the huge island countertop. A double oven was already heating up. So was their impending battle over who was the better cook. Emilia eyed up the raw turkey in front of her. She'd sat up last night, watching videos online that promised to teach her how to cook the perfect roast turkey for Thanksgiving dinner and she had all the supplies she needed. She pulled on kitchen gloves before tackling a task she'd never been partial to as she unwrapped and then used paper towels to dry the poultry.

'If I had to do this on a regular basis, I'd probably become a vegetarian,' she muttered, tying the legs of the large bird together with a piece of string.

'Want to swap? You can make the pies.'

'Pie*s*?' Emilia emphasised the last letter of the word. 'Plural?'

'*Sì.*' Dom was tying the strings of his apron. 'My research told me that it was compulsory to have both an apple and a pumpkin pie on the table for dessert. I think my task is going to be harder than yours.'

'Doubt it.' Emilia pushed the turkey's ugly neck and tail skin out of sight and tucked the wings beneath the body to provide the platform for roasting that one of the videos had recommended. 'It's not just the turkey, you know. There are all the side dishes to do and gravy to make.' She dribbled olive oil over the turkey and rubbed

it over the skin with her hands. 'Garlic mashed potatoes, cranberry sauce, Brussels sprouts, green beans—'

'Enough...' Dom was grinning. 'I declare the competition on even ground and I don't want to swap any
more. Here, let me pour you a glass of wine.' He reached
for the bottle of red wine amongst the grocery bags still
on the floor. 'Were you really telling the truth when you
said you'd never cooked a turkey before? At least I have
the excuse of not being American.'

'I don't tell lies.' The words came out sounding curt
and Emilia bit her lip as she saw the wary look that
crossed Dom's face. 'Sorry...' She stripped off her
gloves before taking the glass of wine he was holding
out towards her. 'I'm not accusing you of lying.'

'But I kept my secret and that's just as bad, yes?'
Dom held her gaze. 'No more secrets, Emmy, I promise. Not ever...'

The thought that 'not ever' might not be very long
at all was enough to make Emilia's breath catch in her
throat. At some point in the near future, Dom was going
to disappear from her life and why on earth would the
ruler of a small Mediterranean kingdom have any desire to keep in touch with someone from a life he'd had
to leave far behind? But there was something in that
sombre gaze that told Emilia that the connection would
always be there. They shared a passion for what they
did in life. They also shared a passion for competing
with each other and there was something close enough
to sadness in Dom's eyes to let her know that he was
going to miss so much of his life here. The high-paced
drama that the ER could provide. Perhaps he was realising that he would miss the connection they had, as well.

Would miss *her*...?

Emilia took a sip of her wine to force herself to break that eye contact. To try and distract herself from the swirl of emotion that was threatening to distract her completely. It worked. She found herself blinking in surprise, in fact.

'Oh, wow...that's the nicest wine I've ever tasted.'

'We have some of the best vineyards in Europe on Isola Verde.' Dom smiled. 'And we make the best olive oil and you should taste the limoncello.' He raised his own glass to touch Emilia's. 'Maybe you will someday.'

'Mmm...' Emilia drowned her response with another mouthful of wine but then she put her glass down to reach for the herbs and other seasoning that she was going to use on the turkey. 'I'll have this in the oven in a minute,' she announced. 'The countdown is on. You've only got a few hours to get those pies made and baked. I hope you didn't cheat and buy ready-made pastry?'

The sound Dom made was indignant. 'As if...'

A short time later, the black granite top of the central island bench was a snowstorm of flour to one side where there were several bowls being devoted to pastry making and there was a pumpkin being carved into pieces on the other side. Impressively, Dom was clearly intending to make his pumpkin purée from scratch. When he'd got all the pieces into a pot to boil, he refilled their wine glasses.

'This is nice,' he declared. 'It's good to be away from the hospital for a while.'

Emilia nodded. 'I imagine you're spending a lot of extra time there at the moment.'

'I read an interesting article about talking to people when they are in a coma. There was a study, from back in 2015, I think, where brain scans revealed that some coma patients can hear and understand what is spoken around them. The people who had family members speaking to them every day woke up significantly faster and had a better recovery. So, yes… I visit him as often as I can.'

'How's he doing?'

It was safe ground to discuss Roberto's condition in medical terms and both Dom and Emilia could carry on with their tasks as they talked about every detail of the care Dom's father was receiving. Emilia made cranberry sauce as they debated the pros and cons of an early tracheostomy for patients who were going to need prolonged control of their ventilation.

'It's only been five days. Early is anything up to ten days so we can afford to wait longer.'

'Doesn't an early tracheostomy have benefits in shortening the duration of mechanical ventilation and minimising risks of weaning failure?'

'Yes, but why do such an invasive procedure if it's not absolutely necessary? They're already starting the gradual reduction of ventilatory support. I'm hoping that my father's spontaneous breathing will be adequate before long. He's tough.' Dom looked as though he was focussing hard on rolling out his pastry. 'Determined. He's going to succeed in this fight.' He was blinking rapidly now and his voice was trailing into silence. 'He's going to win…'

'Like father, like son.'

'Scusi?' Dom looked puzzled.

'You're very alike, I think. You and your father. You both like to win.'

His lips curved into a hint of a smile. 'You could be right. And, this time, I *am* going to win. You're going to be blown away by what I'm about to do.' He was picking up a sharp knife. And...a ruler?

'Well, I'm about to make the best gravy in the world.' Emilia found her phone and did a quick search for a recipe she had bookmarked. Moments later, however, she was searching through her grocery bags.

'What are you looking for?' Dom looked up from where he was slicing his pastry into thin strips.

'I need to make stock. The recipe says to boil the neck of my turkey as a base but my turkey didn't *have* a neck.'

'It will be in a plastic bag. With all the other giblets.'

Giblets? Emilia wasn't going to admit she had no idea what that meant. 'I have everything else I need, like flour and sage. I might have to go back to the butcher and ask what happened to the neck.'

'I wouldn't bother. Have a look in the pantry. There's bound to be some ready-made stock in there. My housekeeper often cooks for me and leaves meals for when I need them so there are all sorts of things on the shelves. Chicken stock would do fine, I expect.'

Emilia scowled. 'Ready-made is cheating.'

Dom's smile widened. 'I'll let you off. It's not as if you're going to win, anyway. Look at this work of art.' He had his pastry strips laid across a pie plate filled with sliced apples and he was somehow weaving them into a very professional looking lattice. 'Oops...that goes over, not under. Stop distracting me, Emmy. I need to get these into the oven so we don't have to wait for dessert later.'

Funny how Emilia had always hated anyone calling her 'Emmy'. She was actually liking it today. Liking it a lot. As much as she was enjoying the cooking. And then setting the table later as the aromas from the roasting meat and vegetables and the bubbling gravy and sauce became delicious enough to make her feel very hungry. It smelt like Thanksgiving and, for the first time ever, it felt like she was a real part of it.

It felt like she belonged.

This sleek, modern apartment that had been chosen for its proximity to Seattle General provided a level of luxury that made life outside work comfortable enough for Dom that he was never distracted from his focus on his career.

Mind you, it had never looked like this, with dishes and pots piling up in the sink and surfaces covered with the remnants of the impromptu cooking competition. It had never smelt quite like this, either, with the savoury aromas of roasting meat and bubbling gravy having their own competition with the sweeter scent of baked goods coming from the oven he was using. Dom crouched down to peer through the glass door of the oven. He was going to turn it off very soon to make sure the pastry didn't get too brown on top and that the pies had time to cool before they ate them. Emilia had finished setting the table and she was about to mash potatoes. Another appetising aroma got added to the mix as she squeezed roasted garlic cloves into the pot. Dom found the fresh cream in his fridge that he needed to whip to go with his pies. Nothing was coming out of a can, today.

'I'm starving,' he told Emilia a little later, putting the whipped cream back in the fridge.

'Me, too. This has all taken a lot longer than I thought it would.'

'And I've been boring you talking shop. I think you're as clued up on my father's condition as anybody in his medical team.'

'I'm not bored, Dom. Of course he's on your mind. He's your father and I can understand how worried you must be. It's easy to see how much you love him.'

Was it?

Dom watched as Emilia took the foil covering off the turkey that had been resting on the bench. He'd been driven by his concern for his father ever since Roberto had been wheeled into his ER and his fear had been mixed with a huge amount of guilt for having ducked his own responsibilities for so long. He was trying to keep in touch with his sister and reassure her and trying to ensure that their father knew that they cared but... Emilia had hit the nail on the head with that one, tiny word, hadn't she?

He *did* love his father. And maybe that love had got buried under resentment that the career he loved was eventually going to be taken away from him and the distance that had been created had added another layer that muffled that love, but the near catastrophe of the accident had shattered those barriers.

'You're very lucky, you know.' Emilia's smile was soft as she looked up to catch his gaze. 'You've got a family to be thankful for and that's what Thanksgiving is all about. Family is everything, isn't it?'

She broke their shared gaze and seemed to be blinking hard. 'Now…look at this.' She moved a magnificently browned turkey onto a wooden board. 'You may as well concede defeat, Dom. Have you ever seen anything that looks this good?'

'It does look good.' His tone was cautious, however. Dom wasn't about to let Emilia think she'd won already. And he was still thinking about those softly spoken words that sounded as if they'd come straight from the heart.

Family is everything, isn't it?

He was lucky. He had a father and a sister and a wonderful home waiting for him on a sun-drenched Mediterranean island. How close had Emilia ever been to feeling like she had a family? Or a real home, for that matter? If he'd known more about her years ago, would that have changed their relationship?

He watched as Emilia gathered the other dishes to take to the table. Tendrils of her hair had come loose to float around her face and the glow on her cheeks almost matched the fiery tones of her hair. She had her sleeves rolled up and her apron was grubby and…and she'd never looked as lovely as she did right now.

It took Dom back to the first time he'd ever seen her. When he'd recognised that she presented a risk to his focus. What a relief it had been to find that she was so determined to outdo him and that nothing personal was going to be allowed to interfere with that goal. So, no. It wouldn't have changed their relationship because that wouldn't have been allowed. And now it *had* changed, because there was truth between them but it was too late because this was the beginning of the end of his life here in Seattle. Very soon it would be time for him to re-join the family he was lucky enough to have but, in the meantime, he could enjoy this celebration.

They ate in silence for several minutes.

'Potatoes are good,' he told Emilia. 'And the beans. I even like the sprouts.'

'But…?'

'Um… I hate to say it…'

'But you're going to, anyway.' Emilia sighed heavily as she put her fork down. 'And you're right. The turkey tastes weird.'

'It does a bit.'

'What's wrong with it?'

'I don't know.' Dom ate another mouthful, staring at the rest of the turkey on its board. 'It almost tastes like…plastic.' He could feel himself frowning as his gaze sharpened. 'What's that?'

'What?'

He reached to take hold of what he'd spotted on the carving board. 'You didn't put stuffing in this turkey, did you?'

Emilia shook her head. 'I read that it can be a risk for food poisoning.'

'So what's this?'

Her mouth dropped as he pulled it out.

'What *is* that?'

Dom was laughing now. 'You know how you couldn't find the bag of giblets when you were looking for the neck? Did you think of looking inside the turkey?'

'No…that's gross. Why would you put a plastic bag

in there? Hey…*stop*…' Emilia leaned far enough to thump his arm. 'Stop laughing at me.'

But she was having trouble not smiling herself and Dom couldn't stop. Even when he caught the smoke seeping out of the oven from the corner of his eye, moments before the alarm sounded, he was still laughing. He'd forgotten to turn the oven off, hadn't he? His pies weren't going to be too brown, they were probably incinerated by now.

In the space of what felt like seconds, their Thanksgiving dinner had become an epic disaster.

So why on earth did he feel like he was having what could possibly be the best time of his life?

CHAPTER FIVE

IT WAS STARTING.

As always, the end of Thanksgiving celebrations was the signal for the Christmas season to begin. Conversations in the staffroom included queries about who would be entering the annual Christmas cookie competition that was approaching and reminders that the last tickets for the fundraiser gala ball on the twelfth of December were being snapped up so people needed to hurry if they wanted to attend the glamorous event. Snatches of Christmas music could be heard already in the cafés and shops, and decorations began appearing in corners of departments and wards throughout Seattle General.

It only became official on the first day of December, however, with the installation of Christmas trees in the hospital's huge, glass-walled atrium. One massive spruce tree stretched high into the impressive space of this entrance, with a slightly smaller tree beside it, both wearing identical decorations of sparkling, white fairy lights, frosted glass icicles and silver balls of various sizes. Beneath the trees there was thick, fluffy, white fabric bunched up to look like drifts of snow.

Not that Emilia was taking any notice of the trees as

she rushed past, cheeks still glowing from the early run she and Dom had completed at the park. Her trauma team pager had sounded as she pulled on a clean set of scrubs in the orthopaedic department's surgical locker room but, even if she wasn't already totally focussed on what might be waiting for her in the ER, she would have ignored the blatant symbols of the upcoming celebration. Memories of Thanksgiving days in her childhood were insignificant compared to those surrounding Christmas Day and none of them were happy memories. Emilia had learned that the joy of Christmas was for other people. For children who had their own families. Who were wanted. And loved…

The decorations and the music of the season, festive flashing jewellery and headbands with reindeer antlers or Santa hats attached, gift wrapping and special food were all part of a background clutter that she could ignore or tolerate for a few weeks of every year. It didn't even bother her particularly now. In the same way that Emilia had learned that standing out from the crowd in terms of academic achievement could change your life for the better, she was well practised in the art of distracting herself from any personal emotional disturbance by using mindfulness. And there couldn't be a better way of being entirely present than being involved in the fight to save someone's life.

Becoming totally involved was inevitable from the moment Emilia arrived in the ER. Due to it being a shift change-over period, with the department already busy, things were more chaotic than usual. On top of that, there seemed to have been little warning that a serious trauma case was on its way. The ambulance had already arrived and the patient was being rushed into Resus as both Emilia and Dom came through the doors. Dom probably wasn't even due to start his shift yet and he looked as if he'd not long stepped out of a shower. It also looked like he'd towel dried his hair but hadn't had a chance to comb it.

The thought that looking unusually tousled achieved what should have been impossible—in that it instantly increased the man's attractiveness—was fleeting enough to be no more than a blink as Emilia reached for a pair of gloves from the wall dispenser at the same moment as Dom. They caught each other's gazes for a heartbeat and it was a relief for Emilia that there was nothing personal in that shared glance, like any awareness of appearance or perhaps the recognition of how much closer they'd become in the days since that shared Thanksgiving dinner disaster or even how much more time they'd been spending together. The silent message that flashed between them was a very different kind of recognition. One that acknowledged a shared determination to do their best for this patient, no matter what they might be up against.

Dom snapped his gloves on as he turned towards the ambulance crew. 'Talk to me,' he commanded, stepping closer to the gurney.

'This is a gentleman in his early seventies, we believe. Name's Brian Butcher.' The paramedic leaned down as his patient groaned loudly. 'It's okay, Brian. We're at the hospital. Try not to move…'

His junior crew partner took over. 'Fall from height,' he told Dom. 'Maybe fifteen feet? He was up on his roof, putting one of those Santa Claus decorations up—

the ones where it's just the legs sticking out of the chimney, you know?'

It only took a quirk of Dom's eyebrow to let the EMT know that it was only the clinical details that were needed urgently.

'The fall was partially broken by shrubbery but he landed on a concrete driveway,' the senior paramedic continued. 'GCS was eight on arrival with eye opening to pain, incomprehensible speech and withdrawal to pain. Blood pressure of ninety systolic, tachycardic at one thirty. Initial IV access failed and we were so close we decided it was better to just load and go.'

Emilia had her gloves on now and she also stepped closer. She could understand that IV access had probably been difficult due to the obesity of this patient. It could mean that airway management would also prove challenging but the immediate concern was getting enough staff on hand to move him from the gurney to the bed. Where was everybody? She and Dom had been joined by an intern and two nurses but there were people missing.

'Lucas back yet?' Dom asked. 'Is he with the team in Resus One dealing with that bus versus pedestrian?'

'No. But I can see if they can spare anyone,' a nurse responded.

'Who's rostered to take his place on airway management for the trauma team?'

'Didn't you pencil in the new guy that's starting today?' The intern asked. 'Logan somebody? I don't think he's arrived yet, though.'

'Connors,' Dom murmured. 'But I wouldn't throw him in the deep end like this. Not on his first day, anyway. I was expecting Lucas would be back to get him up to speed with the team.' He shook his head, as if dismissing information that was no more than a distraction. 'I'll do it. Grab a sliding board and see if anyone else is nearby to help for a minute. Let's get Brian onto the bed, stat. I'm not liking the sound of that stridor.'

The noisy breath sounds were a warning that the man's airway was becoming obstructed which could be due to factors such as swelling, bleeding or aspiration of possibly broken teeth. Whatever the cause, stabilising the airway and breathing were the first steps of any major trauma management and this patient was going to be a real challenge.

One that Dom was clearly up for. He was already observing Brian for any further signs of respiratory difficulty as he directed the limited team he had, including the ambulance crew for the moment, to remove clothing, get monitors in place for heart rate and rhythm, blood pressure and oxygen saturation and to stabilise the cervical spine as the hard collar was opened to let him examine the mouth and neck.

'I need some suction here, please.' He took the handle attached to the device from the nurse as he turned back to the paramedic. 'Do we know anything about his medical history?'

The paramedic shook his head. 'No medic alert bracelet. He lives alone but his neighbour—Dierdre— was going to check his house and bring some stuff in for him. We asked her to check for any medication he might be on.'

Dom nodded, peering into the injured man's mouth after clearing the blood that had been obstructing his vision but he looked up to catch Emilia's gaze as Brian's padded jacket and then a knitted sweater and T-shirt were all cut clear to expose the top half of his body.

'Flail chest,' she noted aloud. The paradoxical move- ment of the ribs that went in the opposite direction than they should as a breath was sucked in or released meant that there were multiple fractures that had separated a section of the rib cage from the rest. It was also a sign that the level of difficulty in stabilising this patient might have just gone up several notches.

'We've got accessory muscle use and tachypnoea as well.' Dom was frowning as the figures on the moni- tor appeared. 'And that oxygen saturation is far too low. We need to intubate. I'm going to need the video laryngoscope,' he told the intern. 'And let's have a cri- cothyroidotomy kit on standby as well, thanks. Emmy, it would be awesome if you could get IV access while I'm getting the drugs drawn up. And then I'd like you to assist me with the intubation, please.'

Emilia knew that Dom probably had no idea he'd used the familiar version of her name but, if anything, it just cemented the bond they needed to work as closely and rapidly as possible right now with their patient's condition deteriorating in front of them. Just the first step of stabilising this patient by securing IV access and an airway was a battle that would require their best efforts.

It wasn't her usual role on this team, of course. Her specialist orthopaedic and trauma skills meant that she should be evaluating that chest and looking for any other life-threatening injuries a fall could have produced, such as a fractured pelvis, but she couldn't move on to that stage of a primary or secondary survey until the patient was able to breathe. It was a matter of priorities. Even trying to keep the alignment of Brian's neck completely stable was less important than securing an airway because the risk of brain injury from a lack of oxygen was greater than making a spinal injury worse by extending the neck for intubation.

The next few minutes were chaotic. Staff were still removing the last pieces of clothing, getting ECG leads stuck on and manoeuvring the trolleys that were needed to supply the drugs and medical equipment that were about to be used. Dom was drawing up the drugs that would sedate and paralyse Brian so that they could take over his breathing. Emilia had the IV trolley beside her and she was trying to locate a vein she could access so that those drugs could be administered. It was no easy task but if they needed to place a central line or an intraosseus needle directly into bone marrow, it would take time they might not have.

There was a fair amount of luck that coated whatever skills Emilia used to find a vein so she could hook Brian up to a running line of saline. The glance and nod of approval from Dom when she looked up was all the acknowledgment she needed to know that she'd done well. Now it was time to do everything she could to assist Dom in his task of placing a flexible, plastic tube into Brian's trachea to ensure that adequate levels of oxygen could be delivered to Brian's lungs.

As the first drugs were administered, Emilia preoxygenated using a bag mask, making sure that everything needed was at hand and that the monitor could be easily seen.

The first attempt to insert the tube did fail.

'Let's optimise the position,' Dom said calmly. 'I want a thirty-degree tilt on the upper body so that we have the ears in line with the sternal notch. I'll try a different blade and, Emilia, I'm going to need some anterior tracheal pressure, please.'

Emilia had to locate the cricoid cartilage, stabilise it between her fingers and then apply enough pressure to help Dom slide the tube into the correct position. She had to keep holding that pressure, as well, until the position of the tube had been checked.

She could see the mix of satisfaction and relief on Dom's face as they confirmed that the airway was in place but his focus didn't slip for a second because, with the pressure of air entering their patient's lungs, it became obvious that the rib fractures had caused damage. Either air or blood was in the chest cavity to a degree that would prevent adequate oxygenation and this was as life-threatening as not having a patent airway.

As a surgeon, Emilia took the lead on the next urgent task of inserting a chest tube to clear the obstruction and this time, as a rush of blood confirmed that her incision and blunt dissection had reached the pleural space and that they could deal with the problems the bleeding was causing, there was more than a fleeting gleam of satisfaction when Dom's gaze caught her own as he helped her secure the tube that would continue the drainage.

The figures on the monitors were already improving enough that they both knew the odds were turning in their favour. They still needed to perform a thorough secondary survey and find whatever other injuries Brian might have sustained and he was very likely to need to go to Theatre soon but it felt like they were winning.

As always, this was the best feeling in the world.

Their eye contact held for a heartbeat longer than it might have, even as recently as a week or two ago. Because Dom knew that she knew more than she had before? Because they had acknowledged their connection? She could hear an echo of his voice in that tiny moment of time their gazes were touching.

'We're the same, you and me... We both give everything we've got—and more—to our careers. To the people who put their trust and their lives into our hands...'

How hard was it going to be for Dom to walk away from this job? It would have to feel like he was cutting out a piece of his heart—his soul, even—and a piece of Emilia's heart was breaking for him because she could imagine exactly how hard that would be. She couldn't do it.

But, however alike they were in how much they loved their jobs and how determined they were to be the best, that was where their similarity ended, wasn't it? It was when Brian's neighbour, Dierdre, arrived with a plastic bag of medication she'd found in his bathroom cabinet and his wallet containing all the personal details they would need that Emilia was reminded of how different she and Dom really were.

Unlike their patient—and herself—Dom had a family. And, okay, there were some issues there because Dom was expected to do something that wasn't what he would have chosen to do with his life and it was a very different kind of family from that of an ordinary person but at the end of the day...it was *family* and, as she had reminded Dom on Thanksgiving, family was everything. So, there was envy mixed in with that sympathy that Dom was going to have to give up the career that he loved so much in the near future. On top of that, as Emilia prepared to accompany Brian first to a CT scan and then to Theatre, she remembered that weird moment when she'd arrived in the ER earlier, when the sight of Dom's tousled hair had made her aware of something so inappropriately unprofessional that she was ashamed of herself.

Oh, man…life had been a lot less complicated when the only feelings that Domenico Di Rossi inspired had been those that made her so determined to prove herself and earn his—along with everybody else's—respect. Even the annoyance that his teasing and the forbidden use of that shortened form of her name had created would be preferable to this…this *knot* of emotion that seemed to have taken up residence deep in her gut, full of things she could almost, but not quite identify clearly. And Emilia had no intention of trying to analyse them any further. What was the point, when they would be irrelevant before very long anyway? And when admitting something could potentially make it real…?

It was a relief to be able to follow Brian's trolley through the doors and head for the elevators. She would be in the CT scanning room within minutes and, with the information the scan could provide, would be planning what was going to happen a short time later in Theatre—a place where she could make sure she was in control. A place where unsettling personal emotions could be totally, albeit perhaps only temporarily, banished.

Exactly the place Emilia needed to be as soon as possible. She knew that Dom was watching her leave Resus but she deliberately kept her gaze on the monitor attached to the end of the trolley so that she didn't look back. She didn't want to notice that tousled hair again, or to have that link from those dark, dark eyes to her own, even for a heartbeat. She didn't want to feel any of those emotions that were powerful enough to feel physical.

Weird how hard it was not to turn her head, though…

What a day…

It was well after the time his shift should have ended when Dom managed to get in a visit to his father in ICU and it was only then that he realised he'd missed lunch. After the extra physical activity of that run with Emilia early this morning, it was no wonder that he was experiencing symptoms of hypoglycaemia with a headache and vague dizziness but Dom knew that a coffee with a couple of sugars would keep him going until he could get home.

He paused for a moment on his way to the ICU staffroom, however, because something had been niggling at the back of his mind ever since that dramatic case in the ER this morning. Why wasn't Lucas back from his unexpected leave of absence yet? And what could be serious enough have kept him away for this long already?

He'd had a response to that voicemail he'd left the day Lucas had disappeared, more than a week ago now, but all Lucas had said was that he had some stuff to sort out and that he'd be in touch soon.

Not knowing where on earth his friend was, and what

time zone he might be in, Dom sent a text message this time instead of trying to phone. He also tried to make it clear he didn't want to pry.

You missed a good case this morning, bro. Flail chest, haemopneumothorax and a challenging airway thrown in just for fun. You would've loved it.

Surprisingly, a response pinged back by the time Dom had started walking again.

Sounds like you're having fun, all right. I'm sure you're coping without me but I'll be back soon. In time for the ball at the latest, if you can remember to grab me a ticket.

It was reassuring that he'd been able to make contact so easily but Dom still had no idea where Lucas was or what the problem in his life might be. Should he be worried? Or was the fact that Lucas was even thinking of attending a social function enough to reassure him that it couldn't be anything too serious?

He was still distracted as he reached the ICU staff-room and suddenly he had to pause again, startled enough to completely let go of his train of thought concerning Lucas. Emilia Featherstone was in the staff-room, paperwork spread out in front of her on the table.

'What on earth are you doing here?'

'I've got a patient in ICU. Our man from this morning who fell off his roof. Two, actually, if we count your...' Emilia's eyes widened as she stopped herself. 'Your...um...patient Mr Baresi.'

A glance over his shoulder showed Dom that there was nobody around who might overhear their conversation, but it was an automatic instinct to be extra careful at work.

'His leg seems to be healing well.'

'It is. And Max Granger seems happy enough with how stable he is neurologically.'

'Mmm… I'll be a lot happier when he wakes up.' Dom closed his eyes in a long blink. 'It's been a long day. I just came in for a coffee. And maybe a cookie. I forgot lunch.'

'What? You must be dead on your feet. Look, there's a whole box of cookies here. I think someone's practising for the competition.'

'Gingerbread men?' Dom picked up one of the cookies.

'No…turn it up the other way. It's a reindeer.'

Dom peered at the shape. A gingerbread man cutter had clearly been used but it had been decorated so that the legs were antlers, the arms were ears and there was a red candy button for a nose where the head would have been.

'Clever,' he murmured, biting off one of the antlers. 'How's our man from this morning?'

'Good.' Emilia was gathering her paperwork. 'I'm just sorting copies of the data I need to enter him in an ongoing study for surgical stabilisation of rib fractures.'

Dom took another bite. 'I'm going to blame my lack of brain function on low blood sugar. I was just reading about it the other day. About bioabsorbable plates for a fixation device?'

'I used a pre-contoured locking plate,' Emilia told

him but there was a gleam in her eye. 'We can compare the merits some other time, when you've had enough to eat.'

'These cookies are good.'

That gleam in Emilia's eyes got brighter. 'Your baking skills are pretty unique. Why don't you enter the competition?'

Dom ate the reindeer's nose. 'Why don't you? There could be someone on the judging panel that appreciates plastic-flavoured Christmas cookies.'

She was having difficulty stifling a grin. 'That's a cruel blow, Dom. You could be doing irreparable damage to my self-esteem, you know?'

Maybe it was the lighting in this staffroom and the way it was picking out the flame-coloured highlights in Emilia's hair and making her eyes sparkle. Or maybe it was because something fundamental had changed in their relationship ever since he had told her the truth and she'd got past her initial shock and anger. On the other hand, it could be that his mental abilities were foggy thanks to a lack of food and those automatic defence mechanisms had been accidentally switched off. Whatever the cause, the net result hit Dom in the gut like a sledgehammer. Emilia had to be the most attractive woman he'd ever met. How on earth had he not noticed that before?

The kick in his gut was rapidly morphing into something Dom had certainly noticed before.

Attraction.

No...worse than that. This was more like *desire*...

The last thing he needed in his life right now was another complication. He should walk away. Fast. Ex-

cept that Emilia was saying something. About food…?
He tuned back in and tried to rewind what he'd missed.

'I haven't tried it yet but it sounds good.' A tiny, puzzled frown appeared on Emilia's brow as she clocked
how distracted he was. 'The new Asian fusion restaurant down at the Pike Place Fish Market?' Those astonishing blue eyes were darkening with what looked like
concern now. 'Boy, you really do need some food, don't
you? Come on…it's time we were out of here. My treat.'

'What? No… I'm not letting you pay for dinner.' Had
he somehow just agreed to have dinner with Emilia—
only seconds after realising that it would be wise to get
away from her until his head was functioning a little
more normally?

'Consider it compensation.' Emilia was on her feet
smiling at him. 'To make up for plastic-flavoured turkey?'

The gingerbread cookie didn't seem to have raised
his blood sugar levels enough to dispel the fuzziness
in his head. Or perhaps Emilia's smile always had this
kind of effect on men and it was just that his own im-
munity was compromised. In either case, the net result
was that he was powerless to resist.

'Dinner sounds great,' he heard himself saying.
'Let's go.'

He'd looked so tired. And then he'd said that he hadn't
eaten all day. Was it any wonder that Emilia had let her
concern for Dom override her common sense? That
she'd not only smothered any warning bells about letting that emotional knot get pulled any tighter, she'd
made it a whole lot more intense by engineering time

alone with him in a restaurant that allowed every table a view into a bustling kitchen but somehow divided the spaces to make every group feel like they were having a private party.

They both seemed to be making an effort to keep things at least a little professional, though, with their conversation focussed on the case they'd shared today as they waited for their order to arrive.

'So, tell me about this study that Brian qualifies for. You said it's ongoing? What trends are being identified?'

'Initially, the study was looking at surgical stabilisation compared to the conservative, non-surgical treatment that was standard a couple of decades ago.'

'Like oral analgesia, mechanical ventilation and intercostal nerve blocks?'

Emilia nodded. 'But now, it's more about how early the surgery should take place. The benefits are significant—lower mortality, shorter stay in ICU and less time under mechanical ventilation. Lower rates of pneumonia...'

She was counting off her points on her fingers but Dom wasn't watching her hands. His gaze was fixed on hers and the look in his eyes gave her an odd tingle. Were the results of the study she was talking about really that fascinating?

It was a relief when their food arrived but, a short time later, Emilia realised she might have been more wary of trying this new restaurant if she'd also known that they specialised in platters of food for sharing and that cutlery was optional. There was something rather intimate in reaching for a delicious taste of twice-fried crispy potato skin or tiny, melt-in-the-mouth pulled beef slider when your hand could brush that of the person you were sharing the meal with. They had finger bowls that came with a tray of barbecued ribs to clean sticky fingers so they both managed to eat all they desired without picking up a fork.

More than all they desired, in fact.

'I'm stuffed,' Emilia finally announced.

'Me, too. But I'm still going to eat that last rib. Unless you'd like it?'

She shook her head. 'I would explode. It wouldn't be pretty.'

Dom grinned and then closed his eyes as he tore into the succulent meat. 'I think this might be the best dinner I've ever had,' he said as he discarded the bone.

'It helps to have not eaten all day. They say that hunger is the best condiment for anything.' Emilia couldn't take her eyes off Dom's face. The sweep of those dark, dark lashes on his cheeks beneath that still rumpled hair and the way his lips curled up at the corners even though they looked completely relaxed...

He'd look like this when he was asleep, wouldn't he? In bed...

Emilia was sure she almost visibly jumped as Dom's eyes opened again.

'What? Have I got something on my face?'

'Ah...actually, yes...' Emilia found what she hoped was a casual smile. 'Barbecue sauce, probably.'

'Oh...' Dom picked up his napkin and wiped his mouth. 'Is it gone?'

'Mmm...'

'You've got some as well.' But Dom was reaching

across the table as he spoke so Emilia didn't have a chance to pick up her own napkin. He wiped the bottom of her cheek, right at the corner of her mouth, with the back of his thumb. 'There you go. All gone.'

Emilia couldn't say anything. That touch, so close to her lips, had stolen her breath completely. Maybe she was looking a little strange, as well, because Dom was staring at her and she'd never seen quite that expression on his face before.

'What?' she finally managed. 'There's more sauce?'

He shook his head. Looked away but then back to catch her gaze. The tone of his voice was curiously hesitant.

'I was just wondering,' he murmured.

'Wondering what?'

'Why you're still single. You're beautiful, Emmy...'

Emilia swallowed hard. Again, she was lost for words. She couldn't look away from those dark eyes, either. It felt like she could fall into them.

And drown...

'Not only that, you're damn good at what you do. And you're independent and ambitious and successful and— What?' Dom broke off. 'Why are you shaking your head like that?'

'You're answering your own question,' Emilia said. 'About why I'm single? It's not necessarily a good thing for a woman to be ambitious and successful.'

Dom's breath came out in a disbelieving huff.

'It's true,' she insisted. 'It's precisely why my last relationship didn't work out. He—Chandler—got more and more resentful of my achievements. When I got promoted over him, that was the end...' She couldn't bring herself to tell him what else Chandler had said—that no man would ever want to be with someone like her. Someone who had to prove herself to be better all the time by putting someone else down. A...ballbreaker.

But it seemed like she didn't need to tell him the worst of it. His gaze had already darkened noticeably.

'He was an idiot,' he growled. 'And a *bastardo*.'

The word didn't need translating. And the vehemence with which he was taking her side made the corners of Emilia's mouth curl up.

'I don't even understand,' he continued. 'We fought like...do you say tooth and nail? Or cats and dogs perhaps, to be the best at medical school, didn't we?' He didn't wait for her response. 'I hated it when you beat me but...you know what?'

'What?'

'I was proud of you, too, in the end. I hated losing but, at the same time, I was so happy that you were winning because you deserved to win.' His mouth twitched. 'Not that I would have ever told you that, of course.'

Oh... He'd been proud of her, back then, when she'd won a race to first place? He'd hidden it well, that was for sure, but knowing that he'd felt like that was melting something inside Emilia. It also made complete sense because she'd had the same sort of reaction when he'd won, hadn't she? She'd decided it was simply grudging admiration but perhaps she'd never recognised it for what it had actually been.

'You can't ever be with someone like that again,' Dom said softly. 'It's hard enough to fight for what you need to achieve without someone pulling you down.'

Emilia nodded slowly. 'That's so true. I already knew

that I had to rely on myself and believe in my ambition. I'll never let anybody else pull me down. I'm happier on my own, anyway.'

'Even then, it can be hard.' Dom's breath came out in a sigh. 'I've had to fight, too. I feel like I'm still fighting but maybe now it's against myself instead of my father. A battle between what I want to do and what I have to do.'

Emilia swallowed hard. She should break this eye contact but she couldn't. What she wanted more than anything, in this moment, was to help Dom. To give him a gift as meaningful as the one he'd just given her, in telling her that she was special enough for him to have been proud of her. And, if he was going to believe her, he needed to see how genuine she was, so she held his gaze.

'There must be a way you can be true to yourself and still do your duty,' she said quietly. 'You're too good a doctor to walk away from your career. You still have lives to save and...and maybe continuing your work is something that you need to save what's so important in your own life.' She took a deep breath. 'I read about Isola Verde. About the wonderful new hospital that's been built there.'

Dom nodded. 'That's Giada's doing,' he told her. 'Despite how young she is, she has a passion for our country and she wanted the best health care to be available for our people.'

'Couldn't you work there? Even if it was only part-time? Find a compromise between what you have to do and what you want to do?'

This time Dom shook his head. 'I don't do compromise,' he said. 'It has to be all or nothing for me. If I choose to do something, I will give it my whole heart and soul. My everything. There can be no half measures. When I commit, that's for ever.'

Wow... Emilia let her breath out very slowly. The sincerity in those words. The passion that they advertised. She could imagine him being this genuine when he committed to a woman he loved. Whoever she turned out to be, Emilia hoped she would know that she was the luckiest woman on earth...

It was Dom who broke the eye contact. And, as if he realised that the atmosphere was getting too heavy, he cleared his throat.

'Speaking of Giada, she tells me that she's going to be back in time to come to the fundraising gala. So is Lucas, apparently. I must remember to get some more tickets for them tomorrow. Are you coming, Emmy?'

'No. I usually work during events like that, so other people get to go. Like I always work on Christmas Day. Not that they needed any extras on the night of gala this time, though.'

'You don't like dressing up?' Dom's glance grazed hers again. 'Now that I come to think of it, I don't think I've ever seen you wearing a dress.'

Emilia shrugged. 'I don't wear them often. And I don't own a cocktail dress, let alone a ballgown.'

'So buy one. Or rent one?'

'Why would I do that?'

Dom had her pinned with his gaze again. 'So that you can come to the gala with me, of course.'

Emilia's jaw sagged. 'Are you asking me out on a *date*?'

That flicker in his gaze...it almost looked like...

desire? Oh, dear Lord…that knot in her gut hadn't just tightened. It felt like it might be disintegrating in a small explosion that was sending waves of sensation to parts of her body that had been peacefully shut away for a long time now.

But Dom was smiling now. 'I'm asking you as a friend,' he told her. 'My best friend. Maybe the only one who'll ever know me for just who I really am. In here…' He touched his chest in that gesture that was becoming so familiar but Emilia could see the muscles in his throat move at the same time, as he swallowed carefully.

They did have something totally unique between them.

Something that couldn't last.

But, right now…it felt like someone was waving a magic wand. Creating a snippet of a fairy tale that cast Emilia Featherstone in a Cinderella role. She was being offered the chance of going to the ball and she already knew that she would be dancing with a prince…

It was such a fantasy that it made her smile. If she was someone who cried, she might well have been fighting back tears right now but, instead, she just smiled more—although the edges of that smile felt a bit wobbly.

'I'd love to come,' she said.

CHAPTER SIX

THE CHRISTMAS CHARITY fundraising gala was still days away but Emilia had already had far too much time to think about it.

To think about Domenico.

Not that she'd seen much of him since the night they'd had dinner together. Even when their schedules could have allowed them to meet for a run in the park, the weather had been cold and wet enough to prevent that happening. There'd even been sleet one day and weather forecasts were predicting snow before Christmas. Trauma team callouts had been few and far between as well and Emilia had missed two of them because she'd been in Theatre and the cases had been complicated enough not to be able to let her senior resident take over. Their paths had crossed yesterday in the ICU when Emilia had been making one of her regular visits to follow the progress of Roberto's recovery from his leg injury but that had been a strictly professional interaction. Until, that was, Dom had tilted his head and lowered his voice as if he was saying something about the notes Emilia had made in Roberto's patient file that he didn't want anybody else to hear.

'Got that dress yet?' he'd murmured.

Emilia had shaken her head. 'Haven't had time to go shopping,' she said quietly. 'And I'm not really sure I want to go. I don't even know how to dance.'

The amused glint in Dom's eyes had told her that he thought he knew exactly what was bothering her— that, like him perhaps, she hated doing something in public unless she knew she could do it very, very well.

'You're coming,' he'd said softly. 'You're going to show the world that you're capable of doing anything, Dr Featherstone.' His lips twitched. 'Even wearing a dress…'

So, here she was. In one of Seattle's largest department stores, in the area devoted to evening dresses and ballgowns. With spacious changing rooms and a huge, gilt-framed mirror for anyone who wanted to come out of the private cubicles to get the full effect of the gown they were trying on.

'Do you need some help in there?'

'No… I'm good. I don't think I like this, though.'

'Come out and look in the big mirror. It can make a difference.'

But the classic 'little black dress' Emilia was trying didn't look any better from a distance, even when she held her hair up to pretend she had a sophisticated evening updo to go with it. The black fabric made her skin look far too pale and there was rather too much of it on show with that short skirt length.

'It makes me look like a member of the Addams family,' she sighed. 'Or like I'm on my way to a Hollywood funeral. It's not right for a Christmas ball, is it?'

'Hmm…' The grey-haired senior shop assistant—

Margie, according to her name badge—pursed her lips as the gaze she had focussed on Emilia became thoughtful. 'It's not the Seattle General Christmas gala that you're going to, is it?'

'It is.'

'Lucky you. That's the most A-list party we get around these parts. Where's it being held this year?'

'At the Polar Club Hotel, I believe.'

'Oh…' The older woman actually clasped her hands in awe. 'I've been in there. That room with the dome ceiling and the chandeliers is incredible…' She let her breath out in a long sigh. That thoughtful expression had given way to something more like determination. 'Right… Take that dress off, love. I've got something else I think you definitely have to try on.'

Emilia went back into the small changing room and it was a relief to peel the black dress from her body. Imagine what Dom would have thought if she'd turned up with her legs on display like that? Would she have seen that spark of whatever it was she'd seen the other night rekindled in his gaze? That mutual physical awareness that had launched shafts of desire, the aftermath of which was still powerful enough to be disturbing.

Did she *want* to see that?

Oh, man… For a long moment, Emilia held the dress against her bare midriff as she felt the now familiar spiral of sensations deep within. Fragments of many conversations she'd had with herself in the last few days—mostly in that quiet space of sleepless hours when it wasn't possible to distract yourself—were swirling in her head again now.

She'd always known that Domenico di Rossi was

dangerous. Right from that first moment she'd seen his effect on the women around him at medical school. It had been at that moment that she'd vowed to ignore him on a personal level because nothing was going to distract her from her dream of becoming a doctor and escaping every dark thing her life had included so far.

Those reasons were no longer valid, however. Emilia had long since arrived at where she'd dreamed of being. She'd escaped her past to the extent that the only contact with anybody from her early life was the annual Christmas card she sent to Mrs Delaney—the person who'd encouraged her to believe that she could escape. What would her eleventh-grade teacher think of her now, she wondered, if she could see her getting ready to try on a ballgown to wear to attend one of Seattle's most glittering nights of the year in the prestigious and historic Polar Club Hotel?

No…any danger that Dom represented now had nothing to do with her ambitions. As her sleepless nights had forced Emilia to pick at the knot of emotions that were building and try to understand what was going on, she recognised that the danger now was that she was playing with fire. That what was going on here had the potential to hurt her enough to cause some lasting damage.

She cared about Dom. She had done for far longer than she'd ever realised. Their rivalry and their banter had been protection and a very effective disguise for the significance their connection had always had the potential to have. Had she really thought that these new feelings were nothing like having a crush on someone or falling in love? Maybe if she'd faced this earlier, she could have stopped herself before she'd travelled too far down that path of falling in love but it felt like she'd passed the point of no return now. She couldn't stop thinking about him. Couldn't stop her body from letting her know just how much it wanted to be a whole lot closer to the man.

How many girls at medical school had felt like this about Dom? The lucky ones had enjoyed a brief time in his life and presumably in his bed but, even back then, she'd been aware of a curious level of control on Dom's part. Despite his popularity and charm, he'd always kept an emotional distance and ended relationships before they became anything serious. She understood why now. Dom couldn't afford to fall in love with just anyone, could he? Not when the woman he chose to share his life would eventually become the Queen of his country?

At least Emilia had an advantage that none of those girls had had, because she knew that the path of falling in love with Domenico di Rossi had that dead end. And thank goodness Dom had no idea how she felt. She'd told him she was happy on her own and it was true. She *was* happy on her own. She certainly wasn't about to invent any fantasies based on a future with him because she knew what was coming and that it was quite possible that Dom would vanish from her life before Christmas, which wasn't that far away. There were children all over the world who had started counting down how many sleeps until then. Waiting for the magic to happen.

'Here I am…' Margie the shop assistant sounded breathless. 'Sorry to take so long. This dress had been put out the back. It's actually from the season before last but…it's special…and, as a bonus, we'll be able to give you a great discount on it.'

Emilia opened the door of her changing area and actually laughed aloud. 'It's *red*. Haven't you noticed my hair?'

'Pfft… Who listens to old-fashioned rules like that these days? For goodness sake, some girls have blue or green hair now. Nobody's making rules about what colours they're allowed or not allowed to wear, are they?'

Emilia couldn't argue with that. And Margie was looking so excited, she had to humour her by trying on the dress. Her legs certainly weren't visible under the mass of floor length ripples of silk and the embroidered and beaded bodice with its low, sweetheart neckline fitted like a glove as it got zipped up. With a built-in bra there was nothing to detract from the delicate, lace straps that put the colour right beside the loose waves of Emilia's hair.

And, if anything, this shade of scarlet was like a celebration of her hair colour rather than anything that clashed horribly.

'Come out and look in the big mirror again,' Margie urged.

Emilia could feel the skirt rippling around her legs as she moved. When she stepped up to look at herself in the mirror, she instinctively smoothed her hands over her hips, where the dress clung before exploding into what felt like miles of fabric that was so fine it still hung close to her body. And maybe it was the feel of her hands on silk that was like a second skin that started the fairy dust. That made her imagine so clearly how it would feel if it was Dom's hands on her hips instead of her own. The thought took her breath away completely.

She didn't need to wait for any form of Christmas magic because she had her own magic happening right now.

A red Cinderella ballgown to wear.

A prince waiting to dance with her.

'Oh, love...' Margie's voice was no more than a whisper. 'Don't you look like a princess?'

That should have added to the fairy dust but, instead, Emilia was aware of a wash of something like panic. She kept her gaze on her reflection but pressed her fingers against her lips. What did she think she was doing—planning to go out with a prince for the evening? What if there were paparazzi around and photos came out everywhere and people found out where she'd come from and Dom ended up being embarrassed by her?

Emilia could feel that odd prickle at the back of her eyes again. Why was her body suddenly remembering how to form tears? If she wasn't careful, they might escape one of these days and what would that do for the tough, confident image she'd cultivated so well for so long? The tears weren't going to fall this time but they did smudge her reflection in the mirror enough to make it dreamlike.

And that's all this was. A small step out of real life for a very limited amount of time. A once-in-a-lifetime opportunity, in fact, because Dom's identity couldn't stay secret for ever. But it was still secret now and that meant there wouldn't be any paparazzi. The only thing that would shock anybody from Seattle General would be that she and Dom were attending a social event together instead of baiting each other or competing in some way.

They weren't to know how much further from real life Emilia's evening out was. How she really felt about Dom. Or that she was still a little dubious about wearing this colour for the first time in her life. She'd always been told to never wear red. Along with being told that she'd never amount to anything. That she'd end up just like her no-good mother.

She could hear a dismissive huff at the back of her mind and it sounded a lot like Mrs Delaney. She could even imagine exactly what her beloved teacher might say if she was standing here beside her.

You've already proved all those small-minded people wrong so why on earth would you think you can't wear red? You can do anything you want, Emilia Featherstone. Be whoever you want. Get out there and celebrate, my girl. Believe in yourself. Be proud of yourself...

Dom had told her she was capable of doing anything. He wanted to see her wearing a dress. It had to be *this* dress because even if it was an imagined conversation with Mrs Delaney, her words rang true.

Emilia *was* proud of herself.

And she wanted Dom to be proud of her again as well—the way he said he had been when she'd shown that she could beat him academically. Maybe this could be an escape from real life for him, too—before he had to face the unimaginable responsibilities of ruling a country. A small fantasy that he would remember—a magic night together with her—for many years after he was gone. One that she, Emilia, suspected she would be remembering for the rest of her life.

She swallowed hard but then turned to smile brightly at Margie. 'This dress is perfect,' she said. 'Just the colour for Christmas.'

The Northern Star Dome Room of the Polar Club Hotel was a colourful scene—impressive even for someone who'd grown up being a part of lavish royal events. The glittering chandelier, the rococo motifs, the massive leaded, stained glass, domed ceiling that was subtly illuminated in festive shades of red and green made a wonderful backdrop for tables that had crisp, white linen cloths, floral decorations and sparkling silverware and crystal.

The colour that was impressing Dom the most, however, was the bright hue of Emilia's gorgeous red dress. It wasn't just the dress, either. The pale skin of her bare arms and shoulders seemed to have been dusted with some kind of shimmery powder. Her make-up was flawless but Dom liked that it was still natural enough for her distinctive freckles to show through. That fiery hair of hers had been cleverly looped up into a sort of bun although curly strands had been left to float down her neck and softly frame her face. There were even tiny red jewelled flowers that were somehow wound into her hair and sparkled every time she moved her head.

Emilia wasn't just a very attractive woman.

Dio bono... She was *stunning...*

And she was his partner for the evening. Dom normally kept as low a profile as possible at any events like this, where photographers were keen to get shots for the social pages of local publications but tonight he didn't care. It wasn't just that his identity was not going to stay secret for much longer, given that he would be returning to rule Isola Verde very soon, it was that he was proud to be Emilia's partner. Proud of her, doing something that he suspected was well out of her comfort zone. Proud of how beautiful she was, as well. He wanted to show her off to the world.

And this small corner of the world was most definitely looking astonished that he and Emilia had apparently come as partners when they were always giving each other such a hard time at work. Well...wait until they saw them dancing together later, Dom thought, as he chose a delicious looking risotto ball from the tray of hors-d'oeuvres a waiter was offering on a silver tray. As long as Emilia allowed him to lead her, of course, and didn't decide it was some sort of competition that she needed to win. Dom knew that if she could suppress her desire to be the best, for once, he could make her look fabulous on the dance floor. He was actually looking forward to that part of the evening with a surprisingly delicious anticipation.

In the meantime, he had to wonder why Ayanna Franklin was staring at him with such concentration. A quirk of his eyebrow had her apologising instantly.

'Sorry... I was just wondering if you liked that risotto ball.'

'It was delicious.'

'And have you tried the smoked salmon? Or the chicken satay skewers?'

'I've tried the chicken skewers,' Emilia told Ayanna. 'They're delicious, too.'

'Oh…thank goodness for that.' Ayanna let out a relieved breath. 'I haven't had time to try them myself yet. There's a lot to do to make sure an event this size goes well.'

'Relax,' Emilia told her. 'Enjoy yourself. You've done a wonderful job of organising this gala—I'm so impressed.'

'Me too,' Dom said, turning his head as he noticed his father's neurosurgeon coming towards them. 'Hi, Max… We're just saying what an amazing job Ayanna's done with the decorations and catering for tonight.'

Max Granger's nod was polite but Ayanna didn't look reassured by either Dom's praise or Max's agreement. If anything, she was looking even more tense.

'Excuse me… I'd better go and check up on how things are going in the kitchens.'

Ayanna's green dress vanished amongst the crowd as Dom let his gaze scan the room.

'I wonder if Giada's here yet?'

'She is,' Max told him, and then lowered his voice. 'I've spoken to her and told her what I told you earlier today—that if…ah… Mr Baresi's condition continues to improve we can look at going ahead with his original surgery very soon. Maybe as soon as the planned date of the fifteenth. I should have a better idea after the scan that's booked in for first thing tomorrow.'

Dom acknowledged the information with no more than a single nod. 'I'll see her soon enough,' he murmured. 'I believe we're seated at the same table for dinner and it looks as though they're getting ready to serve the first course.'

Max turned to move away but then looked back.

'Don't miss the dessert,' he told them. 'It's something very special. Worth all the effort it took to find.'

Emilia watched him walk away. 'I wonder how he knows that?' she said. 'I thought the food tonight was Ayanna's responsibility.'

'One of them,' Dom agreed. 'She's had rather a lot of responsibility lately what with trying to ensure that information that needs to stay private stays that way. And part of that is the reason why Max is here, of course. I believe she's been working closely with him.'

'Well, I hope she gets to enjoy tonight. It would be unfair if it's just stressful for her. Oh…look…there's Lucas. I haven't seen him since the day of the accident.'

'No…' Dom was delighted to see his best friend again. And his sister, who was approaching with Lucas, although he couldn't advertise their relationship by anything as personal as a hug. He was smiling warmly as he greeted her, however.

'You're looking good, Gigi.'

Better than good, he thought. It was more than the lovely, purple dress she was wearing, with the sparkly top that left one shoulder bare. Or the earrings that looked as if they were part of the royal family's famous collection of rare jewels. His sister probably didn't need the accessories to make her look so good because she was almost glowing.

'You look like you've caught a nice bit of sunshine,' he added.

Giada was smiling back at him. 'Hard not to in Isola Verde,' she said. 'Even in winter.'

'It's the most beautiful place,' Lucas agreed. He was

looking at Giada as he spoke but then looked back to catch Dom's raised eyebrow.

'Or so Gigi's told me,' he added hurriedly.

Dom blinked this time. There weren't that many people who got to call the Crown Princess of Isola Verde by her pet name.

'Your dress is beautiful,' Emilia was saying to Giada.

'So is yours. That red is spectacular.' Giada slid a sideways look at her brother and then back at Emilia, clearly wondering what their connection was. 'You work together, yes? Didn't I see you in the ER on the day of the accident?'

'Yes, but we only work together sometimes. I'm a trauma surgeon with the orthopaedic department at Seattle General.'

'We went to medical school together,' Dom put in. 'We're old friends, Gigi, that's all.'

The idea of even being 'old friends' would have seemed presumptuous just a few weeks ago, but things between them had changed so much that the idea that someone would think they were actually a couple didn't seem far-fetched at all. The idea was not unpleasant, either. Impossible, of course, but what man wouldn't want to follow through on an attraction that had been taken to an entirely new level this evening?

'Oh…' Giada's response was drawn out just enough to suggest she didn't quite believe that. The glance she shared with Lucas suggested that they had a silent conversation thing going on which made Dom wonder about connections between people but Giada turned away before he could ask any leading questions and he was distracted by her profile. His sister wasn't just looking good because of the sunshine she'd been enjoying, it looked as though she'd made the most of the wonderful Italian food while she'd been at home. Or maybe it was just the cut of her dress that was making the most of her curves. Either way, it certainly wasn't something Dom was going to mention.

Between courses, people were changing places or walking amongst the tables to chat with friends and toast what they hoped was going to be a record-breaking fund-raising event.

'Those tickets were well worth that hefty price tag,' one of Seattle General's obstetricians said to Dom and Emilia. 'This place is amazing. And the food... I can't wait for the dessert I saw on the menu. I have no idea what a London Fog Cake could be but I suspect I might have to start my New Year's diet before Christmas at this rate.'

'It's all delicious,' Emilia agreed. 'That salad we started with...mmm... What was it called again?'

'Caprese,' Dom said. 'It's an Italian classic.'

'Ah...' The obstetrician smiled at Dom. 'That would be right up your alley, then. You've got Italian heritage, haven't you?'

'It's been a while since I've been there.' Dom didn't want to discuss his heritage and he was well-practised in deflecting awkward questions. 'I'm more than half American now, I reckon. I didn't realise that Seattle had a gem like this amongst its hotels, though. Do you know anything about its history?'

'Not much. I do know it's just over a hundred years old because they had some centenary celebrations not that long ago.'

Another Seattle General specialist stepped close to join the conversation. 'I heard a story that the name came from a group of men who'd struck it rich in the Yukon gold rush and they formed a group and called it the Polar Club.'

'Makes sense,' Emilia put in. 'The Yukon's on the border with Alaska, isn't it? With a coast on the Arctic Ocean? That must have been pretty cold...'

Dom excused himself to visit the restrooms and, by the time he returned, he saw that dessert was being served. Waiters were carrying silver trays with the most extraordinary looking cakes on top. With the smoky looking, streaked grey icing on the cakes, it was obvious where that unusual name had come from.

He stepped back to let a waiter walk past and found his steps slowing to a halt as he watched and listened for a moment. All around him he could hear animated conversation and laughter and cries of admiration as each table's dessert was served. He could also hear the music from the small, live band, who'd been playing mostly classical music so far but seemed to be changing to popular music now, perhaps as a prelude to encouraging people to use the dance floor. It was still a brightly coloured, happy scene but right now, Dom didn't feel a part of it at all.

Maybe it was because his sister was here, having just returned from Isola Verde and it was a reminder of how his life was about to be tipped upside down and that disturbing feeling had been dramatically heightened by the salad they'd been served this evening. A Caprese, for heaven's sake. Tomatoes and mozzarella cheese and basil with a delicious olive oil that could have come straight from his homeland. Every bite had been full of the flavour of his former life—a life he was about to reluctantly step back into.

Most of the people in this spectacular ballroom were his colleagues. People who shared his passion for medicine and were as proud as he was of working in such a prestigious hospital. Dom's gaze travelled back to the table nearest the dance floor. To the splash of vivid red that was Emilia's dress. Of all the people here, she was the one who understood the most. Who was his soul mate as far as how important their careers were to who *they* actually were. The only other person he knew who'd needed to escape their background to be who they really were.

Dom didn't want things to change but it was happening. With what Max had told him this evening, that process of change could be about to speed up. Whatever the outcome of his father's next surgery, they would have to share the news and that would be the moment that Domenico di Rossi would have to become Domenico Baresi again. When he'd have to walk away from the life he loved so much here. From the people he loved working with.

From Emilia…

Another waiter went past where Dom was standing, this time carrying a tray of full champagne flutes. Dom reached out to accept the offer of a glass.

He still had tonight, he told himself, as he took a long sip and then another of the champagne. And maybe this was going to be his last chance to cling to everything he loved about this life, so he'd better make the most of it, hadn't he?

Another long sip emptied his glass and another waiter took it from his hand as Dom walked back to his table.

To Emmy...

Dessert could wait, as far as he was concerned, anyway. If he was to make the most of what time he had left and not think about what was coming he had the best distraction of all waiting for him. Watching him walk towards her with a smile on her face, in fact. He held his hand out as he reached the table.

'Come and dance with me,' he invited.

CHAPTER SEVEN

Yes...

No...

Time seemed to stop for a long, long moment as Emilia stared at Dom's outstretched hand.

She'd noticed him off to one side of the ballroom in the last few minutes, standing alone as he drank a glass of champagne. She'd been instantly aware of him as soon as he'd started moving back towards their table, too, and it had taken quite some effort not to watch every step he took.

Almost any man could look good in a formal, black tie outfit but Dom looked as though he'd been born to wear a superbly cut tuxedo and matching trousers, the snowy white shirt with pin tucks, hidden buttons and the flash of gold cufflinks and, of course, the black silk bow tie.

But he *had* been born to wear it, hadn't he? Born to shine at events just like this charity gala, as part of a royal family which was pretty much as A-list as anyone could ever be. Emilia had no doubts at all that Dom would know how to dance very well. Infinitely better than she could hope to, despite the secret practice in the privacy of her apartment, with the help of online tutorials that she'd made time for ever since she'd accepted his invitation to be his partner tonight.

Which was why her brain had suddenly become a battleground, with the two sides slugging it out so fast, nobody would guess what was going on behind her smile as Dom put out his hand.

Yes…one side wanted nothing more than to be close enough to touch this man. To be touched *by* him… To feel his hands on the silk of her dress the way her own hands had been when she'd first tried it on. She had to find out if that sensation was anything like as breathtaking as it had been in her imagination, not only when she'd put this astonishing dress on that first time, but every time she'd seen it hanging in the corner of her bedroom since then.

But no… The other side was putting up a valiant opposition. Emilia had known there would be dancing involved but she'd imagined that she'd be amongst enough people on a crowded dance floor that it wouldn't matter that she didn't really know how to dance. This invitation had come too early in the evening and there were only a few couples who were already on the polished wooden floor in front of the band which meant that Emilia would be being watched by a large number of people. Many of her colleagues had already been unable to hide their surprise that she was here with Dom in the first place so she could be sure that more than a few jaws would be dropping to see them dancing together.

This was a challenge, for sure.

But this was also Dom and when had she ever backed down from any kind of challenge he'd presented?

This might be a good time to make an exception and back down, that voice in her head warned. She might be in danger of making a complete fool of herself. Or worse, taking herself back to the time in her life when being in a spotlight had been far worse than simply embarrassing. When it had meant that she was being taken to a new family because her current foster parents no longer wanted such a difficult child. Or that she was being sent to the principal's office because she was in trouble. Again. Even recently, the spotlight of her professional success had come with the pain of a failed relationship.

With that kind of background, mustering a defensive barrier was something that could be done in the blink of an eye but Emilia had never had to put that barrier up in the face of something so strong on the other side—a desire that was powerful enough to be sweeping anything else aside. Not only that, she was wearing the red dress. Her Cinderella dress. The one that told her that she could be anyone she wanted to be.

And, right now, Emilia wanted to be the person who was taking hold of Dom's hand. The woman that was about to be held in his arms. A princess for just a blink of time. She wanted it so much that her hand was reaching out to touch his even before she could consciously choose to shut down the protest in her head. It was quite possible that no one had noticed the tiny hesitation she'd had in taking Dom's hand but he'd obviously seen something in her eyes.

Thankfully, he couldn't possibly know why that internal battle had been so convincingly won but he must have guessed that her inner turmoil was due to a fear of some kind of failure, because, as he took her in his arms moments later, he put his mouth close to Emilia's ear and said a few words that changed everything.

'Trust me, Emmy... I've got this...'

His voice tickled her ear. One of his hands was covering hers and the other was against the small of her back and she could feel the heat of it, as though the silk of her dress had evaporated. And his touch was everything she'd imagined it might be. And more... Emilia could feel it in every cell of her body and she was melting. Muscles that had been poised for a physical challenge were relaxing and she even closed her eyes as she felt the power in Dom's hands. Guiding her. Holding her. Making a promise that he was not going to let her fall.

Except she was. As the sweet notes of Celine Dion's 'Think Twice' created the ocean of sound they were floating on, Emilia could feel herself falling. She'd been halfway in love with Dom before this and had been afraid that going any further could be dangerous but there was no stopping what was happening here.

This feeling of complete trust was something she'd never experienced before and there was more there as well. She was feeling protected. Cared for. Respected.

As she responded to the push and pull of his arms, Dom turned her away from him and then twirled her under his arm before drawing her close again. She caught a glimpse of his face, of the gleam in those dark eyes that told her she was doing much better than he might have expected.

That he was proud of her...?

That did it. Emilia hit the bottom of wherever that fall had been taking her and...it didn't hurt a bit. Quite the opposite. She'd never felt this happy in her life. And maybe this would be the only time in her life that she would ever feel this happy so she was going to hang onto every single second of it for as long as it lasted.

Oh, mio Dio...

The feel of this woman in his arms...

Emilia was perfectly capable of fighting as hard as it took to try and prove that she was the best at anything she attempted but she must have instinctively known that that would have been the worst approach to dancing. That what she had to do was trust enough to let someone lead her. She had to listen to what his body and hands were telling her and not to argue back—to simply follow where he led. And that was exactly what she was doing.

She was trusting him...

It was enough to make Dom's heart feel full to bursting because he knew that this wasn't a small thing for Emilia. After seeing that flash of something that could have even been fear in her eyes when he'd invited her onto the dance floor, he wouldn't have been at all surprised if she'd found an excuse to stay seated at their table, but here she was, melting in his arms when he held her close but with exactly the tension that was needed when he wanted to turn and spin her to show her off.

A spin that he could keep complete control of, unlike the way his life was beginning to turn in on itself. At least almost nobody here knew anything about how his life was about to change. They knew him only as a doctor who was striving—and succeeding—in being at the top of his challenging field of emergency medicine. The way Emilia had known him only as a fellow medical student and now her colleague until he'd dropped that bombshell and revealed his true identity.

This wasn't the first time that Dom realised that his relationship with Emilia was the only one he would ever be able to trust as being completely genuine. She was also inextricably woven into the world he'd fought so hard to join.

She was one of the most memorable parts of all those years at medical school.

She was a part of his work that he loved the most, when he was faced with the huge challenges of dealing with major trauma.

Even for just those two reasons, she was—and always would be—a part of *him*.

It was just as well that his instincts had warned him to stay away from personal involvement with her all those years ago because it was blatantly obvious to him at this moment that, in another world, he would have fallen in love with Emilia.

He still could…

And he certainly wasn't helping anything by discovering the delicious curves of her body with his hand shaping her waist and hip beneath the slippery fabric of that amazing dress. By being close enough to catch the scent of her skin and to feel the touch of her hand inside his. Most of all, to be aware of just how much she was trusting him.

If only he was the kind of prince who belonged in a fairy tale and had a fairy godmother who could wave a magic wand to make any obstacles melt away. He would not only be more than happy to give up his career to become King, but Emilia would also walk away from the job that was the most important thing in her life so that she could be by his side for ever.

It was never going to work, of course, but…just for a little while, Dom could pretend, couldn't he?

That he wasn't a prince. That his life wasn't going to change so completely he was sure he would never be truly happy again. He could cling to the things he loved for a little longer. It was only one night. A few magical hours where he could hold the most beautiful woman in the world in his arms and they could lose themselves in this romantic music and a dream or two of what might have been.

The rest of Seattle General's fundraising charity gala went past in a blur for Emilia. There were snatches of conversation she was never going to remember, a glass or two of champagne that fizzed and evaporated on her tongue almost instantly and a swirl of colours and music that was the dance floor she found herself on again and again and almost always with Dom. The one thing that Emilia was sure of, as she finally went outside to find a taxi, was that the only word that could ever sum up what this evening had been like was: *magic*.

And it seemed that the fairy tale hadn't quite ended.

The tall man in the tuxedo who had flagged down a taxi and was now holding the back door open for her was none other than her Prince. Domenico di Rossi.

'Jump in,' he told her. 'But do you mind if I share?'

Of course she didn't. What could be a better ending to such a magical evening than being in the back seat of a taxi beside Dom, with the cloud of red silk spilling onto his dark suit and the strobe effect of the street lights overhead making his eyes sparkle as she caught his gaze.

The taxi stopped for a red light, somewhere very close to the Space Needle and Emilia had to tilt her head to gaze up and admire the elegant structure that held what looked like a spaceship with all its lights on. Dom had done exactly the same thing and then, as if they couldn't resist the magnetic pull, they both turned their heads enough to look at each other.

For the second time in the space of one evening, time stopped for Emilia. But this was way bigger than looking at Dom's outstretched hand and the internal battle that it had generated.

There was no battle here. Nothing could break a connection that felt powerful enough to tilt the world's axis. Nothing was going to interfere with the inevitability that this was going to happen.

This…kiss…

A physical touch that Emilia hadn't realised she'd been waiting for forever. A touch that made her understand exactly what had always been missing from her life—this connection with another human. This feeling that she was wanted. Needed. Loved…?

The jerk of the taxi moving away on the green light wasn't enough for that kiss to be broken. It took the taxi driver's loud clearing of his throat when the taxi had stopped again a short time later for Emilia and Dom to finally break apart.

'This is the first stop,' the driver said. 'Who's getting out here?'

'I am.' Dom handed some bills to the driver and opened the door. He stepped out, then leaned down so that he could catch Emilia's gaze again. He wasn't smiling but there was a warmth in his eyes that made it impossible to look away and Emilia's senses were suddenly so heightened that it didn't matter that his words were no more than a murmur against the background of traffic noise. She could hear what he said, as he held out his hand to her for the second time that evening, as clearly as if his lips had been brushing her ear.

'Come with me?'

Oh...

Everything was spinning. A kaleidoscope of the entire evening. The gorgeous ballroom, the swish of a dress that Emilia was going to keep for ever, the wonderful food, the delicious champagne, the beautiful dresses of all the women and the music that had kept her dancing all night. The whole—incredible—fairy tale and the man who had been at the centre of everything was inviting her to make it last a little longer.

He'd just kissed her senseless and now he wanted more.

And, dear Lord, so did Emilia.

She wanted everything. She wanted it so much that she didn't hesitate for more than a heartbeat and she knew, by the way Dom's hand closed around her own, that she'd made the only choice she could have made.

Like that kiss, it felt like Emilia had been waiting her whole life for this...

He'd always known it was there, hadn't he?

And he'd been right to be afraid of it.

This...*connection*...

This feeling that *this* person, and only this person, could touch your soul, as much as your body, and make it feel like you'd...come home. That you'd finally found the place you truly belonged.

Dom had to kiss Emilia again, the moment the elevator doors closed behind them, because he couldn't wait until they reached the privacy of his apartment to find out if that kiss in the taxi had actually been what it had seemed to be, or if it had simply been his imagination, the combination of an evening full of pleasure or perhaps the frustration of having waited for so many years to kiss Emilia Featherstone that had created nothing short of a magic spell. Would kissing her now be like kissing any other attractive woman? He'd certainly had enough practice to be able to make that judgement.

Unbelievably, this second kiss was even more astonishing. Reaching the penthouse level of this apartment block, the elevator doors slid open, stayed open and then closed again without either of them noticing. The touch and taste of her lips, the seductive dance of her tongue was driving any conscious thought from Dom's mind. It was only the need for a little more oxygen that made him finally pull back, to find Emilia looking just as stunned as he was feeling.

Her lips were still parted a little and her eyes glazed by desire and the only thing Dom wanted to do was to kiss her again. To kiss every inch of her body, in fact, and he certainly couldn't do that in this elevator which seemed to have stopped. Was it stuck? He pushed the button to open the doors to find that they had already

arrived at his floor and that he had absolutely no concept of how much time had passed during that kiss.

Oh, *sì*… He hadn't been wrong that first time he'd
laid eyes on Emilia back at medical school. When he'd
known instantly that it would be dangerous to get close
to her in any personal way. As he held his apartment
door open for her and she went past him with a swish
of silk and a lingering upward glance, Dom could remember vividly that first sight of this woman. Those
blue, blue eyes that made him think of the sea that surrounded Isola Verde. The glorious glint of so many different shades of red in that magnificent hair, including
the copper that was reflected in the freckles that dusted
her pale skin.

Distraction…

Destruction…

He'd put up the fences right there and then. Had
mentally painted the word 'Danger' across the palings
in the same shade of red as Emilia's dress was tonight.
Moments after shoving his door shut behind him with
his foot, Dom's hands were on the smooth silk of that
dress again. Emilia was standing on tiptoe, her arms
around his neck as he kissed her yet again. Dom had
found the zip that was falling open beneath his fingers.
A zip that went far enough for his fingertips to brush
her buttocks and get lost in all the folds of her skirt. Not
too lost, though, because he could cup his hand around
a firm curve and pull her just close enough to leave her
in no doubt about how much he wanted her.

Her tiny gasp beneath his lips and the way she
pressed herself even closer was Dom's undoing.

It wasn't that those warnings weren't still there. If

anything, in the last few minutes, the danger level had gone off the Richter scale because being with Emilia was everything he'd been afraid it would be and there would be no going back after this. Things were going to come crashing down around them and people might well be going to get hurt.

But that was going to happen anyway, wasn't it?

And he could handle the fallout. The hurt. But what about Emilia? The last thing Dom wanted to do was to hurt her. It might be the hardest thing he'd ever done but he could stop now, if that was what it took to protect her.

He held her face between his hands and waited for her eyes to focus.

'Do you want this, Emmy?' His voice was rough. Raw, even. 'Because if we should stop, it needs to be now…'

'No…' Her voice was no more than a whisper. Almost a whimper. 'Please…don't stop… I do want this…' He heard the way her breath hitched. 'Even if it is just for tonight…'

Just for tonight. He'd thought that tonight was his last chance, too. The last opportunity to cling to all the things he loved about the life he'd created away from his home and his royal heritage. Maybe it was the same for Emilia? That she wanted to cling to what they'd had between them that they'd never been brave—or perhaps foolish—enough to confirm?

He'd told himself that he had to make the most of this magic night and this…being able to be as physically close as it was possible to be to another human would make this night one that he was going to remember for the rest of his life. Emilia wanted it as much as he did so this was going to be his gift to the most amazing woman he was ever going to know.

A night that she would also remember for the rest of her life.

Sliding his hands up her back again, it took only a nudge from his thumbs on her shoulders to dislodge the lace straps that were still holding her dress up. The fabric rippled free and tumbled into a huge puddle on the marble tiles of this entranceway. The only under-wear Emilia was wearing were a pair of lace panties the same colour as that dress and, as Dom dragged his gaze back to her eyes, he could see the hint of fear in them. *Dio mio*…did she think that he might not find her beautiful enough? Or change his mind about how much he wanted her?

He scooped her into his arms to carry her into his bedroom.

'You have no idea, do you, *mi amore*?' he murmured.

Her head was tucked in beneath his collar bone. Right against his heart. 'Of what?'

Dom kicked the bedroom door shut behind them. 'Of just how perfect you are…'

Oh… Dear Lord…

Emilia had never been so…what on earth was the word she needed? She was physically, emotionally, *sexually* exhausted and yet she'd never felt so alive. Or so happy.

So…so *whole*…

The way that Dom's breathing had slowed suggested that he had already fallen asleep and Emilia should fol-low his example because, while she had no idea of the time, dawn couldn't be that far away. She'd lost count of how many times they'd made love since Dom had carried her to his bed and the need for each other had been equally fierce on both sides. They both knew that their lives were going to go in such different directions very soon and it seemed that they'd made a tacit agreement to make the most of this one night because it could be the only one they ever got.

And it was a night that Emilia would never, ever forget.

With her eyes closed, tucked under Dom's arm, she rested her cheek against his chest where she could both feel and hear the steady beat of his heart. It was a big thing for her to be this close to someone else. When she'd told Dom about her past relationship with Chandler and said that she was happier on her own, anyway, she'd been quite sincere.

One of Emilia's earliest memories was a place where she'd discovered she could be completely alone and nobody could find her—a hole in the bottom of a hedge, just big enough for a little girl to crawl into and hide away from angry voices or frightening things. Being lonely was worth it to feel safe. At school, libraries became a haven away from bullies and her preferred exercise of running had always been a solitary activity. When she'd escaped that disastrous relationship with Chandler, there was such enormous relief to be found in being alone that Emilia had been able to ignore the loneliness that went with it. To close her eyes to the emptiness that her future threatened to include.

Yes…it had been well ingrained, that belief that she was happier on her own.

Until now…

Now, she knew what it was like to feel like *this*… As if she was hiding away in the safest place possible but she could never feel lonely again. She had someone with her who understood exactly who she was and why she was like that and he still wanted to be with her. Someone who thought she was…perfect?

Emilia lifted her head just enough to see Dom's face in the soft light of this room. *He* was the perfect one and she was missing him already. How crazy was that? He was right here but he had retreated into sleep. The black lashes that matched his, oh, so rumpled hair right now were resting on his cheeks. Deep, even breaths were coming through that gorgeously defined, Italian nose of his and his lips were ever so slightly parted and curled up at the corners, as if he was already dreaming of something very pleasant.

The temptation to touch those lips—kiss them again, perhaps—was strong but Emilia knew she wasn't going to risk waking him. She didn't want him to look at her and see what she was thinking. To know just how much she was going to miss him. Because, if he saw that, he would feel sorry for her because they both knew how unlikely it was that they would ever see each other again in the future. And Emilia didn't want to see that sympathy because that would be the end of this magical night and she wanted to feel like this for a little longer.

To feel safe. And loved. And whole…

Very gently, she let her head settle again in that spot where she could hear every beat of Dom's heart. A soft drum that was already pulling her into sleep but

Emilia was fighting the pull. Because she didn't need to sleep—she was already dreaming…

It was the vibration from his ringing phone that woke Dom and he was startled to find his bedroom bathed in the first fingers of daylight through windows whose curtains had not been pulled. Sunrise at this time of year in Seattle didn't happen before about eight a.m. and he never normally slept this late. But then again, last night had been anything but normal, hadn't it? He could feel the weight of Emilia's head on his arm and it was obvious that she was still soundly asleep which was hardly surprising after he'd kept her awake for most of the night.

But…*oddio*…it had been a night he was definitely never, ever going to forget.

Carefully, Dom eased his arm from beneath her head and rolled away, picking up his phone as he got out of bed and moving swiftly towards the door of his en suite bathroom so as not to disturb Emilia just yet.

He had to take this call because he'd seen the name of caller on the screen.

'What is it, Max?'

'We've just completed the scan on your father,' Max Granger told him. 'I'm sorry Dom, but it's not good news…'

CHAPTER EIGHT

SPLASHING SO MUCH cold water on his face in the wake of that phone call should have been enough to bring Dom firmly back into the present but, as he knotted a towel around his waist for decency, he found himself standing beside his bed, pausing to take a deep, deep breath as his gaze rested on Emilia.

Taking a moment to forget everything that was rushing towards him and soak in the beauty of this woman. The flicker of fire that her hair made, tumbling against the crisp white of his bed linen. That pale, perfect skin that tasted as good as it looked and those freckles... He had a vague memory of vowing to kiss every single one of them...

Dom could almost feel himself being torn in two, here.

What half of him wanted, so much it felt like a shade of desperation, was to turn the clock back. Just a few hours. To when he'd scooped Emilia into his arms to carry her off to bed. This time, however, he'd close the curtains and turn his phone off and give them complete privacy for a little longer.

But time had run out.

The other half of himself was just as desperate to be near his father as Roberto faced a new crisis. And to talk to his sister, as he'd told Max he would do as soon as possible. It was a no-brainer where his duty lay and what his priorities were and Dom absolutely wanted to be there for his family immediately but he knew, too well, how hard it was going to be to walk away from Emilia.

Because he sensed that this would mark the beginning of the end.

If he had a choice, Dom would never want this to end. It had occurred to him during the gala last night that Emilia was someone that he could easily fall in love with if circumstances were very different. He'd taken the risk of playing with that fantasy, even, and giving himself a night of pretending that things *could* be that different only to find that it wasn't simply a possibility. He'd hidden it so well he hadn't even seen it himself but he was already in love with her and he probably had been for far longer than he knew. Not that that was likely to change anything, of course. Reality was hovering, ready to crash all around him. Around them both…

As if she sensed that she was being watched, Emilia stirred in her sleep and stretched like a cat. Perhaps she was instinctively reaching out to touch him because Dom could see her muscles tense and pause as her arm swept the space that was probably still warm from his body. Her eyes flew open but it took a moment for her to register where she was and that he was standing beside the bed, and then to chase enough sleep from her eyes to really focus.

For a heartbeat, and then another, as he saw the

dream filled haze lifting in her gaze, Dom couldn't help taking this fraction of time to snatch the last piece of that fantasy. To imagine an entirely different world, where he would see this transformation in her face every single morning for the rest of his life. That softening around her eyes that was reaching her lips now to become the beginnings of a smile, as if seeing *him* was the best thing that could possibly happen in those first moments of waking up to a new day. It looked… and felt…an awful lot like love. Was it possible that Emilia felt the same way about him as he was feeling about her? That, if she had her choice, she would want him to stay here? To stay with *her*?

He could fight for that. Somehow…

But, in just another heartbeat, Emilia's face changed again. The focus was far more intense and the embryonic smile vanished.

'What's wrong, Dom? What's happened?'

How could she read him so easily when he hadn't even been consciously thinking about what was worrying him so much?

'I just got a call from Max,' he told her. 'They've finished the scan on my father and he's not happy with what they've found. The tumour is growing and it's starting to cause problems. His intracranial pressure is rising.'

'Oh, no…' Emilia sat up, pulling the sheet to wrap around herself like a toga. 'They were hoping he'd recover more from the last surgery before they went ahead with removing the tumour, weren't they?'

Dom nodded. 'There's a few more tests to run and then a detailed plan has to be made for a challenging surgery like this. He's wanting to print a 3D anatomical model for a physical simulation of the surgery.'

'Wow...' Emilia looked fascinated. 'I've heard about that technology. I'll bet I could use it myself in some cases.'

It was so much easier to ease back into reality by slipping into a familiar, professional space. 'I'm sure you could. It'll certainly help Max and his team by letting them see exactly what the tumour looks like and how it sits in relation to blood vessels and surrounding brain structures.'

'How urgent is the surgery?'

'I guess that will depend on whether his condition remains stable or not but Max said something about the fifteenth—the day after tomorrow. Ironically, that's the date that his elective surgery was originally scheduled for.'

'I'll go and see him today,' Emilia said. 'I've been more than happy with the way his leg has been healing but I'd like to make sure the fixation is robust enough to cope with any movement that might be involved in the surgery.' She glanced towards the windows and blinked. 'What time *is* it?'

'Just before eight. What time are you due at work?'

'I've got a late start at eleven a.m. I thought it might be prudent after a big night out.'

She caught his gaze and, for a long moment, a silence hung between them. A silence that acknowledged everything that had happened in the last twelve, life-changing hours. Dom could feel that tearing sensation again, forcing the two halves of himself further apart.

'I'm due at nine a.m.,' he said. 'And I'll need to be a

lot earlier if I can be so I can see my father and talk to my sister. I'm sorry... I'll have to jump into the shower and get going.' He cleared his throat, still holding that gaze. Clinging to it, in fact, with his words no more than a murmur. 'I'd rather be jumping back into bed...'

Emilia got to her feet. The look she was giving him was sharp enough to make him remember the countless times she had needled him into responding to a challenge or teased him because she'd already won.

'You're not a very good listener, are you? Or maybe you've just forgotten the pearls of wisdom I bestowed on you when we were discussing Thanksgiving that day?' She shook her head. 'I guess it was a long time ago. Nearly three weeks.' Her lips quirked and then she held his gaze and spoke slowly, enunciating every word separately as if she was speaking to someone of very limited intelligence. She even put her hand flat against his bare chest, near his heart, as if she wanted to emphasise just how important this was.

'Family. Is. Everything.'

There was a gleam in her eyes that softened any put down and her voice softened as well. 'Your family needs you and you need them, Dom. That has to come above absolutely everything else.'

Still he hesitated. Was he hoping that Emilia would arrange a time and space they could meet again later today? Or that she might offer to go with him?

Instead, her breath came out in a sigh. 'You still don't realise how lucky you are to have a family, Dom. It's something I always dreamed of having but I never have. I never will have...'

Dom shook his head. 'You could. You could make your own.'

Maybe it wouldn't be with him but he still wanted this astonishing woman to find the happiness she deserved in life.

But now it was Emilia who was shaking her head. 'I tried that, remember? With Chandler. Didn't work and I should have known it wouldn't. I can look after myself, Dom. Always have and always will be able to. And I'm happy on my own. It's better this way.'

The touch of her hand on his chest increased in pressure enough to become a shove to send him on his way. 'Go... Get clean. I'm going to find some of your gym gear or something to borrow so I don't have to do the taxi ride of shame in my ballgown.'

Was it possible that the memory of a single touch could be powerful enough to become a kind of scar?

Dom was beginning to think that it was possible, given that he was losing count of how many times he could still feel the imprint of Emilia's hand on his chest as he juggled the next, difficult forty-eight hours. There had been intense conversations with his sister and their father's neurosurgeon as results came in from examinations and tests and more scans. Time spent by his father's bedside were coloured by all the anxiety and guilt and even grief in knowing that these could be their last moments together and Dom had not been able to let his father know how much he was loved.

There were flashes of more guilt because he hadn't seen or spoken to Emilia since they'd spent that extraordinary night together but he knew she would understand that his family had to come first right now. She had, after all, reminded him of that in no uncertain terms.

He'd been successful in barely missing a beat in his beloved ER as well, because keeping himself as busy as possible and as distracted from any personal issues as possible was by far the best way he could deal with such enormous pressure. It meant that when he wasn't needed in the ER, he had to find other things that were challenging or interesting enough to take his entire focus and that was why he'd come up to one of Seattle General's operating theatres this morning. Not to check out where his own father was going to be, for probably many, many hours, later today but to follow up on a patient who'd captured his interest weeks ago.

Fourteen-year-old Jason, who had technically died when his heart had stopped beating almost as soon as he'd arrived by ambulance after his fainting episode at school, was due to have an implantable defibrillator inserted into his chest because extensive testing had shown that he had an inherited condition that had thickened the muscle of his heart enough to disrupt the way its electrical system worked. It was a procedure that Dom had never got around to watching so what better way to fill in some of the time before he was due to start his shift in the ER. He would still be able to visit his father before his surgery was scheduled to begin.

Dom pulled a hat and mask from the dispensers in the scrubbing in room adjacent to the theatre. He could see Jason already on the table in front of him and the anaesthetist was administering his sedation and watching vital signs, adjusting the volume of an alarm on one of the monitors. The beeping from the machine reminded

Dom of that cardiac arrest alarm he'd heard that had signalled the moment he'd become involved in this case.

He'd been in his office. Talking to Emilia in the wake of her reaction to learning the truth about who he was. It wasn't just an echo of the alarm he could hear, however. He could hear some of his own words.

I guess I just don't want to lose what we have, Emmy. Something that's real. Something I can trust...

And...there it was again. The imprint of her hand burning the skin beneath the cotton of his scrub tunic. Disturbing enough to make him touch the spot himself to try and erase the sensation by rubbing at it.

The movement earned him a sharp sideways glance from the attending cardiologist who was reaching for a sterile towel to dry his hands.

'Chest pain, Dom?' He raised his eyebrows. 'You've come to the right place, then. Shall I see if we've got a spare defibrillator lying around that we could bung in?'

'I only came to watch, Rick.' But Dom felt like he was smiling for the first time in the last two days. Maybe because the physician's remark reminded him of the kind of banter he and Emilia had always shared? 'I like your bedside manner, though. It's true what they say about you, isn't it?'

Both men were grinning as they entered the theatre for what should be a routine and relatively minor procedure but one that had the potential to ensure that young Jason would go on to live a normal life that wasn't shadowed by the threat of sudden death.

Dom's smile faded as he stood back to watch the team's well-practised routine of implanting the cardio-verter defibrillator. An incision was made under Jason's collarbone to form the pocket for the small device and wires were threaded through a large vein to be positioned in the heart's chambers under X-ray. Then it was time to test the device.

'These things are getting more sophisticated all the time,' Rick told him. 'You'll see, when we get him into VF.'

Dom glanced to where the electrophysiology technician was ready with his equipment.

'We synchronise a small shock to hit the T wave in the ECG,' the technician told him. 'It's the fastest and most effective way to induce ventricular fibrillation.'

'Don't worry...' Rick must have seen the look on Dom's face at the idea of deliberately causing a potentially fatal heart rhythm. 'We've got back up to deal with a cardiac arrest if the internal defib doesn't do its job.'

It took a few minutes to test the device that was capable of delivering a series of low-voltage electrical impulses to pace the heart, a small shock to try and correct the rhythm or a larger shock to deal with the heart stopping completely. Dom found himself holding his breath as he watched the screens of the monitors, waiting for that small device to do what it had taken a whole team in the ER to achieve that day that Jason had been his patient.

'And that's it,' Rick announced a short time later. 'We just need to close the incision and it'll be a wrap. We'll keep him in overnight, though, just to keep an eye on him.'

As Dom was leaving the suite of operating theatres, he passed an area where relatives were allowed to wait until they could visit the recovery room and be re-assured that their loved one had made it through their surgery. He recognised Jason's mother, even though she was sitting with her head bowed, one hand on her forehead. He wanted to stop and reassure her but he'd misjudged the timing of the procedure a little and he was running late to be in the ER. He also knew that she wouldn't have to suffer much longer because Rick would be coming to see her within minutes to tell her how well the procedure had gone.

That pushing the elevator button would trigger yet another memory of Emilia's touch on his chest was un-expected. Was it the pushing sensation or the fact that he'd just seen a mother who was desperately worried about her son which was an echo of more than Emilia's touch? He could hear *her* words this time.

'Family is everything...'

And, in turn, that brought a flood of memories of Thanksgiving Day. The laughter. The terrible cooking. The way Emilia had made him feel lucky to have a fam-ily, because even with their problems, it was so much more than she'd ever had in her life. Her relationship with that bastard, who couldn't recognise what he'd been lucky enough to have and had undermined her ability to achieve everything she was capable of achiev-ing, had been an attempt to create a family of her own, hadn't it? And its failure had been damaging enough to make her believe she was better off—and would be happier—on her own?

Oh...*sì*... Dom could feel that push on his chest with vivid clarity.

The sensation of being pushed out of Emilia's life.

She didn't feel the same way about him as he did about her. She wasn't remotely interested in forming another permanent relationship and even if she was, she wouldn't want any part of the future that now lay before him.

Abruptly, Dom turned away from the elevator that still hadn't arrived. He gave the firestop door at the entrance to the staircase a firm shove and then took the steps at a fast pace. He needed to be somewhere else. Somewhere he'd be too busy to keep thinking about Emilia like this.

Of course she wouldn't want a part of his future. She loved her work here as much as he did. And she'd always been a private person when it came to her personal life. Dom could be quite sure he wasn't the only person who'd known her for so many years but had no clue what her early life had been like. Imagine if she was put under the scrutiny of the media who would stop at nothing to reveal information that would sell their publications? What could be better than a princess with a past that was far juicier than simply being a commoner?

He wouldn't want that for Emilia. And he knew that it would be the last thing she would want for herself. She'd learned to hide that part of her life. She'd said herself that she'd learned to look after herself and succeed against the odds and Dom could be sure that she would continue to do that. And that she'd thrive.

Dom was almost at the ER now and he would be able to immerse himself in what would hopefully be a very busy shift. He had cover, as well, so he could take breaks to be with Giada as she waited for their father to come out of surgery—probably in the same room that Jason's mother had been waiting.

Emilia was quite right. Family *was* everything and he had to look after his, especially today. Memories of his night with Emilia and any dreams of her being a part of his life in the future had to be dismissed. He'd managed before, when he'd totally dismissed his attraction to Emilia when he'd first seen her at medical school. He could do it again now.

Because the persona of Dr Domenico di Rossi was getting ready to leave the building. His Royal Highness Domenico Baresi was about to step into those shoes and begin a totally different life.

He, too, needed to learn to look after himself. And thrive. Because he owed that, not only to his family, but to his country as well. Emilia would understand because she understood *him*, probably better than anyone else ever had. Or ever would.

Trauma Team to ER. Stat.

The clock felt like it was being rewound as Emilia responded to her pager. Back to the day before any of this had started. Before she'd known Dom's secret and before she'd revealed so much about her own background. Before she'd fallen in love with someone she'd only ever seen as a rival and a colleague and so far before they'd become close enough to *make* love it felt like a different century.

The case was not that dissimilar to the one that had brought Dom's father and sister into the emergency room of Seattle General. A car had gone out of control, presumably because the flurries of snow happening today had made the surface slippery, and the driver had been powerless to stop the vehicle hitting a pedestrian at high speed.

The scene in Resus One was almost identical. Dom was there, gathering his team around him as they all donned their protective gear of gowns, gloves and goggles. He was supervising drugs being drawn up and ensuring that specialised trolleys were available, including the equipment for a FAST scan to look for internal bleeding following abdominal or chest trauma. Dom being here was unexpected given that Emilia knew today was the day his father was facing the challenge of the surgery to remove his brain tumour. She'd been to see the King more than once in the last two days to confirm that she was happy with the stability of his healing femoral fracture but this was the first time she'd seen Dom since she'd left his apartment on the morning after the gala ball.

The usual heightened senses of the adrenaline rush of a trauma team code made Emilia's response to seeing Dom so acute it felt more physical than emotional. And there were far deeper layers than mere surprise. There was delight to be found but apprehension as well. And hope…? She'd been fine with not having heard anything from him in the last forty-eight hours because she'd told herself that he had too much going on with his family and she hadn't wanted to intrude by contacting him for the same reason.

She knew she was staring as she stepped into the resuscitation area and she knew that Dom was aware that she was here. The moment of truth came in the split second before Emilia turned to reach for a pair of gloves from the wall dispenser and Dom looked up and directly at her. Again, it was only for a blink of time but it was long enough for Emilia to feel a shiver run down her spine. The clock really had rewound and her apprehension had not been misplaced. This was purely professional. She had reverted to being nothing more than a colleague. A rival. Whatever barriers had been there before any of this had started were back in place and the connection that had been so powerful such a short time ago was nowhere to be seen or felt.

And it *hurt*, dammit…

It was far more than a slap in the face. It was devastating. Even though Emilia had known that there was never going to be anything more than that one night together, she would have expected there to be an acknowledgment that that private connection would always be there. That it was now rather more significant than it ever had been, in fact.

It would be totally unprofessional to let a personal emotional issue distract her right before the arrival of a probably critically injured patient. It was not something that had ever threatened Emilia's focus before and she wasn't about to let it happen now. Maybe she was actually wrong and Dom was only as focussed as he ever was when he was leading the trauma team with the added tension of his family worries in the background. They'd always had their own way of dealing with tension and old habits often became an automatic response.

'You've been busy,' Emilia said lightly. 'I love what you've done to the place.'

He was frowning at her in bemusement. Emilia tilted

her head towards the fat string of red tinsel that was wound around an IV pole and the bunches of fake holly that adorned the twelve-lead ECG trolley.

Dom's frown became a scowl as he turned to snap at a nurse. 'Who did this? It's totally inappropriate to have Christmas decorations in an area where we bring critically ill patients. Get rid of them. Stat.'

With her arms full of tinsel and holly, the nurse crossed paths with the stretcher that was rushed in moments later so Emilia had no time to dwell on a side of Dom she'd never seen before and wonder just how much stress he was under to have reacted like that. Worse, to feel that, despite feeling so hurt herself, she wanted to help him. Just to touch his arm, perhaps, and catch his gaze for long enough to somehow let him know that she was here if he needed her. That she understood...

Perhaps it was just as well that the familiar chaos of an incoming patient required the absolute attention of every member of the medical team ready to treat them. And this patient, Simon, a thirty-five-year-old man most definitely needed a lot of help if he was going to survive. Paramedics had applied a pelvic binder because they suspected Simon had a fractured pelvis and everyone here knew that the force needed to cause a significant injury to this solid bony structure made it very likely that he would have other significant injuries. Like chest trauma. Broken bones. A ruptured spleen could explain why Simon's blood pressure was dropping to an alarming level if there were no major vessels damaged as a result of the blunt force of a car hitting his pelvis.

Everybody was flat out from the moment Simon was brought in.

'Let's get another large bore IV in, stat, please.' Dom was watching the readings on the monitors coming into focus. 'And get some fluids up. Simon, can you hear me? Do you know where you are?'

The response was no more than an agonised groan.

'We need some more analgesia on board. Have we got some fentanyl drawn up yet? Ketamine?'

Technicians, interns and nurses were working around each other in a familiar, well-rehearsed dance as soon as Simon had been transferred from the ambulance gurney. Clothing was being removed. Blood taken. Electrodes attached for monitoring.

'I want a chest X-ray,' Dom ordered. 'A FAST scan. Pelvic X-ray.' His instructions were crisp and clear. 'What's the blood pressure now?'

'Systolic ninety.'

'Type and cross match. We're going to need some blood. Don't rock the pelvis. And no log roll, please. We don't want any unnecessary movement.'

It was Dom who placed his gloved hands gently under Simon's back to palpate for any major wounds or bone deformity.

'It's clear,' he said, standing back as the overhead X-ray machines were rolled in to take images. 'Okay... anyone without a lead apron step outside, please.'

Emilia had been close enough to examine Simon's chest and found some probably broken lower ribs which could well have lacerated his spleen or liver but she was holding her breath to see what the X-rays would reveal was going on much lower in his abdomen. Despite the aggressive fluid resuscitation this young man was receiving, his blood pressure indicated that he was in hypovolaemic shock which could rapidly prove fatal if they couldn't find and stop whatever internal bleeding was going on.

'Look. There and there…' Dom had come to look over Emilia's shoulder as soon as she had the image up on the computer screen. 'Nasty pelvic ring fracture. Clearly unstable with that anteroposterior displacement of at least a centimetre. Maybe one point five.'

'We need to get him to Theatre for a laparotomy. There might not be enough blood to be showing up on the FAST scan but I'd put money on his spleen being ruptured thanks to those rib fractures. I'm going to aspirate next but his BP's already so low it's not safe to wait for a CT scan.'

'He needs external fixation to stabilise his pelvis before anyone goes near his spleen. The pelvic binder has to come off to allow access and if you open up the abdomen and start shifting organs around without fixation, it could disrupt the pelvic fractures and he could lose his entire blood volume into the pelvic cavity before anyone gets near his spleen.'

'You want to do that here?'

'Can do, if he's haemodynamically stable enough. It'll take me ten to fifteen minutes once we're set up and I can do it without X-ray.'

Emilia could actually feel Dom's focus. Could feel the way they were welded together as a team with a single focus and the absolute determination that they were going to win this battle. It didn't occur to her until later that this might well be the last time they could work together like this but it wouldn't have made any difference at the time, anyway. They always worked together like this.

Dom scrubbed in to help her. Simon was unconscious and oblivious to the preparations around him as staff numbers were reduced to a minimum, his body was draped and the skin of his lower abdomen prepped for the surgical procedure. The sterile packs had been rolled open on the top of a trolley, with an impressive array of steel pins and bars and a drill along with scalpels and sutures but it was a felt pen marker that Emilia reached for first.

'I'm marking the anterior superior iliac spine with an X,' she told Dom. 'And the inferior with a circle. I'll do that on both sides before I make my first incision.'

It took fifteen minutes to construct a frame that would make it possible to move Simon and perform the open surgery he was going to need without exacerbating an injury that could easily prove fatal. It was a challenging fifteen minutes that had trickles of sweat dampening the back of Emilia's tunic and she blew out a relieved breath as she tightened the last bolt.

'You can let go now, thanks, Dom. We should be completely stable now.' Grasping the top of the triangular frame, she tipped it carefully a little to one side. The whole of Simon's pelvis moved as one piece. This frame would not only keep his bones in position until they healed, it meant it was safe to shift him to Theatre and tackle any other sources of blood loss.

'Let's get him up to Theatre,' Dom instructed, stepping back. But then he turned, with a smile and spoke quietly. 'Good job. Thanks, Emmy.'

The glow of that praise stayed with Emilia as she followed her patient to the theatre suite. Or maybe it was because the adrenaline rush of this case still had her senses heightened and she wasn't walking alone. Dom was staying with Simon until he could be handed over to the general surgeon who was waiting in an operating theatre for their arrival.

It wasn't as though it meant anything, though. Dom had always acknowledged the skills of anyone he worked with and a dramatic case like this was exactly what they both loved so much about their work. This was no more than the old dynamic between them but Emilia had new insight about why it had worked so well. They'd always competed so fiercely and baited each other so mercilessly because that kind of a relationship could actually be passionate but still completely safe. Had they both instinctively known how painful it would be to take those protective barriers away only to have to rebuild them?

There was a new team to take over the management of the next stage of Simon's treatment but Emilia was going to stay in Theatre. It was quite possible that this pelvic injury would need internal fixation and, while she would normally want to wait a few days for bleeding and swelling to be under control, if the patient was having abdominal surgery for other reasons, it might be preferable to take the opportunity for any further orthopaedic work.

'I might stay for a while, too,' Dom said. 'I've got cover in the ER anyway, because I knew I'd have to leave at some point today.'

'Is your...? I mean, has the surgery started?'

A single nod. 'It's been going for some time already. I

get progress reports and pass them on to Giada. They'll
tell me when it's over but, until then, I really need to
keep busy.'

Emilia's lips curved gently in sympathy. 'It helps,
doesn't it?'

Another nod. A flash of something in his eyes that
told her he *was* still feeling their connection but it was
drowned instantly by something that looked a lot like
sadness.

'I don't need to scrub in so I'll leave you to get on
with it.'

He turned away but Emilia paused before entering the theatre's anteroom. She wanted to call softly to
Dom. To make him turn around again so that she could
get another glimpse of what she knew was still there.

She wanted to whisper something.

I love you...

I miss you already...

But what did she expect to happen? That he would
reject what his family—his whole country probably—
wanted? Or that she would decide she could walk away
from what had been the total focus of her life for as long
as she wanted to remember? Her dedication to her career had already destroyed a relationship. She'd spent
too long putting herself and her ambitions above everything else. Prince Domenico Baresi deserved far more
than that in a partner.

She might be doing them both a favour by letting
him go.

Figuratively and literally. At least for now, when he
was clearly struggling to cope with everything life was
throwing at him. It wasn't as if she had a choice, any-

way, because a nurse was coming along the corridor towards Dom.

'Dr di Rossi? I was just coming down to the ER to find you. Your patient that you asked to be informed about—Mr Baresi? He's out of Theatre and has been taken through to Recovery.'

Dom walked away from Emilia without a backward glance.

And she turned to walk away as well. Into Theatre. A place that felt like a sanctuary right now. Like home. But then, this was the place where she really belonged, after all.

Perhaps it was destined to be the only place that would ever feel like home.

CHAPTER NINE

Okay. It was official.

Emilia hated Christmas.

For some reason that ability she had honed during her life to ignore or tolerate all the hype of the season had deserted her this year in the final run up to the big day.

There was a palpable pressure to keep such negativity private but Emilia knew she wasn't alone in feeling like a Grinch. There were so many people out there for whom the inescapable message that this was the time for families to come together and show their love for each other by bestowing gifts and sharing a fabulous feast would rub salt into wounds that could never properly heal. People who had lost a loved one at this time of year, perhaps. At worst, a child or baby, which would make this all the more agonising with small faces radiating excitement as they counted down the sleeps. There were the people who were estranged from their families for whatever reasons. And then there were those who simply didn't have a family.

People like Emilia.

So, yeah… Christmas was something to be endured, not enjoyed for her and it seemed to be getting more intense with every passing day. It was going to be Christmas Eve tomorrow so it had to be peaking any moment now but it couldn't come soon enough for Emilia and she was beginning to rethink her usual strategy of trying to bury herself in her work. Maybe next year she would take a month off to go to a place that didn't celebrate Christmas. Like Vietnam, perhaps. Or Qatar. Or Outer Mongolia? That way she wouldn't be faced with constant reminders of what she would prefer to ignore. The resuscitation areas in the ER and the operating theatres might be mercifully free of decorations or music or flashing lights but the rest of Seattle General had become more and more festive as the countdown to Christmas ramped up.

Gifts were piling up under the huge trees in the atrium, ready to be distributed to inpatients in the children's wards. Every second person was wearing something festive like the snowman earrings a young woman at the main reception desk had on today. Yesterday, Emilia had even seen an orderly dressed in an adult-sized elf suit, for heaven's sake. There was tinsel everywhere, like the green, ECG rhythm strip that someone had cleverly stuck along the wall of the corridor she turned into. Her own patients who were admitted to the fracture clinic to have broken bones set or progress monitored and casts applied or changed were leaving with tartan bows or sprigs of plastic mistletoe attached to their casts and the only choice of colours at present were, of course, red or green.

Children were apparently embracing the season by wearing any favourite dress-up outfits. Like the small girl Emilia could see coming towards her now, dressed in a rather spectacular pink princess outfit, complete with a miniature crown and glittery shoes.

A *princess* costume?

Was this a cruel twist of fate, designed to mock the brief fantasy she had indulged in on the night of the gala, that she and Dom could be together for ever? That she could actually become a real princess?

It was almost the last straw. Emilia ducked into a staff toilet and turned on the cold water at the first basin. As she cupped her hands to catch some water, she caught sight of herself in the mirror and she was shocked to see her inner turmoil reflected so clearly in the tight lines of her face and the stormy blue of her eyes. The hurt was still there but there was something darker now, as well. Anger...

She hadn't seen or heard from Dom in a week now. Not since they'd worked together in the initial management of Simon's fractured pelvis—the patient she was on her way to see at the moment, in fact. And, okay, she knew he had a hell of a lot going on in his own life right now but she didn't deserve to be treated like this. Pushing her out of his life was his prerogative and had, no doubt, been inevitable in the long run but surely he could see that, for her, this would be tapping into a lot of old stuff that had had such a negative impact on her life and still had the ability to do her head in. Being pushed out of families. Changing schools. Feeling unwanted and unloved. Dreaming that life could magically become perfect with a fresh start until the dream had been shattered too many times to bother dusting it off.

The splash of cold water helped disperse the fragments of unpleasant emotions. Hurt. Anger. Sadness.

By the time Emilia reached for some paper towels to pat her face dry she could see the difference in her reflection. Nobody would guess that she had any kind of struggle going on. She was the calm, skilled, professional doctor she had fought so hard to become. Which meant that at least one of her dreams had come true. Clearly the most important one, given that it was a dream she could still believe in and one that would last for the rest of her life.

The smile that appeared slowly on the face of her patient when she entered Simon's room to check on him was enough to brighten what was left of Emilia's day.

'You look like you're feeling a whole lot better, Simon.'

He nodded. 'I even got out of bed this morning for long enough to use the chair instead of a bedpan.'

'How was that?' Emilia picked up the patient file clipped to the end of Jason's bed in the post-surgical orthopaedic ward.

'A bit rough,' Simon admitted.

'Did you use your pump to give yourself some more pain medication?'

'Yeah...'

'I know it's not easy.' After a quick scan of the notes and vital signs being recorded on the file, Emilia put it down and perched one hip on the end of Simon's bed. 'Especially at this stage of your healing, given that you've got quite a bit of hardware with those plates and screws that are holding your pelvis together, but it is very important that you are moving. Lying still for too long can lead to complications and we don't want you getting pneumonia or something.'

'I just want to get home, Doc. It's not going to be in time for Christmas, though, is it?'

'Afraid not,' she agreed. 'We can't let you go home until you can transfer yourself independently and have wheelchair mobility or are able to use crutches without weight bearing. That might take a couple of weeks but your physical therapist will be able to monitor your progress and make that call.'

'Is it true what the nurse told me today? That I'm lucky to be alive and that what you did in the ER for me would have saved my life? He said if someone had moved me the wrong way, I could have bled to death in no time at all.'

'You were certainly in a bad way.' Emilia nodded. 'But it wasn't just me. There was a whole team of us looking after you that day.'

Including Dom… She wouldn't have been able to do her own job as well as she had if it hadn't been for the way the two of them could work as a team. Aside from anything more personal, she was going to miss having him leading Seattle General's ER trauma team.

'Can't believe it's been a week.' Simon lay back against his pillows and closed his eyes. 'I can only remember bits of it, so it feels like it's only been a couple of days.'

'Mmm…' Emilia found a smile. She had had the opposite impression in that this last week had felt far, far longer. 'Keep up the good work, Simon, and hopefully the rest of your stay with us will feel like it's gone just as quickly.'

* * *

The route Emilia took having left the ward took her close to the ER and the pull became too strong. But it would only be professional courtesy to let Dom know about the progress of a case that had come through his resuscitation area, wouldn't it? Especially when he always took an interest in following patients up.

His office was empty.

'He's not here,' a nurse told her, walking past to get to the staffroom.

'Do you know when he'll be back?'

'No idea. He's taken some leave. I did hear a rumour that he had some family visiting? Or a close friend of the family in hospital, perhaps? He might not be back until after Christmas if that's true. Did you need him for something urgent?'

'No.' Emilia shook her head. She didn't need Dom for anything urgent. What she needed him for was more like something impossible.

It made sense that Dom would have taken leave to be by his father's bedside and to support his sister. She knew that Roberto was being cared for in the most private area that this large hospital could provide and Dom would be being careful to keep his business equally private—especially if things weren't going so well in the aftermath of his father's brain surgery?

There was no reason for Emilia to stay here but, for a long moment, she stood in the doorway, thinking back to when she'd come into this office that day without knocking first, to see Dom with his head in his hands, looking shockingly broken. That had been the start of finding out just how little she knew about him, as a man rather than simply a rival. The start of new feelings that had, almost from the beginning, included huge empathy for what his future would hold, for the breakdown of his relationship with a father he clearly loved very much and also for how hard it was going to be for him to give up his beloved career.

Where had that empathy gone? It was pretty selfish to be indulging in feeling so hurt and angry given that such major areas of her own life weren't hanging in the balance. She wasn't in danger of losing a parent, having to protect a sibling or contemplating the responsibility of ruling a country. Dom was probably exhausted, she thought, both emotionally and physically. He probably didn't have anything left that would allow him to face any complication that she might be representing in his life. The best thing Emilia could do for both of them was to get out of the way but knowing that Dom might be hurting and not being able to offer any comfort was enough to bring the prickle of tears that were never going to fall.

This was by no means the first time in her life that Emilia had needed to pull herself together and to sort out a messed-up head and bruised heart and, as she prepared to make her way home on this freezing winter evening, she realised that she already knew the best first step to deal with all of this. Mind you, it could be a bit more difficult to tap into that resource at this time of year, especially after the snowfalls of the last few days.

Emilia went online in her office to check the weather forecast for tomorrow and, while it would be cold enough for any snow lying around to be in no danger of melting, the forecast was for clear skies and to be calm enough to not present too much of an obstacle with the windchill factor. She clicked onto other websites after that, checking both road conditions around Seattle and the timetable for the ferries that crossed Puget Sound to Bainbridge Island or Southport.

A few minutes later, Emilia sat back in her chair, closed her eyes and breathed out a long sigh of relief.

She still had a spot of shopping to do on her way home but she now had a plan in place to get to the one space that was almost guaranteed to offer her the peace of mind she so desperately needed.

She could do this.

He couldn't do this any longer.

Not for today. He should have gone home long ago for a shower and some sleep but Dom had lingered by his father's bedside this evening. Something was different and his instincts as a physician were keeping him here. Watching every monitor. And yes…there were more blips than usual in the tracing of his father's heart rate and rhythm. Missed beats and an acceleration here and there in the rates of both heart and breathing. His father's temperature had risen a fraction too.

Was this the beginning of the end? A sign of an infection? Or was Roberto in so much pain he was aware of it even though he was still unconscious? Whatever it was, Dom wasn't about to leave until he figured it out. Even as one hour bled into another as the first hours of Christmas Eve approached. He was exhausted to the point of barely functioning so, when he saw it, he thought it was simply wishful thinking. A figment of his imagination.

Until he saw it again.

Along with another, unsettling, disruption of the cardiac monitor, he saw a twitch of his father's fingers as they curled and then relaxed again. Dom was holding his breath as he raised his head to look at his father's face where he could see the flutter of his eyelids as they opened. For the longest moment, Roberto stared at his son without any sign of recognition and then his eyes drifted shut again.

Oddio... Dom closed his eyes, dipping his head against the sudden wave of pain that was threatening to overwhelm him. Was this the worst thing that could happen? That his father would regain consciousness but be so brain-damaged he wouldn't even recognise his own son?

He called Max, who arrived in the private room with commendable swiftness and he stayed as Max performed a thorough neurological examination. Roberto might look as if he was still in a coma but he was responsive to painful stimuli and even talking to him could create subtle differences in his vital signs like heart rate and blood pressure.

'He's waking up,' Max agreed when they discussed the results. 'He's slipped back into unconsciousness now but it's still very good news. His LOC is a lot lighter and he could wake up more definitively at any time. I'll stay in the hospital and come and look in every couple of hours. Unless you'd like me to stay?

Dom shook his head. 'I'd like to be the first person he sees when he wakes up.'

'Of course.' Max shook his hand. 'Just page me if you're worried about anything.'

Dom dozed on and off in the comfortable armchair beside the bed for an hour. And then another. He was getting a minimal amount of rest but it wasn't real sleep—he was still aware and alert for any changes in the soft beeping from the monitors around the bed. And the sound of his father taking an uneven breath and letting it out in a sigh.

'...Dom? You're here...?'

Dom's eyes flew open as he jerked his head up to find that Roberto's eyes were also open. This time, he could see the recognition in them and relief flooded his heart so much it felt like it might burst.

'Papa? Are you in pain? I'll call Max...'

'No... Don't go, Dom...'

'But I must contact Giada. She's been so worried. We've...' Dom had to clear his throat. 'We've been waiting a while for you to wake up, you know?'

'What day is it, son?'

'Christmas Eve. Very early. It's...' Dom checked his watch. 'Coming up to four a.m. now.'

Roberto blinked slowly, his head sinking back into his pillow. 'Don't disturb her, then,' he said softly. 'Not yet. Don't disturb anyone. It's you I need to talk to, Domenico. It's why I came here. I... I've been asleep too long, haven't I?' He was frowning now as he looked up at Dom. 'What happened?'

'There was a car accident the day you arrived. You broke your leg and had a head injury.'

Roberto reached out to grip Dom's hand. 'Giada? Was she hurt?'

'No. She's fine. She went back home to look after things. She's been back to see you, of course, but she's in Isola Verde again now. She's been very worried and we've been talking every day...but...you're going to be fine, Papa. The surgery to remove your tumour went perfectly. We were just waiting for you to wake up...' Dom's voice trailed into silence and he had to blink back the tears that were filling his eyes.

Neither man said anything for a minute. And then another. Dom scanned every monitor but couldn't see anything that was alarming so there was no need to call Max in. Roberto still needed to rest but Dom wasn't going anywhere because this time, with just a father and son, was undeniably precious. He'd be here when Roberto woke up again. And...even if his father was falling asleep again now, this was an opportunity he couldn't miss.

'I love you, Papa... I'm sorry I've never told you that before...'

Roberto's eyes opened slowly—eyes that were exactly the same dark shade as Dom's—and he held Dom's gaze.

'That's not your fault,' he told his son. 'It was mine. I never said it to you, did I? I was too hard on you. You and your sister. We lost your mother too early, I think, and... I didn't handle it well. I'm sorry, Dom. That was why I came here early. To talk to you about...' He closed his eyes again, as if too fatigued.

'I know,' Dom murmured. 'You came to tell me that it's time I did my duty. I should have stepped up long ago and let you have the abdication you deserve. I'm ready...'

But Roberto rolled his head slowly, from one side to the other, making a negative gesture even though it was clearly painful for him.

'No... I came to tell you that, of course, I want you to succeed me but I will respect whatever choice you make. That I will still love you...'

Dom swallowed hard. He had a choice? Was his father offering him the chance to stay here and keep his career? To be with *Emilia*?

'I've been dreaming,' Roberto told him. 'So much. Of you. I understand now why your career is so important to you. Why it's so much of who you are... I respect that passion, my son. And your gift...'

A weight was falling off Dom's shoulders. He didn't think his father had been dreaming, however. At some level, had he been listening to and absorbing all those late-night conversations as he lay in that coma for week after week? Did he understand things that Dom had never thought he could even explain well enough?

It was enough to feel that the distance between them had evaporated. That there was a bond here like no other and it was one that Dom couldn't turn his back on again, no matter what he was leaving behind.

'I understand things now, too.' He took his father's hand in his own and then put his other hand over the top of it as well. 'Someone...someone very special to me... has reminded me how lucky I am to have my family. To have a place that I belong and a chance to put things right. And yes... I've been able to do what I wanted to do so much. To *be* who I wanted to be for a long time. Longer than I deserved, perhaps. But I meant what I said, Papa. I'm ready to come home. I'm ready to accept my destiny. To rule Isola Verde and make you proud.'

'I've always been proud of you, Domenico. And we have a wonderful new hospital too, you know. They would be so proud to have their King as their patron.'

This time, as Roberto closed his eyes, Dom knew it was time to let him rest properly. A normal sleep, thank goodness, and not a pathological unconsciousness. He needed to call Giada and to let Max know that his father was awake and alert and there didn't seem to be any obvious deterioration in his mental faculties. He didn't want to disturb his father by making the calls in here, however.

'I'm going to go and let you sleep for a while, Papa.' Dom pushed himself to his feet, stiff and sore after sitting for so long. 'Max will be here soon to check on you again. It won't be long before it's a new day and there's going to be a lot of people who will be so happy to know that you're awake and on the road to a real recovery.'

Roberto gave a very slow nod, this time, but he didn't open his eyes when he spoke.

'This special person you talk of,' he murmured. 'Will she come home with you and be your Queen?'

'I...don't think that's possible. She's happy here. She's like me, Papa. She cares about her work more than anything else.'

'Are you sure?' There was a frown line between the King's eyes. 'You have to be sure, Dom. It's hard to do it alone. Believe me... I know...'

Was he sure?

Dom was sitting at the desk in his office some time

later, his head in his hands as he fought off a weariness that was going to overwhelm him anytime now. There was no point in going home because he had made arrangements for an encrypted phone call that could maintain complete secrecy to happen between the hospital and the palace in Isola Verde which was timed for seven a.m., Seattle time. He'd already texted Giada to give her the wonderful news about their father but they couldn't go public yet. Palace officials would be gathering for the conference call because there were many decisions and plans to be made as they prepared statements about what was happening with the royal family in order to make an announcement about the succession of the throne of Isola Verde.

Rubbing at eyes that felt full of grit, Dom remembered that he'd sat like this, in this office, once before, hadn't he? When he'd been grappling with a similar sense of being overwhelmed. When Emilia had come in and he'd known that she'd seen past the protective shield he'd always had in place—especially with regard to her.

With a heartfelt sigh, Dom put his arms on his desk and lowered his head to rest his forehead on the cushion they provided. He'd learned to catnap as an intern and knew how valuable even a few minutes' sleep could be when he had to keep functioning for a double shift. It would only take seconds to fall into a state where his body—and mind—could gather enough new strength to keep him going.

Those few seconds were enough, however.

Enough for Dom to realise that his father had spoken wise words. It would be so hard to cope with his new future alone and he didn't want to. And…in spite of everything Emilia had told him, he wasn't at all sure that she really believed that she was happier facing life alone. She was too good at putting on a brave face, wasn't she? Of hiding how she really felt?

Maybe he was wrong and the career and home Emilia had struggled to win was more important than anything else in her life but the very least she deserved was to know that someone understood and respected that. That she had choices, if she wanted them.

And that she was loved *this* much…

CHAPTER TEN

A LITTLE SLEEP and a lot of strong coffee and handling the conference call to the palace was no problem. Dom felt even more awake as the group conversation ended, knowing that there was now a team of experts at work drafting the statements and press releases.

His private chat to Giada after the palace business had lifted his spirits even further. She would be on a plane as soon as she could tomorrow so that she would be able to see her father on Christmas Day. It would, in fact, be the first time in many years that the three of them would be together as a family for Christmas and that was going to be something to celebrate.

But he couldn't relax completely yet even if he was still on leave. There was something even more important to do and it was nearly eight a.m. Emilia could very well be at work already and Dom had to talk to her. He drained the mug of coffee on his desk, ran his fingers through his hair to try and comb it roughly, rubbed at his chin and decided not to worry about the stubble he had accumulated since yesterday, and got to his feet to open his office door.

Not that he could step out. Ayanna was standing in

front of him. She had a laptop computer in her arms and…she didn't look happy.

'I'm so sorry, Dr di Rossi,' she said. 'But there's something you've got to see.'

It was unwanted publicity about Max. Someone had recognised the world-famous neurosurgeon and started asking questions about why he was here at Seattle General and why was there so much secrecy surrounding his extended visit. There were photographs of him leaving the hospital, of him and Ayanna leaving the gala ball and one of his wife who'd died a couple of years ago, with her famous husband having been unable to save her from the brain aneurysm she had suffered. It was horrible publicity for Max and Dom winced at seeing such private information being spread.

'This is my fault,' Ayanna said miserably. 'I was so focussed on keeping your family's information private that it never occurred to me that the press would go after Max.'

'It's unfortunate,' Dom agreed. 'And I'm very sorry Max has to go through this but it could have been a lot worse.' He smiled at Ayanna. 'You did one part of your job extremely well. We're going public with an announcement but it's going to take some time to get everything in place. Giada won't be back until tomorrow evening probably and we want the family to be together when the announcement is made so it's planned for the morning of the twenty-sixth.'

Ayanna nodded. 'I'll be ready. Do you want a press conference set up?'

'Yes. Thank you.' Dom glanced at his watch. 'I should go and check on my father and I expect Max won't be far away. Have you heard the great news that my father's awake now? That everything's looking very good?'

Ayanna nodded again. 'I'm so happy for you. I was so worried that he hadn't woken up yet.'

'Come with me,' Dom invited. 'And see for yourself. I'll introduce you, because my father will want some input into how the press conference is going to be handled.'

It would have to be a very brief introduction, however, because Dom was increasingly impatient to go and find Emilia before she got caught up, for hours perhaps, in an operating theatre.

He didn't even stop to sympathise with Max about the intrusion into his private life, when he came out of Roberto's room with Ayanna a short time later. He just shook the neurosurgeon's hand warmly.

'Thank you, Max, for everything you've done for my father. My family is in your debt for ever. Now, if you'll excuse me, I have something urgent to do…'

So urgent, he had to stop himself running down the last corridor that led to the orthopaedic department. The receptionist said she hadn't seen Dr Featherstone so far this morning but he could try the fracture room— a space that was already busy with the medical staff dealing with people who needed a new cast or urgent adjustments done in time for Christmas Day.

'Emilia's not here,' her senior resident told Dom. 'She's been working about ten days straight but even then we had to force her to take a day off. She only agreed because she's rostered on for Christmas Day tomorrow. Ah…here we are.' He opened a drawer and picked up what looked like a bag of plastic leaves and berries. 'We thought we'd run out of bits of mistletoe to stick on the casts today.'

'Ah…okay…' Dom knew about mistletoe but couldn't see the point of putting it on a plaster cast. Weren't you supposed to stand beneath it to kiss someone? Anyway, he was already planning his next step which involved charming Emilia's secretary into providing the address of her boss's apartment. He didn't want to send a text message. What he wanted to say had to be done face to face. 'Thanks, anyway.'

'Hey…' the younger doctor was grinning. 'Take one of these.' He put a sprig of the plastic leaves into Dom's hand. 'You never know when you might need one. Merry Christmas…'

Dom didn't want to be rude so he smiled and shoved the plastic token into the back pocket of the jeans he was wearing. Emilia's office was nearby and her secretary was quite happy to provide her address to a close colleague on the trauma team. A short time after that, Dom was moving fast towards the nearest exit of Seattle General. It might still be early in the day but it felt like time was starting to run out.

Emilia's apartment block was within walking distance of the hospital. The sidewalks were damp and there was slushy snow filling the gutters but the sky was crisp and clear above. Dom filled his lungs with the cold air and kept his hands in the pockets of his jacket, walking as fast as he could past other pedestrians and across busy roads. He didn't need to waste time trying to find Emilia's name and doorbell on the bank of letterboxes in the entrance to her apartment block, because there was an elderly concierge in a small office right beside the automatic doors.

'Could you tell me which box belongs to Dr Featherstone, please?' he asked.

'Third one down in the second row,' the concierge told him helpfully.

Dom pressed the button, leaning closer to the small grill beside the button that would allow Emilia to ask who it was.

'She won't answer that,' the concierge said.

'Oh?' Dom turned back. 'Why not?'

'She headed out real early this morning.'

'Oh...' It was more than disappointment that Dom could feel wash over him. There was anxiety there, as well. And a sinking feeling that he really might be too late. 'Um...she didn't say when she'd be back, did she?'

'Nah...' The elderly man scratched at his chin. 'But she was carrying a whole load of stuff. Like she was going camping or some such.' He shook his head. 'She even had a pair of snow shoes, would you believe? I didn't know what they were so I had to ask.'

It seemed logical to head back to the hospital until he could come up with a new plan but, as Dom turned a corner, he caught a glimpse of a view between the tall sides of central city buildings. The kind of view you could get from the roof of Seattle General with a glimpse of the waters of Elliot Bay in front of the impressive range of the Olympic mountains. The snow-capped peaks were reflecting this morning's sunshine as if they were lit from within.

It made Dom remember taking Emilia up to the hospital roof to have that very private conversation.

It also made him remember what she'd told him that day they went jogging together in Discovery Park.

'That over there...' She'd been pointing at those very peaks. *'That's the Olympic National Park. If you want to clear your head and put your world to rights properly, then that's the place to go... It's my absolute favourite place in the world...'*

She'd said something else, too. About how long it took to get there. Hours to drive, even if you took a ferry to cut off some of the road distance.

He took his phone out and, by the time he was back at Seattle General, he had sourced what he needed. An elite private helicopter service which promised discretion along with meeting every need of their clients. Dom had never blatantly wielded either his wealth or his royal status but this was a situation he'd never found himself in before.

And it was more than urgent now. It was beginning to feel almost a matter of life or death.

How lucky was she?

Emilia stopped and raised her face to the winter sunshine as she took in the spectacular view surrounding her. She'd had to walk further than usual to get to this trail because the road was partially closed and she'd been worried when she'd gone to sign in at the Visitors' Centre that the trails might be closed as well but she'd been lucky. Not only were they open but, because it was the day before Christmas, it was unlikely there would be many other people out hiking.

So here she was, on her way to the top of this hill, feeling like the luckiest person on earth, as she took deep breaths of the icy, clean air, gazing across a snow-covered meadow at a forest of fir trees whose branches were drooping under the weight of snow. Beyond the forest, rocky snow-capped mountain peaks made a jagged horizon against the brightest blue sky Emilia had ever seen. She wanted to capture this moment for ever.

No...

What she really wanted was to share it. Because that's what made moments like this truly perfect, wasn't it?

And it had to be the right person. Someone who could understand how something like this could make you feel. How the sheer beauty of nature and the privilege of being able to become a part of it like this was enough to give you a huge lump in your throat and bring tears to the back of your eyes.

Someone who could make almost anything so much more meaningful. Who could share the thrill of facing what could seem an almost impossible medical challenge, like securing the airway and breathing of that man who'd fallen off the roof, and then share that blissful moment of success. Of knowing that you'd won. That you had the best job in the world and this was what mattered the most. *This* was who you were...

Yeah...someone who made the best moments even better.

But someone who made the not so good moments okay as well. Like when you did something stupid like cooking a turkey with the plastic bag still inside it. Or made your nervousness evaporate instantly with just a few words like, *'Trust me, Emmy... I've got this...'*

The picture-postcard scene of the mountains was blurring in front of her eyes and, to her astonishment, Emilia could feel her eyes overflowing. She actually had tears trickling down her cheeks for the first time since she had been a very young child.

Because she knew that it wasn't just 'someone' that she needed.

It was one person.

The man she would love for ever, even if it was impossible for them to be together.

Dom...

The squeeze in her chest was so painful that Emilia opened her mouth to cry out into the profound silence of the mountains but, as she did so, she became aware of another sound. A distant, rapid thumping that was getting steadily louder as it got closer.

'Wow...'

'Impressive, isn't it?' The pilot's voice was loud in Dom's ears through the headphones. 'Bit of a treat to get over here at this time of year.'

'Do you know the Olympic National Park well?'

'Sure do. Grew up in these parts and I've hiked every trail. Love the Grey Wolf Deer Loop and the Klahhane Ridge. Look...that's Steeple Rock down on our left. You can see where it got its name from, can't you?'

'Mmm...' The tall rock pillar was certainly distinctive. 'What's the building coming up?'

'The Hurricane Ridge Visitor Centre. I reckon your friend will have picked the Hurricane Hill trail. It's got everything you want on a day like this. Forest walks, snow, a good climb and the best view ever from the top of the hill.'

'And there'll be a place to land? Even if there's snow?'

'No worries. You might have to walk a bit. Can't land too close to trees.'

'I'll walk as far as I need to.'

The pilot grinned at Dom. 'Does she know you're coming?'

'How do you know it's a "she"?'

His grin widened. 'Just a hunch.'

Dom turned to stare down at the ground beneath them. 'This park is massive. I just hope we can find her.'

'If she's not in the forest, it won't be hard. You'll see…people stand out against snow.'

Especially when they were wearing bright colours like the solitary figure standing on a ridge. A bright red anorak that was the same shade as that gorgeous ballgown had been. A shade of red that was going to be Dom's favourite colour for the rest of his life.

'Looks like this might be where you need to be, mate.'

'Oh, yeah…' Dom kept his gaze locked onto that small patch of red, even when it almost vanished behind flakes of snow stirred up by the rotors. He didn't want to let Emilia out of his sight, for even a heartbeat.

She knew who it was, of course.

Getting dropped off by a helicopter into a remote wilderness area was something only somebody like a superstar or a prince would think of doing, wasn't it?

But that was irrelevant.

Because Emilia couldn't see a superstar or a prince walking towards her from the other side of this meadow as the helicopter took off again. She could just see a man. The man who, until very recently, she had known only as a colleague and rival—a person as ordinary as herself. And that was the man she had fallen in love with. That she'd been waiting for the chance to fall in love with for more than ten years…

She couldn't wait any longer.

It was pretty much impossible to run in snow shoes but Emilia gave it a shot. So did Dom. They almost made it but somehow both managed to lose their balance at the same time, falling into the cushion of soft snow but close enough that it took only a roll to be in each other's arms.

To hold. And be held.

To take turns to murmur, 'I love you…', 'I love you, too…' and 'So, so much…'

And to kiss…

Dear Lord…had anybody ever kissed like this? For this long? The heat of Dom's mouth and tongue was only increasing as the rest of Emilia's skin grew steadily colder but it wasn't until she shivered that Dom finally pulled back.

'You're cold… Here…take my coat…'

'Don't be daft. You need that yourself. We just need to start moving, that's all.'

'Where to?' Dom was smiling as he pulled Emilia to her feet.

'There's a great view from the top of this hill.'

They eyed each other. They could turn this into a

competition to see who could go the fastest in snow shoes with the blink of an eye. Emilia was up for it. She knew she would win so she gave Dom what she hoped was an inviting smile.

But he just laughed. 'I like the view I've got right now,' he said, bending his head to kiss her again.

'Mmm…' Emilia had to catch her breath when he released her. 'We could go home but it's a long drive. Do you need to call your helicopter to come back?'

'Why would I do that when that would mean you'd be driving back alone?' He held Emilia's chin in his hands. 'If I had my wish, it's that you would never be alone ever again. That I will always be with you.'

'You will…' Emilia had to blink back new tears. 'Even when you're not with me, you'll be in here…' She touched her gloved hand to her chest, over her heart, in a gesture she had learned from Dom. 'Always…but…'

A crease appeared between Dom's eyes. '…but?'

'But you have important things you need to do. Family things…'

'Ah…' Dom nodded. 'Family. *Sì*…that is something I need to talk to you about, *mio amore*.'

By tacit consent, they started walking. Back down the hill towards the road.

'You were right,' Dom told her.

'I always am,' Emilia murmured as she threw a grin in his direction. 'What about this time?'

'You said that family is everything.'

Emilia swallowed. Hard. Her heart skipped a beat but she wasn't going to buy into a fear that Dom was about to tell her he had to leave her to be with his family. She could feel the warmth of his touch, even through the thick wool of their gloves. She could hear the sincerity in his voice and she could see nothing but pure love in those beautiful, dark eyes.

'I want you to be part of my family.' Dom pulled Emilia to a halt again. 'I want us to create a family of our very own but…most of all… I just want to be with you. For the rest of my life. I want us to challenge each other like we always have so that we can always be our best in whatever we do. I want to dance with you. And make love with you…'

He kissed her again and Emilia's heart felt like it could split into a million pieces with how tender that kiss was. She wanted to tell him she felt exactly the same way but he wasn't finished yet.

'I used to think that being a doctor would be all I needed to be true to myself,' he told her softly. 'To be the person I always dreamed of being but that's not true now. Because I know I could never be everything I could be if I don't have you in my life.' His face was serious now. 'I know it won't be easy for you to make such big changes in your life but…we have a wonderful new hospital in Isola Verde so you could still work. And tell me about it every day when you come home. I'll be waiting for you if you'll let me. Marry me, Emmy… please?'

There were so many things Emilia wanted to say to Dom but there would be time for that later. So much time. The rest of their lives kind of time. For now, there was really only one thing she wanted to say. That she had to say.

'*Yes...*' Her throat was closing up as joy created more tears but she hadn't said *quite* enough yet.

'Yes, yes...*yes*...'

* * * * *

NEUROSURGEON'S CHRISTMAS TO REMEMBER

TRACI DOUGLASS

MILLS & BOON

To all the healthcare angels out there
who rush in where fools fear to tread.
Thank you for all you do to keep us safe!

CHAPTER ONE

CONTROLLED CHAOS.

Two words that described both the scene playing out before Ayanna Franklin's eyes and her stressful first day as Head of Public Relations for Seattle General Hospital.

Of course, she'd expected the mess she'd walked into first thing this morning. After all, she'd been hired last minute to replace the outgoing director, who'd resigned abruptly to deal with a personal crisis and left Ayanna to deal with preparing for the hospital's huge Christmas ball in a few weeks. Because of said personal crisis, her predecessor had dropped the ball on pretty much everything, meaning Ayanna had to somehow organize the biggest fundraiser event of the year with a limited budget and even more limited time.

What she hadn't expected was the text she'd received from the head nurse in the ER, telling her that not only had one of the hospital's high-profile patients arrived in Seattle three weeks early without warning, he'd also been involved in a serious car accident. The patient was currently in the ER, badly injured and unconscious, and basically all hell had broken loose. If Ayanna didn't stay on top of her part in it, the whole situation had the potential to explode into an enormous catastrophe.

Okay. Calm down. You've got this.

Handling problems was her specialty. Growing up with five younger siblings, all of whom she'd had to keep under her watchful eye as babysitter while her busy parents had worked during their childhood, had prepared Ayanna for anything.

Well, almost anything…

After a deep breath to steady her raging pulse, Ayanna headed through the automatic sliding doors into a cacophony of doctors, nurses, gurneys, and patients, making a beeline for the main workstation hub at the center of it all. Most of the staff here she'd met only briefly, but in her peripheral vision she spotted a few familiar faces—Emelia Featherstone, Head of Orthopedics, and Lucas Beaufort, one of the ER doctors. She'd met them both on a tour of the facility earlier in the week. Now they were both working on Seattle General's VIP patient—Roberto Baresi, King of Isola Verde. No one seemed to know why the man had arrived early and, based on the King's unresponsiveness despite the doctors' repeated attempts to awaken him, it didn't look like they'd find out anytime soon.

Blood stained the sheet covering the King's legs and though the sight might've turned some people's stomachs, Ayanna wasn't squeamish. Between her younger siblings' minor scraped knees from bike accidents to more major broken bones from falling out of trees or mishaps at Little League practice, she'd basically seen and heard it all. Plus, their mother was a retired nurse.

She sidestepped another gurney rushing in through

the ambulance bay doors on her way to the central workstation. This new patient was a woman, her dark curly hair and features similar enough to the King's to mark her as Giada Baresi, Princess of Isola Verde, Roberto's daughter. Both of them had been mentioned in the brief she'd received from Dr. Dominic di Rossi this morning. The public relations firms she'd worked for had always made dossiers for visits by their high-profile clients to cover things like security and public relations protocol, staff confidentiality, etc., so that was nothing new either. The only differences at Seattle General now were the confidentiality of the medical setting and the fact these people were royalty, not just CEOs or celebrities.

Nearby stood Dr. di Rossi himself, looking strangely pale as he stared at their unconscious patient. He glanced up then and caught Ayanna's eye then headed in her direction.

"Good thing you're here," the head nurse said, diverting Ayanna's attention away from Dr. di Rossi's approach. The woman gestured impatiently from behind the desk toward Ayanna, beckoning her over. "This place is a zoo already."

Ayanna focused on her part here and not the life or death situations playing out around her. It was her duty to keep the King and this accident out of the press, no matter how unexpected his arrival, and she planned to do just that. Ayanna hated failing, so she didn't. At least professionally. In her personal life, though? That was another story.

Shaking off those errant thoughts, she glanced over at Dr. di Rossi, who was still weaving his way toward her through gurneys and staff, then looked back at the nurse. "Have there been any calls from reporters?"

"Not yet." The nurse stepped closer to allow a crash cart to pass behind her. "But the local news teams have scanners and they'd have picked up the 911 dispatcher's call to the ambulance and police."

"Right." Ayanna's stomach lurched and she swallowed hard against her dry throat, a surge of adrenaline prepping her for proverbial battle. Okay. First priority—keep the press off the scent of the King's accident until she had a better idea of how this would all play out. "If anyone from the media calls, refer them to my office."

"Will do." The nurse nodded. "I also contacted the neurosurgeon, per Dr. di Rossi's protocol. He's left his conference in Vancouver and is flying in now."

"Perfect." Among her other duties, Ayanna had been assigned to retrieve said neurosurgeon, Dr. Max Granger, from the airport before the King's scheduled brain surgery on December fifteenth, still several weeks away. Now, with the accident, he'd be arriving today and so she pulled up the calendar on her phone to try to work him into her already overflowing schedule. "What time is he landing?"

"About an hour from now," the nurse said, then rattled off the flight info.

"Got it." Ayanna typed all the details into her phone then glanced over at the King again. Her heart went out to the man and his daughter. They were injured and in a foreign country. It must be terrifying, royalty or not. Plus, with it being so near the holidays, that would make things even more difficult. "Is he doing all right?"

"The King's holding his own. For now." The nurse

started around the desk to help another patient then said to Ayanna over her shoulder, "I'll text you if anything changes."

"Thanks." Ayanna slid her phone back into the pocket of her blazer just as Dr. di Rossi reached her. Given his worried expression, he could probably use a moment of quiet, and her caretaker instincts took over as she led the man across the hall to a small private conference room. The door closed, shutting out the barrage of noise behind them, and Ayanna relaxed her tense shoulders a bit. "We've got this covered. Nobody knows that the royal family is here. It's still a secret, as originally planned, and all hospital staff are under strict instructions not to talk about their identities, as per the King's demand."

Dr. di Rossi scrubbed a hand over his face. "Why are they here so early? It's three weeks until his scheduled surgery."

"I don't know. Perhaps he wanted to settle in," Ayanna speculated. "To feel comfortable in the place he's going to be recuperating?"

He shook his head, frowning. Maybe she was wrong. Honestly, she had no idea what royalty normally did with their lives.

"At least we already had all the plans in place. I've contacted his neurosurgeon as well. Max Granger? He was attending a conference in Vancouver but he's already on his way back. He was very concerned to hear that the King may have a head injury. I'm going to collect him at the airport and bring him here."

"Good. Thank you, Ms. Franklin. I need to get back

out there now and see what's happening. Excuse me."
Dr. di Rossi gave her a curt nod before exiting.

Alone again, Ayanna waited a few moments before
opening the door, the scent of antiseptic and bleach
stinging her nose. Her high heels clacked on the shiny
linoleum floor as she hurried out of the ER and headed
back toward her office.

At least I'll get my exercise, working here.

As she walked, Ayanna shoved aside the fatigue
threatening to overwhelm her. She thrived on a challenge. The busier she was, the better. It was one reason she was so good at her job. And probably another
mark against her in the romance department. At least
that was what her ex, Will, had said when he'd broken
off their engagement and left Ayanna for her best friend
six months ago.

*"Maybe if you paid as much attention to me as you
do your career, I wouldn't have cheated."*

Will's words still haunted her, usually when she was
tired or at night when she was alone. As though his
sleeping with her best friend could ever be Ayanna's
fault.

Honestly, Ayanna had thought she'd done everything
right with Will, and that was the problem. She couldn't
trust herself any more, or her emotions. And without
her instincts to rely on where her heart was concerned,
she tended to shut anyone other than her family out just
to be safe. She never wanted to go through having her
heart broken again and didn't plan on opening herself
up like that again for a very long time, if ever.

Ayanna shook off the lingering ache of loneliness in
her chest. Will was a disloyal idiot and she was better

off without him. The only person responsible for his actions was him. He'd known what her crazy schedule was like before they'd become involved. For him to throw it in her face like that as an excuse for his deplorable behavior was nonsense.

Maybe if she repeated that to herself enough times, she'd finally believe it.

She gave herself a mental shake. No time to dwell on the past. There was too much to do today, starting with prioritizing her current workload now that she had to include a trip to the airport to pick up Dr. Granger.

An image of the stacks of files waiting for her to sort through for the upcoming annual charity Christmas ball put on by Seattle General flashed in her head. This year it was being held at the luxurious four-diamond Polar Club Hotel. The place was an historic treasure in the Pacific Northwest and at least her predecessor had managed to reserve the grand ballroom before their swift departure. The locale gave Ayanna a good canvas to work with, but she had less than a month until the event and the menu and décor were still up in the air, not to mention the musicians. It was a lot to get done in a short amount of time. And with her staff tied up trying to prevent the information about the King's accident from getting out now, they wouldn't be much help either.

But somehow it would all work out. Because the alternative wasn't an option.

Besides, she'd handled worse situations in her days in the PR trenches. In fact, her ability to think on her feet was what had landed her on the list of "Top PR Professionals Under Forty", according to the *Washington Post*. She worked hard and played harder.

Or not at all.

Restless, Ayanna boarded an elevator to her office on the fourth floor. The car jolted upward, and she pulled out her phone again to check her app that was tracking Dr. Granger's flight in real time. On a good day, it took twenty minutes to get to the airport from Seattle General, but with Thanksgiving less than a week away, the city was more packed than usual with tourists. She'd grab her purse and leave now, just to make sure she arrived in plenty of time. The last thing she needed today were more unexpected issues because she somehow missed picking up the King's neurosurgeon.

"Please place your trays in the upright and secure position as we prepare for landing. Thank you." The pilot's voice crackled over the PA system as the "Seatbelt Fastened" signs were illuminated overhead. Dr. Max Granger shut down his laptop and stared out the window at the city below. Afternoon sunlight glinted off the Space Needle in the distance, but he had little time to appreciate the beauty of Seattle and even less inclination.

Since his wife's death two years previously, Max preferred to stay busy. Busy and famous, apparently, if those ridiculous TV tabloid shows that had recently dubbed him the "Brain Surgeon to the Stars" were believed. He sighed and shifted in his seat. Yes, many of his patients were celebrities and dignitaries, including the patient he was flying in to see now—King Roberto Baresi of Isolde Verde—but that was because he was a world-renowned neurosurgeon at the pinnacle of his profession. He was the best at what he did. His upbringing had ensured it. The fact his late parents would've been proud of all he'd accomplished brought him little joy, though. He could count on two hands the number of times they'd spent any quality time with him as he'd been growing up.

Greatness comes at a price.

That had been the motto his parents had taught him as a child and their rationale for leaving him behind with nannies expected to raise him to adulthood. For a long time Max had bought it too. At least until he'd met his late wife, Laura.

Familiar loneliness weighed him down. Two years was a long time to be alone.

But now wasn't the time to get bogged down in the past or his emotions. He had a case to prepare for, one that had just become far more complicated due to the King's accident. Originally, the King's tumor hadn't been a cause for immediate surgical intervention. Meningiomas were generally slow growing and benign. The only real concerning factor had been its location near the sagittal sinus, which—if infiltrated by the tumor—could jeopardize blood flow through the major vein running across the top of the brain. Max had been keeping tabs on his patient through CT scans and had planned to go ahead with a scheduled procedure to remove the meningioma on December fifteenth, still almost a month away.

The accident today, however, had changed those plans. According to the latest update he'd received from the ER staff, his patient's current Glasgow Coma Score was seven. The King had no visual or verbal responses but did show purposeful movement to painful stimuli.

An emergency scan of his brain had shown a temporal bleed into the epidural space and Max suspected a hematoma. Given the man's age and the fact the King already had slightly increased intracranial pressure due to his tumor, time was of the essence to restore normal blood flow and avoid permanent damage to the tissues.

The sooner Max got off this plane and to Seattle General, the sooner he could prep for surgery.

"Happy Holidays," a passing flight attendant said, handing him a Santa pin.

He took it from the guy and stuffed it in his pocket without looking at it. He didn't have the time for Christmas cheer. He didn't celebrate the holidays anyway. Not since losing Laura.

His ears popped as the plane descended and his memories returned against his wishes. The irony of his own wife dying of an aneurysm wasn't lost on Max. Rationally, he knew there was little chance anyone could have known of the existence of the weakened blood vessel in Laura's brain. But the knowledge did little to relieve the remorse of not being there for her, the one patient he should have tried his hardest to save.

Now he lived alone. Alone was better anyway. He was too busy for a relationship. Between his speaking engagements and seminars and patients, Max couldn't remember the last time he'd spent more than one night in his apartment back in New York.

The tires jolted on the runway and he rubbed his palm down the leg of his trousers. As the plane taxied toward the gate, Max gathered his carry-on from the overhead bin then checked his phone again for any new updates on the King's condition. Nothing yet.

Finally, the attendant opened the door and Max pushed out of first class. Footsteps pounding up the rampway, he emerged into the busy gate at Seattle-Tacoma International Airport and looked around for the person the hospital had sent to pick him up. Unfortunately, no one made eye contact with him except a perky guy dressed as an elf. Definitely not who he was looking for. They were supposed to have a sign with his name on it for identification. But none of the signs he could see said Max Granger.

Dammit.

Overhead, an announcement proclaimed Santa's helicopter would land soon and North Pole Village was opening in the gallery at the end of Concourse B. Max glanced up at the sign hanging above the walkway and dread welled inside him. Sure enough, he was smack dab at the epicenter of what would soon be a madhouse of kids and parents rushing to see the big man in red.

Guess that explained the elf.

Soon families converged, milling about the area with luggage and children in tow, the little ones clamoring to visit Saint Nick. To add insult to injury, peppy Christmas tunes drifted down from the speaker system, and Max felt more Grinch-like by the second.

Why can't the holidays get out of my way already?

He didn't have time for this. Pulse thudding, he battled his way through the crowds toward the glowing exit sign, switching into strict surgeon mode and turning the invisible dial on his inner turmoil down to zero before firing off a quick text to let the ER staff know

his ride hadn't arrived and that he was getting a taxi
to the hospital.

He'd failed once to save someone important because
of a late arrival. He refused to do so again.

CHAPTER TWO

"Santa and Ms. Claus are landing now, kids! Be sure to get in line!"

Ayanna stared at the increasing mob of people between her and the gate ahead with growing dread. Traffic had been even worse than she'd expected and she'd arrived twenty minutes late. Then she'd had to find a spot in the garage because she hadn't had time to prebook and she'd ended up far away from the terminal. She'd raced down here as fast as her high heels would allow, but Dr. Granger's plane had already landed and the passengers had disembarked.

Dealing with Santa's arrival on top of everything else was the last straw. It was like some bizarre comedy movie, except none of this was funny. Not to her.

Her phone buzzed with an update from the ER. The King's condition had not improved, and Dr. Granger was needed onsite stat. After trying to cut through the throngs of people ahead of her with little luck, Ayanna finally managed to flag down a ticketing agent. "Can you page someone for me, please? It's an emergency."

"Sorry, ma'am. You'll need to go to Customer Service." The woman pointed back toward the direction Ayanna had come.

Great.

Staying one step ahead was what she normally did best, but today it seemed she'd fallen ten steps behind. Heart hammering against her ribcage, Ayanna slipped out of the line she was in and headed back the way she'd come. She needed to find Dr. Granger and get him to Seattle General. She could stew over the rest of this mess later, once this awful day was over.

Dodging passengers and their rolling suitcases while Bing Crosby crooned "White Christmas," she stood in yet another line behind a woman with a stroller and three small kids. Normally Ayanna loved Christmas, but right now she felt decidedly unjolly.

After a small eternity, she finally reached the counter. "I need to page someone, please."

"Name?" the service agent asked.

Ayanna's phone buzzed in her hand and she looked down to see another message from the ER.

Neurosurgeon on the way in a taxi. Where are you?

"Ma'am?" the customer service rep asked again. "What's the name of the party you're looking for?"

Damn.

She buzzed with an odd mix of relief and irritation. The missing surgeon had been found. That was good. But he'd found his own ride instead of waiting for her to pick him up, which meant she'd screwed up one of her first major tasks as PR director. That was bad. "Uh, I'm sorry. He's been located. Thank you."

She moved out of line to send her reply to her staff.

Still at SeaTac. Long story. On my way now.

Her phone buzzed again, but she was already on her way out of the airport, more angry at herself than anyone. She didn't let people down like this.

Will's stupid face flashed in her head again.

"You're always doing stuff for other people, but what about me?"

The last thing she needed in her mind was her ex and his spiteful last words to her. And the fact they held a tiny kernel of truth didn't make her feel any better. Yes, she was a caretaker. Yes, it made her feel worthwhile. That wasn't a bad thing, was it? Helping others was good.

Besides, her can-do attitude was what had had her graduating with an MBA from Washington University at just twenty-four and landing internships and jobs with the best companies and brightest people in the marketing world. Yes, maybe she had neglected her relationship with Will because of work, but that didn't mean he'd been free to sleep with her best friend.

Disappointment squeezed her chest as she exited the terminal and headed for the parking garage. She'd had her problems, but Will wasn't perfect either. Nope. Not at all. And he'd never understood or appreciated how hard she tried to make everyone else's life easier.

She took the elevator up four levels then strode across the pavement toward her car. After tossing her purse on the passenger seat and buckling her seatbelt, she started the engine then pulled out of the lot and merged back into traffic heading toward downtown Seattle, fielding calls through her Bluetooth as she sat in traffic on the I5, heading north.

"Call the Polar Club Hotel," she said, then waited for it to connect.

With the King's original surgery scheduled for a few weeks in the future, the hotel reservations for Dr. Granger's room needed to be changed to accommodate his earlier arrival and she hadn't had time to do it before she'd left the office.

"Thank you for calling. How may I help you?" the clerk said.

"Yes, my name is Ayanna Franklin and I need to modify reservations made on behalf of Seattle General Hospital for Dr. Maxwell Granger. He's arrived in town earlier than expected and will need the room tonight through at least December twenty-fifth, please."

"Of course, Ms. Franklin," the clerk said, his tone solicitous over the sound of clacking computer keys. "Yes, I've pulled that reservation up. A single room with a king-sized bed."

"Yes."

"Unfortunately, however, with the holidays I'm afraid we're completely booked."

Crap. Could nothing go right today?

Ayanna signaled and changed lanes, then slowed for more stopped vehicles. In the distance, sunlight glinted off the Seattle skyline, but her usual joy at seeing her beloved hometown was dimmed. "What about another room type?"

The clerk typed again. "No. I'm sorry. It looks like we're full up through Christmas. Unless..." Ayanna held her breath as the clerk trailed off, tapping furiously on his keyboard.

One of her greatest strengths was coming up with creative solutions to seemingly insurmountable problems. She could try another hotel, but if the Polar Club was full up, chances were good they all were. Maybe Dr. Granger could stay with her? But, no, that wouldn't work either. Her apartment was too small and they were getting ready to do some electrical work on her place anyway, which meant she was going to have to find a place to stay for a few weeks herself. Perhaps temporary rental then or…

"Ma'am?" the clerk said, breaking into her thoughts. "I do see our Denali Suite is available for the date range you specified. It's a bit larger, though, with two bedrooms, and more expensive than the room originally booked for Dr. Granger."

He rattled off the room price and her mind ticked through the budget set aside for the surgeon's visit. It was more than the hospital had wanted to spend, but if it was the only room available, there wasn't much they could do at this point.

"Fine. We'll take it," she said, staring at the red taillights ahead.

One problem down, a gazillion more to go.

"Marvelous. Anything else I can do for you, Ms. Franklin?"

"No, thank you." She ended the call then exhaled. Right now, she needed to get back to her office and keep an eye on Dr. Granger so he didn't disappear on her again.

She passed a sign for the Redmond exit and the knot

in her gut tightened. Her parents lived in Redmond. They'd offered Ayanna her old room to stay in while the work at her apartment was being done, but being home during the holidays was stressful enough without actually living there, what with her five siblings and their significant others filling the space.

She'd find another solution.

I could stay with Dr. Granger. In the extra bedroom.

Wait. What?

Where in the world had *that* come from? She didn't even know the man.

Maybe she'd just sleep in her office. Lord knew, she had enough work to do to get ready for the ball to keep her there round the clock for the next few weeks. She snorted and veered off the highway at her exit, relaxing her death grip on the steering wheel. She had this. Forget the mishap in the airport. From this moment forward, Ayanna was back on her game.

"Could I get some suction here, please?" Max said as he placed the last tiny screw into the bone plate over the temporal region of the King's skull. "And give Radiology thirty minutes' notice also."

"Yes, Doctor," one of the nurses said, while another provided the requested suction to the area he'd indicated.

Max continued suturing in the drain he'd placed. "How are the patient's vitals?"

"Good," the anesthesiologist replied. "Heart rate steady and blood oxygen levels normal."

"Excellent." He handed the last of his instruments to the surgical nurse then stepped away. "And we're done.

Thank you, team. Let's get the patient back to CT to make sure the hematoma's gone."

The nurses took over, cleaning up the area before wheeling the patient away to Radiology. Closure hadn't taken thirty minutes after all, but Max always liked to err on the side of caution. Once the room was empty, he walked out of the OR and into the small room attached to remove his soiled gown and gloves then scrub up post-op.

The King was stable. Tension eased inside him and the tightness in his gut uncoiled. It was probably the fatigue of travel but he felt raw and restless. He didn't do vulnerability well. Never had, really. Not since he'd been eight and his parents had come home unexpectedly from a trip to China. He'd loved his parents so much back then and had been unable to wait to tell them all about the friends he'd made in school and how well he'd done on his math test. Of course, they'd only been interested in whether or not he'd gotten into the fancy boarding school they'd attended. After New Year, they'd gone off to travel the world again and he'd been shipped off to school. From then on out, he'd lived there year round until he'd graduated and headed off to Harvard. At least his parents had shown up to his commencement. Guess he should've been grateful for that.

Max sighed. Maybe it was Christmas that had him on edge. Really, the only time he'd even remotely enjoyed this time of year had been with Laura. She'd loved Christmas and used to decorate their house back in Long Island to within an inch of its life. To this day, he couldn't see reindeer and twinkle lights without thinking of her. Come to think of it, it had been holiday time when he'd last seen his parents too, all those years ago.

He finished washing his hands and arms before yanking a few paper towels from the dispenser. His shoulders gave a painful twinge and he rolled his neck to release the crick there. Man, what he wouldn't give for a hot shower and a long nap. The clock on the wall showed it was well after midnight and between work and seminars he hadn't slept for more than a few hours at a stretch in days.

Stifling a yawn, he pressed the metal accessibility button on the wall with his hip to open the door then backed out into the hallway, only to collide backend first with a woman.

"Sorry," he said, swiveling fast. "Didn't see you there."

"Unless you've got eyes in the back of your head, I'd say not," she said, giving him a small smile. "Then again, I swear my mother always seems to know what's going on behind her, so…"

Max stared at the petite black woman with her stylish blue business suit and killer high heels. His first thought was that she was cute. Really cute. In fact, she reminded him of an actress he'd seen in a movie recently during one of his many flights. Same smooth skin. Same bright smile. Same adorable dimples.

Whoa. What?

Max shook his head. He didn't care about her cuteness or her dimples or anything else. That wasn't what he was here for. He was here to work. Period.

Still they stared at each other across the span of a few feet and Max swallowed hard against the unwanted interest clawing inside him. Then his old work ethic intervened, bringing him back to his senses. He had no business noticing anything about this woman, other than the fact she was currently in his way. The King's results from the post-op CT scan should be back soon and he needed to check them. No time to stand here gawking over a beautiful woman with wide brown eyes and a smile that made the dark clouds around him vanish for a moment. Before he could contemplate why, one of the surgical nurses called to him from down the hall.

"Films are ready, Dr. Granger."

"Right." He looked back at the woman who was still standing there with her head tilted and her arms crossed, one brow still raised at him as if he were a naughty schoolboy and not an accomplished brain surgeon. "Excuse me," he said, frowning. "Sorry again."

Instead of leaving her behind, however, the woman followed him to the nurses' station. "I'm sorry too, Dr. Granger, but you're not getting away from me again so easily."

"What?" Baffled, he glanced over at her. "Look, I have a patient to deal with, Miss…?"

"Franklin. And, please, do your work," she said, then pulled out her phone and leaned against the wall behind her. "I'll wait, don't worry."

He glanced around to see if anyone else had noticed this strange conversation, but the nurses were all busy. One of them waved him over to a computer. "Doctor."

Max walked around the desk and took a seat to click through the CT images of the King's brain, irritated with himself for getting distracted. Thankfully, everything looked clear and he nodded at the surgical nurse who'd assisted him in the OR. "Looks good. Thanks for your help on such short notice."

"Thank you, Dr. Granger, for being so appreciative," she said, smiling. "Not everyone is."

"Of course." He let her have her seat back. Nurses were the heart and soul of the hospital and could be a doctor's staunchest ally or his worst nightmare. He preferred the former and always tried to be kind and courteous no matter what the situation. He moved to a private corner of the desk to phone Dr. di Rossi and update him on the King's condition. Max was one of the few people at the hospital who knew that the head of the ER was actually King Roberto's son and therefore Prince of Isolde Verde, heir apparent to the throne. He couldn't treat the King properly without a full and accurate medical and family history. As he spoke in hushed tones to Dr. di Rossi, Max could still feel the weight of Miss Franklin's gaze on the nape of his neck, burning a hole through his skin along with his composure. Annoyed, he rubbed the area, as if that might make her go away. She was persistent. He'd give her that.

Finally, he turned around, determined to put a swift end to this odd encounter. "Look, Miss Franklin," Max said, doing his best to keep the annoyance from his voice and failing miserably, if her flat stare was any indication, "I'm not sure who you are or—"

"I'm the PR Director for this hospital and the woman who was supposed to pick you up at the airport. But you left without me and I've spent the last few hours tracking you down. You've already disrupted my busy schedule enough and I won't let that happen again. So, here are some ground rules going forward," she said, her crisp words scraping against his already overtaxed nervous system.

"Once you're changed, I'm taking you to your hotel for the night. Next, I'll pick you up tomorrow morning and each day following to deliver you here to the hospital to see the King. At the end of the day, I'll take you back to your hotel again. Until the King's case is closed and my office has a firm lid on the press about this accident, we'll be seeing a lot more of each other. Any questions?"

CHAPTER THREE

SEVERAL OF THE nurses cast curious looks in her direction at that statement, and Ayanna could've kicked herself. She hadn't meant to blurt it out like that, but it was too late now. Something about this guy ruffled all her feathers and she didn't like it. Not one bit.

"Yeah, I've got a question." Those icy gray eyes of his lit with cold fire. "Who do I speak with to get off lockdown? I don't need a babysitter. Especially one I don't even know."

"Maybe you should've thought of that before you went rogue at SeaTac." So much for biting her tongue. She crossed her arms and waited for him to walk around the desk, taking a deep breath to get herself under control and avoid drawing any more unwanted attention from the staff, who were now whispering amongst themselves and pointing in Ayanna's direction. Perfect. Add "starting a scandal" to her growing list of first-day accomplishments.

"Rogue?" Dr. Granger scrunched his nose then stalked off toward the staff changing room down the hall, leaving her behind. "My patient needed immediate treatment. There was no time to waste." He stopped halfway down the hall and glanced back at her with a chilly glare. "Pardon me if I happen to care more about people's lives than your precious schedule, Ms. Franklin."

Appalled, Ayanna blinked at him several moments before following him. *Oh. No. He. Didn't.* She was doing her best here. "Excuse me, Dr. Granger, but I do care about people's lives, especially those of Seattle General's high-profile patients whose privacy I've been tasked with protecting. And as for us not knowing each other, that should solve itself as we'll be seeing more of each other on a daily basis." She paused a moment to collect her thoughts and lower her defensiveness below red zone levels. "Look, believe me when I say this isn't my ideal situation either, but until your work here is done, I am your new shadow."

Heat pulsed off her cheeks with each beat of her heart and their gazes remained locked. Standing just a few feet away from him, she couldn't help noticing that he was...well, he was *gorgeous*, darn it. Even with those dark shadows under his eyes. Tall, dark hair, piercing gray-green eyes. Man, oh, man. If this guy wasn't on her naughty list, he'd have been just her type.

Except she wasn't looking. Especially at Dr. Granger.

Besides, Will had been handsome as heck too and look how that had turned out. Not well. Not well at all. Nope. Ayanna didn't care if this man was a gift sent straight from the North Pole, she had enough on her plate to deal with at present without a booty call from Dr. Distraction.

"Again, I don't need a babysitter, Ms. Franklin," he growled as he pushed inside the changing room. "I'm a board-certified neurosurgeon with a world-class client list. I'm perfectly capable of getting around on my own, thank you very much."

"Great," she said, her voice dripping with faux cheerfulness. "Then you should have no problem dealing with me."

Ayanna followed him inside the private staffroom, completely unfazed by his grumpiness. She'd seen far worse from her siblings growing up. This late at night the area was deserted except for them, which was good considering their argument had already drawn more attention than she wanted, but she couldn't seem to help herself. For some reason, this man pushed all her buttons without even trying.

"Also, Dr. di Rossi's orders stated you are to be made available at a moment's notice should the King require your services. The only way I can ensure that, after your disappearing act at the airport, is to keep you under my watch until the King's surgery is complete on the fifteenth. So, the sooner you accept it, the easier it will be for both of us. Now, get changed so we can get you checked into your hotel."

With a low growl he yanked open one of the metal lockers against the wall with a clatter, not looking at her. "First of all, I didn't disappear on you, Ms. Franklin. As I've already explained, the King's condition was critical and required my immediate assistance. I didn't have time to go searching for you. I'd appreciate it if you don't make me repeat that information again." Jaw tight, he picked up a wheeled suitcase nearby and sat it atop the wooden bench in front of a row of lockers against one wall, then clicked it open before tugging off his scrub shirt, leaving him naked from the waist up. "Also, there's no need for you to ferry me around town like a chauffeur. I can make my own way to and from the hospital as needed. I'm a grown man."

Grown man indeed.

Her eyes widened as he rummaged around in his suitcase for a shirt. Flushed and flustered, Ayanna turned away fast but not before she'd gotten a peek at all those rippling muscles and smooth, tanned skin.

Sweet Santa on a sleigh, why is it so hot in here?

She resisted the urge to fan herself and stared at the white wall opposite her instead.

Get a grip, girl. He's just a man.

A man who obviously kept himself in peak physical condition despite his busy schedule.

"Why do you need keep tabs on my every move anyway, Ms. Franklin?" he grumbled from behind her as he changed. She only half listened to him, doing her best not to imagine him stripping off those scrub pants too, and didn't dare turn around for fear of seeing her wicked fantasies realized. Lord, this was ridiculous. Okay, sure. She hadn't been with a man since Will. And, yes, maybe six months of celibacy was too long for a red-blooded woman like her. That had to be the reason why this man was affecting her so strongly, right? Thankfully, his sharp tone jarred her out of the smutty pool she'd fallen into and back to reality. "Please don't tell me you're some kind of control freak."

The label struck a painful chord, reminding her of Will's spiteful attitude toward her work hours. She wasn't a control freak. People depended on her to handle things. It's what she did, who she was.

But she wasn't about to stand here and defend herself to this man who couldn't be bothered to follow the simplest of directions. No. At this point the best thing was to get Dr. Bah Humbug to the hotel and checked in, then part ways for the evening. Maybe after some sleep they could meet again on better terms. She cleared her throat and squared her shoulders. "I'll wait for you outside."

"Sure you don't want to stay and help me tie my shoes?" he called from behind her as she headed for the door. "I might find a way out of here through the ceiling tiles and escape again."

Ayanna couldn't resist glancing back at him then, one hand on the cool metal door handle as she tried to bite back a smile and saw he had regular black pants on and was buttoning up a white dress shirt, tiny splotches of crimson dotting his high cheekbones.

"I'll take my chances," she said, mimicking his sarcastic tone with one of her own. "Five minutes."

She exited the room head held high, far too aware of the weight of his gaze on her back as she walked out into the brightly lit hallway once more. Her throat felt tight and for some reason that image of his long fingers fastening the front of his shirt was burned into her brain. Those were good hands. Sturdy and strong. Her traitorous mind had her imagining all the things those hands could do to her before she stopped herself.

What is wrong with me?

The cooler air felt good on her heated cheeks. She slumped back against the wall several feet down from the door and closed her eyes, searching in vain for her missing composure. This wasn't like her at all. She was always the go-to gal in a crisis. Yet one encounter with

Dr. Granger had thrown her entire ordered world asunder. Well, no more.

Inhaling deeply, Ayanna straightened and smoothed a hand down the front of her cerulean blue pantsuit. She'd bought it last month and had been so excited to wear it for the first time today. The salesgirl had said the color highlighted the pink tones in her complexion and made her skin glow. She could sure as hell use all the shine she could get at the moment.

Fine. Enough. Yes, she and Dr. Granger had gotten off to a rocky start, but they were both professionals and while the current circumstances weren't ideal, they would make the best of them. Starting with reaching an accord before she dropped the man off at his hotel for the night.

Dr. Granger exited the changing room a few moments later, still scowling and muttering under his breath as he made a beeline for the elevators, wheeling his suitcase right past her as if she weren't there. Undeterred, Ayanna quickly caught up with him and waited beside him in front of the gleaming metal doors. He felt big next to her, the heat of him penetrating the sleeve of her jacket as their arms brushed. With that grim set to his lips and the faint lines of tension around his mouth and eyes, his presence screamed alpha male dominance.

To her chagrin, her ovaries gave a tiny squeeze before she put a quick kibosh on that. The last thing she needed was input from her reproductive system.

She'd hoped to have babies with Will, until she'd discovered he was a lying, cheating snake beneath his slick exterior and she knew she could still have kids.

She was only thirty-two, for goodness' sake. Now, if she could just ignore that tick-tick-tick of her biological clock and the well-meaning hints her parents kept dropping about grandchildren, she'd be all set.

"We've booked you a suite at the Polar Club," she said, both to distract herself and to break the near-stifling silence that had fallen between them. When he didn't respond, Ayanna side-eyed him from beneath her lashes. "With you arriving earlier than originally planned, I upgraded your accommodations to a suite."

"I'm perfectly fine with a standard room." He exhaled slowly through his nose, as if summoning the last of his patience. Then he shook his head and his broad shoulders relaxed slightly, the corners of his firm lips turning down. "But thank you for making the adjustment."

"You're welcome." Given the reluctance in his voice, she'd bet that concession had cost him a lot. He was tired, that much was plain, given the dark circles beneath his eyes and his slightly rumpled appearance. She was exhausted too. Still, she couldn't help wondering if his prickly demeanor was caused by more than lack of sleep. "And the suite was the only room they had left. All the local hotels are booked solid through the holidays."

The elevator dinged and the doors swished open. Ayanna held them for him while he trundled himself and his suitcase on, then followed him. She pushed the button for the walkway level then stepped back and clasped her hands in front of her, her tote over her shoulder.

As they descended, Dr. Granger's posture remained stiff. "So we're stuck with each other, then?"

"We are." The elevator dinged and the doors opened once more. As they walked, she pointed out different areas of interest to him, including the cafeteria and where his interim office would be located in the neurology department, just down the hall from her own.

Finally, they reached the parking lot across the street where her car was parked. Dr. Granger hadn't said much as they walked and now that she really looked at him again, he seemed almost forlorn without his gruff bravado. It was endearing, in an odd sort of way that pulled at her heartstrings, and before she knew it Ayanna's fixer mode kicked in and an apology fizzed to the tip of her tongue before she could stop it. "We started on the wrong foot earlier at the nurses' station and I'm sorry."

They crossed the street, the late-November air crisp, the starry sky above clear for a change. Weather in Seattle was nothing if not unpredictable at this time of year. When he didn't respond, she continued, feeling the need to make him understand, though she couldn't say exactly why. "I'm under a bit more stress than usual as it's my first day at Seattle General and I apologize if I took some of that out on you. And I don't mean to act like a mother hen, but Dr. di Rossi's orders were clear. My only concern is making sure you get where you need to be as conveniently as possible. I'm here to make your life easier."

He looked over at her, the orange glow from the streetlight above casting deep shadows on his face. For a moment she worried he might argue again, but then he sighed and shook his head. "I'm sorry too. I should've have looked harder for you at the airport, but as I said my patient's condition is my priority, and I needed to get to Seattle General immediately."

After loading his luggage into the back of her vehicle, they headed out of the lot, Ayanna scanning her badge at the exit before turning out onto the street. Trying to fill the conversational void, she asked, "Is this your first visit to the Pacific Northwest, Dr. Granger?"

"No," he said, the dashboard GPS screen highlighting his profile as he stared out of the window beside him. "I was here a few months ago for a seminar on improved accuracy in frameless stereotaxy."

"Oh." Ayanna had no idea what that meant, but now that he was talking again she wanted to keep it going. "Seminars probably don't allow much time to explore your location, though, do they?"

That got her a low grunt in response. After a moment he looked over at her once more. "You should probably call me Max since we'll be seeing more of each other."

She blinked straight ahead. "Okay, Max. And please call me Ayanna."

Minutes later, they pulled up to the curb on Third Avenue in front of the Polar Club and she got out, handing her keys to a waiting valet. After a bellman retrieved Dr. Granger's suitcase, they went inside to check in.

Ayanna had always loved this place. The lobby looked like something out of a turn-of-the-century gentlemen's club, all dark woods and plush velvet upholstery, with thick oriental rugs under foot and a fire crackling in the fireplace. Golden Christmas lights twinkled from the mantel and a large, plump spruce was decorated in one corner in tasteful shades of gold and green.

Beside her, Max's expression was pleasingly awed. Maybe she'd finally gotten something right with him. The thought she'd made him happy caused an unexpected prickle of satisfaction inside Ayanna before she quickly shoved it aside. This was her job. That's all.

They approached the large, carved wooden reservation desk across from the fireplace and she smiled at the clerk. "Hello, reservation for Dr. Maxwell Granger. I called earlier."

"Ah, yes. Ms. Franklin," the clerk said. "We spoke on the phone."

"Right. Thank you for your help."

"My pleasure," His gaze flicked to Max, who'd moved in beside Ayanna. "Will you be staying in the suite as well, Miss Franklin?"

"No!" they both said in unison, a bit louder than necessary.

Ayanna cleared her throat. "The room belongs to Dr. Granger. He'll be in town for the next few weeks, working on a case."

"Very good." If the clerk thought that statement was odd, he didn't show it. Then again, Ayanna figured he probably got lots of practice hiding his reactions to people's strange arrangements in his job. The clerk printed out the paperwork and Ayanna signed it on behalf of Seattle General then waited while Max got his key card and a map of the hotel. "The elevators are down the hall. Please enjoy your stay with us, Dr. Granger. Happy Holidays."

Max grunted again then started off down the corridor.

"Thank you. Happy Holidays to you too," Ayanna said, before racing off after Max. Whatever the guy had against the season she didn't know, but the idea of finding out why intrigued her far more than it should.

Max set his suitcase against the wall and stared at the spacious suite before him. Floor-to-ceiling windows across one wall led to a large balcony spanning the entire length of the room that showcased spectacular views of downtown Seattle. From the custom wallpaper to the shiny hardwood floors, the room was amazing and held a special touch of Northwest flavor.

"This is even nicer than I expected," Ayanna said, sidling past him into the nicely appointed kitchen area and setting her bag on the counter. The black leather matched her shoes, he noticed. In fact, everything about her appearance was precise and perfectly coordinated, from her silky dark shoulder-length hair to her expertly applied makeup. Based on what he'd seen so far, he'd say Ayanna Franklin left little to chance when it came to her life. Not that he cared. Her life and how she chose to live it were none of his business. He was here to care for the King. That was all.

Ayanna peered inside the empty stainless-steel fridge and the smaller mini-fridge. The latter was brimming with assorted snacks and booze. She peered back at him over her shoulder, her pretty smile expectant, and something coiled tight inside him before he brushed it away. "What do you think?"

"It's fine," he mumbled, scowling down at his shoes. The room was far more than fine, but he likely wouldn't get to enjoy it too much. He was here to work, not to lounge in his luxury accommodation.

Max turned away, but not before he caught the flicker of hurt in her expression. Guilt pinched his ribcage. Dammit. She'd interpreted his remoteness as rudeness, but it wasn't personal towards her. He didn't allow anyone close these days. The difficulty of his cases required peace, quiet and intense concentration. Distractions could be lethal, so he avoided them at all costs. Yet for some reason Ayanna Franklin seemed to have gotten further under his skin in a few hours than anyone had since his wife's passing.

It was baffling. It was bewildering. It was very bad indeed.

Normally, he tried his best to be cordial to everyone. And while he traveled often for his job, never staying in one place long enough to make real connections, most people liked him. Max Granger, they said, was easy to get along with. A team player. But something about this woman tonight had set his nerves on edge and nothing since had put them right.

She closed the mini-fridge then grabbed her bag off the counter. "Well, Dr. Granger, you look exhausted. If everything is satisfactory here with your room, I'll be going."

A hint of her scent—spice and cloves and a hint of rose—filled the air as she passed him, teasing his senses and driving his awareness of her higher. For a crazy second he was tempted to ask her stay, but why? They were both obviously ruffled and spending more time together wouldn't end this evening any sooner and get him the privacy he craved. So, instead he said, "Yes, if you'll excuse me, I'd like to shower then get some sleep. I'm very tired."

"Great." Ayanna hesitated near the door, watching him across the span of a few feet, her dark eyes wide. She licked her lips and damn if he couldn't stop himself from tracking that tiny movement, his jumbled mind immediately wondering what her mouth would taste like, if those lips felt as soft as they looked, what sounds she might make if he pulled her against him and kissed her…

Whoa. What the—?

Max stepped back and turned away, coughing to relieve the pressure of his heart lodged in his throat. He never acted like this. There was no excuse for his behavior. Not exhaustion. Not unwanted lust.

Confused, he took a step back, then another, until his butt hit the edge of the granite-topped island in the kitchen and his suitcase bumped against his leg. He needed time alone to clear his head and sort out this mess, to get showered and changed, then get some sleep. Whatever was going on here could wait until the morning when, hopefully, he'd be thinking and acting more rationally again. "Thank you for all you've done for me tonight."

It took a moment, but finally she opened the door and headed back out into the hall. "I'll be back at seven tomorrow morning to take you to work."

After she left, Max went to the master bedroom to unpack. This wasn't like him. Not at all. But there was something about Ayanna that set him alight inside like a roman candle. Which was damned inconvenient. He didn't need this in his life right now. Didn't want it. He was more than happy living in his self-imposed, emotionless bubble. Things were easier that way.

Determined to put tonight and Ms. Franklin out of his mind, Max finished putting away his things then strode into the attached bathroom to turn on the walk-in shower. Steam filled the room while he stripped down then stepped beneath the shower head and let the hot water ease away the tension from his stiff muscles.

Regardless of this unwanted awareness where Ayanna was concerned, his best move was to ignore it. There were already far too many things that could go wrong here in Seattle with the King's case.

His personal life didn't need to be added to the list.

CHAPTER FOUR

AN HOUR LATER, Ayanna slumped down on the cushy sofa in her apartment and toed off her pumps. Dealing with Max Granger had been an unexpected challenge in an already difficult day.

With a sigh, she took off her jacket and got out her laptop to pull up the spreadsheets she'd downloaded from her work computer earlier. It was going on two a.m. now and she should really try to sleep, but she had too much to do. Plus, she needed to start packing some of her stuff, since she needed to be out of her apartment by the end of the week so the workmen could get in. Not to mention the fact she was far too amped to sleep at this point from her earlier encounter with Max. She hoped maybe being productive would help lower her stress levels.

She started going over the lists of decorations needed for the ball and the menus and the musical selections, but time and again her mind kept circling back to Max Granger. For some reason, arguing with him had gotten her blood boiling, in more ways than one. Even now, if she closed her eyes, Ayanna could still remember the heat of him scorching through her clothes, could still smell the soap and cedar scent of his skin, could still hear the snarkiness in his tone during his comment in the changing room. And those icy gray-green eyes of his? They hadn't been frigid at all then. Nope. His gaze had been hot. Hot as the flames licking inside her now and…

Oh, boy.

She didn't *want* to want Dr. Max Granger that way. They'd just met. She didn't do love or romance or relationships anymore. Not after Will. She didn't believe in happily ever after. Having your fiancé run off with your best friend weeks before the wedding did that to a girl.

These days she was all about her career and fully intended to keep it that way, thanks so much. Never mind Max's growly, brooding alpha act called to her inner fixer. The only reason she was shadowing him was because that was her job. Dr. di Rossi expected her to keep the neurosurgeon reined in and that's exactly what she intended to do, whether Max liked it or not.

Taking a deep breath, she sat forward, determined to think about something else other than her infuriating new charge. The ball. That should be her focus. She'd throw the biggest and best holiday fundraising ball Seattle General had ever seen.

Fingers flying across her keyboard as she typed, Ayanna periodically checked her phone for updates and emails, and soon enough lost herself in her work. By the time she looked up again, it was almost five in the morning. Her muscles felt stiff from sitting in one spot too long and a glance out the window above her kitchen sink showed the first streaks of pink and purple near the horizon. So much for sleep. She stood and stretched, then froze in place at the sound of her phone buzzing on the coffee table. The number wasn't one she recognized, and she frowned down at the text message on her screen.

Not her family. Not her staff. Her pulse tripped.

Max.

She'd left a sheet of important numbers on the counter in the suite when they'd first arrived, hers being one of them, but she'd never expected him to use it. Her stomach dropped. Oh, God. What if the King had taken a turn for the worse? What if Max had once more rushed off, leaving her to scramble after him?

But as she read the message, her worry turned to surprise. Not an emergency at all, but an apology.

Thank you again for getting this suite. It's very nice and I appreciate it.

Stunned, Ayanna just blinked at her phone. Just when she'd put him squarely in the lump-of-coal-in-his-stocking category he went and did something nice. Not just nice—sweet. And that was…wow. The tension between her shoulder blades eased and her thumbs shook slightly as she typed in a response.

My pleasure. See you soon. A

After hitting "send" Ayanna sank back down on to the sofa and stared out the window for a long moment. She'd seen him be kind and solicitous to the nurses at the hospital, but that was the first time he'd done so with her and darn if that didn't make her see him in a better light. Maybe there was a chance they could make this work after all. Maybe they were both just trying to get through a difficult time as best they could. And maybe being around Max Granger wouldn't be quiet so tedious after all.

Early the next morning, Max ate his eggs and turkey sausage and drank his coffee, periodically peeking at his breakfast guest across the table from him over the top of his *New York Times.* Ayanna hadn't eaten a thing since she'd arrived promptly at seven, had just sat there working on her laptop and drinking coffee. Honestly, it was none of his business. He shouldn't say anything, especially after establishing their uneasy accord with his apology earlier, but he couldn't seem to stop himself.

"Are you feeling all right?' he asked, staring at his paper and not at her.

"Fine." She glanced up at him then continued typing. "Why?"

"No reason." He picked up his own buzzing phone to see another update from the ICU nurse on duty. The King was still stable and unconscious, but that wasn't uncommon after a bad concussion. The most important thing, his intracranial pressure, was holding at pre-accident levels, meaning no new clots had formed. Max clicked off his device and placed it face down on the table. "You aren't hungry?"

"Nah. I hardly ever eat in the morning." She leaned in closer to her screen and squinted at it before tapping a few more keys then smiling. That weird buzz flared inside him again. Things were finally smoothed over between them and he didn't need to ruffle them up again by drooling over the last person on earth he should be attracted to. Besides, Ayanna was too bright and bold and bubbly. He preferred quiet, calm, and routine these days. Bad enough they were sharing commutes, which meant seeing her each morning and evening. Restlessness niggled inside him again, but before it could take hold Ayanna's voice broke through the gathering shadows inside him like the rays of persistent sunshine burst through the clouds outside.

"Breakfast slows me down and makes me feel sluggish. I usually don't have time anyway." Ayanna glanced at his plate of eggs and meat. "You on a keto diet?"

"No." He swallowed another bite of turkey sausage. "Just like to get my protein. Helps my energy levels during long, busy days."

"Hmm." Sounding skeptical, she closed her laptop then nabbed a wedge of whole wheat toast from the plate he'd ordered, in case she wanted something. "Thanks again for your message this morning, by the way. I'm glad we're on better terms now."

He nodded, focusing on his scrambled eggs and not her. He still couldn't quite believe he'd sent that text, but in the moment it had seemed like the right thing to do. One of them had to give, and he could accept defeat. What he couldn't accept, however, were these appalling bad eggs. He wrinkled his nose.

"What's wrong?" Ayanna asked, giving him a wary look. "Don't tell me you're rescinding the apology now."

"What?" Max looked up and blinked at her, taking a second to connect the dots. "No. Nothing's wrong. Not about that, anyway. It's just these eggs aren't nearly as good as the ones I make."

Her expression turned dubious. "You cook?"

"I do." For some reason, people didn't expect him to know his way around a kitchen, but after his wife had died he'd had to fend for himself. Now Max considered himself a foodie. It was one of the few hobbies he had and he treasured his time in the kitchen, tinkering with new recipes. It helped relax him. "At first out of necessity and now because I enjoy it."

"Huh." She swallowed another bite of toast. "Well, your wife probably appreciates that."

He winced before he could stop himself. "My wife died two years ago."

"Oh." Ayanna flushed, setting the rest of her toast aside, uneaten. "I'm sorry. I had no idea."

"It's fine." Max shoved a whole sausage link in his mouth, chewing without tasting it. He expected the same hollow emptiness to fill him each time he thought of his life post-Laura, but for the first time in recent memory it didn't. He didn't stop to consider why, though, just swallowed his food with gulp of hot decaf tea, the scald on his throat a welcome distraction. "Anyway, eating out a lot isn't healthy, so I started buying a few cookbooks and trying my hand at things."

Ayanna tilted her head, her gaze narrowed. "And how'd that go?"

"At first? Not good." Max chuckled. "Right out of the gate I ruined an expensive set of pans because I burned everything I touched. Eventually, though, I got better. Even took some classes at Le Cordon Bleu in New York between cases. Now, I make a mean *coq au vin* and my scrambled eggs are the best in Manhattan."

"Huh. Maybe you can make me dinner some time."

Ayanna's smile froze then faltered and she looked away fast, the silence between them turning awkward. To cover it, she refilled her coffee cup, for the third time by his estimation. He wasn't sure what she did with all that caffeine, but he avoided the stuff in order to hold his instruments steady.

While finishing the rest of his breakfast, Max studied her more closely as she frowned down into her mug. Dark smudges marred the delicate skin beneath her eyes today and there were new faint lines of stress at the corners of her lips. A pang of guilt stabbed his chest. He hoped their argument the night before hadn't been the cause of her lost sleep. She glanced up and caught him staring and he looked away.

She shrugged and sat back crossing her legs away from him. "Personally, I don't really cook at all, which is an affront to my mother who makes enormous meals whenever she can."

"You come from a big family?" he asked, glad to have a talking point again. Chatting with her was nice, normal. Ayanna was surprisingly easy to talk to—when she wasn't arguing with him, of course. "Are you married?"

"Yes and no," Ayanna said. "I have five younger siblings, two brothers and three sisters, and we all love to eat. And I was engaged once, but things didn't work out."

He wanted to ask more, but her firm tone effectively shut the door on that topic. Just as well, since he had no business getting more involved with her life. He stood to set the room service tray in the kitchen. Truth was, he'd missed this kind of morning routine. Missed making small talk over the table. Missed connecting with another person, no matter how trivial the topic.

When he'd met Laura, she'd pulled him out of the isolation of his youth. Being with her had taught him that love and affection were normal and nice and needed. Now that she was gone, deep down part of him feared falling back into that same trap again, feared squeezing back inside the cold, unfeeling shell his parents had raised him in. After living with his wife, those tight confines of emotionlessness didn't fit as comfortably anymore and that knowledge both worried and terrified him.

"If cooking is your thing, I can call today and have groceries delivered so you can use the kitchen here in the suite. All of the appliances work," Ayanna said, following him into the kitchen to rinse out her cup in the sink. "Just give me a list of what you need and I'll make sure it's all here this evening."

At first, he was going to tell her not to bother, since he planned to talk to the head of neurosurgery today about consulting on some additional cases to keep busy—there was also no telling if or when the King's condition might change—but then he reconsidered. Cooking was his go-to stress reliever. No matter what, he still had to eat. Making food helped clear his head and he could use a breather right now. "Okay. That would be nice. Thank you for offering."

"You're welcome." Ayanna checked her watch. "We should get going. Traffic's a bear in the mornings and I've got a pile of work to get done today."

"Sure." Max tugged on his jacket while Ayanna gathered her computer and bag. Maybe this whole carpool thing would work out better than he'd imagined. "And if I cook, maybe I can get you to eat."

Ayanna glanced up at him, flashing that sunny smile of hers again, and his day got a tad brighter. "Maybe. We'll see. You've got a few weeks to try anyway."

CHAPTER FIVE

LATER THAT MORNING, after checking in on the King's condition—stable but still unconscious—and reporting his finding to Dr. di Rossi, Max headed between buildings at Seattle General. He liked to stay busy and since the King's prognosis was still uncertain, Max had cleared his calendar until after the first of the new year and planned to hunker down here in Seattle until then.

Luckily, the chief of neurosurgery was running short on staff with the holidays. Many of the doctors took time off to be with their families, so the department was eager to have Max's help. In fact, he'd barely finished filling out his paperwork downstairs in HR and got hold of his staff pass when a call came in from the ER that they had a new patient who needed a neuro consult.

He headed through the maze of brightly lit halls, his attention split between the busy Seattle streets below and the facilities around him. Max was still learning his way around the place, but so far he'd been impressed. They had state-of-the-art equipment and were participating in several prominent clinical trials. Dr. di Rossi ran a tight ship in the ER as well, erasing any doubts

Max might have had that the King had only chosen this facility for his surgery because of his son.

And, much as he hated to admit it, part of his mind was still focused on Ayanna. He wasn't sure why exactly, but she intrigued him far more than anyone else had in a long time. Delicious smells wafted from the cafeteria and he pulled out his phone to add some baking ingredients to the list of items he'd asked Ayanna to order for him earlier.

Truthfully, he looked forward to cooking like some men looked forward to the NFL playoffs. He hadn't been kidding about getting her to eat better while he was here either. In fact, he took it as a personal challenge to get her have breakfast each day when she came to pick him up. He'd already asked her to get the necessary ingredients to make his signature roasted vegetable frittata for her tomorrow: zucchini, bell peppers, onions, garlic, cream, eggs and Parmesan cheese. Seeing the look of ecstasy on her face when she tasted the first bite would be reward enough for getting up extra early to prepare it.

But as he continued on through the busy corridors toward the ER, Max's visions of Ayanna groaning with delight over his food suddenly morphed into something else entirely, his mind filling with images of the two of them entwined in his sheets, her soft moans parting those delectable lips as she called out his name when she came apart in his arms…

What the…?

Max stopped short, narrowly avoiding crashing into several other people walking towards him.

Thinking about sex with Ayanna made no sense. They barely knew each other. They had been thrown together because of the King's case, that was all. Besides, he wasn't looking for intimacy. Things were complicated enough in his life without opening himself up to that too. And, yes, he was a normal, straight guy. He dealt with his libido by sleeping only with women who understood the rules—no fuss, no muss, and certainly no emotions or strings attached. From the brief time he'd spent with Ayanna, she didn't seem like the type of woman who had affairs or flings.

The whole idea was insane. Impossible. Yet far more compelling than he cared to admit.

He stepped around the group of visitors blocking his path, then continued toward the ER. Keeping things strictly professional with Ayanna during his stay in Seattle was priority one. After losing Laura, Max never wanted to open himself up to being emotionally vulnerable again. He was perfectly happy in his isolated, rational bubble. There was safety in being alone. He'd much rather deal with that than have his heart shredded. No. His parents had had it right. Emotions only caused trouble. Rubbing his hand over his tight chest, he jogged down the remaining stairs, resignation dogging his heels as he entered the emergency department.

"What's the rundown?" Max asked Dr. Cho, the resident who'd called him in for a consult, while he clicked through the case file at a computer terminal in the hall.

"Seventeen-year-old male with positive loss of consciousness after being slammed into the boards while playing hockey," Dr. Cho said, her dark spiky hair gleaming midnight blue beneath the lights.

"How long was he out?"

"About three minutes, according to witnesses."

Max scrolled through the patient's vitals, which all looked good, then headed into the room where the kid was now awake and talking to his parents, who sat anxiously by his bedside. He shook their hands, then turned to the patient. "Hi. there. I'm Dr. Granger. Can you tell me your name?"

"Josh Whitaker." The kid frowned. "Why am I here?"

"Because you hit your head." Max took a penlight from the pocket of his scrub shirt and checked the teen's pupils—both equal and reactive to light—then gently examined the patient's skull for signs of a possible fracture. There was a nasty cut over his left eyebrow, but otherwise the boy seemed uninjured. "Can you tell me if anything hurts where I'm pushing?"

"Nothing hurts." Josh winced as his arm hit the bed rail. "My hand's numb, though, and I feel dizzy."

"Okay." Max finished examining Josh then stepped back to record his findings in the electronic file. Head injuries were always concerning in someone this young. Unfortunately, they weren't all that uncommon, especially in contact sports like hockey, football and soccer. As Max typed, he continued to ask questions over his shoulder. "Josh, do you remember anything about what happened?"

"Uh…" Josh scowled then ran his fingers through his messy blond hair. "The last thing I remember was… I don't know. No, I don't think I remember anything at all."

"Okay." Max glanced at the parents. "Has he had previous concussions?"

"Yes," Josh's mother said, her tone concerned. "About

two years ago, when he was playing lacrosse. Will my son be okay, Doctor?"

Max wanted to say yes but the fact that Josh had had multiple head injuries prior to today wasn't ideal. Still, he tried to be as encouraging as possible. "We'll do everything we can, Mrs. Whitaker."

She closed her eyes as her husband put his arm around her. "I've seen my son get hit a lot, but I didn't think it was that bad this time. But he just lay there on the ice, not moving, and they called the coach and then 911..." Her shoulders shook with sobs and Mr. Whitaker handed her a tissue.

"As I said, we'll do everything we can for Josh." Max did his best to reassure her. The teen was young and strong and he should be fine.

Laura should've been fine too.

Max coughed and shoved aside his past failings and guilt to focus on the case at hand. "We'll get an MRI to have an idea of what's happening in his brain. If that's clear, then I'd say your son likely has a concussion. Let's wait on the results then go from there, all right?"

"Yes." Ms. Whitaker reached over and took Max's hand. "Thank you, Doctor."

"My pleasure." Helping others was why Max had gone into neurosurgery in the first place and the fact these poor people were spending their day in a hospital instead of out preparing for the holidays like everyone else only made him more determined to do what he could. Just because he didn't do Christmas anymore, it didn't mean the Whitakers didn't deserve to have their son home and healthy for the season. "Let me call Radiology and get things rolling."

At the nurses' station Max put in a stat call for an MRI then waited until the technicians wheeled Josh away. While he waited for results, Max went upstairs to ICU to check in on King Roberto again. Still no change. Disappointing but not too discouraging, since short-term comas weren't uncommon after a craniotomy.

Twenty minutes later Max got a text that Josh's MRI was complete, and the results were ready for him to view. He returned to the ER and brought up the images on the computer in Josh's trauma bay.

Josh seemed to be in a bit better spirits at least, which was a good sign.

"Do I have a brain, Doc?" he joked.

Max snorted. "Yep. It's still in there."

He scrolled through the images then turned to the anxious parents. "The good news is there's no sign of any internal bleeding in the brain or clotting and no skull fractures either. But given his pain and dizziness and the fact he hit a wall hard with his head, your son most likely has a concussion." Max shut off the computer and crossed his arms, narrowing his gaze on the patient. "Which means no hockey for a while, son."

Josh gave a disappointed sigh.

"I know it's hard, but you need time to heal," Max continued. "A few weeks at least, until your brain recovers, and you can have a checkup with your regular doctor. Then when you do go back on the ice, make sure you have on your safety gear. Understood?"

"Understood, Doc," Josh said, then turned to his dad. "Did we at least win?"

His dad laughed. "Yep, son. Three to nothing."

Max exited the trauma bay to finish Josh's discharge paperwork, relief lifting a bit of burden off his shoulders. Cases like King Roberto's, where progress was slow, made for long days and worrisome nights. Having a case like Josh's with a swifter positive outcome helped ease the strain. After he completed his documentation, he turned the case back over to Dr. Cho then decided to take a walk.

Being cooped up in one place too long made him stir crazy, another unexpected side effect of his hectic work schedule. He grabbed a lab coat off one of the racks of spare scrubs against the wall, then pushed outside through a side exit door. For a Sunday in late November, the temperatures in Seattle were surprisingly moderate, though the sky was a typical overcast gray. Weak sunlight filtered through the clouds above and people rushed down the busy sidewalks, even on a weekend. Heading down Terry Street toward Madison, his stomach growled, and he checked his watch. Yep, it was lunchtime. Maybe he'd sample some local cuisine while he was out and about.

Passing by a sign for Zipcar, his thought returned to Ayanna. Zippy certainly described her. She seemed to go twenty-four seven, always working, always moving. Not that he had any room to talk. He was Type A through and through as well. Neurosurgery wasn't for slackers, as his parents used to remind him all the time. Too bad, since he could've used a little more downtime with them to just be a kid, just enjoy his childhood and feel like he was loved.

An image of Josh and his family flashed through his head. They'd been so easy and affectionate with each other, so different from how *he* had grown up. His thoughts circled around to what Ayanna had told him earlier about her own family. Five siblings. Wow. He couldn't imagine what that must've been like, growing up with all that noise and togetherness and love. He'd grown up with loneliness and nannies. Yet even from a distance his parents had pushed him to succeed, to do better, to be better. They'd cared little for his heart. For them, it was all about his mind. Looking back, he supposed they'd meant to encourage him, but he didn't really know for sure. All he knew was that they'd remained remote and emotionally distant from him when what he'd really craved was closeness and compassion. Eventually, when his repeated efforts to engage them emotionally had failed, he'd learned to switch off his emotions and interact with them on a purely cerebral level in order to get any attention at all.

Laura had used to joke with him about being able to "flip the switch", as she'd called it, when he was working, but honestly, it hadn't been until he'd married her that he'd finally escaped that buttoned-up, locked-down emotional state and learned to feel again.

Now, though, since her death, he'd retreated back into isolation again.

An image of Ayanna this morning popped into his head, with her perfectly pressed crimson pantsuit, her sunny smile and her bright eyes. Maybe that's why he couldn't seem to stop thinking about her. She reminded him of the connection and vitality he'd lost. First with his parents and then again two years ago when Laura had died.

A door opened nearby and warm air gusted around

him, scented with fresh baked bread and cinnamon. Memories of making cinnamon rolls with Laura on Christmas morning flooded his mind and for a moment it felt like a hug from the beyond. Max blinked hard to stem the yearning inside him. He was happy alone. He didn't need anyone else in his life.

He didn't *want* to need anyone else again.

Through the glass windows of the bakery, golden lights beckoned him inside. A handwritten chalk menu by the door listed all sorts of delicious-sounding sandwiches and Max went inside to grab lunch. As he waited to order, Christmas carols drifted from the stereo system, though he found them less annoying today, for some reason.

While he stood in line, he pulled out his phone to check for updates and instead found a text from Ayanna. The sight of her name on his screen sent a thrill of adrenaline through his system, which was weird. According to the message, she was running late, buried under work, and she might not be ready to go at five, as originally scheduled. She also said she'd placed his delivery order and it would be waiting at the suite once they arrived.

All righty, then. He knew from personal experience how easy it was to let things like meals slide when you got busy. But as a physician he also knew the importance of good nutrition for keeping a healthy immune system. With winter on their doorstep and her being his ride to and from the hospital, he needed her to stay healthy. Besides, the idea of Ayanna neglecting herself bothered Max more than he cared to admit. She'd already skipped breakfast. He refused to let her skip lunch too, as he suspected she would from her text.

"Welcome to the Thunderbird Café," a woman behind the counter greeted him. "May I take your order?"

Max stepped up and ordered two Turkey Havarti sandwiches, and kale chips to go. Honestly, he had no idea what Ayanna liked, other than coffee, but figured it was worth a shot. After paying and grabbing their food, he headed back to Seattle General.

Ayanna ended her call and laid her head atop her arms on the desk in her office. As if she didn't have enough to deal with at present, that had been the Polar Club stating that due to a staff error the ballroom had been double-booked for December twelfth, the night of the hospital's ball. After a battle with the functions manager at the hotel the ballroom was theirs, but still. A girl only had so much time and patience to go around and Ayanna had not planned to spend all hers on that.

With a sigh, she straightened and smoothed a hand down the front of her new wool suit, taking a deep breath before staring at the stack of files on her desk once more. Her hands shook slightly from low blood sugar, so she took another swig of her energy drink before diving back into planning the ball décor again. She'd barely begun on the table centerpieces when a knock on the door interrupted her.

"Yes?" she called, without looking up, doing her best to keep the irritation from her tone and failing. The door opened and Ayanna expected to see one of her staff walk in with yet another problem for her to solve, but instead she was greeted by the sight of Max Granger holding food and two bottles of water. How the man managed to make a plain white lab coat and scrubs look so sexy was a mystery.

"Good afternoon," he said, smiling then closing the door behind him before taking a seat in one of the chairs in front of her desk. She'd been around enough powerful men in her line of work to know they tended to act like they owned the place, no matter where they went. Will had been that way too, working in finance. With her ex it had rubbed her up the wrong way on occasion, but then again Will had never brought her lunch on a hectic day either. Of course, he'd been fine with her doing it for him, though. Even though he'd complained about her busy schedule, he'd never once complained about her doing all sorts of little things to make his life easier. Nope. In fact, he'd taken her generosity for granted.

Max, though, had been nothing but sweet to her since they'd made peace. He placed one of the bags and a bottle of water on the desk beside her energy drink and grinned, the color of his eyes reminding her of the waters of Puget Sound during a storm. "It's past lunchtime and I thought you might be hungry now. Can't having you missing another meal."

Ayanna blinked at him for a moment, then spotted the logo from her favorite café. Growing up, she'd always been the caretaker, the one looking out for everyone else. It felt odd to receive that sort of attention from someone else. Odd and a bit scary, to be honest. Because having someone take care of her for a change scratched an invisible itch she hadn't even known she had until now. Her stomach growled and she peeked inside the bag. "Um, thank you."

"My pleasure," he said, winking as he opened his own bag and pulled out a paper-wrapped sandwich and a bag of kale chips. "I did warn you."

"Warn me?" Her brows drew together as she discovered the same turkey sandwich and a bag of chips inside her own sack. Ayanna quickly unwrapped it and took a bite, chewing and swallowing before she asked, "About what?"

"About you eating properly." He gulped down a large swig of water. "At breakfast this morning. Studies show keeping your blood sugar levels steady through the day by eating regularly helps increase productivity. Coffee and energy drinks only solve the problem temporarily. Eventually you crash, harder than you would have with food. It's a vicious cycle."

She snorted around a mouthful of salty kale chips. "Thanks, Mr. Food Police."

"Anytime." Max grinned and her insides gave a tiny, unwanted flutter. She stared down at her food, anywhere but at him, as she ate. Whatever this weird attraction was, she needed to get over it quickly. She had far too much to deal with as it was. She didn't need her neglected girly parts chiming in.

Max ate another large bite of his sandwich then pointed to the files on her overflowing desktop. "What are you working on?"

"One issue after another, unfortunately." She started to tell him all about her problems with the ball, but then stopped. Sharing her burdens wasn't exactly a skill she'd honed. It was hard enough delegating things to her staff, let alone telling someone about issues with her new job. Even if he did seem to be a good listener, the last thing he probably wanted to hear about were flowers and hors d'oeuvres. So she dodged his with a question of her own. "How is the King?"

"Stable. Tell me more about this ball. What's your menu?" Max asked, refusing to be deterred. He was stubborn too, apparently. A good trait in a surgeon. Maybe not so much in a lunch companion. "I'm a foodie, remember? Maybe I can help."

"You want to help me with the planning?" She gave him a dubious stare, but it made sense. And much as she hated to admit it, she was used to designing global PR campaigns, not picking out entrées and desserts. Maybe she should take him up on his offer. He was sitting here in her office anyway, so what could it hurt? She set her sandwich down and flipped open a folder again before turning it to face him. "Well, since you insist, I'm having fits trying to get the hospital's big fundraising ball planned in half the time it normally takes."

"Hmm." He finished off his kale chips then stuffed the debris back inside his sack before reaching for the centerpiece photos. "Sounds stressful. What have you done so far?"

"The only thing that's locked down at this point is the venue. It's being held in the ballroom of the hotel where you're staying. I just got off the phone with the Polar Club, actually. Apparently, they double booked our ballroom for the same evening, but my predecessor made our reservation first, so the was crisis averted, thankfully. Now, I'm going over décor options for the ballroom then I need to pick menus for the night and book musicians and—"

Her cellphone rang, cutting her off. Par for the course

when it came to interruptions today. Ayanna held up a finger for Max to wait, then answered without checking the caller ID. "Ayanna Franklin."

"Hi, honey. How are you?" her mother said, the sound of cooking in the background as usual. Ayanna loved her mom, loved her whole family, but this was another time suck she didn't need, especially since she was pretty sure her mother was calling about Thanksgiving, and also about Ayanna staying there while her apartment was being worked on. More things to add to her to-do list.

"I'm fine, Mom. Busy." Ayanna swiveled away from Max for a modicum of privacy and faced the bookshelves covering one wall of her office. "What did you need?"

"I wanted to let you know your room's ready to go," her mother said. "We can talk about Thanksgiving after you get moved in again."

"I'm not moving back in, Mom." Ayanna glanced back over her shoulder at Max, who'd grown suspiciously quiet, only to find him riffling through more event files on her desk. Shocked, she swung her chair around to smack his hand away. "At most I'll only be staying there a few weeks until the electrical work is done at my place."

Max glanced up at her and quirked an inquisitive brow, which she ignored. She gave him a "don't touch" look then turned back to face her bookcases again.

"And where else are you going to stay, huh?" her mom said. "James is out of town. So are Clarissa and Tonya. I don't know about LaTasha or Brandon, but you know how they are. So that counts out your siblings, which leaves your old room, honey."

"I'm thinking maybe I'll get a hotel room," Ayanna said, cradling the phone between her shoulder and wincing at her mother's outraged gasp. "It's not that I don't want to see you guys, it's just that I've got a lot of work to do over the next couple of weeks and I really need a distraction-free space to do it in."

"Distraction, huh?" Her mother gave an imperious sniff. "Is that how you see us now?"

Ayanna closed her eyes and rubbed the bridge of her nose. No one played the guilt card better than a mother. "No, Mom. It's not that at all, it's just—"

"Just what?" her mom asked, her tone skeptical. "If you think you're going to worm your way out of Thanksgiving dinner with us, you've got another think coming. I've already bought the turkey and all the stuff for side dishes. I will not waste all this food because you think your fancy job is more important than being home for the holidays—you got me, young lady?"

And just like that, Ayanna was back to being ten years old again, getting a dressing down from Momma because she'd let her brothers make a mess in the garage when she was supposed to be watching them. Shame flared hot in her chest before she tamped it down. "No. I'll be there for Thanksgiving."

She actually *had* been planning on cancelling, not because she didn't want to see her family but because of her crazy schedule. But if showing up got her off the hook with her mom about staying with them during her apartment work, then so be it. Even if she didn't have another place to stay. Yet.

"Well, I suppose that's something, at least," her mother said, banging a pan on the stove. "Your father just bought a thirty-pound turkey. Do you know how many people a thirty-pound turkey feeds?"

"No."

"Twenty-five people, that's how many," her mother continued over Ayanna's answer. "Plus, I've got potatoes and stuffing and rolls and pie. Three pumpkin pies. Darn right you'll be here on the holiday because who else is going to help me get all this ready?"

Ayanna was tempted to give a smartass answer then reconsidered. Sassing her mother when she was pissed was taking her life into her hands. Thankfully, she was saved by the call-waiting beep. "Hang on, Mom."

She abruptly switched lines, cutting off her mother's continued speech about starving people in Africa, and said in her best PR director tone, "Ayanna Franklin, how may I help you?"

All the while Max sat across from her, watching her with an inscrutable expression. Her cheeks heated and she did her best to concentrate on the person talking on the other end of the line. She didn't like appearing anything less that poised in front of other people, especially Max.

"Yes, Ms. Franklin. This is Gerry Miller with the Thunderbird Orchestra returning your call," the guy on the other end of the line said.

Right. The musicians. She sifted through the paperwork in front of her, searching for their fact sheet as her mother's call buzzed on the other line. Her breath hitched and she bumped her water bottle, nearly knocking it over, but Max caught it. Dammit. Where was that paper?

Buzz. Buzz. Buzz.

"Sorry," she said, forcing the words past her tight vocal cords. "Can you hang on a moment, Mr. Miller? I'm just finishing up with another call."

She put the musician back on hold then picked up with her mother again. "Sorry, Mom. I have to go. I'll call you later, okay?"

"Okay," her mother huffed out. "And let me know what time you'll be here on Thanksgiving too."

"I will."

As soon as I figure that out myself.

Ayanna stared over at Max as she ended the call, then picked up again with the musician. By the time she'd gotten the band sorted out, Max had thrown away his trash. Ayanna had expected him to leave once he'd eaten, but instead he flopped back down in his chair and steepled his fingers. "What's happening at your apartment?"

"They're doing some electrical work. I need to stay elsewhere until it's done." She took another drink of water to dislodge the lingering lump of stress from her throat. "Why?"

"You don't want to stay with your parents?"

"No, I'd rather not sleep in my tiny twin bed again. Besides, I need some privacy while I sort out this mess with the ball and that's in short supply at my parents' house most of the time."

"Hmm." Max tapped his fingers against his lips, seemingly deep in thought. "You told your mother you were getting a hotel room."

"Yeah?" Ayanna sat back, taking another bite of her sandwich. "So?"

"So you told me the other night that mine was the only room left in town."

Ayanna swallowed. Dammit. Why did he have to be so observant? She could've told Will the same information fifty times and he still wouldn't have remembered. But Max Granger had a memory like a steel trap. Just one more annoying trait on her growing list of things about him that got under her skin, and it bothered her more than she cared to admit. Straightening slightly, she finished the last bite of her sandwich before answering. "And?"

"And you just lied to your mother."

Out of patience, she balled up her empty wrapper and tossed it in the bin with more force than necessary. She'd save the kale chips for a snack later. "Why is my private life any of your business? And like you never lied to your parents. Everyone has at one time or another."

"Not mine." A shadow passed over his face, sadness maybe or resignation. Either way, his broad shoulders slumped a bit. "I wasn't close enough to lie to them."

She took that in, not sure what to say. That sounded really odd. And horrible. How could someone not be close to their own parents? Her family drove her nuts sometimes, but they were always there whenever she needed them. Ayanna didn't like the fact she'd lied to her mom, but she liked even less that Dr. Granger now looked like someone had kicked his puppy. "I'm sorry."

Max exhaled, watching her a moment as if coming to some decision. "You should stay with me."

"Excuse me?" She couldn't have heard that right.

"The suite has two bedrooms. Seems a waste of space to leave one empty when you're in need of lodgings." He sat forward. "Plus, since we're riding together to and from work, it makes sense for you to stay there. We don't have to interact any more than we already are. You'll have separate sleeping quarters and a separate bathroom. You can work on your ball preparations and I can continue to plan for the King's surgery on the fifteenth." Max stood and pointed at the files on her desk. "Plus, you'll be onsite to meet with the musicians and chefs for the party."

"Well, I..." Ayanna wanted to argue with him about it, but damn if he wasn't right. It did make sense, no matter how much she might wish it didn't.

"Think about it," he said, walking to the door. "Let me know tonight. See you in the Seneca Lot when you're ready. Just text me. Oh." He turned to look at her over his shoulder. "And thanks for ordering the groceries."

After he'd gone, she sat staring at the closed door, wondering what the hell had just happened.

CHAPTER SIX

MAX FINISHED PUTTING away the groceries Ayanna had ordered, still a bit shocked at himself for suggesting that they share the suite. Too late now, though, since she'd accepted his offer and was currently on her way back here with her bags. He checked the cupboards in the kitchen then pulled out several frying pans and a couple of mixing bowls and set them on the granite island beside the package of skinless chicken breasts and fresh veggies he planned to cook for dinner.

As he cleaned and chopped and prepared the food to stir fry it, he felt some of the stress from his day leave his body. After his lunch with Ayanna in her office, he'd gone back to his interim office down the hall in Neurology and gotten to work on plans to have a 3D model of the King's brain tumor made from the MRIs and CT scans his patient had had done recently by a company affiliated with Seattle General. It was cutting-edge technology and would help Max better prepare for the surgery ahead.

Once he'd heated the sesame oil in the pan, he dumped the veggies in and stirred them around until their heavenly scents filled the air. He also started a pot of water to make the rice. Before he knew it, the suite smelled fantastic and there was a knock on the door.

An unexpected jolt of eagerness jangled through him as he hurried to let Ayanna into the suite. Normally, he prized his alone time above all else, but tonight he looked forward to getting to know her better.

"Here, let me help you with those." He took the case from over her shoulder as she trundled into the suite with what looked like enough luggage for three people. Ayanna headed toward the second bedroom with a large wheeled suitcase in one hand and two smaller ones in the other, stacked one atop the other. "You're only planning on staying a few weeks, right?"

"Less, if I can help it," Ayanna said. How she maneuvered all this stuff with her small frame and in those ridiculous heels, he had no idea. "As soon as another room opens up here, I'm taking it. Why?"

"You seem to have enough clothes for the next year." Max chuckled.

"I like to have options in what I wear." He followed her down the hall and watched as she set her bags near the end of the queen-sized bed. "And in my job, appearance is important."

"Sure." He nodded, still not completely convinced but smart enough not to argue with a woman about clothing. "Right. Well, I'll let you settle in while I check on dinner."

"What are you making? It smells amazing."

"Chicken stir fry. Hope you're hungry."

"I am." Ayanna turned to unzip the closest suitcase to her. "And thank you for letting me stay here."

"No problem." He backed away slowly, reluctant to

leave. It wasn't like they were anything more than acquaintances, yet he felt drawn to her far more than he had to anyone in a long time. Warmth spread upward from beneath the collar of the gray sweatshirt he'd changed into after work. He smoothed the palm of his hand down the thigh of his jeans then reached for the door handle. "See you in a bit."

"Yep." She grinned at him over her shoulder as she unpacked. "See you."

Want fizzed alongside the adrenaline in his system now.

This was bad. Very, very bad. He didn't *want* to want Ayanna that way. Didn't care to get close to anyone that way again. And yet he'd invited her to stay here, with him, in the same suite.

God, I'm an idiot.

As he finished cooking then dished up dinner onto serving plates, Max searched in vain for a way to make this work that wouldn't involve his libido getting any more involved where Ayanna was concerned. His analytical brain said they'd eat meals together, ride to and from the hospital. Maybe pass in the hall sometimes. That was all. He could do this.

But his heart pinched with the loneliness he'd kept buried for so long and that's what had him worried. Logically he could keep Ayanna in a tidy little box. But emotionally she awakened things in him without even trying—yearning, need, desire—things he'd thought he'd safely buried with Laura. All of them came surging back whenever Ayanna was around and that scared him more than any life-threatening surgery ever had.

* * *

Ayanna unpacked then changed into jeans and an oversized black Seahawks sweatshirt. Staying here was ideal in a lot of ways, but less so in others. Namely the fact that she was sharing space with Max, the one man who'd made her sit up and take notice when she'd been able to avoid romance altogether since Will.

She'd done everything she could to stop her unwanted attraction to him in its tracks, but so far nothing had worked. So she planned to be kind and courteous and stay in her own lane while she was here. Not get any friendlier than necessary. Given how busy they both were, it shouldn't be a problem.

Except when she walked out of her room and down the hall and caught sight of Max in the kitchen, her heart gave a little flip. Man, oh, man. He had his back to her as he cooked, his lithe, muscled build and graceful movements captivating her. He was just her type, if she'd been looking. Tall, dark and gorgeous, with that whole brooding thing going on.

Down, girl. Down. Remember what happened with Will. He was your type too. Until he wasn't anymore.

Will's betrayal had left Ayanna questioning everything, most of all her instincts. She'd been wrong once. What's to say she wouldn't be wrong again? And no matter how Max's inner demons might pull on her heartstrings and make her want to take care of him, she couldn't do that again. Will's betrayal had almost broken her. Going through that again might just end her, once and for all.

Forcing a cheerful smile she didn't quite feel, Ayanna squared her shoulders and headed into the living room in her stockinged feet. Fake it till you make it, wasn't that the motto? She cleared her throat to alert Max to her presence then rubbed her hands on the thighs of her faded jeans. "Anything I can help with?"

"You can set the table, if you want," he said, pointing with his spatula to a stack of plates and silverware on the island. "Drinks too. I'm good with water, but there's also soda in the mini-bar. Or liquor, if you prefer."

"Water's good for me too," Ayanna said, grabbing the plates, grateful she'd tied her hair back into a low pony-tail to keep it out of the way. At work, she dressed to kill, but at home she liked to be comfy and cozy. Wanting to keep the relaxed vibe going, she asked, "How was the rest of your afternoon?"

"Good." Max dished up their food then set the bowls on the table while Ayanna grabbed the bottles of water from the fridge. "Consulted on a couple of new patients, checked on the King again. Designed a model of his tumor for pre-surgery prep."

"A model?" Ayanna asked, as they sat down to eat. She dished herself up a large portion of rice and stir fry then dug into the spicy, savory sweetness with appreciation. "This is… Wow. You are a fabulous cook, Dr. Granger."

"Thanks, Ms. Franklin." He grinned and her toes curled. One of his front teeth was slightly crooked, overlapping the one next to it a bit. She'd never noticed that before. Instead of detracting from his handsomeness, the small imperfection only made him more gorgeous.

To distract herself, she frowned down at her food and continued their conversation. "Tell me more about this model thing. Sounds fascinating."

He went on about brain tumors and axial models and 3D printing while she did her best to take in all the details. Some of the terms were familiar from her mom's nursing work, but some of it went right over her head. Still, it was good to have someone else do the talking instead of her carrying the conversation load for a change. At first, getting Will to talk about his days had been like pulling teeth. Then later he'd only wanted to talk about himself. She squeezed her fork harder than necessary and glanced up at Max. He was looking at her expectantly and it took her a moment to realize he'd asked her something. Crap. She gulped some water to hide her embarrassment. "I'm sorry?"

"I asked how your afternoon went," he said around a mouthful of chicken and veggies. "Get any more done on the décor?"

"Some." She told him her plans for the lighting and the table runners, surprised and delighted he'd asked. "I'm still deciding on the centerpieces, though. There's a florist here in town who does beautiful work, but I'm not sure we have enough time to use them. When I was preparing for my wedding reception, they were booking four months ahead."

When she'd realized what she'd let slip, Ayanna winced. Damn. She'd not meant to bring up her past or Will again but, knowing Max, now that it was out he wouldn't let it drop. Sure enough, when she glanced over at him, he was watching her with that inscrutable look again.

"What?" she asked, trying to dissemble.

"Nothing." He stabbed more chicken with his fork,

avoiding her gaze. "You'd mentioned you were engaged once before, but you're not married now."

"No. I'm not."

He paused in mid-bite, his gray gaze locked with hers. "I'm sorry."

"It's fine." She waved it off with her fork, shoveling in more food to push down the lingering hurt inside her that always resurfaced when the wedding was mentioned. Since she'd been a little girl, Ayanna had dreamed of her wedding day, how special it would be, how magical. Will had taken all of that away from her.

Bastard.

Max blinked at her for a moment then stared down at his food again. "Doesn't sound fine. I understand if you don't want to talk about it, though. Some painful things are best left in the past."

Ayanna should have stopped talking then. Should've eaten her dinner and been done with it, but for some reason she found herself telling Max all about it instead. "My fiancé's name was Will. Will Barnett. We'd known each other since high school and dated in college. He was in finance. Everyone thought we were the perfect couple. He proposed to me on New Year's Eve at the top of the freaking Space Needle." She drank more water to combat the bile burning in her throat and gave Max a rueful smile. "He was always Mr. Popular. Always knew the right thing to say. That's probably how he kept the affair hidden so long."

"Oh." Max scowled across the table at her. "That's awful."

"Yeah. It was bad. He ran off with my best friend, Rinna, a month before the wedding. Then blamed me for it. Said I wasn't supporting him enough. Said I put my career before everything. Said I was so busy taking care of other people that I never stopped to take care of him and our relationship. Never mind the fact that I bent over backward to always be there for him, to always lend a supporting ear, always doing things for him." She snorted, her laugh decidedly unpleasant. "Anyway. He's gone. They moved to LA two months ago, so…yeah." She cringed at Max's dark expression. "Sorry. Didn't mean to unload like that."

"Not at all." He finished his plate of food then stood to clear their dishes. "Thank you for sharing that with me."

"That's who I am," Ayanna said, getting up to help him clear the table, trying to mask her pain with a joke. "I'm a giver. Just ask Will. Or my family."

"Pardon my French, but he sounds like an ass," Max said, taking the plates from her to put in the sink. "You're well rid of him." He filled one half of the stainless-steel sink with soapy water then began to scrub. "And speaking of your family, did you tell your mother where you're staying?"

"I did." She grabbed a towel. "Not about us being here together or anything." She picked up a clean plate to dry, desperate to change the subject. "What about your family?"

Oh, crap. Why'd I ask that? With his wife and all and…

He set another clean plate in the drainer, the corners of his mouth tightening. "I don't have any family to speak of anymore. My wife passed away two years ago, and my parents died when I was eighteen."

Ayanna nodded, feeling terrible but not sure what to say. Her family were constantly in each other's business. She couldn't imagine a life where that wasn't the case. She shouldn't ask but couldn't seem to stop herself. He seemed so lonely and forlorn, standing there all alone, and her fixer genes kicked into overdrive. "What are you doing for Thanksgiving?"

"Working. Same as any other day." He shrugged, not looking up from the sink. "Why?"

"My mother has got plenty of food and she loves having guests to fawn over." Ayanna dried the last dish then set her towel aside to put the clean plates away. "You're welcome to come with me to my parents' house, if you're not busy."

Maybe having him around would divert attention away from her and avoid the dreaded questions about her love life. His being there wouldn't hurt anything, would it? Of course, he'd have to say yes first.

"I don't know." Max drained the sink then hung the dishcloth over the center divider to dry. "I don't really do holidays anymore, like I said."

"Well, the invitation is open, if you change your mind." They finished up in the kitchen then went out into the living room. Ayanna shuffled her feet, the cold hardwood chilling her toes even through her socks. "Well, uh, I should go work on the plans for the ball some more, I guess. Thanks again for dinner."

"You're welcome," Max said, as she backed away toward the hall. "And thanks for the invitation. I'll think about it. Don't work too hard."

"Same to you." She watched him sit back down on the sofa and open his laptop. She hadn't even been there one night yet and already this all felt natural, normal. And if that wasn't a sign to keep to herself even more, she didn't know what was. She had no business getting all comfortable and homey with Max Granger. Not now, not ever. "Goodnight."

"'Night." He smiled over at her. And darn if that little flutter in her gut didn't start all over again.

CHAPTER SEVEN

"OKAY. ANY QUESTIONS before we walk in there?" Ayanna asked on Thursday morning as they pulled up to the curb outside her parents' blue and white craftsman-style home in the Seattle suburb of Redmond. Outside, the air was misty from the recent rain and clumps of snow from the last storm still dotted the ground. Typical Washington state weather for late November. At least the temperature wasn't bad at fifty-five. Several other cars already clogged the driveway and lined the curb out front, meaning the rest of her siblings had already arrived.

She parked then cut the engine, taking a few slow breaths to calm the rise in her pulse. She loved her family, but they could be...*a lot*. Especially for someone from the outside like Max. Honestly, Ayanna had second-guessed her decision to invite him along today at least a billion times since their dinner together on Sunday night, but in the end she just couldn't stand the thought of him sitting alone in the suite during the holiday, since they were both off work today. Besides, he'd been nice enough to cook for her and let her stay in his suite. The least she could do was repay the favor.

A glance at the front bay windows in her parents' living room showed the gauzy drapes fluttering back into place, meaning they'd already been spotted. Too late to turn around and head back to the hotel. If they didn't go into the house soon, her family would send a search party out to retrieve them.

Ayanna's chest pinched and she resisted the urge to take Max's hand. They were friendly now, or at least friendlier than they'd been at the beginning of this, but she didn't want him getting the wrong idea. She'd been specific with her mother as well, when she'd called to tell her to expect her plus one. This wasn't a romantic thing. It was just a nice gesture from one person to another. No one should be alone on the holidays, even if they didn't celebrate. And, sure, Max was a hottie, no two ways about that, but Ayanna had things well in control now regarding her errant sexy thoughts about him. Today was a meal shared with a friend. With her family. Who were nosy as all get out and now stood on the porch craning their necks, trying to get a better look at the guy she'd brought to Thanksgiving and... *Ugh.*

With a sigh, Ayanna undid her seatbelt, turning slightly to face Max in the passenger seat. "They're probably going to ask you lots of questions, but don't feel like you have to share anything you don't want to, okay?"

"I wouldn't want to be rude," he said, peering out the windshield at her brother Brandon, who had a beer in one hand and a blue and green foam finger that said "Seahawks Number One Fan" on the other. "They're into football, huh?"

"Yeah." Her sister Clarissa stepped out from behind

Brandon in her favorite player's jersey and a Seahawks logo temporary tattoo displayed on one cheek. "It's a tradition around here. Do you watch?"

"Not really." Max frowned and sank back in his seat. "Usually I'm working."

"Oh. Well…" She grabbed her purse. "At least I got you out of the suite today. And my mom's food is excellent. Maybe you guys can swap recipes."

"Maybe." His eyes widened slightly.

She checked her makeup in the mirror then pulled out a tube of lip balm to slick some on. "I'm sure you'll be fine." She tossed her lip balm back in her bag then zipped it up. "Ready?"

"Ready."

Ayanna gripped the handles of her purse tightly, more on edge than she cared to admit. She was probably overreacting and her family might very well ignore Max after the introductions were made, but after the whole debacle with Will and the endless litanies of *I told you so* from her siblings, followed by them gathering the wagons around her in support, she wasn't sure, especially since he was the first man she'd brought home since the breakup, date or not.

Besides, she liked Max, more than she had liked anyone in a while. After getting past their initial rocky start and moving into the suite with him, they'd actually discovered they had a lot in common. Both of them were hard workers, both of them loved to watch science documentaries on TV and both of them thought avocados were icky. She didn't want him to feel uncomfortable or out of place today.

Honestly, it had been a long time since she'd found

someone she clicked so well with personality-wise in such a short time. Not even Will had meshed into her life so well, especially after he'd started taking her for granted then nitpicking every little thing she did. It would've been almost scary how much she synched with Max Granger if it wasn't for the fact all this was only temporary. As long as she remembered he'd be gone after the King's case was done, she was fine. She flashed him what she hoped was a confident smile. "Okay. Let's get inside before they come over here and drag us out."

He exhaled hard through his nose then turned away to stare out the window beside him, his dark brows drawing together, looking as anxious as she felt. Poor guy. "Okay. I haven't spent time with a family on Thanksgiving since my wife was around."

This time she couldn't resist touching him. His hand felt warm and soft beneath hers. "Losing someone you care for is terrible, and especially hard around this time of year. But I'm glad you're here."

Their gazes locked and the moment stretched tautly between them. Finally, Max gave a small nod, his broad shoulders relaxing beneath the navy-blue sweater he'd worn over a black T-shirt and jeans. He frowned down at her hand covering his. "Is it just the breakup that's making you nervous today?"

"It's just hard, being here. My mom depends on me more than my siblings and I feel like I need to take care of everyone, make sure they're comfortable and happy before I can enjoy myself. Guess it's a holdover from when I used to babysit them when we were younger," she said, sitting back in her own seat to stare out the windshield as truth swelled inside her.

"Don't get me wrong. I love my family. It would just be nice to not have to worry about everyone else all the time." She darted a quick look at him, realizing how that must sound. "Not that I'm complaining. I love my family. I just... I don't know." She shook her head and gave a small shrug. "Anyway, enough about that. My dad's a retired high school history teacher. He'll talk your ear off with long stories about the civil war and the Praetorian Guard, his two favorite subjects. And my mom's a retired ER nurse who's seen and done it all. There isn't a boundary she's afraid to cross when it comes to finding out what she wants to know.

"Then there's James. His partner David is in tech, but he won't be here today. And my other brother Brandon." She pointed out the window at them all, still standing on the porch. "And my sisters Tonya, LaTasha and Clarissa. We're all pretty close." She finally stopped babbling and just sat there.

Max seemed to take that in for a moment. "I guess the holidays aren't easy for you either, huh?"

"Nope." She laughed, the sound forced and brittle. "It's all fine, though."

"Hmm." Max gave her fingers a gentle squeeze and damn if those nerve endings of hers didn't sizzle again, despite her wishes. Her breath caught and her mouth dried. If he noticed the same rush, he didn't show it. Max just smiled, small and sweet. "Well, in case I forget to say it later, thank you for inviting me. I look forward to meeting Clan Franklin."

She met his eyes again and their gazes snagged, held, the space between them crackling with possibilities.

Ayanna wasn't sure which of them leaned closer first, but then Max licked his lips and she tracked the tiny movement, imagining how his mouth might feel, how his tongue might lick her in all the right spots, how…

Knock, knock, knock.

Startled, Ayanna spun to see Brandon's face pressed to the driver's side window. Dazed, she pressed the button to lower it, hoping her face didn't look as hot as it felt. Thankfully, her brother didn't mention it.

"You guys gonna sit out here all day or come inside?" He raised a brow at her, then glanced at Max as if sizing him up. "Mom said she needs help in the kitchen."

"Right," Ayanna said, the word emerging breathier than she intended. Duty called. As always. She waited until her brother went back inside before closing the window then hazarding a glance over at Max, who'd remained silent. "Are we doing this?"

Tiny patches of crimson dotted his high cheekbones and his Adam's apple bobbed as he swallowed. "Yep. Let's do it."

Max entered the house already feeling off-kilter after their almost-kiss in the car. Now, confronted with hugs and kisses and questions from people he barely knew, to say he was overwhelmed was the understatement of the century.

Still, it wasn't as unpleasant as he'd expected, even when Ayanna disappeared into the kitchen with her mother, presumably to help with dinner and probably talk about him. In fact, as they all gathered around a huge dining room table laden with every kind of food imaginable, from roast turkey and dressing to three kinds of potatoes—mashed, sweet, and baked—along with corn, carrots, green bean casserole, collard greens, fried okra, and a large crockpot full of homemade macaroni and cheese, Max felt something he hadn't felt in a long time. Included. Which was crazy, since he'd just met these people, but there it was. Everything was delicious too, just like Ayanna had promised. He made a mental note to ask her mother for several recipes before they left.

"So, a neurosurgeon, eh?" Ayanna's father said from where he sat at the end of the long dining table. "Ever work with war veterans? There's a lot of documentation about head injuries during the civil war."

"Dad!" Ayanna said from beside Max, placing her hand on his forearm. The warmth of her touch felt much nicer than he cared to admit. "Please, he just got here. Plus, this is his day off. I'm sure Max doesn't want to talk about work stuff today."

"It's fine," Max said, swallowing another bit of succulent turkey and dressing. Growing up, his nannies had always had holiday dinners delivered from a local restaurant. The food had been fine, but nothing like all this homemade fare. His mother had never cooked. She'd been too busy traveling or working out the specifics of a new procedure.

He'd already cleared one plate of food and gone back for second helpings of everything, not missing the way Ayanna's mother kept a watchful eye on him, her smile widening the more he ate. He finished dishing up more mac and cheese and candied sweet potatoes, then took a swig of water. Ayanna didn't know it, but he was a bit of a civil war buff himself. "I did know, Mr. Franklin. In fact, my paper for one of my classes in med school was on battlefield treatments of closed head injuries during that time period."

"Interesting!" Her father smiled beneath his white mustache. The knot of tension between Max's shoulder blades eased a tad. "We'll talk after dinner then, son. And, please, call me Harry."

Max felt like he'd just won a huge prize, though he couldn't say exactly why. After all, this was just one meal, one day. He probably wouldn't see these people again after he left Seattle. Still, the thought of being accepted by Ayanna's family banished his shadows for a while.

"Thank you, Harry," Max said, then turned to Ayanna's mother. "And thank you, Mrs. Franklin, for having me today. Everything is delicious and your home is beautiful. I like to cook a fair bit myself. Perhaps we can talk food later, if you don't mind."

"My, my. Gotta love a man who's confident in the kitchen." The older woman beamed then gave her oldest daughter a pointed look. Max could certainly see where Ayanna got her beauty from. Their smiles were so similar it caused Max's chest to tighten. "And thank you for the compliments. Please, call me Narissa. We can absolutely talk turkey today. And you're always welcome in our home, Max. Any friend of my daughter's is a friend of ours too." Max didn't miss the unspoken hint of warning in her tone, though.

Unless you hurt Ayanna, then all bets are off.

He thought about her ex's actions and his dislike for

the man grew, even though they'd never met. He and Ayanna were still getting to know each other, but from what Max had seen so far she was a wonderful woman. Smart, funny, hard-working, loyal. Her ex must've been an idiot to take her for granted then run out on her the way he had.

"Maybe after dinner Ayanna can give you a full tour of the place," Narissa said, breaking Max out of his thoughts. Then she reached over and took her husband's hand, the affection between them clear. "Harry and I built this place when Ayanna was just a baby. Back then real estate prices around here were more reasonable. We were lucky to get in before the big housing boom in Seattle, when we could still afford this land on a nurse's and teacher's salaries."

"Dude," Brandon said to Max from across the table, cutting his mom off. "Can you take a look at my shoulder later? I pulled something shooting hoops last month and my hand keeps tingling at night when I'm trying to sleep."

"Seriously, Bran?" Ayanna tossed her napkin on the table, giving her brother a look. "Which part of he's not working today did you not understand?"

Max stifled a laugh and stared down at his food. Ayanna was cute when she was feisty, which was basically all the time.

Wait. What?

The thought stopped him short. He had no business thinking of Ayanna like that, especially now that they were sharing the suite. Yes, they'd spent more time together since Sunday and he knew more about her—like how she liked her eggs and what perfume she wore and how she had to have socks on at night in order to sleep. That wasn't an invitation to cross an invisible line from friendship to something more. In fact, if anything, that moment in the car earlier when they'd almost kissed should've sent him fleeing far and fast in the opposite direction. He didn't want to get involved romantically ever again. Didn't want to open himself up to that kind of vulnerability and pain. He was perfectly happy in his self-imposed workaholic isolation.

Aren't I?

He certainly had been when he'd arrived here in Seattle. Now, though, sitting in a raucous dining room filled with family and laughter and food, he wasn't so sure. Brandon was still looking at him expectantly from across the table and Max nodded. "Sure, I can take a look at your shoulder. My specialty is the brain, but the nervous system is the nervous system."

Max felt Ayanna's stare tingling on his skin so he focused on finishing the last of his mashed potatoes and gravy instead of looking at her for fear she might see the conflicting emotions in his eyes—joy, fear, hope, hesitation. Luckily, the conversation picked up again and continued around him as he finished his food then pushed away his empty plate. Stomach full and suddenly feeling in need of a nap, he took a deep breath then sat back, careful to keep his arms close to his sides to avoid brushing against Ayanna again. For some reason, he was having even more trouble battling his deepening attraction to her. He didn't want to deal with that right now, though, just wanted to enjoy what was left of today.

"All right, then," Narissa said, standing to begin

clearing away the dishes. "Kids, help your mama clear this table, then we've got pumpkin pie for dessert." Ayanna started to get up, along with her siblings, but her mother stopped her. "Not you, Ayanna. You take your Max and show him the rest of Casa Franklin."

"He's not my Max, Mom," Ayanna said, giving him an apologetic side glance. "I told you we're just working together while he's in town. Are you sure you don't want my help? I'm usually your go-to gal."

"You usually don't have a guest with you either, honey," Narissa said, shaking her head. "I know you like to take care of everyone else, but let us take care of you today, okay? Now, go show Max around our house." She stopped in the hallway through the doorway into the kitchen, arms laden with dirty dishes, and glanced back at Ayanna with a stern look. "And don't get any ideas about rushing through things to hurry back down here to take over. We will survive without you, honey. I don't want to see either of you in my kitchen until it's time for pie. Go on. The rest of you, dish duty. Now."

Her siblings whined and grumbled, but not one of them refused their momma. They all knew better.

Max pushed to his feet beside Ayanna, taking in her somewhat shocked expression. "Sounds like she means business."

"I guess she does." Ayanna moved out behind her chair then pushed it in before gesturing for him to proceed her out of the open dining room. "After you."

"You looked surprised she's letting you out of dish duty," he joked as they headed back toward the front of the house.

"I am," Ayanna said, giving him a half-grin. "It's

like winning the lottery or something. You must be good luck."

Warmth spread from his core to his extremities and he found himself grinning along with her. "Well, I don't know about that, but I'll take it."

They started back at the foyer, with its pickled pine floors and high cathedral ceiling. A staircase sat back against the far wall and above a loft overlooked the whole area. The house overall was bright and open and inviting and reminded Max of the home he and Laura had bought in Jericho, Long Island, when he'd been working regularly out of Manhattan. It had been a craftsmen-style too, though not nearly as large as this home. Then again, it had just been the two of them.

"See that loft up there?" Ayanna pointed to the second floor. "James and Brandon jumped off there one time after seeing *Iron Man*. Good thing they dragged the couch cushions out here first to break their fall. I thought Mom was going to kill them herself after that."

"I bet," Max said, following her into the living room to stand before said couch. This room too was light and airy, decorated in shades of light grays and blues. One wall was taken up by windows and the other held a large flat-screen TV. Recessed lighting in the ceiling, along with speakers and deep, overstuffed furniture marked this as a home theater as well as a place for guests to gather. Next they visited a small office that belonged to her father before heading upstairs to the loft.

From up here the noise and laughter of her family were muted, and it seemed like they were in their own tiny world. Ayanna looked over the railing then turned to him. "Did you enjoy dinner?"

"I did. I like your family." He was surprised to find he meant it. Honestly, today was the first time in recent memory that he'd been able to just relax. Being here with Ayanna and her family had been nice and comfortable, and for that he was grateful. "Today's been kind of wonderful, actually."

"Yeah?" She smiled back at him and tilted her head. His heart tripped. They stared at each other for a moment and the same invisible cord that had connected them in the car returned, drawing them closer, closer, until Ayanna cleared her throat and moved away to continue the tour, saying under her breath, "That's enough of that."

She showed him the master bedroom and bath, a small library with a reading nook, and a guest bath followed by several smaller bedrooms, pointing out which had belonged to her siblings, before stopping at one room in the corner. "And this used to be my old bedroom."

He stepped inside, taking in the pastel purple walls and shiny wood floors, the twin bed and the picture hanging above it with a quote in white, "I love you, a bushel and a peck."

"Yeah." Ayanna snorted. "My mom bought it at a flea market. She used to sing me that song when I was little."

Max frowned. "Uh, don't think I've heard that one."

"Really?" She started to sing. At his befuddled look, she laughed. "Well, anyway, it was her favorite song to sing at night when I couldn't sleep. So when she found this at the flea market, she had to have it."

"That's sweet." He studied some framed photos on the wall showing Ayanna when she'd been younger. Still cute. There was one of her in a cheerleading uniform and one in a ballet tutu. Another of her and a group of other little girls selling cookies. A bittersweet pang stabbed between his ribs. "Looks like you were involved in a lot of activities growing up. The only thing my parents allowed me to participate in were academic clubs. Science, math, things like that. And even then it was the nannies who shuttled me around."

"Nannies?" Ayanna frowned. "You must've been super rich growing up."

"No." Max turned away, shame and defensiveness searing his throat. "My parents were always working and couldn't be home with me, so they hired people. Good thing they only had one child to deal with."

Ayanna walked over and placed her hand on his arm again, the heat of her touch soothing. "That must've been really lonely for you. I'm sorry."

"It was fine." He shifted away, resisting the urge to take her hand again. "They weren't bad parents, just busy. And I never lacked for anything."

"Except love," she whispered, shaking her head. "And connection."

Max took a deep breath then forced a smile, eager to get out of this room that seemed smaller and hotter all of a sudden. "It's in the past. Where to next?"

"That's basically it, I'm afraid." They went back out to the loft and sat on the loveseat against the wall. It was cozy nook, far enough back from the railing that it couldn't be seen from below. Ayanna toed off her shoes and tucked one stockinged foot beneath her, resting her elbow against the back cushion to face him. "There's a deck out back, but since it's raining now, we should probably wait on that."

"Agreed." He stifled a yawn. Between all the food he'd eaten and the ease of being around Ayanna and her family today, he felt sleepy. After pushing himself non-stop for the past two years since his wife's death, it was a welcome, unexpected relief. "Thank you for the tour."

"Thank you for coming." She'd gone with jeans and a sweater, the same as him, though hers was a light pink color and fuzzy. He wondered if it felt as soft as it looked and damn if that didn't set the blood singing in his veins again. Guard down and unable to resist, he reached over and took her hand, the way he'd been wanting to for what felt like forever. Her dark eyes widened and her lips parted slightly as he leaned in once more until her warm breath fanned his face. Max wasn't sure what he was doing, only that it felt necessary, like if he didn't kiss her right then, he'd be missing out on something precious. All the guilt, all the anger, all the darkness that had haunted him disappeared in that moment until there was only now, only them, only this kiss.

He half expected her to pull away again, but this time she didn't. Time seemed to slow. Then his lips brushed hers and the rest of the world fell away. Her breath caught and he pulled back. A dull voice in the back of his head warned him to be careful, to slow down, this was all too much too soon. But then Max saw those soft lips of hers parted and ready and he was lost.

His mouth brushed hers again and Ayanna groaned low in her throat. Her hand slid into the hair at the nape of his neck, holding him close, pulling him tighter against her as if she felt the same rush, the same urgency. She gasped and he took advantage, sweeping his tongue inside to taste her—cinnamon from the sweet potatoes and decadent temptation—and he couldn't get enough. It had been too long since he'd held someone close, since he'd felt their heart race alongside his, since he'd heard their tiny mewls of need, since…

The sound of a clearing throat had them springing apart fast.

Max sat back, blinking hard as Ayanna ran a flustered hand through her hair. She coughed and scowled over at her other brother, James. "What is it?"

"Pie's ready," he said, giving them each a coy look, smirking. "But seems like you two are already having your own special kind of dessert."

"Shut up." Ayanna stood and smoothed the front of her sweater. "Tell Mom we'll be right down."

"Oh, I'll tell her all right." He snickered then started back downstairs, pulling out his phone. "Wait until David hears about this…"

Face flushed, Ayanna turned back to Max. "Sorry. Nosy, like I told you."

"They care about you, that's all." Except as he stood and followed her back down the stairs, all he could think about was the fact that he'd just kissed Ayanna Franklin, the woman he'd sworn not to, and he couldn't quite wrap his head around it. Max wasn't impulsive. He wasn't emotional.

And yet, with Ayanna, *he was*. In fact, his heart was still racing and his lips still tingled from their encounter.

They returned to the dining room and ate pie, but Max could've been chewing plywood for all he tasted it. Each time he licked his lips he'd swear he still tasted

Ayanna, and every time her family looked at him, it seemed like they knew exactly what they'd been up to on that loveseat upstairs. Or maybe that was his own conscience. He was acting like an idiot, pure and simple. He'd gone too long denying his needs, that had to be it.

Logic ruled him most of the time and while that suited him fine, perhaps he'd gone too overboard with it and now he'd acted out because of it. Yes, that made sense. What didn't make sense, though, was the pull he felt to Ayanna even now, maybe more so since their kiss. The yearning to hold her and touch her and taste her that drowned out everything else. For a man who lived by his mind and not his emotions, it made him question everything.

The next few hours passed in a blur. Max watched sports with her family without paying much attention. Checked her brother's shoulder and advised him to see his family doctor for an X-ray and possibly PT. Then the afternoon was gone and it was time to go. He and Ayanna said their goodbyes and he got more hugs and kisses from her family, plus handwritten recipes from Narissa. By the time they were back in her SUV and heading for the hotel, his thoughts were jumbled worse than the traffic jam they ran into on the highway. The conflict inside him had reached a crescendo and he needed answers. Needed clarity. Needed to figure out a way beyond this mess and back to the logical world he loved. "Listen, about what happened in the loft—"

"Forget it, okay?" Ayanna said, not looking at him, seemingly as disturbed as he was by their kiss. "Don't mention it again. It's better that way."

Right. Good. Forget about it. That made sense. He nodded then stared out the window beside him. Forgetting it was the best possible thing they could do. The kiss had been a mistake. An aberration. They should both move on and never look back again.

But as they drove through downtown Seattle, all Max could seem to think about now was Ayanna, for better or worse.

CHAPTER EIGHT

"NO, I'M SORRY. We have no information to report about the accident victims from last week," Ayanna said to the reporter on the other end of the line. She'd been fielding calls, along with her staff, for most of the day and yet they still kept coming in. "Yes, that's an official statement. Thank you."

She hung up then covered her face with her hands. It was nearly four o'clock and she'd gotten almost nothing accomplished on her to-do list for the ball. Then again, her lack of productivity could also have had something to do with the fact she'd slept like crap the night before. Tossing and turning and replaying that stupid kiss with Max over and over in her head.

Why exactly she'd let him kiss her, Ayanna wasn't sure. But she was certain it wouldn't be happening again. For one, getting involved with him was one more complication she did not need right now. Sure, Max was wonderful. Yes, her family had taken to him like a polar bear to snow. In fact, they'd been blowing up her cellphone with texts all day. But neither of those things were good reasons to go all gaga over the guy.

Right?

She put her head down atop her arms on her desk. If only she could rely on what her instincts were telling her—that Max wasn't like Will, that he appreciated her, that he understood her in a way Will never had—but she couldn't. Even now, months after the breakup, her ability to trust herself was still shredded. Shredded by the hurt. The embarrassment. The stupidity of not knowing what she should've seen right in front of her face.

Ayanna groaned and squeezed her eyes shut. No. She couldn't go through that again. Will's betrayal had made her doubt herself. Doubt her instincts about people. And if she couldn't trust herself to make good choices about who to let into her life, who's to say letting Max in wouldn't be a mistake too?

Her head hurt and her heart ached. Not that she needed to worry about things going too far with Max because they'd both agreed to forget all about that kiss last night. It was over. Done.

Except each time she closed her eyes, images of them on the loveseat had filled her head.

She sat back and sighed. This was what her life had become these days. Stolen kisses and forbidden fumbles. The fact she knew Max was just down the hall from her in his office hadn't helped either.

A knock sounded on the door and she straightened, smoothing her hair before calling, "Come in."

"Hey." The man in question stuck his head into her office, setting her traitorous pulse fluttering again. "Are we still leaving at five?"

"Uh…" At the sight of him, her usual gift of the gab went right out the window. Man, she was in serious trouble here. To distract herself, she frowned down at her phone instead of drooling over him, and pulled up the calendar, only to wince. "Oops. Can we do four-thirty instead? I need to make a stop for the ball planning on the way to the hotel, if you don't mind."

Max pulled out his own phone to check, the overhead lights revealing dark shadows beneath his eyes, suggesting maybe she hadn't been the only one with kiss-induced insomnia last night. The thought made her feel slightly better, for reasons she didn't want to analyze. "Um, yeah. Four-thirty should be doable for me. I've got documentation and follow-ups to get done on a couple of cases, then I should be able to leave early. I'll come back here when I'm ready."

"Sounds good." He left and she released her pent-up breath. Things between them had seemed normal just then. Maybe too normal. Or maybe she was reading too much into this because that's what she did. Overanalyzed everything to try and stay two steps ahead of everyone else. Anticipating their wants and needs. Putting those possible outcomes before her own agenda. And…

Oh, God. She covered her face again. Max was right. She did try to fix everything. She was all for self-actualization but, man, couldn't a girl catch a break for once? She frowned at the Charlie Brown Christmas tree on her desk, its one red ornament drooping, just like her mood. Even her family had seemed to treat her differently when Max was around, not expecting her to take care of all their problems for once, just letting her enjoy her day. It had been weird and wonderful and completely discombobulating.

Tired and irritable, she did her best to get back to work on the menus for the ball. The errand she'd mentioned to Max involved the dessert. Considering he was a self-proclaimed foodie, she thought she might as well put his skills to the test by picking out the dessert for the ball. Now, if she could just make up her mind on the rest of the food, she'd be all set. They were down to the wire, with less than two weeks left until the fundraiser, and if she didn't finalize the catering menu soon, they'd end up having cheese and crackers from the local grocery store. Not exactly a good way to impress her new bosses or the donors.

The next thirty minutes dragged by in another tangle of phone calls and budgets and descriptions of gourmet dishes that either sounded way too fancy or way too expensive for what she needed. One of the keys to a successful event was giving people the same, but different. Whacky designer dishes might seem like a great idea on paper, but if no one knew what they were eating, it wouldn't go down well—literally or figuratively. Finally, she'd narrowed the choices down to a few items and made notes to request them from the kitchens at the Polar Club to sample before placing her final order. Maybe Max could help her with those as well.

And speaking of Max, he tapped on her door at that moment to let her know he was ready.

Perfect.

She gathered her bag and phone then shut down her computer and said goodbye to her staff before heading out of her office to meet Max in the hall by the elevators.

He'd changed out of scrubs into khakis and a soft-looking black turtleneck. Her fingertips itched with a weird urge to stroke his chest and see if he felt as solid and warm as she remembered from the day before. Ayanna stopped herself clenching the handles of her brown leather satchel and stared straight ahead at the elevator doors.

Get a grip, girl.

The elevator dinged and he held the door for her to board first. As she passed him, Ayanna caught a hint of sandalwood and cedar soap on his skin. And just like that all her good intentions fell by the wayside. Goosebumps of awareness rose on her arms and the backs of her knees buzzed with adrenaline. Memories of his mouth on hers, the sweep of his tongue, the flavor of salt and sweetness in his kisses swamped her.

Oh, boy. This was bad. So, so bad. What if she'd read it all wrong? What if Max wasn't the good guy she thought he was? What if he couldn't be trusted, just like Will? What if…?

"Where are we going?" Max asked, his words jarring her out of her downward spiral. "On that ball-related errand you mentioned."

"Oh." She gathered her red trench coat closer around her like a shield. "A local bakery. I thought you could help me choose the dessert for the evening." At his surprised look, she smiled. "What? You said you wanted to help, and I could use a second set of taste buds to make sure I'm picking out the right one."

"Okay."

"And don't worry about cooking dinner tonight. I'll order in samples of the dinner menu selections for us to try."

"Sounds good." Max gave a curt nod. "It's been quite a day and cake makes everything better."

"Amen to that," she said, then stopped herself. "Sorry. Nothing new with the King, I hope?"

"No. His condition is still the same." He didn't elaborate and that was good. HIPAA laws were there for a reason, namely to protect patient privacy. "Just hectic."

The elevator dinged and the doors slid open on the first floor. They walked outside and across the street to her car. Max got in and buckled his seatbelt while Ayanna climbed in behind the wheel and tossed her bag on the backseat.

"Is this the same place I went to the other day for lunch?" Max asked. "The Thunderbird Café?"

"No. Different place. This one specializes in cakes and they do some really innovative things with flavor profiles, so I'm excited to check it out. They were rated as the top bakery in Seattle by one of the local food magazines too. Figured having them do our desserts for the gala might score me some bonus points with the big money donors."

"Good thinking." Max grinned then faced front again, yawning. "Man, I'm beat."

"Me too," she said, as they headed through the streets of Seattle toward Seahawk Sweets and Confections, glad the awkwardness had abated for the time being. They chatted about nothing in particular. He told her about a couple of consults he'd done in the ER—a car accident victim and a schoolteacher who'd collapsed at work—and they both steered clear of the subject of their kiss the previous evening, thank goodness.

Finally, they arrived at the bakery and she pulled

into a spot alongside the brick building on Carlton Avenue then cut the engine. Ayanna checked her watch and grabbed her purse, feeling like she'd dodged a bullet. "Here we are. Let's get inside before we're late."

"First we have our peach bourbon cake," the owner, a woman in her mid-thirties with glasses and a thunderbird tattoo on her arm, said half an hour later. "It's made with a ricotta olive oil cake and a bourbon soak. The filling is dark salted caramel and peach, topped with cream cheese frosting."

Max took a bite of his small slice and thought he'd died and gone to heaven. Sweet and boozy with just a hint of salt from the filling. He glanced over at Ayanna beside him for her reaction then and oops. Big mistake. He'd been doing so well too, avoiding thinking about her lips and all. But one look at her, her eyes closed and head tipped back in ecstasy, and boom. His blood pumped and his heart galloped like a racehorse at the Derby. He wiped his damp palms on the legs of his pants and did his best to ignore her throaty little moan.

No. No, no, no.

This wasn't him. He wasn't ruled by his emotions. He didn't lead with his heart.

Mind out of the gutter, head in the game. He was here to help Ayanna pick a cake for the ball. That was all. Now, if someone could just convey that message to his tightening body, he'd be all set.

Thankfully, Ayanna didn't seem notice his raging response. "What do you think?"

I think I'd like to continue where we left off last night with that kiss...

Dammit. He bit back the words, coughing then sipping water from the plastic cup the owner had set in front of each of them to cover it. "This one's marvelous," he said, his words gruffer than normal from the testosterone tearing through his body. He cleared his throat and tried again. "But we should try them all first before deciding."

"Agreed."

The owner took their plates away to replace them with new slices of cake. This new one had dark chocolate frosting and a slight hint of pine. Intrigued, Max took a bite, glad for a distraction from the adorable way Ayanna was tilting her head as she concentrated. It was one of things he loved about her.

Love?

His thoughts screeched to a halt while Ayanna asked the owner, "And what's this one?"

"This is our PNW chocolate. Dark chocolate cake infused with pine oil and porter beer then covered with a semi-sweet chocolate ganache also flavored with pine."

Max only half heard that, his mind still churning over the fact he'd used the L-word, even casually, where Ayanna was concerned. He liked her, yes, way more than he probably should, but he had no business going further than that. They were friends. Nothing more.

Friends who kissed.

He scowled and chewed his bite of cake and did his best to concentrate on the unique flavor profile instead of his memories of how Ayanna had tasted—like cinnamon and spice and everything nice. Frowning, he focused his attention on his taste buds. There was a slight bitterness to this cake, offset by the sweeter ganache frosting. The addition of pine and porter balanced all the flavors out with a brightness he'd never thought possible. He dug it. Based on Ayanna's reaction, however, she didn't.

"Gotta say it's not my favorite." She pushed her plate away without another bite. "I love chocolate, but the pine reminds me too much of my mom's floor cleaner. Sorry."

"Not at all." The owner laughed. "It's an acquired taste. Let's move on to the last one, shall we?" She placed a new small slice in front of each of them, this one with a dark gray marbled frosting. "We call this one London Fog. Earl Grey tea infused cake soaked in honey and Earl Grey syrup, bergamot mascarpone cream filling and topped with cream cheese frosting. It's our newest creation and the one I'm most proud of."

Ayanna took a bite and her dark eyes widened. She quickly gobbled down a second and third bite. "Wow. I love this one."

Max had to agree. The hint of tea flavor wasn't overpowering, as he'd feared. Instead, the bergamot and mascarpone cream filling balanced it out to perfection. The addition of the slight tang from the cream cheese frosting was a great finish to a glorious cake. He polished off his slice too. "I vote this one."

"I think we have a winner." Ayanna grinned. "Our ball is on the evening of December twelfth at the Polar Club. We'll need to have enough to serve two hundred. Is that possible?"

The owner opened a binder and leafed through a few pages. "Yes. We should be able to accommodate that, though you just made it in under the wire."

"Should you consider doing half and half?" Max asked, pointing to one of the vegan cakes they'd sampled earlier. "Just in case some donors have food allergies or dietary preferences."

"Oh, good idea." Ayanna nodded. "Sorry. I've had so much on my mind I didn't think of that. Yes. Can I change the order to half London Fog cake and half the vegan option, please? Honestly, that vegan cake is so tasty, I didn't even miss the eggs and butter."

"Sure." The owner made a few more notes then wrote up the paperwork. "Anything else? If you change your mind after tonight, there's a fifteen percent surcharge."

"Nope. We're good." Ayanna signed off and handed the woman her corporate credit card.

Once that was done, they went back outside. Dusk had settled in and the streetlights gave an orange glow as they returned to her vehicle. Ayanna got in then started the car before looking over at him as he buckled his seatbelt. "Thanks for your help in there."

"No problem." He chuckled. "I mean, eating gourmet cake is a hardship, but I'm willing to suffer."

"Right." Her smile beamed through the darkness, and that darned connection, the one he'd tried so hard to avoid, tugged a little tighter in his gut. "And good catch on the vegan thing," Ayanna said. "It could've cost me a lot more tomorrow to change the order."

"No problem," he said, resisting the urge to brush back the curls that had fallen across her cheek. "Guess we make a pretty good team, huh?"

"Yes, we do." She swallowed hard, heat flickering through her gaze, so fast he would've missed it if he hadn't been concentrating on her so intently. Her breath hitched and his pulse stumbled. Then Ayanna faced front again, signaling then pulling out of their parking spot to merge into traffic. "Now on to those dinner samples at the hotel."

"Yep." Max watched the passing scenery, knowing avoidance when he saw it. Seemed they were both becoming experts in it these days.

CHAPTER NINE

"TODD, CAN YOU hand me another ornament, please?"
Ayanna said from the top of a ladder in the hospital's
glass-walled atrium. Beside her was a towering artifi-
cial spruce. It was a yearly tradition here at Seattle General now that December first had arrived, though the
addition of the handmade ornaments from childhood
cancer patients around the country was new, as were
the gifts being left beneath the tree by staff to give to
be distributed in the children's wards.

Both ideas had been Ayanna's, to help boost the hospital's standing as one of the city's top philanthropic
organizations. So far, the tree and the gifts were prov-
ing immensely popular, with many people stopping to
take photos, even though the final decorations were
only now being put up. "How about one from Indiana?
I don't think that state's represented here yet."

"Uh, will Ohio do?" a familiar male voice said from
below, and Ayanna froze. She glanced down to see Max
holding up a brightly painted glass globe with the name
"Justin" scrawled in red and green across the middle
with rainbow glitter around the edges. Each child was

encouraged to make the ornament their own. "It looks like it would fit the space you're filling."

"It does. Thanks. What are you doing here?" she asked, taking it from him to hang on the branch she'd chosen. He was right. It fit perfectly. Ayanna climbed down and matched his grin with one of her own. "No patients this afternoon?"

"Finished my rounds early." He took her arm to steady her as she slipped her shoes back on then walked across the atrium with her to see how the trees looked from a distance. "A day without many neurological emergencies is both rare and much appreciated."

"I bet." She squinted at the tree, searching for any bare spots or clumps of decorations. The silver and gold garlands caught the sunlight filtering in through the glass atrium above and twinkled nearly as brightly as the white fairy lights strung through the branches. People riding up and down the escalators behind the tree seemed appropriately awed, she noted. However, there was one area where the décor wasn't quite balanced.

Ayanna held up a finger to stop Max's continued explanation about his day, then called across the space, "Hey, Todd? Can you please spread out those ornaments a bit more so they're evenly spaced? No. Not there. A bit more to the left and up about three branches. Yes! Good. Thanks."

Satisfied, she turned back to Max. "Are you ready to go now? I've got some time yet until things are done here in the lobby. We still need to hang the mistletoe and add lights and garland to the rest of the room." She narrowed her gaze on him. "Don't suppose you'd want to help, would you?"

"Eh, I don't want to get in the way," Max said. "I'm sure I can find something to occupy my time until you're ready to leave."

Ayanna opened her mouth to tell him he wouldn't be in the way at all but was cut off by the sound of shattering glass. Her attention snapped back to the tree again, where Todd gave her a sheepish look.

"Sorry, boss," he said. "At least it wasn't one of the handmade ones. Just a glass icicle from the store."

"Be careful," Ayanna called back, shaking her head before looking at Max once more.

He was still scowling at Todd and the tree. "He's doing that wrong."

"Huh?" She scrunched her nose and glanced back at her staffer. "How can you hang ornaments wrong?"

"There's a proper way to loop the wires around the branches for maximum support and safety. Plus, the ratios are all wrong."

"Ratios? Seriously?" Ayanna raised a brow. "Not to sound clichéd, but this isn't brain surgery, Max."

"Funny." He rolled his eyes then placed his hands on her shoulders to turn her around to face the tree again, keeping her directly in front of him. Warmth from his touch penetrated her black blazer, making her knees wobble and her blood sizzle. Part of her brain told Ayanna to step away from temptation, but damn if she could get her feet to move. Max reached past her to point at where Todd was working. His forearm brushed her ear and her core gave a tiny squeeze of want before she could stop it.

"Squint. See how the sizes are too similar on the right-hand side and the colors are all the same in that area, making the composition unbalanced? Mixing them up helps the overall design and keeps it looking fresh."

Ayanna opened her mouth to make another snarky comment but, man. He was right again. "For a guy who hates Christmas, you sure seem to know a lot about it. Your wife must've trained you well."

The minute the words were out, she wished she could take them back. What a stupid, insensitive thing for her to say, knowing what he'd been through, losing his wife. She was the gal who always knew the right words to say, but with Max they always seemed to come out wrong. He stepped away and she missed the heat of him immediately. Ayanna looked back over her shoulder. "I'm sorry. I didn't mean to—"

"No. It's fine." His remote expression said otherwise. "I'm going to go back up to my office to finish a few things. I'll meet you by the elevators at six as planned."

Ayanna watched him walk away, the attraction inside her quickly shifting to a need to atone. Dammit. Things between them had finally settled back into a nice, normal rhythm after their mistaken kiss and then she had to go and ruin things by blurting out what she had.

And, sure, maybe she still couldn't seem to forget about what had happened in her parents' loft and move on, but that was her problem, not his. She liked Max. Way more than she should, but again it was her issue to deal with. She liked talking with him, spending time with him, having him help her with the ball prep. He'd been way more assistance than she'd ever thought possible and she didn't like to see him unhappy, especially because of her.

She wanted him to smile. Wanted to see him relaxed and joyful. Not because she was coming to care for him in ways that had nothing to do with friendship. She was fixer, that was all. And being around him so much brought out her caretaker side.

And maybe if you tell yourself that enough times it'll make it true.

Sighing, she went over to help Todd redistribute the decorations based on Max's advice.

Two hours later, the tree and the rest of the lobby looked amazing and Ayanna felt worse than ever about her flippant comment to Max. She wanted to do something to make it up to him but wasn't sure what. She couldn't cook. That was Max's area. Obviously design wasn't her forte either, since he'd just bested her there too. By the time she made it back to her office, Ayanna began to wonder if there was anything Max Granger wasn't good at. Then Wham's "Last Christmas" came on the overhead sound system and a deep, off-key male voice bellowed down the hall from the direction of his office and... *Whoa!* Yeah. That was awful. Like am angry cat caught in a shower drain. Ayanna cringed on Max's behalf.

Ding! Ding! Ding! We have a winner. The man couldn't carry a tune to save his life.

She stood in the empty hall and stifled her laugh while her ears rang from his sour notes. Good thing the rest of the staff on the floor had cleared out earlier. It was after six, so she and staff from Housekeeping were the only ones there. Finally, the last chorus died away, and Ayanna couldn't resist teasing him any longer. Moving silently down the hall, she pushed open his office door then leaned her shoulder against the wall. "Wow. That was... Wow. Words can't accurately describe what I just heard."

"What?" He swiveled fast in his chair to face her, tiny splotches of crimson dotting his cheekbones. "Uh, sorry. I didn't know you were back. I don't usually sing in front of other people."

"Thank you, Lord." They both cracked up, laughing for a moment before Ayanna set aside the box of leftover decorations she'd carried back with her from the lobby. "I get it, though. I love Wham too."

He bit his lips then shook his head, losing the battle as another bark of laughter escaped him. "You caught me. I guess maybe I don't *entirely* hate Christmas after all. Just parts of it." He shrugged. "Does that make sense?"

"Sure. I mean, I still can't stand the sight of all those bridal shows and spring wedding commercials on TV."

Max winced. "Yeah. I can't imagine."

Ayanna took a deep breath to ward off the usual knot of anger and betrayal that tightened her chest whenever she thought of Will, but for some reason it didn't come. Instead, she just felt hollow. Like her hurt had burned away a hole that was waiting to be refilled. "Listen, I'm sorry again about what I said downstairs."

"Don't worry about it. Really." He ran a hand through his hair, leaving the dark, thick strands spiked atop his head. He looked messy and completely adorable. A tiny quiver of need vibrated through her like a tuning fork and... Uh-oh. Yeah. Whether she wanted to admit it or not, her feelings for Max Granger had gone way past like and tumbled straight into lust. He stood and grabbed his jacket off the back of his chair. "I'm good."

Yes, you are. She swallowed hard and turned away from the sight of his muscles rippling as he tugged on his coat. "Let me just grab my stuff and we can leave."

Ayanna made a hasty retreat and didn't breathe again until she was alone in her office. Oh, boy. She didn't want to want Max that way. What if he turned out to be a player? The last thing she wanted was to trust the wrong man again and have her heart broken again. Except her heart wasn't on the line this time.

Wasn't it?

"Ready when you are," Max said from her office door, jolting her out of her thoughts.

"Great," Ayanna said with a burst of fake cheerfulness. She pulled on her coat and grabbed her purse, making sure she had her phone before heading back downstairs with him to the parking lot. "Uh, thanks again for your advice on the tree. It really did make a difference."

"You're welcome." He held the door for her in the lobby then followed Ayanna outside into the chilly, damp evening air. Even though the temperature was above freezing, the breeze blowing in off Puget Sound felt cold enough for snow. "Instead of me cooking tonight, want to stop on the way back to the hotel and pick up some dinner? My treat."

"Oh, I'm not very hungry," she said, the lights of her vehicle blinking as she unlocked the doors using her key fob. Not a lie. Her gut was churning from the unexpected realization that she wanted Max as way more than just a friend. "Besides, I've, uh, got more work to do tonight, so I'll probably just heat up some soup or something later."

"Okay. But no skipping meals," he said, sliding into the seat next to her and giving her a stern look. "We talked about that. Maybe I can call down for room service. Or I think there might still be some leftovers from the menu tasting we did the other day. I know there's some butternut squash ravioli left. Maybe some Caprese salad too."

"That's fine." She could've eaten dust bunnies for all she cared at the moment. Her brain was still stuck on the fact that somehow Max had slipped beneath her defenses and now there didn't seem to be anything she could do about it. She started the car then pulled out of the lot. "I don't need much. Whatever makes you happy."

His expression turned thoughtful as Max stared out the window beside him while she drove. "What makes you happy, Ayanna?"

"Huh?" She looked over at him, her heart in her throat. She felt vulnerable enough where he was concerned without getting into this at the moment. "I'm happy."

"Are you?" His gaze shifted back to her, those gray-green eyes of his far too perceptive for her comfort. "I know it's probably none of my business, but in the short time I've known you, you always seem far more concerned about making other people comfortable than you do about yourself."

She jammed on her turn signal, not looking at him. "Catering to other people's needs is my job."

"Hmm." He exhaled slowly as a few stray snowflakes began to fall and stick to the windshield. "Did you learn that growing up?"

Yes. "No." *Liar.*

Max shifted slightly to rest one elbow on the window ledge, the seatbelt stretching tautly across his broad chest. "You know, part of my job as a surgeon is to figure out why things are the way they are and the best way to correct them. Take the King's tumor. I had that model made so I could see the problem from all angles then decide on the best course of action surgically to remove it all with the least risk possible." He blinked at her. "If only all life's problems were that easy to correct."

"Brain tumors are easy?" Ayanna gave him a skeptical glance, desperately trying to change the subject away from her personal life and failing, if Max's flat stare was any indication.

He took a deep breath and faced the window beside him again, the glass fogging slightly when he exhaled. "It was my fault my wife died."

"What? No." Ayanna slowed for a red light before focusing on him again. "I don't believe that."

"It's true." Max rubbed his hand over his jaw. "She had an aneurysm. I, of all people, should've recognized the symptoms when they started and had her tested. The headaches, the stiffness in her neck, the extreme fatigue. But we were both working so much. Me with my traveling and teaching and her with her OB/GYN practice. She swore to me that it was nothing." He gave a sad snort and scrubbed his hand over his face. "I did exactly what I warn my patients not to do. I ignored the warning signs. As it was, I wasn't even there when she died. I was stuck across town in a lecture and with traffic I didn't arrive at the hospital until she'd already slipped away." He shook his head and scowled at the snow outside. "How ironic is that? The world-renowned neurosurgeon can't even save his own wife."

"Oh, Max." Ayanna reached over to take his hand, only to have the car behind her honk when the light turned green. Cursing under her breath, she accelerated through the intersection then pulled over into a nearby parking lot without paying much attention to the location. "There's no way you could've known what would happen. I'm not a medical professional, but I remember hearing stories from my mom growing up of patients with aneurysms coming into the ER. By nature, they're unpredictable. You can't feel guilty over something you can't control."

"I know that. Logically." He stared down at his hands in his lap. "But knowing it doesn't make it any easier to believe."

"I get it. I do." She put the car into park then leaned back in her seat. "I still don't trust myself after what happened with Will. Looking back, there were so many red flags that things weren't right between us. His secretiveness, the way he gaslighted me into thinking it was my fault. Even now, I can't let my instincts dictate my actions."

They sat there in silence for a while, staring out into the night, watching the snow gather on the windshield.

"We make quite a pair, don't we?" Max said at last, followed by a small, sad chuckle.

"Yeah, we do." She flipped on the wipers and the snow disappeared to reveal a Christmas tree lot across the parking area from them. Ayanna laughed. "Looks like the holidays are haunting you today."

Max grinned and shook his head. "It does, doesn't it? Maybe this is a sign I should give in to the spirit of Santa."

Ayanna looked over at him, her gaze narrowed. "Are you thinking what I'm thinking?"

"That we should decorate the suite so I can show you exactly what I mean about my superior Christmas tree composition theory?" Max gave a curt nod. "Yes. I say we do it. If you can squeeze it in around your work, that is."

She couldn't help smiling back. "With a challenge like that, how could I refuse?"

They got out and walked over to the brightly lit area. It was busy tonight, with several couples as well as a few families milling about to find "their" tree.

"How about these?" Ayanna said, appraising several small Douglas firs. "What do you think?"

Max checked them out then crossed his arms. "Too small. And the needles are dry. They'll all fall off before Christmas."

"Hmm." She bit back a grin. "Don't tell me your expertise extends to arborist as well."

"I just know my way around a spruce." He walked over to another specimen across the aisle, this one taller and plumper. "See, now this one is better. Lots of branches for ornaments, and the needles are strong and healthy. If you want a tree, this is the one to get. Should fit perfectly in that corner in the living room between the TV and the windows."

"You remind me of my dad. He used to give us lectures every year," Ayanna said, waving over one of the attendants so she could buy the tree Max had approved. "Drove my mom nuts. Him bossing her around with the lights and tinsel. Add in my brothers breaking every other ornament and my sisters fighting over who'd put the star on the top and that was pretty much every Christmas at Casa Franklin."

Max's smiled widened and Ayanna couldn't help grinning herself. So much so she didn't even notice the attendant behind her until she crashed into him. Flustered, she paid the guy then stood off to the side with Max while they ran the tree through the bundler to make it easier to load on top of the car with the bungee cords she kept in her trunk to hold cargo and boxes.

"I'll pay you for half the tree," Max said while they waited.

"Don't be ridiculous." Ayanna waved off his suggestion. "Consider this my thanks to you for helping me pick out the food for the ball. I seriously could not have gotten all that done without you."

"Fine. But since we stopped here, I insist we stop for food on the way back. And I will pay for it. We'll need fuel to get that thing decorated. Speaking of which, do we need to buy decorations too?"

"I actually have several boxes of them in storage while they're working on my apartment. We can pick them up after we get dinner." At his smug look she conceded, "What? All this activity has made me hungry."

"Whatever." Max held out his hand. "Deal?"

"Deal." They shook on it, the heat of him warming her through her red knit mitten. The attendant finished bundling up their tree and they each grabbed a side to haul it back across the lot to the car. Max had just finished fastening the last bungee cord when a shout went out from the tree lot behind them.

"Help! Someone, please help me! My husband's collapsed!"

Max sprinted across the lot with Ayanna following close on his heels. They found an older woman kneeling on the ground beside a man who'd collapsed. Max knelt and checked for a heartbeat on the man's neck. "He's not breathing and his pulse is weak. Ayanna, call 911. Ma'am, I'm a doctor. Can you tell me if your husband has a heart condition?"

"Yes," the woman said, through her sobs. "He's got stents and is on blood thinners. Please help him. I don't know what I'd do if I lost him."

"I'll do everything I can, ma'am. Promise." Max positioned the man's head properly then puffed a breath into his patient's lungs before beginning compressions. "Ayanna, ETA on that ambulance, please?"

"911 Dispatch. What's your emergency?" the operator said over the line, and Ayanna's adrenaline skyrocketed.

"Yes, we're at the Christmas tree lot on Holman Road, near Soundview Playfield, and there's a man who's collapsed. We think he might have had a heart attack. He's not breathing, and his pulse is weak. There's a doctor on scene, but we need an ambulance."

"I've got your coordinates on GPS, ma'am, and the EMTs are on the way. Please stay on the line with me until they arrive."

"I could use some help," Max said, looking up at Ayanna. "Do you know CPR?"

"I do." She'd had the mandatory training every year at her jobs, plus she had learned early on from her mother. Had never had to put it into practice, though, until tonight. She handed her phone to the man's wife. "Stay on the line with them until the ambulance arrives. I'm going to help the doctor with your husband."

The woman nodded, her hands shaking as she took the phone from Ayanna.

Ayanna was shaking pretty badly herself, but she needed to stay calm. Panic was your worst enemy in a crisis, her mom always said, and she would know. Not caring about the snowy wet pavement staining her designer pants, she knelt beside Max and helped get the man's coat and shirt open while Max pulled out his wallet to remove a face shield.

"Always carry one with me," he said at her questioning look. "Just in case."

Max repositioned the man's neck to open his airway again after placing the face shield then waited while Ayanna positioned her hands correctly on the guy's chest to begin compressions. "Ready?"

"Ready." Not really, but this was life or death. She nodded and Max puffed two breaths into the man's mouth before Ayanna started her compressions. To make sure she kept the correct rhythm and rate of one hundred to one hundred and twenty compressions per minute, she sang the Bee Gees song "Stayin' Alive" in her head.

"You're doing great," Max said, giving her an encouraging smile as the wail of a siren grew louder in the distance. "Let me know if you get tired and we can switch. Shouldn't be too long now."

"Yes," the man's wife said into Ayanna's phone. "They're doing CPR on him now. Please hurry!"

Time narrowed to just one second, then the next, as Ayanna helped Max try to save this man's life. He continued to check their patient's vitals and give breaths between her compressions. She had no idea how long they worked, but once the EMTs arrived and took over CPR from them, Ayanna's arms ached and her own chest felt tight from stress.

Max gave the medics a rundown on the man's condition then helped them load the man and his wife into the back of the waiting ambulance.

"Oh," the wife said, handing Ayanna back her phone. "Thank you both so much for all you've done."

Ayanna was still too stunned by everything that she couldn't do more than nod to the woman. Sirens wailed again as the ambulance took off, leaving her and Max standing in the parking lot while the gathered crowd around them dispersed. Several people shook her hand or clapped Max on the back as they left, congratulating them on a job well done.

She still couldn't wrap her head around what had happened. It seemed unreal. One minute they'd bought a tree, the next they were trying to save a life. As they walked back to the car again, her feet felt numb, not from cold but from shock.

"Maybe I should drive?" Max asked as she stopped in front of the SUV and just stood there. Ayanna didn't usually allow other people to take charge, but tonight it seemed like a good idea. She handed the keys to him. "Right," he said, opening her door for her. "You'd better sit down before you fall down."

They got into her vehicle and she fumbled with her seatbelt, the distinctive scent from the tree strapped to the roof mixing with the antiseptic from the wipes the medics had used still swirling around her. Ayanna's fingers shook so badly Max ended up buckling her in. She felt shaken and stirred and yet oddly triumphant.

He started the engine, watching her. "You sure you're okay?"

"Yes. That was…" She had no words. "Wow."

"Let's just hope he'll survive and make a full recovery." He ran his hand through his hair again, melting snowflakes making the strands sparkle in the darkness. "Emergency situations like that are always tough, but you did well."

"So did you." Ayanna blinked at him. He'd done something miraculous and she was even more astonished by him than she'd been before. Every day since she'd known him, Max Granger had surprised her in the best possible ways. "You were amazing. Is your life that exciting every day?"

"Uh, no." His slow smile went a long way toward chasing away the chill that had settled in her bones during their ordeal. "And you were pretty spectacular yourself. Taking the classes for CPR and actually performing it in a crisis are two different things. Well done, Ayanna."

Heat crept up her cheeks and a bubble of joy swelled inside her. Before she could consider the wisdom of her actions, Ayanna leaned over and kissed him, soft and quick. When she pulled back, the air between them stilled and the world dropped away.

Say something.

Except when she opened her mouth, nothing came out.

Max looked as stunned as she felt, but recovered faster, facing front again and pulling out of the lot. "Right. Let's get your decorations and some food and get back to the suite before we get into more trouble."

Max's thoughts continued to whirl once they were back in the suite. At least wrestling the tree into position before the windows in the living room gave him some welcome space to breathe.

It wasn't the situation with the heart-attack victim the bothered him as he was used to dealing with emergencies in his line of work. What he wasn't used to dealing with were the emotions now roiling through him like a pot at full boil—need, nervousness, want, wariness. He'd kissed Ayanna Franklin twice and each time had left him questioning everything about himself and what he wanted.

He'd planned to stay alone, to keep his feelings safely tucked away where they couldn't hurt him. But one touch, one look, one valiant rescue effort on Ayanna's part had sent all his well-ordered, well-intentioned plans straight to hell.

She made him want to open up his heart and live and love again. And that was terrifying.

"Okay," Ayanna said, after she'd tightened the screws on the tree stand to lock their spruce into place. "Let's this gal beautified."

"Beautified?" Max squinted one eye. "Is that even a word?"

"It is in my family," she said, opening one of the boxes they'd retrieved from her storage pod. "Growing up, whenever I or my sisters went to get our hair done, my mom said we were getting beautified."

"Hmm." Max shrugged off his jacket and tossed it over the back of the sofa. "If we're going to decorate first, I'll put our food in the oven to keep it warm."

"Good idea." Ayanna set out ornaments on the coffee table and sofa cushions, along with several strings of multi-colored lights. "Speaking of my mom, she really enjoyed having you there on Thanksgiving."

"I liked her too," he said as he stuck their bags of burgers and fries into the warming oven. "And I'm excited to try those recipes she gave me. She's an interesting lady."

"That's one way to put it." Ayanna chuckled and damn if he didn't feel that low, throaty sound straight in his groin. Man, he needed to get a grip on this thing between them before he did something stupid, like haul her into his arms and right into his bedroom. Thankfully, once he got back into the living room, Ayanna's mood seemed to have shifted from teasing to pensive. She continued while she set out more ornaments on the coffee table. "But you were right. I did learn to put other people's needs above my own when I was growing up. In some ways, I guess that's what makes me good at my job. I know what my clients want before they do sometimes."

Her self-reflection was good, even if it hurt his heart to see her smile disappear. Man, he loved that smile. "Anticipating others' needs isn't always a bad thing."

She gave a sad little snort. "True, but it isn't always such a great trait in relationships. Especially when your partner uses it against you. When we first started dat-

ing, Will appreciated all the little things I did for him—
making sure I kept his favorite tea in stock, arranging
his calendar so he had time to hit the gym when he
wanted, ordering supplies for his office so he never
ran out.

"But then, after a few months, he came to expect it
from me and if I got behind or forgot, he'd get angry.
Then, finally, he turned it on me and began to tear me
down for my caretaker tendencies, nitpicking at me
about how he wished I wasn't such a control freak all
the time and how I'd be so much more fun if I loosened
up. Near the end, right before he ran off with Rinna,
he told me I was lucky to have him because he put up
with all my issues. He said another man wouldn't even
consider getting involved with me."

She exhaled slowly and set the empty ornament container aside before picking up a ball of tangled lights
from the sofa. "After the breakup and the wedding that
wasn't, I didn't know what to think."

A small muscle spasmed near Max's tight jaw. The
more she talked about her selfish ass of an ex, the more
he wanted to punch the guy in the face. Ayanna was
wonderful and witty and way too caring about everyone
else's comfort but her own. If this Will guy couldn't see
that, then he hadn't deserved her. Max went back to the
kitchen for a pitcher of water to pour into the tree stand
before they started decorating, talking to Ayanna over
his shoulder as he went. "Please, tell me you didn't believe those awful things he said."

"I wish I could, at least at first, but honestly, I was too
close to the situation." She shook her head. "My family
had tried to warn me about him, especially my mom, but

I blew her off. Said she was being too overprotective. I even accused her of being jealous because I was doing for Will what I'd always done for the family—taking care of him like I used to take care of them."

Max returned with the water, the plastic handle of the water pitcher clenched tightly in his fist to stop himself from reaching over and pulling Ayanna into his arms instead.

"Just one more way I was completely blind to what was really going on. God, I'm such an idiot. That night I walked in on him and Rinna in our bed…" She swallowed hard, her brows drawing together and her lips tightening. "Anyway, now, in hindsight, I can see that it was Will and not me who caused the breakup, but still. I have a hard time trusting my instincts. Back then, I thought I was helping, thought I was making things better, but I wasn't. It makes it difficult to open up again, you know?"

"I do." Max poured the water around the base of the tree then set the empty pitcher aside before grabbing a non-tangled string of lights to weave through the tree branches. "With the way I was raised, my parents being so cold and clinical around me, meeting Laura was a shock to my system. She was so different, like a bright light after years of darkness. But she was so easy to be around, so kind and caring, she made it easy for me to open up around her." He scowled as he disappeared around the back of the tree, then glanced over again at Ayanna when he emerged on the other side. "And it made it so much harder when she died. Sometimes I wonder if it would've been better not to have met her at all."

Ayanna stopped fiddling with the lights and gave him an astonished look. "You can't mean that. From what you've told me, you loved her a great deal. What's that saying? 'It's better to have loved and lost than never to have loved at all'?"

"I hate that saying." He cringed and gave a full-body shake then finished placing the last of his string of lights before walking over to grab another. "Up until I'd met her, I'd learned to live my life alone. Logically. Analytically. I was happy that way. After being married to Laura and seeing a different way, making myself open and vulnerable to that and then losing her, it was…" He searched for the right word. *Unnerving? Eviscerating? Excruciating?* Finally, he settled on, "The most difficult thing I've ever been through."

"I can't imagine," Ayanna said, frowning down at the knotted lights in her hands. "I mean, having Will run away with my ex-best friend right before our wedding was bad, and there are still days I wish karma would hurry up and do her thing where he's concerned, but death?" She sighed. "You mentioned in the car the other day that you felt responsible for what happened to your wife. I hope you know that Laura's passing wasn't your fault either."

Max compressed his lips. "I'm a doctor. I should have known."

"Exactly. You're a doctor, not a psychic." She laid her string of lights on the coffee table and fixed him with a steady stare. "Is what happened with her why you don't celebrate the holidays now?"

He turned away to tuck more lights into the upper sections of the tree. "Partly, I suppose."

"Tell me more about her. What was she like? You said she was kind and caring."

"She was. Basically, the opposite of me," Max said, trying to ease the seriousness in the room with humor and failing, if the look Ayanna gave him was any indication. Finally, he gave in and sighed. "Fine. Let's see. We got married six months after we met. I knew right away she was the one. Laura used to tease me that it took her a lot longer." He chuckled, the old sting of guilt in his chest whenever he thought of his late wife easing slightly the more he talked to Ayanna.

"We bought a little house in Jericho, Long Island, since we both worked in Manhattan, and we started a life together." He pictured their little white two-story Tudor-style house. "We were happy there." Rather than rehash his painful past again, he changed course. "Laura loved Christmas. Loved all the holidays, really. If there was a reason to decorate and buy candy, she was on it."

"She sounds like my kind of lady." Ayanna grinned. "Cookies too. Don't forget the cookies."

"Never." A slow smile formed on his lips. "By the way, I've got a recipe to try out later. Don't let me forget."

She tapped her temple. "Got it in my internal calendar."

"Good." He grabbed the string of lights she'd been working on off the table and tugged them free himself, the words flowing out now before he could stop them. Max didn't stop to consider why talking to Ayanna seemed so easy, just enjoyed the rare and delightful fact that it was. "Before Laura, I wasn't used to being a priority in someone's life. I got so used to being alone when I was a kid, I figured that's the way it would always be. That life was meant to be lived alone, that emotions were bad. But when I was with my wife, she made it okay to open up, to be vulnerable. Then that safety net disappeared."

He stuck the remaining lights on the upper branches of the trees then lowered his arms. "After she was gone, I closed myself off again, tried to lose myself in my work. I wanted that to be enough. I wanted to not feel anymore."

"Oh, Max." Ayanna moved in beside him, her lovely dark eyes filled with concern. "I'm so sorry."

"It's okay." He placed the last of the lights, then reached for one of her garlands. "But being at your parents' house on Thanksgiving was nice. Reminded me that things could be different, brighter."

Man, he'd not intended to share all this with her, but now that it was out there, he was glad. "How about we finish decorating later? I'm starving."

Ayanna watched him a moment, then nodded. "Okay, but first I'm going to change. Be right back."

Max gathered their dinner then sat at the dining table to wait, his thoughts ticking through the event of the night and wondering how exactly he was going to handle things with Ayanna from now on. Even with all they'd shared tonight, there were still secrets between them. Like how he was starting to care for her more than as just a friend. How he felt more connected to her every day. Most of all, how much he'd miss her after he left Seattle.

CHAPTER TEN

THE REST OF the week passed by in a blur of phone calls and appointments for Ayanna. Between hiring the small orchestra for the ball and finalizing the menus at the hotel, she'd been up to her eyeballs in work. Max had continued to help, though, and they both had the entire weekend ahead off, so she was looking forward to relaxing in the suite.

She glanced at him over the top of her book and bit back a smile. The man took his decorating seriously, that was for sure. He hadn't been kidding about his theory of composition thing either, considering it had taken him days to perfect the tree and he'd been standing there at least five minutes staring at one spot or another to decide where to hang the last ornament. Must be a surgeon thing, she figured.

Finally, he chose a branch and carefully looped the tiny string around the needles then stood back.

"There. Done!"

Ayanna set her book aside and stood, her arm brushing his as she moved in beside him. She ignored the tingle of heat skittering across her skin from the brief contact and focused on his masterpiece instead. "Looks great."

He grinned down at her and damn if her insides didn't melt into a puddle of goo. "Thanks. Hey, what are your plans this afternoon?"

"Nothing, really." She blinked up at him, far too comfy in her cozy sweats to want to change. "Just stay here and read. Why?"

"Well…" He reached over to grab the newspaper off the coffee table. "I saw in here there's a Christmas parade downtown today. I've never been to one and thought maybe we could go."

Surprised, she blinked at him. "You. The former Grinch. Want to go to a Christmas parade?"

He shrugged and flashed her a crooked little half-smile, the one that made her heart dance a besotted jig. Lord, the man was adorable, and he wasn't even trying. She was in major trouble here.

"C'mon," he said, his tone turning pleading. "Just to see what it is, that's all. We have to go out anyway to get a couple of missing ingredients for my cookie recipe that I forgot to add to the grocery list the other day, and from the map on my phone it looks like the parade route is close by the store, so…" He flipped through more pages to the entertainment section. "Oh, and there's also a showing of *It's a Wonderful Life* across the street in Myrtle Edwards Park after the parade."

She checked the area behind him then glanced around the room.

"What are you doing?" Max frowned.

"Searching for the real Max Granger?"

"Funny. Not." He gave her a deadpan look. "I figured

since we both had the weekend off, maybe you could show me around more of Seattle. I don't usually get the chance to sightsee when I'm traveling, and I like this city. Not my fault if it happens to be the holidays too." Max shrugged. "I mean, if you don't want to, that's fine. I can go by myself."

She probably should say no. Ayanna was getting far too attached to him already. But she couldn't bring herself to do it. Her book was good, but reality was even better today. "Fine. I'll go. I think they offer picnic meals at those movies too, if I'm not mistaken. James and his partner David go to them a lot and said they're a lot of fun. They have them year round, since the winters are generally mild here in the PNW."

"Pacific Northwest," he said, with pride. "See? I'm even getting the lingo."

"You are." She winked then headed around the couch toward the hall. "Let me put my jeans on. Be right back."

"No rush. The parade doesn't start for another hour, so you've got time." He headed for the kitchen. "I'll clean up from breakfast while you get ready."

He'd made them yummy waffles with strawberries, whipped cream and thick-cut bacon and Ayanna thought she'd died and gone to heaven. The man had a way with food, no doubt about it. Had a way with people too, especially her. Yep. She had it bad for her brooding surgeon and that wasn't good.

Flustered and frustrated, in more ways than one, Ayanna changed into a fresh pair of jeans and a festive emerald-green turtleneck then headed into her bathroom to fix her hair and apply a light coat of makeup

before going back out to find Max. He was just finishing up with the dishes and had put on a black sweater
over his gray henley and faded jeans, she noticed.

He straightened after closing the dishwasher and
caught sight of her, giving her a slow once-over that
had her heart tripping. "You look... *Wow.* Green is definitely your color."

"Thanks." She ran a self-conscious hand down the
front of her turtleneck. "You look nice too."

The black sweater clung to his torso in all the right
spots and made her fingertips itch to slide beneath it
to stroke his warm, soft skin. She tugged on her jacket
and to keep from reaching for him instead.

"Should we go?" She slung her purse over her shoulder then turned fast, only to freeze in place as Max
came over to slide his hands beneath the collar of her
brown leather bomber jacket to free her curls trapped
there. Ayanna's breath caught and her lips parted. If
she rose up on tiptoe, she could kiss him. They could
forget about the parade and the movie and stay in bed
all day and...

Max's eyes flickered to her mouth then back to her
eyes, the flames banked there matching her own. Then
he took a deep breath and stepped back. "Ready?"

"Ready."

For more than you know.

She followed him out the door, excitement buzzing
in her bloodstream.

"This is great," Max said later as they stood near the
curb on Fourth Avenue and watched another high school

marching band go by, this one playing the theme from *Home Alone*. "Not sure about the moose, though."

"You mean Mariner Moose and the Moosemobile?" Ayanna laughed. "They're a Seattle tradition!"

"Right. Sure." He chuckled, then put his arm around her shoulders to keep them from getting separated in the crowds. Or at least that was the excuse he was going with anyway. Honestly, it felt so damned good to touch her he couldn't seem to stop. "Looks like the big guy in red is coming."

"Yes!" Ayanna clapped and pointed, excited as any of the kids nearby. It was great to see her enjoy herself. She worked too hard and he was determined to see her take better care of herself. Soon the booming strains of "Santa Claus is Coming to Town" filled the air and he pulled Ayanna closer as they waved to St. Nick and caught a few candy canes tossed by the elves on board the sleigh. Finally, she turned to him, her smile glowing brighter than the lights decorating the storefront windows. "That was awesome! I haven't been to one of these since I was a kid. Thanks for bringing me."

"Thanks for coming." Without thinking, he looped his other arm around her waist and clasped his hands at the small of her back. "Ready to see the movie now?"

"Absolutely. Lead the way!" She hugged him then took his hand as they walked down the street and over to the park. They picked up a free blanket at a concession stand nearby then spread it out on the grass beneath a tree, so they'd have something to rest back on. A vendor came around with sandwiches and chips and Max bought them each a sack lunch and a bottled water to enjoy. The park filled up quickly with couples and he couldn't remember the last time he'd sat outside like this and relaxed. In the distance, boats filled Puget Sound for a nautical holiday celebration and the low toots of their horns reminded him that they were still on the coast and not lost at the North Pole.

Being here with Ayanna, happiness coursing through his veins, made him reconsider. Maybe there was something to be said for the holidays after all. For the first time in a long time Max realized he didn't dread Christmas. And it was all thanks to the woman beside him.

For the next few hours, they sat side by side, his arm around Ayanna and her head on his shoulder, chatting and eating and watching Jimmy Stewart and Clarence, his guardian angel, come to the conclusion that as hard as things had been in the past, there'd been good times too. Everything had led them to that point in time. One difference and it would all change.

The irony wasn't lost on Max.

After the final scene of Jimmy and his onscreen family standing in a snowy Bedford Falls, staring up at the starry sky as Clarence got his wings, Ayanna gave a happy sigh and swiped the back of her hand across her damp cheeks. "Man, no matter how many times I see that movie, it always gets me. How about you, Grinch? Did you like it?"

"Seriously? That's your nickname for me?" He laughed and squeezed her closer into his side for a minute. "Fine. I can live with it. And, yes, I liked it." He'd seen it before. Who hadn't? But today, for some reason, its message really hit home. After letting her go and clambering to his feet, Max helped Ayanna up then turned to throw away their trash while she folded up their blanket to return it to the concession booth. "My favorite old holiday movie, though, is *The Bishop's Wife*, with Cary Grant."

"Oh, that's a good one too." She walked alongside him back toward the street "Anything with Cary Grant is great, really. Where to now?"

"Now we stop at the grocery store so I can pick up a few last things to make my special cookies." He took her hand as they crossed the street. Today they weren't busy professionals with stressful jobs and people depending on them. They were just two people out for a day of fun and holiday cheer. It felt good. And right.

They got his supplies then returned to the hotel. Once he'd removed his coat and helped Ayanna with hers, he checked his phone while Ayanna got out mixing bowls and set the oven to preheat to the temperature he'd given her. After dialing the number for the nurses' station in ICU, Max turned away to make his call.

The ICU charge nurse picked up on the second ring. "Intensive Care, Laurel speaking."

"Hi, Laurel. Dr. Granger checking in on the condition of my patient, please." He paced the small area while he waited for the nurse to pull up the King's file on the computer. After a busy day, Max usually felt drained. But now he was restless with energy. He found it harder to resist the pull he felt toward Ayanna. If he'd been looking, she was everything he wanted—smart, funny, outgoing, caring, loyal. But he wasn't looking.

Am I?

"Yes, Dr. Granger," Laurel said, bringing him back

to reality. "The King's condition is still stable. His GCS is holding steady at six and he's breathing well with the ventilator."

"Okay." The fact that some weeks had passed and the King still hadn't regained consciousness yet wasn't ideal, but they had him under constant monitoring and his latest CT scans hadn't shown any new bleeding or clot formation, so that was promising. Plus, the King's son, Dr. di Rossi, had spent a lot of his time at his father's bedside, speaking to him and holding his hands. Research showed such actions helped many coma patients recover more quickly and several articles cited how coma patients could still hear things being said to and around them. Max was a firm believer in the power and support of community to help heal patients' wounds and new theories about the mind-body-immune-system connection arose each day. "Good. Continue the current protocol then. And be sure to call me right away if anything changes."

"Will do, Doctor," Laurel said, and ended the call.

Max then spoke with Dr. di Rossi about his father's condition before putting his phone on the charging pad. Time to bake. With Ayanna. The thought thrilled him more than he'd expected.

"So, where's the recipe?" Ayanna had taken off her shoes, he noticed, leaving her in stockinged feet. A sudden urge to make her cute little toes curl with ecstasy had his throat constricting with need again before he swallowed hard.

"Uh." Max turned his attention to measuring out ingredients to distract himself. "It's in my head."

"You sound like my mom. She's got her favorites

memorized too. I'm actually surprised she wrote them down for you. She must like you, since she doesn't do that for just anyone." She moved in beside him at the island, her warmth sending a fresh wave of want through him. His hands shook slightly as he cracked eggs into the bowl. Lord, the woman affected him in the best, and worst, way. Ayanna threw away the empty eggshells then washed her hands. "What can I do?"

"Give me a minute to get all this mixed together," he said, reaching into the fridge for the milk and butter and a bag of crushed pecans, grateful for the blast of chilly air on his overheated body. "Then you can help me get the dough on those cookies sheets. Go ahead and line them with parchment paper, if you want."

"Will do."

Once ready, they each took a tablespoon and scooped out small balls of dough, rolling them into one-inch spheres and coating each in crushed pecans before placing them on the cookie sheets. Max glanced over at her batch of twelve. "Good. Now go down each row and stick your thumb into the center of each ball."

She did, licking her thumb after she'd finished. And damn if Max couldn't stop thinking about where else he'd like her to use that soft pink tongue of hers now. Heat prickled up his neck from beneath the collar of his sweater and he wondered when the heck it had gotten so hot in the suite. He quickly shoved the cookie sheets into the oven and set the timer.

"Now we wait eight minutes until they're done then do it all again." He turned away to wash his hands, his body screaming for him to forget about his good intentions and just take Ayanna to bed. But his analytical mind still urged caution. This wouldn't be another emotionless one-night stand. He cared for Ayanna, more than he'd been willing to admit until now, and he wasn't used to all these feelings roiling around inside him.

It was exhilarating. It was exhausting. It was unlike anything he'd ever experienced.

He dried his hands then fiddled with the towel, avoiding facing Ayanna again until he was certain he had himself back under control.

"So," she said behind him, her tone quiet. "What do you call these cookies?"

Right. The cookies. Their sweet, familiar scent wafted from the oven as they baked. He reached back into the fridge to pull out a jar of currant jelly. "Thumbprint Cookies."

"Imagine that." Ayanna snorted and took the jar from him. "And what's this for?"

"To put a dollop in the center of each cookie after they've cooled." He twisted off the lid then got out two clean teaspoons. "You can help me fill them, if you want."

"Absolutely."

The buzzer went off a short time later and he pulled the pans out of the oven with an oven mitt, setting them atop the stove to cool before removing the baked cookies and freeing up the pans for another round. They worked side by side, making a surprisingly good team. So good, in fact, Max couldn't help thinking about where else they might make fine partners. He shook his head and cracked a joke to distract himself from the tsunami of desire threatening to pull him under. "I think you're eating more dough than you're putting on the cookie sheets."

"Maybe." She laughed. "But these are so good. Seriously. You should enter them in the staff cookie contest tomorrow."

Max scrunched his nose. "I'm not really part of the staff."

"You are for now. It'll be fun. And maybe you'll even win."

He sighed and tried to bite back the grin threatening to break through his stoic façade. "What's the prize?"

"Besides bragging rights? Michelin-starred dinner for two." She shoved another bite of dough in her mouth then winked. "For a foodie like you, that's like nirvana, right?"

Hell, yeah, he wanted to win that prize. "Consider me convinced."

"Cool!" Ayanna fisted pumped the air. "I'm getting you out of your shell at last."

"Are you always like this?" he teased, already knowing the answer.

"Only when it's something important to me," she said, their gazes catching and holding before they both looked away. He'd not missed the flicker of heat in her dark eyes or the answering flare of need in his gut. They each retreated to their own corners of the kitchen, the air between them sparking like a live wire.

Finally, after what seemed a small eternity, all the cookies were done, half of them filled with currant jelly, and the oven was off. The suite smelled like the holidays and Max still had no idea what to do about this thing between him and Ayanna. She was still beside him, spooning jelly into their cookies and occasionally licking the sugar off her fingers. Each time he watched her suck on a fingertip, he moved that much closer to moaning, his body taut with need. She was going to kill him if this didn't stop soon. Death by desire.

"There," she said, filling the last cookie. "All done. What do you think?"

I think I'd like to spread that jelly on you next and lick it off every square inch of you.

Max cleared his throat. "I think that's enough baking for now."

He turned away to fill the sink with soapy water, then shoved the cookie sheets and utensils in to soak. "Thanks for your help."

"Thanks for letting me." Ayanna leaned her hip against the counter beside him and crossed her arms. "And thanks for today too. I think you might have even enjoyed yourself."

"I did." He shut off the faucet and swiped a hand through his hair. "It was fun."

"Oh." She bit her lips, stifling a laugh. "You've got suds on your forehead."

Ayanna brushed her finger across his skin to remove the soap and his mouth dried to sandpaper. Oh, God. Every cell in his body raged to have her. Teeth clenched, he forced himself not pick her up and take her right there on the counter. He might've kept his control too, if her touch hadn't traveled down his cheek then around to the nape of his neck, ruffling his hair and making him shiver.

Yep. Every man had his limits and Max Granger had just reached his.

Before he could second-guess his actions, he tugged Ayanna against him, kissing her hard and hot and deep. His free hand slid down to pull her hips against his, letting her feel just how much he wanted her. Instead of objecting to his advances, Ayanna couldn't seem to get enough, sliding her fingers into his hair and holding him tighter, her legs wrapping around his waist. He hoisted her up and instead of taking her in the kitchen he headed for the master bedroom, not wanting to rush their first time together.

Max set her in the middle of his huge king-sized bed and tore off his sweater and T-shirt before joining Ayanna. Her clothes and his jeans and boxer briefs vanished in a tangle of kisses and caresses and soon they were both naked atop the down-filled comforter. She felt every bit as amazing against him as he'd imagined, and Max took his time exploring her beautiful body. Worshiped her gorgeous breasts, then kissed his way down her body to make love to her with his mouth and tongue, showing her how much he cared, all the things he couldn't say.

Ayanna moaned and writhed beneath him, crying out her pleasure as the soft glow of twinkle lights filtered in from the tree in the living room.

Once she'd settled back to earth, Max slowly kissed his way back up to her lips, loving the dreamy look in her lovely eyes. Loving even more that he'd been the one to put it there. He rested his forehead against hers, his breathing heavy and his body tense, needing release of its own. "Hang on."

He fumbled in the nightstand drawer for the complimentary condom packets he'd found in there on his first night. Originally, he'd thought them a frivolous amenity. Now he couldn't be happier this five-star hotel had thought of everything. While he put it on, Ayanna raised up on her elbows to watch. Knowing she wanted him every bit as much as he wanted her only made the whole thing hotter. Still, he wanted to be sure before they took the final step. There was no going back after this.

"Are you sure?" He held himself above her with one forearm, his hard length poised at her wet entrance. "I need to know—"

Ayanna growled and pulled him down for another kiss. "Get inside me, Max. Now."

She didn't have to ask twice. He drove into her in one long thrust then held still to allow her body to adjust to his size. Then she dug her heels into his backside and rocked her hips and he set up a rhythm that had them both teetering on the edge of ecstasy. He couldn't stop kissing her. Her mouth. Her cheeks. Her throat. Her breasts. Ayanna met him thrust for thrust, those long, manicured nails of hers scoring his back and bringing him closer and closer to orgasm.

At first he'd been worried about it not being good between them. But now he worried he might never find another person who matched him so perfectly. She seemed to know, instinctively, exactly what he wanted, how to move to draw every single last shred of feeling from him. Ayanna cried out again and he reached between them to stroke her most sensitive flesh. That was all it took. She arched hard, reaching her second climax and spurring him on to his own fulfillment. He thrust once, twice, then went whipcord tight as wave after wave of pleasure drowned him in an explosion of sensation.

Afterward, they lay sated in each other's arms, Ayanna stroking her fingers through his hair while he dozed with his head on her breast, the steady beat of her heart lulling him into blissful sleep.

CHAPTER ELEVEN

AYANNA WOKE EARLY the next morning and stared around the unfamiliar bedroom, taking a moment to register where she was. Max's bedroom. They'd made love. Several times. The warm weight of his arm wrapped around her waist as he spooned her from behind, his soft snores stirring the hair near her temple. Slowly, she turned over to face him, taking in his relaxed features, so unguarded in sleep.

Last night had been wonderful. Magical. And more than a tad scary.

The most terrifying part was that she hadn't felt this way about anyone since Will. She liked Max. Liked talking to him, liked spending time with him. Liked everything about him, way, way more than she should. Unable to resist, she gently smoothed an errant lock of hair off his forehead, the same one that had started it all in the kitchen last night.

Man, she'd never intended to fall for anyone again, let alone Max Granger, yet here she was, head over heels for him. Her heart felt ten sizes too big for her chest and all she wanted to do was stay in their warm bed, in his warm arms, for the rest of the day.

Except the longer she lay there, the more her old doubt demons kicked in, warning her about how quickly everything had become real between her and Max. Maybe too quickly. Her chest tightened and her throat constricted. Was she wrong again? Could she trust her feelings this time? What if her instincts were leading her astray, the same way they had before, blinding her to what was really happening?

Anxiety rushed through her and she suddenly couldn't stay there any longer. She needed to move, to breathe, to take some time alone to figure all this out. Originally, they'd both had the full weekend off, but after last night...

Nope. She eased out from under Max's arm. Besides, after spending yesterday with Max in a veritable winter wonderland, she had all sorts of new ideas for the centerpieces for the ball tables and décor for the ballroom and she really ought to get them nailed down before she forgot. Time was of the essence now with the big fundraiser in just a few days. She didn't want to lose that creative momentum when Dr. di Rossi and the entire Seattle General board of directors were depending on her.

At least, that's the excuse she was going with.

Ayanna gathered her clothes then headed into her own room to get dressed. After showering and changing, she padded to the kitchen, shoes in hand to keep from making too much noise, and brewed some coffee. Drank a cup of liquid energy while staring at the plate of cookies from the night before, remembering how much fun they'd had making them. She hadn't been kidding about him entering them in the cookie contest today and packed up a plateful to take with her.

Once she'd finished her coffee and eaten an extra cookie or three, Ayanna grabbed her coat and bag and the container full of cookies for the contest, then scribbled a quick note for Max before heading out to Seattle General.

Went in to work for a bit. See you later. And don't worry. I've got your cookies.

The annoying hotel alarm clock on the nightstand buzzed Max awake. He fumbled an arm over to shut it off without opening his eyes then he reached beside him to pull Ayanna closer, only to encounter cold mattress.

Frowning, he squinted over to confirm, yep. She was gone.

Damn. He'd envisioned them staying in bed together all day long.

Disappointed, Max rolled over onto his back and stared up at the white ceiling, listening for sounds of her in the suite, thinking maybe it wasn't too late to convince her to stay beneath the covers with him. But nope. Everything was quiet, indicating she'd already left the suite. With a groan, he got up, hitting the bathroom to take a quick shower then dressing in comfy sweats instead of his usual work clothes. Last night had been...*wonderful.*

Ayanna was beautiful and sexy. Yes, they'd only known each other a short time, but when you clicked with someone, you just clicked. It had been that way with Laura too. They'd only dated a few months before he'd asked her to marry him.

That thought tripped him up a minute. He liked

Ayanna. More than liked her. But was he thinking of more with her? Was he considering forever?

Am I?

Deep in thought, he went out to the kitchen to make himself some tea. Being with Ayanna was great. Even spending the day at her parents' house on Thanksgiving had been nice. Meeting her siblings, enjoying that easy camaraderie of people who knew everything about you—good and bad—and loved you anyway. That had been a concept he'd never known he needed in his life until that day.

But old habits died hard and his analytical mind refused to stop turning things over in his head. As a brain surgeon, Max relied on being able to see and approach his cases from all angles to choose the best direction for treatment. But when it came to romance, nothing was ever that clear or concise. Love was messy and mind-boggling at times. Exactly why he tended to avoid it.

But somehow, with Ayanna, maybe the prospect wouldn't be so daunting.

After filling the kettle and setting it on the stove to boil, Max spotted the note Ayanna had left him.

Went in to work for a bit. See you later. And don't worry. I've got your cookies.

He chuckled and set the note aside, catching a hint of her spicy sweet perfume on the paper. Who knew, maybe she was right. Maybe his recipe would win that contest and they'd dine at a gorgeous seaside gourmet restaurant overlooking Puget Sound before he left to return to Manhattan.

The reminder of life in New York put a bit of a damper on his good mood. He was comfortable here with Ayanna. He didn't want to think about leaving yet. He shook his head and scolded himself. Forget about romance. The real reason he was here was the King's surgery. He had a job to do and a patient to monitor. And if the King's condition continued to improve, he could perform surgery as scheduled. That's where his focus should be. Everything else was irrelevant, no matter how his chest might ache whenever he thought of saying goodbye to Ayanna.

He finished his tea and made himself a quick egg white omelet before deciding to head into the hospital himself. Sitting around the empty suite wasn't his idea of a fun day and, besides, he had work and consults to keep him busy. The weather looked decent too, so the walk would do him good. Seattle General was only a few blocks away after all.

Half an hour later, the brisk morning air slapped his cheeks as he walked out of the hotel and headed east. The skies were overcast as usual, but the temp seemed less chilly. As he passed the storefronts filled with holiday cheer, he wondered about the man they'd saved at the tree lot and made a note to check on his condition when he got to work. More memories filtered into his head as he waited at the corner for the light to change. The way Ayanna had felt last night—against him, beneath him, around him. The soft moan of his name on her lips as she'd come apart in his arms. The sweet taste of her kisses, sugar and a bit of tartness from the currant jelly.

The light turned green and he crossed with a small crowd headed in the same direction. Even this early in the day, the tourists were out, dressed in red and green for the upcoming holiday, laden with shopping bags from the stores downtown. He reached Seattle General and headed straight to the emergency department to change into some scrubs in the staff locker room. From there he went up to ICU to see King Roberto. His last text update from a few hours prior suggested his patient's condition was still unchanged. That was good, considering the King's advanced age and what he'd been through during that accident.

He took the elevator up to the third floor and stepped off into the quiet environment, the rhythmic beeps of monitors and the occasional squeak of the staff's shoes on the gleaming linoleum the only sounds breaking the silence. The scents of antiseptic and lemon floor wax helped center him and focus him on the task at hand as he made his way to the nurses' station.

"Dr. Granger checking in," he said to the middle-aged woman behind the desk. "Any changes with my patient?"

"Still the same, Doc," the nurse said, grinning at him. "Congrats, by the way."

Max frowned. "For what?"

"Those are some fine cookies you entered in the contest, Doc Granger," Laurel said, coming up beside him. "What do we have to do to get the recipe?"

"Uh…" Totally confused, Max frowned at the assembled nurses around him. "You mean I won?"

"You did," the nurse behind the desk said. Her name tag said "Rosie." "Congrats."

"Wow." Max raised his eyebrows. "I didn't expect that."

"So, about that recipe, Doc," Laurel said, her dark skin contrasting with her pink scrub shirt.

"Uh, sure." Max grabbed a piece of copy paper and pen and scribbled it down for them. "Here you guys go."

"Thanks, Doc," Laurel said, taking the paper over to the copy machine. "I'll try it out on my kids this year and see what they think. Enjoy that dinner too."

"Thanks, ladies," he said, heading for the King's room. He'd have to stop by Ayanna's office when he was done and thank her for entering him in the contest. She'd been right. Dinner at a five-star restaurant, just the two of them, was exactly his idea of nirvana.

CHAPTER TWELVE

ON THE NIGHT OF the fundraising ball, Ayanna honestly didn't know if she was coming or going, she was so busy. And nervous. Her caretaker instincts were out of control too, making her run from one corner of the massive ballroom to the other, checking on food and drinks and musicians and décor and any other issues that came up throughout the evening. Not to mention the running was made harder by the form-fitting emerald-green evening gown and silver strappy heels she'd worn for the event.

With a sigh, she stopped near the open bar and surveyed the space. The guests seemed happy. That was the most important thing. Happy donors meant larger donations and tonight was all about raising funds to add a new children's cancer ward at Seattle General. She smoothed a hand down the silky fabric of her dress and scanned the gathering crowd around her for Max.

"Stop worrying," he'd said, kissing her before they'd parted in the suite. "You look amazing and the ball will be amazing too. Enjoy the benefits of all your hard work!"

Except that was easier said than done for Ayanna. Max had been right again. She was used to constantly taking care of everyone else's problems, not relaxing and enjoying herself. They were arriving separately tonight, as she'd been here early to supervise her staff and make sure everything was set up properly ahead of the guests' arrivals. Now, though, she wished he'd come with her. Having Max by her side steadied her, grounded her. And, darn it, she missed him, even though it had only been a few hours since they'd parted.

Other than their working hours, they'd been practically inseparable since the night they'd made love. He'd even taken her for dinner last night. The food had been wonderful and the company even better. And the views from the floor-to-ceiling glass windows to the harbor below had been breathtaking. What she remembered most of all, though, was the warmth in Max's gray eyes and the touch of his skin on hers as he'd held her hand across the table. Things between them this week had been perfect.

Maybe too perfect.

Her heart lurched a bit before she shook it off. Her stupid instincts, mouthing off again. Max wasn't Will, she reminded herself. She could trust Max. And speaking of him, there he stood in the entrance, as if summoned from her thoughts. Her pulse stumbled and her knees went weak. Man, oh, man. Seeing her sexy surgeon in scrubs was a sight to behold. But Max dressed to the nines in a tuxedo? Be still, her racing heart. Talk about a glorious sight to behold. Their gazes caught across the crowded ballroom and held, and that's when she knew for certain.

I love Max Granger.
Totally. Completely. Irrevocably.

Oh, God.

Flustered, Ayanna forced her attention away from him and focused on the important guests milling about the ballroom beneath the beautiful gilded Aurora Dome. The elaborate, art-deco style stained-glass panels and intricate fresco work were illuminated tonight in shades of crimson and forest green for the occasion. On the tables were the elaborate centerpieces she'd chosen after seeing the Christmas parade floats with Max, made of white lilies and red roses. Even the glittering crystal glassware and sparkling silverware held a nineteen-twenties-style flavor. It all looked like a very expensive holiday heaven. Exactly what she was going for and, hopefully, exactly what would get their donors to open up their wallets to support the new children's cancer ward.

Dr. di Rossi and Dr. Featherstone, the King's orthopedic surgeon, stood not far away, and Ayanna made her way over to them, eager for something to distract her from Max and her newly acknowledged feelings for him. Along the way, she stopped to greet their high-profile attendees, everyone from celebrities to politicians to sports stars, using her formidable memory to place names with faces and make everyone feel welcome. Finally, she reached Dr. di Rossi and Dr. Featherstone as they sipped champagne taken from the tray of a passing server. When she didn't immediately say anything Dr. di Rossi quirked one eyebrow in question.

"Sorry… I was just wondering if you liked that risotto ball."

"It was delicious."

"And have you tried the smoked salmon? Or the chicken satay skewers?"

"I've tried the chicken skewers," Dr. Featherstone said. 'They're delicious, too." She looked beautiful in a crimson gown with lace straps and a full skirt of silk cascading from her hips. The color suited the woman's complexion perfectly and if the covert glances Dr. di Rossi kept giving Dr. Featherstone beneath his lashes were any indication, he seemed to agree.

"You've done a wonderful job of organizing this ball—I'm so impressed."

"Me too," Dr. di Rossi said, turning his head to look over Ayanna's shoulder.

Ayanna followed his gaze and caught sight of Max again, heading in her direction now. *Oh, boy.* Her mouth dried and she looked away fast, heat rising in her cheeks. If she wasn't careful, everyone would know by the end of the night exactly how she felt about him, including the man himself, and she wasn't sure if she was ready for that yet.

Get a grip, girl. Stay cool.

Ayanna smoothed a hand down the front of her fitted emerald-green gown. She'd purchased it weeks ago, before she'd met Max. Now she was glad of the color, considering the compliment he'd give her the day of the parade. Thoughts of that day quickly gave way to that night, Max naked and flushed as he'd driven them both to the peak of pleasure and...

Cheeks hot, she looked up to find Dr. Featherstone watching her and Ayanna fumbled to pick up the thread of conversation. Even though she couldn't see him behind her, her skin tingled with anticipation as Max grew closer to them by the second. Was it weird she could sense his presence? She'd never had that happen before and it seemed odd.

Focus, girl. Focus.

Max was right behind her now, his warmth fizzing through her like the bubbles in the expensive champagne in her glass and his scent—sandalwood and cedar and soap—made her want to close her eyes and just inhale his essence. He placed his hand at the small of her back and her pedicured toes curled in her expensive designer sandals.

Get. A. Grip. This is your big night. Don't blow it.

Determined to regain control, Ayanna squared her shoulders and stiffened her spine, causing Max's hand to fall away. It was difficult enough to think with him standing near her. With him touching her, her brain turned to mush.

"Hi, Max," Dr. di Rossi said. "We're just saying what an amazing job Ayanna's done with the decorations and catering for tonight."

Max gave a polite nod to Dr. di Rossi and smiled at Ayanna. If they weren't careful everyone at Seattle General would know they were sleeping together and once the rumor mill got started who knew when it would die down? Gossip was a horrible thing. She knew that from experience. After the whole mess with Will, she'd spent months avoiding people's pitying looks and comments.

This isn't the same.

"Excuse me... I'd better go check on how things are going in the kitchen."

She'd almost reached the doorway when Max caught up to her and grabbed her hand.

"Dance with me," he said.

"I need to check on the food." Ayanna tried to pull away as he tugged her forward, but he held fast. "I've got a lot to do to make sure the guests are happy."

"What about you?" he asked, pulling her into his arms and swaying with her in time to the music, his embrace quieting the stress inside her. "Are you happy?"

Yes.

Instead of answering, she placed her hands on his lapels and smoothed them down his chest.

"Everything is beautiful," Max said against her temple, his warm breath fanning her skin. "Including you."

"Thanks." She wanted to burrow into him and never leave, but that niggle of doubt persisted in the back of her mind. He'd never mentioned feeling the same way about her. Yes, they were happy now, but what if it all disappeared in an instant? That's what had happened with Will. She'd been blind to the truth. What if the same was happening now? Her emotions twisted and tangled, Ayanna forced herself to straighten and step back from him. "Sorry. But I'm working tonight and I really do need to check in on wait staff now. Excuse me."

Before he could stop her, she fled. Yes, she loved Max, but what if love wasn't enough? She took a deep breath then pushed through into the busy back area, the delicious smells of roasting meat and spices surrounding her. Todd and a couple of other members of her staff were already there, overseeing things. She checked in with them then inspected the cakes the bakery had delivered. They all looked perfect, from the smooth fondant frosting in graduated shades of grays and blacks on the London Fog cakes to the creamy white frosting of the vegan chocolate raspberry cake. Edible art, as Max had called them. She turned fast, only to run smack into the man himself, blocking her path.

"Mind telling me why you keep running away?" Max asked, not letting her get away again.

Ayanna opened her mouth then closed it again and Max shook his head. He'd not seen a takeoff that fast since the Indy 500. Something was going on and it was more than just nerves over her big night.

When she still didn't say anything after a few moments, he switched tactics. The last thing he wanted to do during the ball was argue with her. That wouldn't do either of them any good. Instead, he took her hand and gently let her back toward the exit. "Come on, we didn't finish our dance."

"But I need to—"

"No, you don't. Whatever it is, it can wait."

He took her out of the kitchen and onto the balcony just as the orchestra began one of his personal favorites: "Have Yourself A Merry Little Christmas." Its bittersweet lyrics always touched his heart, but now they seemed even more poignant because of the woman in his arms. He tucked her closer against him and her stiff posture relaxed at last, her body sinking into his and sending tingles of sweet awareness through him.

After years of struggle and strain, things were going well for him—with Ayanna and with his case. After his conversation with Dr. di Rossi he'd brought in Dr. Connor, one of the emergency room physicians who'd worked on the King and his family after the accident and a good friend of Dr. di Rossi's, as well and had told them both that as long as the King's condition continued to remain stable, they could proceed with the scheduled surgery on the fifteenth. Max had another CT scan scheduled for the King tomorrow morning and would know more after that. But for now his attention was completely on the woman in his arms. He couldn't resist sliding a hand down to Ayanna's lower back to pull her hips closer to his.

"Max." She pushed at his chest, forcing more space between them. "People will notice."

"So?" He looked down at her. "Who cares?"

"I care." She frowned, glancing through the French doors at the other couples dancing inside. "I have to work with these people."

"So do I," he said, looking down into her beautiful brown eyes. "But how about we forget about that. Just for one night. You've put in hours and hours to get this ball ready. Now it's time to enjoy it."

Ayanna sighed and shook her head. "I know. You're right, and I'm sorry. It's just hard for me. I'm not used to letting go."

"I know." He smiled and rested his forehead against hers, glad she didn't push him away again. "Just know I'll be here to catch you. Don't worry. You can trust me."

"Can I?" she asked, the hesitation in her tone sending a surge of protectiveness through him.

"Yes, you can. I'm here for you, Ayanna. Whatever you need. You can rely on me."

She seemed to contemplate that for a moment, her brows drawing together, and he prayed his sincerity showed through in his voice. When she didn't respond, he exhaled and gazed up at the lighted dome visible inside the ballroom then back at her. "What's the dome called again?"

"The Northern Star."

Max smiled. "Then let me be that for you. Let me be your Northern Star, Ayanna."

She blinked up at him, the flash of hope in her dark eyes making his breath catch. Maybe he'd finally gotten through to her this time. Maybe she'd finally realize she could trust him, let him in, that he wasn't like her ex. Then her walls seemed to come down again, shutting him out. Snorting, Ayanna tried to pull away from him, using humor to keep him at bay. "Like my own personal GPS."

"I'm serious," he said, allowing her to move away from him when she stepped back.

"I know." A small sad smile formed on her lips. "But I'm not lost."

"Aren't you?" Max said, but doubted she'd heard him as she turned and disappeared into the throng of guests. Because he sure as hell felt like he was wandering in a forest of uncomfortable and unexpected feelings with no sense of how he'd ever find his way out again.

CHAPTER THIRTEEN

UNFORTUNATELY, THE KING'S CT scans the following morning did not look good.

In fact, based on the fact the images had shown that his meningioma had grown during the coma and now threatened to infiltrate the sagittal sinus, Max found himself scrubbing down and prepping for surgery to remove the King's tumor on the original date set for the King's operation—December fifteenth. Having blood flow compromised could have lethal consequences, so the procedure needed to happen before the tumor progressed any farther. Thankfully, he'd planned it all ahead of time using his model and other 3D programs on his computer so he was prepared. Dr. di Rossi hadn't been so fortunate, however, when Max had called to tell him the news earlier. Unfortunately, life wasn't always tidy.

The last thing Max wanted was to ignore the warning signs and have disaster strike again.

The old pang of guilt he'd carried with him since his wife's death constricted his ribcage for the first time in weeks. Being with Ayanna had given him hope that he'd put that behind him for good, but it seemed the situation with the King had resurrected his old demons. They were another distraction he couldn't afford now, however, so Max pushed them aside. The long surgery ahead would be grueling enough.

Flipping the switch on his emotions, Max went into neurosurgeon mode and backed out of the prep room into the OR. The King was already on the table and ready to go. While the nurses gowned him up and tied on his mask, Max ran through the surgery in his mind, visualizing each step. Once he was suited up, Max approached the table and checked in with the anesthesiologist.

"Morning, Dr. Chen. Patient doing well?" Max asked. The King was lying face down on the surgical table with his head fixed in place to the right and a portion of his scalp shaved.

"Patient's stable and his vitals look good, Dr. Granger. Ready when you are," Dr. Chen said.

"Right. Let's get started."

Two hours into the four-hour procedure, Max was ready to begin the delicate process of removing the King's tumor, using ultrasonic aspiration.

"Fornices protected?" Max asked the assisting surgeon.

"Yes, Dr. Granger."

"Good. Thank you. Dr. Chen, how are the patient's vitals?"

"Still within normal limits. Blood pressure has dropped slightly, but O2 sat level is good."

"Okay. Proceeding with aspiration." Max held his instruments steady as he worked, occasionally asking for suction or irrigation but otherwise keeping silent. With the King's condition already compromised from the previous emergency craniotomy, he didn't want to take longer than necessary. Finally, an hour later, the tumor had been removed and the OR as a whole released a prolonged sigh of relief. The worst part was over. Now, Max just had to close and—

A shrill beep issued from the heart monitor and his attention snapped to the anesthesiologist. Sudden flashes of the day Laura had died flashed through Max's mind before he could stop them.

"There was nothing we could do."

Max swallowed hard and narrowed his gaze on the monitor. "What's happening, Dr. Chen?"

"Heart rate dropped." The anesthesiologist reached over to check the King's tracheal tube. "Breathing is normal."

"Have Cardiology on standby, please, just in case." Then the alarm stopped and the regular beeps of the King's pulse returned. Max flexed his tense fingers. "Zero-five suture, please."

A further hour and a half later, the King's surgery was over and the patient was on his way back to Radiology for a second MRI to make sure they'd removed the entire tumor. An odd mix of energy and exhaustion flooded Max's system, not uncommon after a complex surgery. Today, though, he also couldn't seem to stop thinking about Ayanna. Normally, he never let his personal life enter his mind during his operations, but now all that had changed.

"Dr. Granger?" One of the nurses waved him over

to the computer monitor on the wall of the OR. "MRI results on the patient are in."

He removed his gloves then scrolled through the images, happy to see they'd gotten all of the tumor and removed the risk. "These look good. Thank you, everyone. The patient is out of danger and should recover nicely."

Max went back into the prep room to remove his soiled gown and mask then washed up before exiting once more into the hallway. After updating Dr. di Rossi on his father's outcome and prognosis—both good—he headed back to his office to type up his report.

Once there, though, he found himself thinking even more about Ayanna. He'd checked her office, but her staff had said she was at a meeting. Now that the surgery was over, Max's future loomed. They hadn't really discussed their relationship beyond the right now but, cheesy as it was, he'd meant what he'd told her at the ball. He'd be her Northern Star. He'd be there for her, if she wanted him. She worked too hard. She needed someone to look out for her best interests.

His heart squeezed. He'd love to be there for her each day, see that smile of hers light up his life like a second sun. Be there for her at night, to cook her dinner and make sure she ate well. Listen to her day and discuss the problems she was dealing with and have her do the same for him.

But his old life in New York still loomed like a specter. All those conferences and lectures and travel he had booked. Long-distance relationships weren't something he'd tried, but from what he'd heard they could be difficult. And perhaps Ayanna wasn't even interested in that with him.

They needed to talk, that much was certain.

As he dictated his surgery notes into the computer, he devised a plan. He'd make her dinner then ask where things stood between them.

"You're quiet tonight," Ayanna said that evening, over a delicious bowl of homemade baked ziti, courtesy of Max's culinary genius. He'd seemed awfully serious since they'd gotten home tonight and it had her on edge. "Everything go okay with the King's surgery?"

"Fine." Max frowned down into his pasta. "How was your day?"

"Good." She tore off another piece of garlic bread and nibbled on the warm crust. Yep, something was definitely off here. Ayanna pressed her knees together under the table and tried not to imagine the worst. The night Will had told her about his affair with Rinna had felt very similar, full of tension and unspoken words. Was she missing something? Was Max leaving sooner than she thought? The King's surgery was done, but she'd expected him to at least stick around until his patient was released. Maybe she'd been wrong. Her stomach cramped and she put the rest of her bread down, uneaten. "Please tell me what's bothering you. I can tell there's a problem."

Max looked up at her then, his eyes stormy. "What's happening here, with us?"

"What do you mean?" Ayanna swallowed hard. "We're enjoying each other's company."

"Is that all?"

"Isn't that enough?"

Max got up to take his plate to the sink and Ayanna's heart sank. She'd apparently said the wrong thing but wasn't sure what. She stood too and moved in beside him at the sink. They bumped arms and Ayanna pulled back. "Sorry. We seem to be in each other's way tonight."

Lips compressed, he looked over at her. "No, I'm sorry. I'm can't seem to find the right way to—"

Her phone buzzed on the table.

Ayanna held up a finger then went back to answer it. On the screen, her mother's face glowed brightly. With a sigh, Ayanna pressed answer, her gaze still locked on Max. "Hey, Mom. What's up?"

"Hi, honey. Just checking on your plans for Christmas," her mother said. "It's less than two weeks away."

"Yes, I know." Ayanna rolled her eyes then turned away from Max, who was still frowning.

"Be sure to invite Max also," her mom said. "You two make such a nice couple and he seemed to really hit it off with everyone."

"We're not a couple, Mom." Ayanna glanced back over her shoulder to see a shadow flicker across his handsome face. Man, something was really wrong, and she had no idea what. The pit in her stomach bottomed out. That old niggle of doubt bored deeper into her gut.

"Hey, Mom. I need to call you back, okay? I'll let you know about Christmas." She hung up before her mother could respond. Max walked past her and into the living room, slumping down on the sofa to stare at the blank TV screen, the glow of the Christmas lights the only other illumination in the room. Feeling like she was walking through a minefield, Ayanna made her way over to him and sat on the opposite end of the sofa, curling her legs up beneath her, anxiety and apprehension stinging like angry bees inside her. She sensed something precious had been lost, but she couldn't say exactly what yet. "What did you want to tell me before at dinner?"

Max blinked a few times, his expression resigned. "I'm flying back to New York on Christmas Day, pending any unforeseen complications with the King's condition."

"Oh." The news punched her right in the heart. So he was leaving sooner than she'd expected. It should've been fine. Good. She'd known eventually he'd return to his other life across the country, but things had been so happy and idyllic here in Seattle for them the past few weeks she'd allowed herself to get lost in their fantasy bubble.

But all happy bubbles burst eventually, don't they?

Man, how stupid could she have been? She of all people should know that after what had happened with Will. Life had seemed happy and idyllic to her then too, until it hadn't anymore. She had no right to feel surprised or hurt now. Max had been nothing but honest with her from the start. She forced words past the lump of sadness and self-recriminations in her throat. "Okay. Thanks for telling me."

He gave a curt nod. "Figured you should know, even though we aren't a couple or anything."

Red flags went up in her mind and defensiveness joined the ball of whirling emotions inside her. "Do you want us to be a couple?"

Max looked over at her again, his expression unreadable. "Do you?"

Yes. No. I don't know.

She couldn't seem to think straight at the moment. She cared for him deeply, but there were a lot of other factors they needed to discuss that hadn't been factored in when all this was just temporary. What about her job? What about his? Could they make a go of it? Did they even want to try? In the end, she told her truth, "I don't know."

"Right." Max stood and headed for the hall. "I'm going to bed. Got early rounds in the morning."

"Goodnight," she said to his retreating back, her voice as dazed as she felt. Long after he'd gone, Ayanna sat there staring at the tree, wondering how in the world everything had come crashing down so fast.

CHAPTER FOURTEEN

BY CHRISTMAS EVE MORNING, things were even more crazy in Ayanna's life, even though the ball was over. The media were still barking at her heels about the accident and the King had woken up after his surgery. She was doing her best to keep the media at bay on both fronts until Dr. di Rossi could make a formal announcement, but it was getting harder by the day.

Then there was Max. Since he'd dropped the bombshell on her about leaving on Christmas Day, to say things between them had been strained would be an understatement. In fact, she hadn't seen Max at all since he'd had the call about the King regaining consciousness in the early hours this morning and had rushed to Seattle General to monitor the King's condition and keep the royal family and Dr. di Rossi updated. She assumed he'd slept there, since she'd woken up alone in bed and there was no sign of his return.

With a sigh, she rolled over and blinked into the darkness. It wasn't yet five. They hadn't made love in almost two weeks. Just kept to their separate sides of the bed, even though every cell in her body had yearned for him. She'd tried to approach him a couple of times, get him to open up and talk, but he'd shut her out, his gray-green gaze as chilly and unreadable as it had been when they'd first met.

Maybe it was for the best. He was leaving and there was no sense in her getting even more attached to him than she already was. She'd known the score going into this and she'd chosen to sleep with him anyway. She'd fallen in love, against her own common sense. If she was miserable now, there was no one to blame but herself.

It was just like the breakup with Will all over again.

She'd blinded herself to the truth then too and look where that had gotten her. Hurt and heartbroken.

Being here in the suite alone gave Ayanna her first taste of what living without Max would be like and it wasn't pleasant. The world felt a bit smaller without him.

Unable to sleep, she finally got up and got ready. Might as well head into work herself. Maybe the busyness of her office would distract her from the pain of losing him. She finished showering and brushing her teeth, then padded into the bedroom to get dressed, clicking on the local morning news in the background while she dressed. According to the weatherman, the temperature had turned chillier and he predicted a chance of light snow later. Perfect. Ayanna chose her black wool designer pantsuit, thinking it would be the warmest choice.

"And in other breaking news..." the anchor said, going to a breaking news story. "We've just learned the identity of this man, seen entering and leaving Seattle General Hospital several times since late November.

He's Dr. Maxwell Granger, a world-renowned neurosurgeon whose patient roster includes celebrities and world dignitaries. We haven't yet confirmed the reason for Dr. Granger's appearance here in Seattle, but we speculate it may have something to do with King Roberto of Isola Verde and an auto accident that occurred back on November twenty-first of this year.

"As we reported last month, Dr. Granger visited the royal palace of the wealthy island nation to provide a medial consultation to the King. Our correspondent has reached out to the public relations office for Seattle General Hospital but the facility had no official comment about the accident at this time. They also refused to give any details as to why Dr. Granger was at their hospital, and our attempts to contact Dr. Granger personally have been unsuccessful. We will continue to bring you updates on the late breaking story as they become available. Interestingly…"

Ayanna lowered the volume then sank down on the edge of the bed, dazed. Thank goodness for her intrepid staff. They'd managed to keep a lid on things, though for how long was anyone's guess. She glanced up at the screen again and spotted a picture of Max and a woman she assumed to be his wife, Laura.

Ayanna raised the volume again to hear the anchor say, "…Dr. Granger's skills as a neurosurgeon are well known, yet he was unable to save his own wife, also a physician, who died two years ago from an undiagnosed brain aneurysm. Let's hope King Roberto fares better under Dr. Granger's care."

She shut the TV off then stared down at her toes. Blood rushed in her ears and her ribcage contracted.

Max guarded his privacy fiercely and would flip when he saw the news story. It would open up old wounds for him and make things between them even worse. She'd told him she had the situation under control, had bragged to him about how good she was at her job.

This was bad. Very, very bad.

She needed to get to the hospital, and fast, both to talk to Dr. di Rossi and make sure Max was okay. Ayanna hurriedly finished dressing, for once not caring that she had no makeup on, then pulled her damp hair back into a ponytail before shoving her feet into her pumps and grabbing her bag before rushing out the door. By the time she reached the elevators, she was already dialing her office.

Her staff picked up on the second ring. "Did you see the news?"

"Yes." Ayanna headed through the parking garage toward her vehicle, climbing in behind the wheel and starting the engine, switching the call over to Bluetooth as she pulled out of her spot and headed up the ramp to street level. "Please contact Dr. di Rossi and tell him I'll meet him at his office as soon as I get to Seattle General."

"Thank you. Keep the change," Max said to the cashier in the cafeteria after paying for his tea. He'd just finished another neurological check on the King. After a month in a coma and two brain surgeries, both the man's sensory and motor functions had all proved normal as did his reflexes. All in all, Roberto was very lucky, recovering well from both the trauma of the car accident and the removal of his brain tumor.

He took a seat at a small table in a secluded corner and tried to feel better about the fact his case had been a success. Prior to coming to Seattle, that would've been enough. In fact, he would've already been planning ahead for his next patient, his next conference, his next international location.

But after the way his conversation with Ayanna had ended just over a week ago, his heart was heavy. She'd not given him any indication she wanted him to stay in Seattle and if he was smart, he'd take that for what it was—goodbye. Except for some reason he couldn't. Even knowing she didn't want a relationship with him, even knowing it would never work between them, he hated the thought of leaving her. He loved Ayanna, but sometimes love wasn't enough. Look at what had happened with him and Laura.

Wincing, he swallowed more of his hot tea, glad of the distracting scald on the back of his throat, then sighed, staring down at his wrinkled scrubs. The best thing for everyone would be for him to get showered and changed, clear his head and look at this situation logically, analytically, without his blasted heart getting in the way and mucking it all up. The King's next check wasn't for another couple of hours and he'd already been removed from the consult rotation for the ER, pending his departure tomorrow, so he had nothing but time on his hands at the moment.

Time and regret.

His heart pinched and his stomach dropped, along with his spirits.

People came and went from the tables around him, but Max barely noticed. Restless, he glanced up at the

TV mounted on the wall nearby. The local morning news was on, but the volume was off. Closed captioning across the bottom showed what the anchor was saying. For a moment the image on the screen didn't register. Then he blinked and squinted, disbelief overriding the shadows inside him. That was him, his picture beside the King's. His body tensed. Ayanna and her staff had worked day and night to keep the King's accident and surgery out of the media. She must be frantic right now.

Then another photo popped up on the screen of him and Laura and his concern for Ayanna quickly morphed into outrage. With the types of patients he treated, Max was no stranger to paparazzi, but how dared they invade his privacy? What gutted him the most, though, were the words scrolling across the bottom of the screen, "…he was unable to save his own wife…"

Guilt that had eased during his weeks here with Ayanna returned hot and heavy in his torso, expanding to fill his extremities. This was exactly why it was better not to feel anything. Because once you opened up the floodgates it all came in, the good and the bad. His breath shallow, he threw away the rest of his tea and headed back to the relative privacy of the ICU, jaw tense and skin too tight for his body. As he stalked through the walkways and halls then took the stairs to the third floor, he couldn't stop berating himself for being such an idiot. He'd learned his lesson growing up—emotions got you nothing but trouble. He should have come here, done his job, then got out. No fuss, no muss, no mess.

We're not a couple.

Ayanna's words to her mother on the phone on the night of the King's surgery haunted him once more and he gave a derisive snort. Good thing he hadn't asked her to start a relationship with him, a real one, told her he loved her, even if it currently felt like he'd taken a bullet straight to the heart. The best thing for both of them was to end things now, cleanly, and go back to the lives waiting for them. End of story.

He pushed out of the stairwell and into the ICU, running a hand through his hair. At the other end of the hall, where the King's room was located, he spotted Ayanna and Dr. di Rossi emerging from Roberto's room. Neither of them noticed him approach as they were deep in conversation, but Max cleared his throat, making his presence known.

Dr. di Rossi extended his hand, leaning in so Ayanna wouldn't hear him. "Thank you, Max, for everything you've done for my father. My family is forever in your debt. Now, if you'll excuse me, I have something urgent to do..."

Once he'd gone, Ayanna led Max into a small private conference room, looking as unhappy as he felt. "I take it you saw the news story."

"I did. It's fine," he said, even though it really wasn't. He couldn't seem to stand still, pacing the small space to diffuse some of the nervous energy rioting through him. Too bad he couldn't seem to flip that switch and turn off his emotions, like he had in the past.

"It's not fine," Ayanna said. "The media needs to stop. This is what I do for a living, Max. I've already spoken to Dr. di Rossi about the King's story in all this. Let me do some damage control for you too and—"

"Damage control?" He gave an unpleasant laugh and shook his head. "God. Is that what these past few weeks together have come to? I thought…" His scowl deepened. "Never mind. It doesn't matter what I thought."

"Max, I'm sorry. I shouldn't have put it like that." The hurt in her eyes made him feel worse, if that were possible. "It's just a turn of phrase. It doesn't mean anything."

"And there's the problem, in a nutshell. None of this really means anything, does it? The time we spent together, making love. It was all just a temporary affair. We go our separate ways and get back to our separate lives."

"Hey. We both knew this was a fling, right? Besides, you're the one leaving tomorrow for New York. Not me." She took a deep breath, her posture as stiff as a board and the toe of her pump tapping soundlessly on the beige carpet. "Look, we're both tired and under a lot of stress. If you've got something to say about us, then say it. I can't read between your lines all the time and guess whatever it is you're feeling. Sorry. I've been there, done that, and don't plan on taking that trip again."

"You want to know what I'm feeling?" he asked. Max struggled to keep his voice down, hating that his anger and frustration were ruling him but unable to tamp them down. "I'm feeling like an idiot. Like this whole affair between us was nothing but a mistake. I let you in, Ayanna, I opened up to you, but I shouldn't have. Because the truth is I'm not available. My work doesn't allow me the time or emotional space for other people in my life. I'm alone for a reason."

"What a load of crap." Ayanna inched closer, her eyes bright with fury. "You know what I think? I think what you're feeling is scared. Scared of your emotions. Scared of taking a chance with me because the truth is that love terrifies you. Well, guess what, mister big-time surgeon. That's the name of the game. Love is scary. It's messy and maddening and magnificent. But you'll never let yourself have that again because you've already closed yourself off again in that tight shell of yours."

"Like you're one to talk." He inched closer to Ayanna as well, crossing a line in the proverbial sand but unable to stop now. "You're scared too. Scared to be less than perfect. Scared to trust yourself and make another mistake. Scared that if you can't be everything to everybody all the time, no one will ever love you."

Her face turned ashen and her mouth opened wordlessly. Yeah, he'd gone too far. He wanted nothing more than to take his hateful words back, but it was too late. They hung in the air, potent and poisonous, eating away at whatever possibilities might have been left between them like acid on metal.

"We're done here," Ayanna finally managed to say, her tone brittle. "Have a nice trip home, Dr. Granger. I'll head back to the suite now to pack my things and disappear from your life forever. Merry Christmas."

Max stared at the door after she walked out, unable to move. He was alone again, just as he'd wanted. Except the gaping black hole where his heart should've been didn't feel like what he wanted at all. He slumped down into a nearby chair and dropped his head into his hands, desperately wishing for the icy monotony of his old façade while fearing it—along with Ayanna—was gone for good.

CHAPTER FIFTEEN

AYANNA HAD RUSHED back to the hotel after leaving Max, shoved things into her bags as quickly as she could then returned to Seattle General. Now, hours later, she sat in her office, trying to finish up some last-minute things before leaving for the holiday and not think about the horrible fight with Max. Funny, but when the breakup with Will had occurred, there'd been no fireworks, no shouting or arguments. She'd been too shocked and Will hadn't cared enough at that point to fight.

If that didn't prove how much she loved Max, Ayanna didn't know what did.

Not that it mattered. He'd be gone soon and she'd be left here to pick up the pieces and go on. Same as always. Chalk up another failure for her stupid instincts.

With a sigh, she closed her eyes and once again her mind replayed their argument. What he'd said about her need for perfection, about her trust issues, about her fearing no one would love her if she didn't take care of them had been hitting below the belt. Trouble was, they also happened to be true.

Darn it.

She hated admitting that, but there it was. Max had always been far too perceptive for his own good. He also happened to know her better than anyone else, even in the short time they'd been together. He got her, more than her parents, more than her family. Way more than Will ever had.

Max was her person. She loved him.

And now he was leaving.

Because I pushed him away.

A knock sounded at the door and one of her staffers, a young intern named Gretchen, popped her head inside, a pair of glittery reindeer antlers on her head. "Hey, boss. Staff party's wrapping up and I wanted to wish you Happy Holidays before I go."

"Thank you." Ayanna forced a smile. "I hope you have a wonderful holiday too, Gretchen."

"Thanks, boss." Gretchen raised a glass of eggnog. "You sure you don't want to take a break and join us? We're probably going to hit the pub down the street after we leave here."

"Aw, thank you for the invitation, but no." Ayanna shook her head. "I'm pretty tired. You guys have fun and be careful. No drinking and driving, all right?"

"Yes, ma'am." Gretchen saluted. "See you in the new year."

"See you." She waited until the office emptied then tried again to get through the stack of papers that hadn't budged since she'd first sat down earlier this afternoon, but it was hopeless.

She covered her face with her hands and slumped back in her seat. God, she'd really messed things up with Max. He had a right to feel however he wanted to feel about the media invading his privacy and his wife's death. She should have supported his decision, whatever it was, and helped him through it, not berated him about it. Man, some PR expert she was.

Sniffling, Ayanna yanked a tissue from the box on her desk. They hadn't been apart a full day yet and already she missed him. Her first instinct was to go to his office down the hall, but he wasn't there anymore. She'd peeked down the hall when she'd returned from the hotel and it looked like he'd already cleared out the space. And speaking of clearing out, she needed to call her parents about staying at their place next week since the suite wasn't an option anymore and the work on her apartment still wasn't finished.

Looked like she'd end up back in her old room after all. She was going to be there tomorrow for Christmas anyway, so it made sense. With a sigh, she picked up her phone and texted her mother.

Mind if I come early and spend the night tonight? I'll stay through next week too, if it's okay.

The response came through quicker than she'd expected.

Oh, no! What happened?

Light snow fell as Ayanna walked across the street to the parking lot alone, the sadness in her heart in direct contrast to the jolly decorations lighting up the city around her. Her thumb trembled slightly as she texted back.

I'll explain later. See you soon.

Late that night, Max was back in the hospital cafeteria. The place was all but deserted now because it was Christmas Eve. He should go back to the hotel to sleep, but he just couldn't. Couldn't face being in the suite without Ayanna. Especially knowing he'd basically destroyed any chance he'd had with her.

God, once again his emotions had cost him dearly. He rubbed his hands over his face then stared out the window at the snowy landscape. It was probably good he was leaving tomorrow. After their awful argument, Ayanna would want nothing to do with him and now that the King was on the mend, there was no reason for him to stay.

He stared down into another cup of tea, this one as cold as ice because it had sat there so long. But instead of seeing the beverage, replays of their time together unspooled in his head.

During the few brief weeks they'd shared, Ayanna had shown him a different way to be—happy, carefree, fun. Sure, he'd still had his work and his obligations to his patients, but the burden of guilt he'd carried so long over his wife's death had lifted. He had Ayanna to thank for that. She'd got him talking about it, got it out in the open and helped him release it. She'd been right today too. He'd been using his busy schedule as a shield against being vulnerable and getting hurt again.

But instead of protecting him, keeping everyone away had only caused him more pain in the end.

Max sat back and scratched the stubble on his jaw, exhausted but unable to sleep.

He'd mucked things up in the worst way. He should never have poked Ayanna's most painful spots. Why did he have to bring up her ex? Why did he have to push the buttons he knew hurt her most? Why couldn't he have just told her he loved her and wanted to spend the rest of his life with her? Maybe if he had, she'd still be here, and the future ahead of him now wouldn't seem as cold and lonely as the Arctic tundra.

CHAPTER SIXTEEN

ON CHRISTMAS MORNING at her parents' house Ayanna got the grilling she'd expected from her family.

"Spill it, sis," her sister LaTasha said over a batch of their mom's superb cinnamon buns. "I can tell something's wrong."

"How?" Ayanna scowled from across the breakfast bar. "Nothing's wrong."

Five incredulous stares met Ayanna's gaze, along with several raised brows.

Maybe she was sitting here with her hair all ratty and uncombed, not a touch of makeup on and her PJs wrinkled. Couldn't a girl just relax without getting the fifth degree? Apparently not, where her family was concerned. "Okay. Fine. Max and I had an argument yesterday at work."

"Oh, no. Was it about that news story? I saw that; they were harsh about his past," James said, giving her a look. "That's none of their business."

"Agreed." Ayanna took a bigger bite than necessary of her roll, not even caring about the crumbs on the front of her shirt. Forget all her fussy perfectionism. She was going full-out mess for a change.

"Sweetie," Tonya, said, handing her a napkin. "Have you tried calling him? Maybe you can still work things out. Max seemed pretty great to me."

Talking about her problems with her siblings wasn't exactly comfortable for Ayanna. In fact, it was downright embarrassing. She was the oldest, the one who was supposed to have it all together. The one who took care of everyone else. But no longer. That was the old her. The her that had driven Max away.

The new her was all about letting it all hang out— mistakes and mussiness and all.

Scared that if you can't be everything to everybody all the time, no one will ever love you...

Max's words looped through her head. Yep. That extreme hadn't worked for her at all. Maybe this other one would. She took a sip of her peppermint tea, the tips of her ears hot as her siblings continued to eyeball her as if she were an alien life form who'd invaded Ayanna's body.

Tonya was right. Max was great. One of the best men she'd ever met. And now he was gone. Loneliness clawed inside her, making her grip her mug tighter. She missed him, so much it ached. She'd not slept a wink last night. Just stared up at the ceiling in her old room and remembered when she and Max had stood in there together on Thanksgiving.

Tears stung her eyes before she could blink them away, all her love for him swamping her at once and drowning her in a whirlpool of sadness. Great, now she could add red and puffy to her growing list of new looks she'd tried.

"Aw, sweetie." Her family gathered around her in a group hug that included her mom and dad. "Don't cry."

Another great thing about families. They always had your back, no matter how you screwed up.

Minutes later, after more hugs and tears, Ayanna blew her nose, then frowned down at her cold tea. "I pushed Max away because I couldn't trust myself and what I was feeling after what happened with Will, and now I've lost him."

"Oh, honey." Her mom rubbed her back. "Don't give up so easy. If I hadn't stuck it out with your dad when we were dating, we never would've ended up together. Believe me, he was not easy to be around all the time. Moody and brooding and then he went and dated another woman behind my back and—"

"Hey!" Her father gave her mom a look. "I didn't date that woman. We went out one time to make you jealous, Nari. Worked too, since you wouldn't leave me alone after that."

"Hush." Her mom tossed a balled-up napkin at his head. Her dad ducked then chuckled, winking at his wife with obvious affection. "Don't listen to him. He pursued me like the queen I am and that's why we got back together. Listen, honey. Will wasn't worth your time. You were always too good for him. But Max? Now, there's a man who appreciates a good woman. The fact he still feels guilty over his late wife is proof of that. What you need to do now is show him what the future for you two could be like. Men are visual creatures. Show him a new path forward." She pushed Ayanna's hair behind her ear then kissed her temple. "But whatever you do, honey, do it fast. Time's aticking."

Ayanna glanced at the clock then picked up her phone. It was ten o'clock now. Max's flight was this afternoon. If she hurried, she might be able to catch him at the airport before he left. She knew what she wanted. Max. Pure and simple. Exactly how they'd make it work she wasn't sure, but, man, she wanted to try.

Determination fluttered inside her and she straightened, pushing aside her cold tea. "I'm going to get him."

"About damned time," her mother said, slipping her arm around her husband's waist. "Might want to take a shower first, though."

Max stood on the porch of Ayanna's parents' house late the next morning, wondering when exactly he'd lost his mind. He hadn't slept more than an hour the night before and felt even more tired now. Tired and empty. He'd never felt so empty before. Not after his parents had died. Not after losing Laura.

It was like there was a huge, gaping, Ayanna-sized hole inside him and the only cure was inside the house before him. But whether or not he could ever get her back was another question. Exhaling slowly, he gripped the handle of the wheeled suitcase beside him and glanced back over his shoulder at the cab still idling at the curb. His flight didn't leave for a few more hours, but he'd checked out of the hotel anyway, thinking he'd head to the airport early. Nothing to keep him in Seattle now. Nothing but all the memories, all the regrets. For the first time in a long time he had nowhere to be. He was adrift and he didn't like it.

He stared at the candy cane wreath on the front door of her parents' house again, its cheerful bright red bow mocking him. Maybe he should just leave and go back to Manhattan, get back into his routine. That usually made him feel better.

Except there was nothing waiting for him in New York either. Nothing except another empty room.

Until he'd come here, he'd never had a problem being alone, but now everything had changed. Because of Ayanna. The woman he loved and had driven away.

To add insult to injury, the head of neurosurgery had stopped him on his way out of the hospital last night and offered him a permanent position on their staff. They'd even been willing to work around Max's hectic travel schedule, since his reputation and expertise would bring in many more high-profile clients to Seattle General. He'd seriously considered it for a moment—the constant travel and work that had driven him the past two years had grown old—but staying in the city now would mean constantly wondering if he might see Ayanna around the next corner. It would've been too painful.

In his mind, scenes from *It's a Wonderful Life* played like a sign from above. What Max wouldn't do for a little angelic intervention right about now.

You see, you've really had a wonderful life. What a mistake it would be to throw it away...

Clarence the angel had said that line to George Bailey in the movie, but to Max now it sounded like it was meant just for him. Life here in Seattle these past few weeks with Ayanna had been pretty wonderful. In fact, she'd made every one of his days brighter just by being there. She'd made him feel like he could climb any mountain, solve any case, be a better man.

And if that wasn't a heavenly gift, and the best Christmas present ever, Max didn't know what was.

Before he could rethink his actions, he pulled out his cellphone to change his flight. There was every chance in the world Ayanna might tell him to get lost, but that was a chance he was willing to take. He'd open his battered heart and be vulnerable, if it meant he might get to spend forever with the woman he loved.

After switching to a later return, after the new year, Max signaled to the cab driver to continue waiting then faced the door of Ayanna's parents' house once more. He rang the bell then glanced upward to the porch roof, saying, "Thanks, Clarence. Wish me luck."

CHAPTER SEVENTEEN

"HURRY BACK, HONEY," Ayanna's mom said. "There's dinner later and I've got so much food. Plus presents."

"I know, Mom. With luck I'll get to SeaTac before his flight leaves." Ayanna tugged her coat on over the jeans and sweatshirt she'd changed into after her shower, her damp hair pulled back into a ponytail, no makeup. She leaned over to peck her mom's cheek on her way to the foyer. "I don't want to miss Max again."

"Fine. But after you find that man of yours, drag him straight back here to eat, you hear me?" The huge ham her mom had been cooking all night in the kitchen had the house smelling like cloves and cinnamon.

"Will do. Mom." Ayanna grabbed her bag.

"You got love in your heart, honey. That's all the luck you need."

Ayanna had just reached for the door handle when the bell rang. Thinking it was David, James's partner, Ayanna opened it up to dash past the guy, only to find Max standing there, looking disheveled and distraught and decidedly delicious.

He stared at her, his cheeks pink from the cold, wariness and surprise warring in his gray-green eyes. "Uh, hey." Max said at last. "Merry Christmas."

"Who is it, sis?" LaTasha asked, moving in beside Ayanna. "Oh!"

"Is that David?" James traipsed up next, his stock-inged feet pounding across the hardwood, his attention focused on his phone and not the person at the door. "He'd better have an excuse for being late, and—"

Her brother looked up and stopped in mid-rant, wide-eyed. James recovered faster than his sisters, though, and nudged Ayanna's ribs. "Girl, go get him."

"Hey, James," Max said, his small smile cautious. "I came to talk to Ayanna."

"Good." James reached past a still frozen Ayanna and tugged Max inside before herding them both into a small library across the foyer. "Whatever's going on with you two, work it out." He started to close the door, leaving them in privacy. "Kiss and make up already."

Alone with Max, Ayanna felt even more tongue-tied and twisted. They looked anywhere but at each other and her cheeks burned hotter than the surface of the sun.

Just tell him, girl. Trust yourself.

"I...uh..." she started, finding it hard to say what she needed with him actually standing there in front of her. Ayanna took a deep breath then forced herself to continue. Now or never. "I'm sorry about what I said during our argument. I was wrong,"

"No, you were right," Max said. "And I'm the one who's sorry. I have been using my work as a shield." He stepped forward and took her hand. "But unless I change and let you in, I'll be alone forever and that's not what I want."

A small tree glowed in the corner of the room, casting them in flickering shades of red and green and blue. Ayanna squeezed his fingers. "You were right too. I was scared to make mistakes, scared to trust myself and what I was feeling." She looked up at him, meeting his gaze with her tear-filled eyes. "But I'm not scared anymore. Because I love you, Max."

"I love you too, Ayanna." Max stepped closer, the heat of him warming her heart. "I want to make a new life with you, here in Seattle, if you'll have me."

He kissed her gently and her breath hitched. It was the sweetest, most wonderful present she ever could have asked for, but there was still one small doubt left in Ayanna's mind. "But what about your life in New York? What about your career there?"

"My career is wherever my patients are. And my life is with you, Ayanna. I can travel anywhere, if need be, but the head of neurosurgery at Seattle General offered me a position on staff last night and I'm going to take it. This place already feels more like more of a home to me than New York ever did, thanks to you."

A scuffle sounded on the other side of the library door and Ayanna chuckled. "I think my family's listening in."

"I think you're right." He chuckled then kissed her again, this time more deeply, wrapping his arms around her and holding her close. "No matter where I go, Ayanna, I'll always come back to you."

"Same." She pulled him down for another kiss until

whoops and hollers echoing from the foyer beyond had them pulling apart again, laughing. "We can share my apartment for a while, maybe save up for a house together."

"Sounds perfect," he said, smiling. "Did I mention that I love you, Ayanna Franklin?"

"Yes, you did, Max Granger." She rose up on tiptoe to kiss him again. "And I love you too."

Then the door opened and her mom stuck her head in. "Now that everyone loves everyone else again, you two get out here and help me with all this food. We've got a Christmas to celebrate."

"C'mon, lovebirds," Tonya said, waving them out. "I want to open my gifts now."

"Me too!" LaTasha chimed in. "Girl, you better have gotten me that book I wanted."

"Since when do you read?" James snorted, shepherding everyone down the hall to the dining room where Brandon, Clarissa and their dad were busy setting the table. He checked his phone again then announced. "David is on his way. And, Tasha, the last thing you read was the back of the box for that dye that turned your hair green. You better get your butt into my salon soon so I can fix that before it all falls out."

"I liked my green hair. Makes me feel like a mermaid," Ayanna's sister said. "At least I have hair. You tell people you shaved your head, but I know the truth."

Gasps and laughter broke out from the group and then her parents got involved and things rapidly deteriorated from there. From the relative quiet of the doorway, Ayanna shook her head then hazarded a glance up at Max, his hand still in hers, just the way she hoped it would always be. "You sure you want to join this crazy family?"

"As long as you're in it…" Max looked down at her, his smile brimming with joy "…absolutely."

* * * * *

MILLS & BOON

Coming next month

MISTLETOE KISS WITH THE HEART DOCTOR
Marion Lennox

Oh, she wanted him. She ached for him. Her whole body felt as if it was surrendering.

She was being kissed and she was kissing. He didn't need to balance on his bad leg because she was holding him.

Maybe it could count as therapy, she thought, almost hysterically. Helping patient stand. Maybe this was a medical tool designed to make him feel better.

It was surely making her feel better. Every sense seemed to have come alive. Every nerve ending was tingling.

More. Every single part of her was screaming that she wanted this man, she needed this man, that she wouldn't mind in the least if they fell back on the bed and...

Um, not in a million years. Not!

Because this was a hospital ward and any minute the door could open as a nurse arrived for routine obs. This was a patient and she was a doctor and...

Shut up, Elsa, she told her inner self fiercely. Just let this moment be.

So she did. Her mind shut down and she let herself just kiss. And be kissed.

The kiss was deep and long and magical, and as it

finally ended it was as much as she could do not to weep. But Marc was still holding her. He had her at arm's length now, smiling into her eyes with such tenderness that…

No! She made a herculean effort to haul herself together. This was way past unprofessional. She could just about get herself struck off the medical register for this.

But right now she was having trouble thinking that it mattered, whether she was struck off or not. For Marc was smiling at her, and that seemed to be the only thing that mattered in the whole world.

But this was still well out of order. This man's life was in Sydney. It could only ever be a casual fling.

Oh, but his smile…

'About that date…' he ventured, and she needed to shake her head but all she could do was look up into his deep eyes and sense went right out the window.

But then reality suddenly slammed back with a vengeance. The hospital speaker system cracked into life and she heard Kim, one of the hospital's junior nurses. Even through the dodgy hospital intercom she heard the fear in Kim's tone.

'Code Blue. Nurses' station. Code Blue.'

Continue reading
MISTLETOE KISS WITH THE HEART DOCTOR
Marion Lennox

Available next month
www.millsandboon.co.uk

COMING SOON!

We really hope you enjoyed reading this book. If you're looking for more romance, be sure to head to the shops when new books are available on

Thursday 26th November

To see which titles are coming soon, please visit

millsandboon.co.uk/nextmonth

WE'RE LOOKING FOR NEW AUTHORS FOR THE MILLS & BOON MEDICAL SERIES!

Whether you're a published author or an aspiring one, our editors would love to read your story.

You can submit the synopsis and first three chapters of your novel online, and find out more about the series, at **harlequin.submittable.com/submit**

We read all submissions and you do not need to have an agent to submit.

IF YOU'RE INTERESTED, WHY NOT HAVE A GO?

Submit your story at:
harlequin.submittable.com/submit

MILLS & BOON